"There's an old inn legend," Abby said.

She glanced at Josh  tood in the inn's yard, was focused intently on art-shaped shadow th tree, they will fall in l their lives."

"Have you ever kissed in the shadow?" a deep voice asked beside her.

She turned to peek at Josh, thankful for the darkness that hid the blush warming her cheeks. "No, I haven't. There— look, Josh, I think the shadow is forming," she whispered, watching the shifting dark patterns on the dazzling white snow.

"We can't waste that," Josh said, taking her hand and hurrying down the steps.

"Josh, we can't—"

He rushed her over to stand in the heart-shaped shadow. "It's only a kiss."

"This is absurd," she said, laughing, her heart pounding wildly. "Suppose it comes true? We don't even know each other. You're tempting fate."

He smiled at her, then pulled her to him.

* * *

is part of *Kissed by a Rancher*

KISSED BY
A RANCHER

BY
SARA ORWIG

MILLS
BOON

Published in Great Britain 2015
by Mills & Boon, an imprint of Harlequin (UK) Limited,
Eton House, 18-24 Paradise Road, Richmond, Surrey, TW9 1SR

© 2015 Sara Orwig

ISBN: 978-0-263-25261-3

51-0515

Harlequin (UK) Limited's policy is to use papers that are natural, renewable and recyclable products and made from wood grown in sustainable forests. The logging and manufacturing processes conform to the legal environmental regulations of the country of origin.

Printed and bound in Spain
by CPI, Barcelona

Sara Orwig lives in Oklahoma. She has a patient husband who will take her on research trips anywhere, from big cities to old forts. She is an avid collector of Western history books. With a master's degree in English, Sara has written historical romance, mainstream fiction and contemporary romance. Books are beloved treasures that take Sara to magical worlds, and she loves both reading and writing them.

To David and my family with love.
Also, with many thanks to Stacy Boyd
and Maureen Walters.

One

Josh Calhoun glanced at the red neon sign glowing through the swirling snow. The windows of the Beckett Café were frosted, so he couldn't see if it had closed for the night. As hungry as he was, he was far more interested in finding a bed. Highway patrol troopers had closed the roads, and he couldn't even get back to the tiny airport to sleep on a cold hangar floor or inside his plane. He glanced at the cab's clock: a few minutes past ten. He felt as if it should be around 1:00 a.m.

The taxi left the two blocks of one-story buildings, shops and neon behind as the main street of Beckett, Texas, was swallowed in a white world of howling wind and blowing snow. In spite of the warmth of the cab, Josh shivered. He pulled his jacket collar up while he peered outside at the uninviting storm.

In minutes he spotted a sign swinging in the wind, a spotlight on the ground throwing a strong beam over the announcement of the Donovan Bed and Breakfast Inn. Glumly he stared at the bright red No Vacancy part of the sign.

Even wind-whipped snow could not hide the three-story Victorian-style house that loomed into view. A light glowed over the wraparound porch. Dark shutters flanked the wide windows spilling warm yellow light outside into the stormy night. The driver pulled to the curb.

"Ask for Abby Donovan. She runs the place," the driver said.

"Will do. I'll be right back."

"I'll wait. Abby's a nice person. I don't think she'll turn you out in the cold. You'll see."

Placing a broad-brimmed Stetson on his head, Josh stepped out of the warmth of the cab into the driving wind and streaming snow. Holding his hat against the battering wind, he trudged to the house to ring the bell. Through a window he could see a big living room with people inside and an inviting roaring fire in the fireplace.

When the door swung open, he momentarily forgot why he was there. A slender woman with huge, thickly lashed cornflower-blue eyes faced him. She wore a powder-blue sweater and jeans. He forgot the time, the howling storm and even his plight. Too captivated by eyes that widened and held him, Josh stood immobilized and silent until he realized how he stared at her.

"Abby Donovan?" His voice was husky, and he still was lost in her gaze.

She blinked as if as captured as he had been. "I'm Abby."

"I'm Josh Calhoun. I flew in to see someone about buying a horse, and then I couldn't get back to the airport. I was told to see you about a place to stay. I know you have a No Vacancy sign out, but at this point, I'm willing to sleep on the floor just to get in out of this blizzard."

"I'm so sorry, but we're overbooked. I already have people sleeping on the floor."

"My cabdriver can't get back to the airport. They've closed the roads."

"I'm sorry, but even the overflow space is taken here. I've let two people come in tonight who will sleep on sofas, and we have two on pallets on the floor. That's the most I can possibly accommodate. I have eighteen adults in rooms, plus nine children. Four other people live here at least part of the time. I don't have extra blankets or pillows now—"

"I stopped and bought blankets and a pillow at the only store open in this town just as they closed. I'm desperate."

"Oh, my," she said, staring at him with a slight frown. Her rosy lips were full, enticing. He tried to focus on getting a bed for the night and stop thinking about the possibility of kissing her. He couldn't recall ever having this type of reaction to a total stranger, much less under his present circumstances. His gaze roamed over her, and he was even more surprised by his attraction to her, because her sandy-blond hair was caught up behind her head in a ponytail, giving her a plain look that shouldn't have done anything to his pulse. All he had to do was gaze into her eyes, though, and a physical response strummed in him. Her riveting blue eyes were unique.

"Abby, I'm desperate. I have bedding. I can sit in a chair. My cabdriver has little kids and wants to get home to them. Just any corner will do. Even a kitchen floor, and I'll get out of your way in the morning. I'll pay you double what you charge for a room."

Her frown deepened. "Come in while we talk. The air is cold."

"Yes, it is," he said as he stepped inside a wide hallway dominated by winding stairs to the second floor. Warmth enveloped him, and his spirits lifted a fraction. A floor mat was close, and he stamped his booted feet. "I can provide payment in advance, an extra fee—whatever you would like. I can't tell you how much I would appreciate this. I really am desperate. I was up until three last night working on a business deal in Arizona and flew in here today on the way home to see about the horse. I didn't have dinner. I'm tired and cold. I can't get home. It's a miserable night and even more miserable without a place to stay. What can I do to help if I stay here? Order in breakfast for everyone?"

Shaking her head, her frown vanished. "There's nowhere in Beckett you could order breakfast. I cook, and it'll be better than trying to order in at this time of night or in the morning. If this snow doesn't stop, no restaurants will be open."

"I'm sure you're right. You're highly praised in town, and I also heard you're softhearted, generous, kind—"

"Stop," she said, a faint smile appearing. "Tell me more about yourself. We're going to be in close quarters, more so than if you just called at an ordinary time and checked in for a room."

Josh was amused by being asked to give a reference, because he was well-known in Texas. "I'm Josh Calhoun from Verity, Texas, and I own a business, Calhoun Hotels."

Her gaze swept over him from his wide-brimmed

Stetson to his hand-tooled boots. "You're buying a horse, but you're in the hotel business?"

"I'm a rancher, too. The hotel headquarters are in Dallas, where I have another home, so you can check that out easily by calling the hotel's front desk. The sheriff of Verity can tell you about me because we've known each other all our lives," Josh said as he withdrew his wallet and flipped it open to show her his driver's license and fishing license. He was turning to the next license when she placed her fingers over his.

The contact sizzled, startling him and causing him to look up. She had stepped closer, and he could detect an old-fashioned lilac perfume. Again, he was caught and held by her stare.

She shook her head slightly. "You don't have to show more identification," she said, stepping away. "All right, you can stay tonight. You can sleep on the sofa in my suite, but I will not share my bathroom, so you'll have to go across the hall to a central one."

"That sounds like paradise," he said, smiling at her. "Thanks, Abby. This means a lot to me, because it's a deplorable night." He wondered if he could talk her into going to dinner with him some night. The cold and relief of acquiring a room must have affected his judgment, because she definitely didn't look like his type of woman. He didn't know her, either, and he didn't ask strangers to go out with him. "I'll get my bedding and pay the cabbie. I'll be back in a minute."

"The front door will be unlocked. I'll lock it after you're back inside."

He stepped closer to her. "You're not going to regret this."

She blinked as if startled. "I certainly hope I don't," she replied breathlessly.

He turned and left, pulling the door closed behind him. Holding his hat squarely on his head again, he sprinted to the taxi and climbed inside. "I got the room. Thanks for the ride," he said, drawing bills out of his wallet. "Thanks for getting me back into town after seeing about the horse. And thanks for your encouragement and for stopping so I could buy a pillow and blanket."

"Glad you found a place. Sorry I couldn't help more, but with the kids plus my in-laws staying, my two-bedroom duplex is not the best place, although you could have come if nothing else had turned up. Good luck to you. When the roads open and you're ready to go back to the airport, call—you have my card. I'll come get you."

"Thanks, Benny," Josh said, glancing at the man's identification card attached to the visor, knowing he would have stayed anywhere he could find before imposing on the cabbie and his family with four little ones plus in-laws in a tiny place. "I won't forget all you've done." Josh tucked an extra-large tip in with the other bills he gave the cabdriver.

"Mister, you made a mistake," the driver said, seeing how much money he had in his hand.

"No, I didn't. That's a thank-you. Take care of yourself and your family," Josh said.

The man smiled. "Thanks. That's a generous tip."

Josh started to step outside but stopped and looked back. "Does Ms. Donovan have a husband who helps her run the inn?"

"No. She's single—from a big family. Her grandmother used to run the place. Now Abby does, and Grandma Donovan lives up on the top floor with some other elderly relatives or over at her daughter's house, which is next door."

"I see," Josh said, deciding the town was small enough that everyone knew everyone else. "Thanks again." He stepped out into the snow to dash back to the inn.

Abby appeared instantly to lock the front door and switch off the porch light. Wind whistled and howled around the house.

"I'll show you where to put your things," she said, walking down the hall and turning as it branched off. "This is my suite." She stepped into a room and turned on a ceiling light. The room had a polished oak floor with a hand-woven area rug, antique mahogany furniture and bookshelves filled with books and family pictures. Green plants gave it an old-fashioned, cozy appearance that made him think of his grandparents' house. A stone fireplace had a smoldering fire with a screen in front of it.

"I started the fire a while ago so my room would be warm after I told everyone good-night," she said. "Most of the guests are in the big living room, and they go to their own rooms about eleven, when I shut everything down. Tonight is a little different because no one can get up and leave in the morning, so I think some will watch a movie. Suit yourself about what you do. You can leave your things and join us, or if you prefer, you can stay in here. There is a door from my bedroom into the hall, so I can come and go that way and not disturb you. You'll have this room to yourself. As soon as I get towels for you and get you registered, I'll go join them again."

"I'll go with you," he said, placing his pillow and blanket on the sofa before shedding his coat. He wore a thick brown sweater over a white dress shirt, jeans and boots and was glad he had dressed warmly.

"You'll be too long for that old-fashioned sofa. Would you rather sleep on the floor?"

"I'll be fine. Just to have a roof over my head is paradise. I don't mind my feet hanging off the sofa," he said, smiling at her. Once again he received a riveting look that momentarily immobilized him until she turned away.

"I'll get your towels," she said and left. He watched her cross the hall and disappear into a room. She returned to hand him clean towels and washcloths.

"If you'll come with me, you can register."

Josh followed her to the front desk of polished dark wood with scratches from what must have been years of use. He glanced around at the decorative staircase rails. "This place looks Victorian."

"It is. It's been in my family for five generations now." She turned a ledger toward him. "Please sign your name. I'll need a credit card. Since you'll be on the sofa, I'll just charge you a discounted rate. Here are the rates and details about staying here," she added, handing a paper to him. "And here's a map of the inn and a map of the town of Beckett, although you won't be leaving tomorrow, because we're supposed to get a lot more snow and possibly sleet."

"No, I'm stuck probably through tomorrow at least."

"Everything has shut down—highways, roads and businesses will be closed tomorrow. They've already had the announcements on television and said schools will be closed Monday." She reached under the desk and produced a small flashlight. "We heard on the radio that half the town is without power because of ice on electric lines. I'm giving all the guests flashlights. This is an old house, and candles are dangerous."

"Thanks." Pocketing the flashlight, Josh barely

glanced at the papers she handed him as he studied her instead. Her smooth, flawless skin and rosy cheeks added to her appeal. What was it about her that fueled this tingling awareness of her? It wasn't her personality, because he barely knew her and had spoken with her only briefly. Her fuzzy sweater came to her thighs and hid her figure, so that wasn't the electrifying draw. She was a nice person who was being helpful. That should be all. Instead, he had a scalding awareness of her that made him think about asking her out, fantasize about dancing with her and holding her, and wonder what it would be like to kiss her and make love with her. She was providing shelter and comfort; maybe it was his long hours of work over the past few days and now the storm that caused his reaction to her. He had slept little for over a week.

When she turned the register around, she read what he had signed. "This gives a Dallas address. Do you consider Dallas home instead of Verity?"

"I live and work in Dallas most of the time. I also have a ranch in west Texas. The closest town is Verity," he replied. She nodded as she gathered more papers to hand to him.

"So you're a hobby rancher," she said.

"Yes, at least for now. Someday I'll move to the ranch and do that full-time and let someone else run the hotel business for me. I go to the ranch when I get a chance, but that rarely happens," he admitted, thinking there weren't many people who knew he missed ranching and wondering why he was telling a stranger.

"Here's the schedule for tomorrow," she said. "Normally breakfast runs from seven-thirty until 9:00 a.m. Since no one can get out tomorrow, we'll start at 8:00 a.m. and go until nine-thirty."

"Thanks. The breakfast time is fine."

"I'll be going back to join the others now unless you have anything else you want to ask me about," she said, looking up, those wide eyes capturing his full attention again.

"Thanks, no. I'll follow you."

"We've been singing. I play the piano or leave it to a guest."

They entered a large living room that ran almost the length of the east side of the house and was furnished in early American maple with a hardwood floor and area rugs. A fire burned low in the fireplace, adding to the inviting appeal of the room. Two small children slept in adults' arms. Five children sprawled on the floor or in an adult's lap. A couple of men stood to offer Abby a seat. Smiling, she thanked them and asked the men to sit.

"We've been waiting. Let's sing some more," someone said.

"Folks, this is another guest—Josh Calhoun of Dallas, Texas," Abby said, smiling and glancing at him while he acknowledged her introduction with a nod and wave of his hand.

People said hi as Abby crossed the room to slide onto the piano bench. She played a song Josh had heard his grandmother play, a song from his childhood that he was surprised to discover he still knew when he joined in the singing.

As they sang, he watched her play. She was not his type in any manner, other than being a woman. He couldn't understand his reaction to her. She was plain, with her hair in an unflattering thick ponytail, and she wore no makeup. She ran a bed-and-breakfast inn in a small west Texas town. He would never ask her out.

He looked out the window at the howling storm blowing heavy snow in horizontal waves. Snowflakes struck the warmer storm window, melted slightly, slid to the bottom and built up along the frame. It was a cozy winter scene, but he wished he were flying home tonight.

Relaxing, he leaned back in the chair and sang with the others while he reflected that he hadn't experienced an evening like this in years. He felt as if he had stepped back to a different time and way of life, and he began to relax and enjoy himself.

After another half hour, Abby turned and slid off the piano bench to take a bow. "That should do for tonight's songfest. Does anyone want hot chocolate? If so, I'll be glad to make some. The entertainment room is open, and Mr. Julius said he will be in charge of the movie. Right now, for hot cocoa, just come to the kitchen."

She left the room. People followed her out until Josh was the only one left. He turned off all the lights except one. He sat again, stretching out his legs and leaning back to gaze at the snow. A few red embers of the dying fire glowed brightly in gray ashes.

He heard tapping and looked again at the window. Sleet struck the glass, building up swiftly on top of the snow at the bottom. He placed his hands behind his head. He couldn't go anywhere or do anything for the rest of the night and probably all day tomorrow. As a peaceful contentment filled him, he thought that an unplanned holiday had befallen him, and he intended to enjoy it.

"You don't want any hot chocolate?"

He glanced around to see Abby entering the room. As he stood, she motioned to him to be seated. "No, thanks," he said. "I'm enjoying the quiet and the storm now that I'm inside and it's outside. I'm beginning to think I'm getting a much-needed vacation."

"That's a good way to look at being stranded. I usually let the fire burn out this time of night. Did you plan to sit here a lot longer?" she asked.

"I'm fine. Let the fire die. I'll turn out the light when I go. If you aren't going to watch the movie, sit and join me," he said.

"Thanks. I will while I can. Mr. Julius knows how to deal with the movie."

"My cabdriver said you're single. This is a big place to run by yourself."

"I'm definitely not by myself," she said, smiling as she sat in a rocker. "I have a long list of people I can rely on for help. I have a brother and a sister nearby, and my grandmother lives here part of the time. I can turn to her for advice if I need it because she used to own and run this place."

"So there are three kids in your family?"

"Right. I'm the oldest. The next is my brother, twenty-year-old Justin, in his second year at a nearby junior college on an academic scholarship. He helps with the bed-and-breakfast and lives at home with Mom. Arden, the youngest at seventeen, is a junior in high school, and she also works here at the inn and lives at home. What about you?"

"I've got two brothers and one sister. This is a big bed-and-breakfast—I'm surprised it doesn't hold more people than you listed earlier."

"I mentioned the people on the third floor who are permanent residents. My grandmother stays here about half of the year. I have two great-aunts who live here part of the year, and I have Mr. Hickman, who is elderly. His family is in Dallas. He's told me that his married sons run a business he had. They have asked him to move to Dallas and live with them, but he grew up here and came back here when he retired and his wife was still living. I think she's the one who wanted to return to Beckett because she still had relatives here. His wife was my grandmother's best friend, so he lives here. He has a little hearing problem, but he's in relatively good health. There is an elevator the elderly residents can take, so they don't use the stairs. My aunts and my grandmother are gone right now—my grandmother at Mom's and my aunts visiting their families."

"Do you have to take care of them?"

"No, not really. I have a van and drive them to town once a week, and I'll take them to church. My brother or sister or I take them for haircuts, little things. They just need someone around. By living here, they have that. My great-aunts' families have scattered and are on both coasts. They don't want to move, but they may have to someday. Right now, they're happy here with my grandmother and our part of the family."

"That's commendable of you to let them live here. You're young to be tied down to a bed-and-breakfast."

"I'm over twenty-one," she said, smiling at him. "Twenty-five to be exact."

"This is a lot of responsibility," he remarked, noting that her attire hid her figure, except for the V-neck of her sweater, which revealed curves. Also, even in suede boots, it was obvious she had long legs as she stretched them out and crossed her feet at her ankles.

"It's fun, and I meet interesting people. I can work here in my hometown, actually work at home."

"For some, working at home in your hometown is a drawback, not a plus," he said, thinking he didn't know a single woman like her with such a simple life.

"For me it's a definite plus. I've never been out of Texas and never been out of my hometown much beyond Dallas or north to Wichita Falls or around west Texas, south to San Antonio once. I don't really want to go anywhere else. Everyone I love is here."

Thinking of his own travels, Josh smiled. "You're a homebody."

"Very much of one," she said. "I suspect you're not, and you sound as if you're a busy man. Are you married, Josh?"

"No, I'm single, not into commitment at this point in my life. I travel a lot, and this is a job I like," he said. "Or have liked. At heart I'm a rancher, which is why I came to Beckett to see about a horse."

Big blue eyes studied him, and he thought again how easy it was to look at her.

"You have two vastly different interests—I guess, vocations—ranching and the corporate world," she said. "Does your family live close?"

My siblings are here in Texas, but our parents retired in California. Are both your parents next door?"

"Mom is. She's divorced. She's Nell Donovan, a hairdresser who has a shop in her house. Her story is well-known in town, so it's no secret—my dad ran off with a younger woman he met on his business travels. That was when I was fourteen. He traveled a lot."

"Sorry that he left your mother and your family."

"We hardly saw him anyway because of his job."

"So besides this inn and family, what do you like to do?"

"Gardening, swimming. I'd like to have a pool here, but so far, that hasn't worked out. I like little kids. Once a week I have a story hour at the library and read to preschool kids. I also like movies and tennis."

The thought flitted to mind again to ask her to dinner when the storm was over and the snow melted. Instantly, he vetoed his own thought. She was the earnest type who would take everything seriously. With a sigh, he turned back to look at the fire, trying to forget her sitting so close. It was even more difficult to ignore the tingly awareness of her that he couldn't shake.

"Is there a guy in your life?"

"Sort of," she said, smiling. "There's someone local. We've grown up knowing each other, and we like the same things, so we occasionally go out together. I always figure someday we'll marry, but we seldom talk about it. Neither of us is in a hurry."

"That doesn't sound too serious," Josh said, wondering what kind of man the guy was to have that type of relationship.

She shrugged. "We're after the same things. He wants never to move from Beckett, and I don't either. Our lives are tied up here. He's an accountant, and we're both busy. It's pretty simple."

They lapsed into silence. Josh wondered if in a few months he would even remember her.

"I hope no one else appears on your doorstep and wants shelter," he remarked after a time. "I have two blankets, and I'd feel compelled to give him a blanket and let him sleep on the floor in the room I have."

"I've turned off the porch light, and I can't take anyone else. In the morning I'll have to cook for thirty-five people. We barely have enough of certain food items, and my brother and sister are both out of town, so I'm without help. I can't handle another person."

"I'll help you cook breakfast," Josh volunteered, the words coming without thought.

She laughed softly. "Thanks. You don't look like the type to have done much kitchen work."

He grinned. "I'm a man of many talents," he joked. "I've cooked. I've camped and cooked, cooked as a kid. Occasionally I cook at home, but rarely, I'll admit. I can help. I can serve and that sort of thing."

"Watch out, I'll take you up on your offer."

"I mean it. I'll help you," he said, still wondering why he was so drawn to her. He should have gone to bed an hour ago or when he arrived. "What time will you begin cooking?"

"About six. You don't have to get up that early."

"I'm usually up that early. I'll set the alarm on my phone," he said, getting his phone from his pocket. "I haven't had a call since I arrived," he added, realizing that was a switch in his life, as different as so many other things about this night.

"You surely don't get many calls at night."

"Sometimes. Not getting any is a unique change in my life, and I can live with it tonight easily." He put away his phone. "It's like a holiday. Tell me more about your family."

He settled back in the chair, listening and talking to her as the fire died into gray ashes. It was after one in the morning when she stood. "I should go to bed. Six a.m. will come soon."

He stood to walk with her, stopping at the door to his room for the night. "I'll see you at six. Thanks again for this room."

"Thanks for offering to help in the morning. Good night, Josh."

"Good night," he replied in a husky voice, gazing into her eyes and as riveted as he had been the first moment he had seen her. Still puzzled by his reaction to her, he turned to his door.

Then he glanced down the hall to see her ponytail swing with each step as she walked away. There was nothing about her that should set his heart racing, but it did. He still wanted her in his arms, wanted to kiss her at least, before he left Beckett forever. What made his heart beat even faster were the slight reactions she'd had—her blue eyes widening, a sudden breathless moment in which neither of them spoke—that told him she had felt something, too. He didn't intend to let that go by without doing something to satisfy his curiosity.

Two

Certain Josh stood watching her, Abby felt her back tingle as she walked to her door. What was it about him that made her heartbeat race and took her breath away? She hadn't had that kind of reaction to anyone since she was a teenager. She occasionally dated Lamont Nealey, who lived close by. She had grown up friends with him, closer friends than with any other man, but he never stirred a quicker heartbeat. A slight physical contact with Lamont never made her tingle all over.

As she changed into flannel pajamas, she kept glancing at the door that separated her from Josh. She couldn't shake her awareness of him so close at hand.

She smiled as she thought about his offer of help with breakfast because he had to be wealthy and influential. He probably had a lot of people working for him and keeping him from everyday tasks. She didn't really expect him to pitch in and help.

* * *

The first thing Abby did on waking was slip into her robe and shove her feet into fuzzy slippers to walk to the window. While the wind continued to howl, she opened the drapes and stared at the falling snow. It meant more business, but she never lacked long for business. It was the third weekend in March. A snowstorm rarely occurred so late, but this had been a cold winter in Beckett. With more snow, no one would be leaving the inn, and her brother and sister couldn't get home, so she had a day of work ahead of her.

She glanced at the closed door to the sitting room and wondered how Josh had fared on her short sofa. Her gaze went to the clock, and she hurried to shower.

She spent too long deciding what to wear, finally giving up and pulling on faded jeans, a green sweater and her suede boots. She had told Josh 6:00 a.m. but went to the kitchen half an hour earlier so she could get started alone.

At six on the dot she heard his boots against the wood floor, and her pulse speeded—something she wished wouldn't happen.

"Good morning," Josh said, bringing a dynamic charge into the air as he smiled at her. He had on a navy sweater, jeans and boots and looked like a cowboy in an ad in one of the Western magazines. "Or at least it's a good snowy morning. I see more of the white stuff coming down."

"Sorry. I think you're stuck for a time. Did you get any sleep on the short sofa?"

"Yes, I did. I'm enormously grateful that I didn't have to sleep in the lobby of your town's only hotel."

"I'm sure they would have let you sit in a chair all night."

"They had some employees who couldn't get home, so they were as booked up and as overcrowded as you. I think I was in the town's only available taxi."

"I know you were. We have only one taxi, with people taking different shifts to drive."

He smiled. "What can I do to help? It looks as if you've been up awhile and working. How about I get the pots and pans washed?"

"Wonderful," she said, surprised he would pick such a job. "I'm getting the breakfast casseroles made. The biscuit dough is rising. I'll get the fruit and coffee soon. The table is ready. We're moving along."

"What you mean is, you're moving along. Pretty good for working without any help. You will make someone a good wife," he said, smiling at her as he crossed the kitchen.

"Are you interested?" she teased, certain there was no way he would have any designs on her—or anyone right now—as a wife. He had been about to pass her, but he stopped and turned to look at her. He stood close, and she wished she could take back her flirty remark.

"If I were looking for a wife, I would want to find out what other qualities you have along with capable, kind-hearted and fun. Without looking for a wife, it might be interesting to find out," he teased back, his eyes twinkling and making her insides flutter.

"I should have stuck to talking about what work needs to be done," she whispered, wishing she weren't breathless. "I don't usually joke like that with the guests."

"You mean flirt like that with the guests," he said with amusement, and she could feel the blush that swept across her cheeks. Something flickered in the depths of his eyes, and his smile vanished as he looked more intently at her. "Now I really do want to find out," he said in a deeper tone of voice.

"No, you don't. It wouldn't possibly interest you. In every way," she whispered, "I lead a quiet life without excitement, without the outside world intruding, without—" She stopped to stare at him.

"Without what?" he prompted, stepping closer, his gaze searching hers.

"If you wait a lifetime, you won't get an answer from me on that one. It's my fault we're on a subject we don't need to discuss. Let's go back to talking about breakfast."

"That makes what you said all the more interesting," he remarked, placing his hands on both sides of her and hemming her in against the counter, leaning even closer. His eyes were a dark brown, his brown hair straight and neatly combed. His jaw was clean-shaven and she could detect the fresh smell of his aftershave. Her heart pounded, and she couldn't get her breath.

"Josh, maybe I should take care of breakfast alone," she said.

"I disturb you?"

"You've disturbed me since you rang the bell last night at ten," she said bluntly. "I need to get back to breakfast before I burn something."

A faint smile lifted one corner of his mouth. "My morning has started out better than I ever dreamed possible," he said quietly and dropped his hands, moving back.

She passed him, going to the dining room even though she had the table set and ready. She opened a drawer in a buffet and got two serving spoons, moving without thinking about what she was doing, trying to give her pounding heart a chance to slow to normal.

For a moment she had thought he was going to kiss her. With the kind of reaction she had to him, she shouldn't be alone with him. She didn't need distraction from her routine life, or a charmer like Josh, a man who'd merely stopped in Beckett because of a storm. He was another man like her father. The charmer, the traveler, the businessman who could not settle or be faithful. Josh had the same knack for making friends with people he met, and any man with a private jet did a lot of traveling, constantly reminding her of her father. She shivered and turned back to work.

When the weather permitted, Josh would leave, and he would not return. Her heart did not need to get caught up with someone who would go on his way without a thought for Beckett or anyone who lived here.

Returning to the kitchen, she glanced at Josh as he stood at the sink filled with soapy water with his sleeves pushed up, his watch on the windowsill while he scrubbed pans. Amazed that he would work on a tedious, routine job he didn't have to do, she went on to get breakfast, trying to forget Josh or her response when he had stood close or when he flirted.

They worked quietly together, but even as she concentrated on breakfast as the morning progressed, she was aware of Josh working nearby.

Though it was still early for breakfast, she heard shuffling in the hall. As she expected, her tenant Mr. Hickman entered the kitchen, smiling at her. "Good morning, Abby. You look as beautiful as ever."

"Good morning, Mr. Hickman. Thank you. What can I do for you?"

He pulled his brown cardigan closer over his white shirt. "The snow has made me hungry. Can I get a poached egg and a piece of French toast? I don't suppose that's on the menu for this morning."

"I'll fix it for you and you can sit in here to eat. You remember our agreement?"

"Certainly. If I ask for something special, I'll eat it in the kitchen so the others do not expect special favors," he said, chuckling. "I brought yesterday's paper because I don't think we'll get one today."

"I don't think we will, either. Josh, our latest guest, is helping. He can eat in here with you and keep you company," she said, and Josh turned around, drying his hands. "Josh, meet Mr. Hickman. Mr. Hickman, this is Josh Calhoun from Verity and Dallas. He came late last night."

"How do you do, Mr. Hickman," Josh said, shaking the elderly man's hand gently.

"Come join me for breakfast," Mr. Hickman said.

"Mr. Hickman's having a poached egg and French toast," Abby told Josh. "Would you like that, too?"

"I've seen the breakfast casserole and the biscuits—I'd like them if you have enough."

"We have plenty," she said. "I'll get coffee and juice for both of you."

"Go on with what you have to do," Josh said, "and I'll take care of us. If you need help with serving out there, I'll do it."

"Thank you," she replied, surprised again that he was willing to work.

It was after eight and she expected people to begin showing for breakfast, so she hurried to get things ready, poaching the egg and making French toast for Mr. Hickman. She wondered whether Josh minded sitting with him, but in minutes she heard them in conversation and realized Josh seemed happy talking to the elderly man and vice versa. She knew Mr. Hickman was happy, because he spent many long hours without anyone to talk to.

When the first guests came downstairs to be seated for breakfast, she picked up a large serving dish holding the casserole. Josh stepped in front of her, his fingers brushing hers as he took the dish from her. "Let me. You just fill the plates or whatever you do. I'll take things to the dining room. I waited tables in college. I told Mr. Hickman I'd be right back, and he's reading his paper."

"You're nice to sit with him," she said.

"He reminds me of a grandfather I was close to. I like Mr. Hickman."

She felt a pang. She realized she had been hoping Josh would disappoint her and not like eating in the kitchen or with the elderly man, which would cause her to lose some of her attraction for him. Instead, she was more drawn to him in spite of wishing she weren't.

She handed the plates to him and went back to fill more. She wondered about his life, and if he had needed a job waiting tables to make the money to go to school. It had been late last night so she hadn't looked him up on the web, but today she would do a little research on him.

Soon she was too busy dealing with her guests to think about Josh. Finally the dining room was empty and Mr. Hickman had gone to the living room, taking his paper with him.

"Now I'm going to have breakfast," she told Josh, helping herself. "Can I get you something else?"

He stood to pour another cup of coffee. "I'll get what I want. When you sit, I'll join you." He headed to the dining room and returned carrying dishes, which he placed in the sink. When she finally sat down at the table to eat, he picked up his cup of steaming coffee and sat facing her.

"So what did you and Mr. Hickman talk about?"

"He's interesting. He's a fisherman, so we talked about fishing holes and fly-fishing and the biggest trout caught around here, which of course was in a pond that had been stocked."

"So you have time to fish on top of being a business-man and a rancher."

"No, not as often as I'd like. I miss it."

"Maybe this snow is good for you—chance to stop the constant work and enjoy life and that sort of thing," she said.

"Oh, I know how to enjoy life," he said quietly, giv-ing her a look that made his remark personal.

"Relax, Josh. Enjoy this snow. I'd be as lost in your busy corporate world as you are in mine."

"Do you like to dance?"

"I love to dance but do little of it. I don't get out often. If I go out, it's with Lamont Nealey, whom I've known forever—the friend I was telling you about last night. When we go out, we go to a movie or something on that order."

"You think I'm missing out on life," Josh said, "and I think you are. At the same time, I think we have a bit of common ground where we view life the same way. You're a family person just as I'm a family person."

"So tell me about your family."

He reached across the table and wrapped his fin-gers lightly around her wrist with his thumb where he could feel her pulse. "Coward," he accused her softly. "I'll leave it alone now, but we'll take up this subject again sometime soon."

"You didn't see the sign when you came in that reads

'Guests do not flirt with the staff,'" she said, smiling at him.

"I sure as hell didn't see any such sign, and if I had, I would pay no attention to it. Not when I get a response from the staff like the one I'm getting right now," he said, his thumb pressing slightly on her wrist. "Your pulse is galloping."

"That means nothing," she said, too aware of his brown eyes that seemed alert, observant and curious.

"Not where I come from," he retorted. "You want me to tell you what it means?"

"No. You tell me about your family or I'm going to join the guests in the living room."

With a faint smile, Josh sat back in his chair. "I have three siblings," he said. "Two older brothers, Mike and Jake, plus a younger sister, Lindsay."

She listened, learning about his family but still knowing little about his background. From what he had said last night, she suspected a lot of Texans knew who he was. She had an idea he was well-known by wealthy Texas businessmen and probably by Texas socialites.

She was interrupted when a guest came for a late breakfast. As she served it, Josh poured coffee.

Through the morning he worked, doing whatever she needed, and he was a big help to her. Breakfast was over and the kitchen cleaned by a quarter past ten.

"Josh, thanks so much," she said. "Now I'll have a break before lunch, which I'm serving because of the weather. No one can get out for lunch."

"I'm getting the hang of it. I can help with lunch."

That surprised her—or maybe it shouldn't have. "I'm taking a short break. Come back in a little while and we can get started."

"Sure," he said, jamming a hand in his pocket and leaving the kitchen.

As she headed out and walked past the library, Mr. Hickman lowered his paper and motioned to her to come in.

"Perhaps you should close the door," he said, stirring her curiosity about what he wanted. "Do you know who your guest Josh Calhoun is? Or his company?"

"I don't know much about him. He said his business is Calhoun Hotels, and he's a rancher occasionally," she said. "He's just staying until the roads open, and then I'm sure he'll be gone forever."

"Oh, no. I think he'll come back to fish with me."

"I hope so, if that's what you want, but he sounds as if he's wrapped up in his work," she said.

Mr. Hickman's brow furrowed, and his watery blue eyes gazed into the distance. "Perhaps at the moment." His attention returned to her, and he stared at her a moment before he smiled. "He asked a few questions about you. He's a very nice young man. A knowledgeable fisherman, from his conversation. I liked him."

"Well, that's good, because he's here for a few days."

Mr. Hickman whispered, "If I were Josh Calhoun, I would ask you out to dinner."

"I think Josh has a girlfriend," she whispered back, not knowing whether he did or not, but wanting to stop Mr. Hickman from pursuing that topic with Josh or anyone else.

Mr. Hickman nodded. "Nice fella. Too bad."

"Mr. Hickman, you like Lamont. That's who I go out with sometimes."

"If I were Lamont, I would not wait two or three months between dates. I would never have won my Barbara if I had done that."

She smiled and patted his hand. "Lamont is nice, and we're very much alike. That's what counts."

"Lamont is my accountant, and you're my landlady. Frankly, I don't think you're as much alike as you seem to think."

"Do not be a matchmaker, Mr. Hickman. I'm very happy with Lamont. Now I'm going to my room. Are you going upstairs?"

"No, I'll sit and read the rest of yesterday's paper," he said. "You may leave the door open when you go."

Smiling, she left to go to her room, but her smile faded when she glanced at the closed door between her bedroom and her sitting room, where Josh had slept. He was in his room now, just on the other side of the door. What was he doing? She thought about her reassurances to Mr. Hickman regarding how alike she and Lamont were and how happy she was going out with him. She gazed at the door as if looking at Josh instead and thought about how he had flirted and what fun she had had with him this morning—something that was totally lacking in her relationship with Lamont. Lamont was an old friend. There was none of the electricity that sparked between Josh and her, no flirting, no fun in that way.

She hadn't stopped to think about it before. Was she really that happy with Lamont? Would they ever marry or just go through life as friends? What did she really want? She had never questioned her relationship with him.

Always, her thoughts turned to her parents—she never wanted to be hurt the way her mother had been when her father had walked out on them. Shaking her head as if she could get rid of thoughts about Josh, she knew Lamont was the type of man she needed in her life: steady, reliable, dependable. Those qualities were what counted and meant a satisfying life.

For an instant, a memory flashed of her father, who could coax a laugh from her and make the whole world seem magical. She focused on the inn, trying to avoid remembering how much she had loved her father. The hurt still came after all these years any time she recalled the shock when he'd suddenly left them.

She went to her computer and pulled up Calhoun Hotels and read about Josh's business, but she found little actual information about him.

When she returned to the kitchen to start on lunch, she was surprised to discover Josh already had the table set and was preparing a pitcher of ice water.

"You're a help. You don't have to keep working. You're a paying guest, so go do something enjoyable," she said.

As he shook his head, he grinned. "I don't mind, and it keeps me busy. It's a change of pace for me and keeps my thoughts off what is piling up in my office while I'm gone." He glanced out the window. "The snow has finally stopped."

"I checked the weather report before coming down— we might get more before morning."

"As soon as the roads open, I'll rent a car and drive home. I can rent a car in Beckett, can't I?"

"Oh, yes. We have car rental at the airport. But I don't think you'll get out tomorrow or the day after."

"I don't think so, either."

She glanced at him. "You were nice to Mr. Hickman this morning. He enjoyed talking to you." Why had she brought up Mr. Hickman when the elderly man was clearly trying to matchmake?

"Edwin Hickman is an interesting fellow, and I

enjoyed talking to him, too. He told me more about Lamont Nealey."

"Pay no attention to whatever Mr. Hickman said about Lamont."

"He said Lamont takes you out about once every three months. He also said you've told him you'll probably marry Lamont someday."

"Mr. Hickman exaggerates, and he doesn't remember accurately. Lamont and I go out when we want. Going out occasionally is good and makes it special," she said, thinking it really wasn't special, just a change from her routine to go to a show she wanted to see or Lamont wanted to attend. She had no intention of sounding as if she wanted Josh to ask her out, although she didn't think there was any chance of that ever happening. He should have no interest in her or a town like Beckett. Not the cosmopolitan Josh Calhoun, head of Calhoun Hotels.

"As for marrying Lamont, that may happen someday. We're compatible, we've known each other forever and Lamont is ideal. He's grown up here, works here and doesn't want to leave here. That description fits me also. How many men would feel that way?"

"Have you ever heard the old saying 'opposites attract'?" Josh asked with a faint smile.

"I've heard the saying, but it's no part of my life. Lamont is the ideal man for me—very plain tastes, will never leave Beckett, tied to his family—which in his case is only his mother and a married aunt and her family. We're alike, we've known each other since we were children and neither of us is in a rush to marry. That's all I want."

"You're damn easy to please. More than any woman I've ever known."

"I'm sure I'm not like women you've known," she

said, smiling at him. "I know you can't imagine such a simple life as Lamont's or mine, but that's what I know and like. My mother falls into your 'opposites attract' category. My dad was a charmer, a traveling salesman. He was delightful, but oh, so unreliable, and after three kids, he finally left Mom for another woman he met in California. When he did, it broke her heart, and I don't like to remember that time. It was sad for all of us."

"That doesn't mean all men with personalities like your dad's won't be faithful or honor their marriage vows."

"I'm not sure I believe that. I've heard he now has his fourth wife. I don't want someone like that in my life. What about you, Josh? You're single. I seriously doubt if you're searching for your opposite," she said, amused. "You would be bored beyond measure."

"I suppose you're right," he said, smiling with her. "Right now, I'm not at the point where I care to get tied down. You're already tied down with this inn— that's 24/7. You work more than I do, and that's saying something."

"It doesn't seem like work," she said. "I enjoy the people and the job and taking care of the inn. I enjoy my family and Mr. Hickman, Aunt Trudy and Aunt Millie."

"Well, you're good at what you do, and I will be forever grateful for getting to stay here."

"I'd better get moving because lunch will come before you know it." As she walked away, her back tingled, and she had to fight the urge to glance over her shoulder. She was certain he watched her. But what was he thinking?

Along with sandwiches that Josh helped her make for lunch, she had a pot of vegetable soup, a salad and

choices of chocolate or lemon cake, yogurt or cookies
for dessert.

All the time she worked, she couldn't lose the sharp
awareness she had of him. She thought it would diminish as she got accustomed to him being at the inn and
working with her, but it didn't diminish one tiny degree.

Far from it—as she felt a constant, tingling con-
sciousness of him wherever he was or whatever he did.

Through lunch she tried to ignore her fluttering insides. Afterward they sat and talked for an hour over
cups of coffee. Then Josh helped her get dinner started,
peeling potatoes while she prepared a roast. By the time
they cleaned up and sat down with cold drinks, the delicious smell of the roast and potatoes in a slow cooker
filled the kitchen.

"You've been such a help. I'll owe you when you
leave."

"No, you won't. Your inn has been a lifesaver."

A clock chimed in the hall. "Oh, my word. I need
to check the inn's email account before dinner. They
begin to drift down after five for a cocktail," she said,
standing and carrying her glass to the sink.

Turning, she almost bumped into him as he did the
same.

"Sorry," she said, causing him to smile.

"Slow down. I'll help with serving dinner and with
the cocktails. Where do you keep glasses? Do you have
a bar?"

"There's a small bar in the corner of the back room.
We were in the living room last night because of the
piano, but usually we gather in the back sitting room
because it's the largest. Through that door. I'll hurry
and be in the kitchen in about twenty minutes."

He set his glass in the sink and caught up with her

to head toward his room. They parted at the door, and she rushed on to her entrance. She had spent the day with him, and it had flown by swiftly. She liked being with him, still had the dizzying response to him physically and anticipated with a growing eagerness being with him again soon.

She knew that Josh would disappear from her life, but it had been fun while he was here—because she wasn't letting herself fall for him.

She showered and dressed in another thick sweater, this time pink. She pulled on jeans and her suede boots and brushed her hair into a fresh ponytail.

With an uncustomary eagerness, Abby went to the kitchen to check on dinner and set the table. Josh was already there in a charcoal sweater, chinos and his Western boots, his straight, short brown hair neatly combed. He hadn't shaved today, and a faint dark shadow of stubble on his jaw gave him a rugged look and added to his appeal. He was handsome enough that she had to fight the temptation to stare. Once again, Josh was helpful, setting the dining room table without even being asked.

When the first guests came downstairs, Josh left to serve them drinks. She was busy all through dinner and afterward until the kitchen was clean and everything put away. She heard Josh join the guests about five minutes before she did. As she went into the big sitting room, she could see through an open door some of the men playing pool in the billiards room. In the sitting room, some of the little girls sat at a table with crayons and coloring books. Other kids worked a puzzle, while two teens were busy with their phones. She looked at the fire Josh had built before dinner and saw it would soon go out.

Crossing the room to a game table, she stopped beside Josh, who sat playing cards with Mr. Hickman.

"Can I trade places briefly with you and get you to bring in some logs from the woodpile so the fire doesn't die?"

"Sure," Josh said, standing. "It's your turn, Mr. Hickman."

"I know, I know," he said without looking up.

She smiled at Josh, who stood only inches away. She hoped he never realized the extent of the reaction she had to his presence. "The woodpile is below the east windows of this room," she said, pointing. "You can go out through the kitchen. Thanks."

She slid onto his seat and watched Mr. Hickman. His wrinkled hands were poised on the edge of the board as he studied his cards.

They each played several cards before Josh returned carrying logs. He paused near Abby. "Folks, there is a huge full moon that you can see rising over the horizon if you step outside and look to the east," he announced, looking around the room. He glanced at Abby. "It's marvelous out," he added, setting down the logs. "Let's go look and then I'll build a fire."

"Mr. Hickman, do you want to look at the moon?" she asked.

"Of course," he said. "I'll get my coat. It's supposed to be seventeen degrees tonight."

"Can I go upstairs and get it for you, sir?" Josh asked.

"It's down here in the hall closet," Abby said.

"Thank you very much anyway," Mr. Hickman said to Josh.

Once Mr. Hickman had on his coat, Abby got hers out of the hall closet, and Josh held it for her as she slipped into it. "Ready, Mr. Hickman?"

"Ready," he replied.

Abby linked arms with Mr. Hickman and was aware

of Josh moving to the other side of him. Josh held the door, and finally they stepped out onto the porch and walked around the house. Her guests were clustered there, some huddled together because they hadn't bothered to get their coats. Some gasped at the wintry scene. The wind had finally died, and the snow had stopped falling. It was a cold, clear night, and an enormous moon hovered over the horizon. The moon was a huge white ball with gray patterns on its surface. Nobody had walked through the snow beyond the house yet, and it was pristine, glistening in the bright moonlight.

"Just a minute," Abby said, releasing Mr. Hickman's arm and walking to one side of the crowd. "Folks, we have an old Texas legend about the moon. If you'll move over here on the porch where I'm standing, you can see two oak trees in the yard with entwined branches." She waited a moment as the group clustered around her.

"The full moon shining on those oak trees sometimes casts a heart-shaped shadow. There's an old legend here that if two people kiss in that shadow, they will fall in love with each other for the rest of their lives. If you want to see the shadow, you have to stand on this part of the porch, or if you're in the yard, stand right in front of the porch at this place."

"Has anyone who has stayed at the inn ever seen it and kissed in the shadow?" someone asked.

"Oh, yes," Abby said. "Including my grandparents. My grandfather died very young, so my grandmother wasn't married long, but she always loved him and has never remarried." Talking softly, people turned to watch as shadows across the snow changed gradually.

"So, have you ever kissed in this shadow?" a deep voice asked beside Abby. She turned to glance at Josh, thankful for the darkness that hid a blush warming her cheeks.

"No, I haven't. There—look, Josh, I think the shadow is forming," she whispered, watching the shifting dark patterns on the dazzling white snow. The crowd became silent, seemingly transfixed.

There was a collective gasp when a heart-shaped shadow became visible. People began to call out about it and hold up their phones to take pictures. One couple ran down the porch steps to kiss in the shadow. Two more couples joined them, and little kids laughed and clapped. Someone whistled.

"We can't waste that," Josh said, taking her hand and hurrying down the steps.

"Josh—"

"It's only a kiss," he said, rushing to stand in the shadow of the heart and pull her to him.

"This is absurd," she said, laughing, her own heart pounding wildly. "Suppose it comes true? We don't even know each other. You're tempting fate. We might not like each other—"

"We'll find out," he said, wrapping his arms around her and leaning down to kiss her. His mouth covered hers.

Shocked, excited, caught off guard, she thought this kiss was the craziest thing she had ever done in her quiet, ordinary life. And then she stopped thinking and was consumed by his kiss, which built a fire deep within her. She couldn't get her breath. She became oblivious to the cold, the snow and the people around her, as well as the knowledge that she barely knew Josh. All she was aware of was his mouth on hers, his arms banding her tightly, holding her against his solid, warm length.

She had never been kissed like this, held like this. She wrapped her arms around his neck and kissed him passionately in return. The reason for their kiss vanished. All she knew was Josh, his hard strength, his tongue that took her breath completely and stirred her desire to a level she hadn't experienced before.

With Josh's kiss, her world and her life underwent a change as subtle as the shifting shadows around her, but in another way, a change far more monumental. Desire burned hotly, enveloping her, permeating her being. She clung tightly to him, kissing him in a way she had never kissed any other man.

At some point she realized where she was and what she was doing. With an effort she stepped back. As they broke apart, people clapped again, laughed and whistled. She was thankful for the darkness, because her face burned from embarrassment as she tried to smile but couldn't.

For once, Josh's ever-ready smile didn't appear. He stared at her.

"We drew a crowd," she said quietly. "That shadow is long gone."

"Yeah."

She turned away. Josh caught her hand as people clapped again. "Bow," he said. "We have an audience. Let's join the fun, and the moment will pass. Sort of."

She curtsied as Josh bowed again.

The crowd broke up. Kids were tossing snowballs, and several had started a snowman. The snow crunched beneath their feet as they walked back to the inn. They stopped to accompany Mr. Hickman.

"Josh is an enterprising young man," Mr. Hickman said, laughter in his voice. "I shall try to prevail upon him to go fishing with me."

"That would be nice," she said, thinking Josh would never come back to Beckett, and he probably was too busy to fish often. When he did, she suspected he flew to Colorado or Idaho or some location where fishing was much more challenging and satisfying than a stocked pond in a small west Texas town.

They went inside and put away their coats. "Want to finish our game?" Josh asked Mr. Hickman.

"Yes, indeed, and then it will be my bedtime."

"See you later," Josh said to her, and the two men turned to go to their game. One of the guests stopped to ask her if they would be having cocoa later.

"Yes. Would you and your family like some now? I can make it now just as easily."

"That would be wonderful. I'll come help."

"You don't need to. I'll announce it as soon as it's ready. It doesn't really take long."

"Thank you, Abby. We all look forward to your homemade hot cocoa," the petite blonde said. "I'll tell my family and the others."

Abby hurried to the kitchen, trying to focus on making hot cocoa for everyone and keeping Josh's kiss out of her thoughts for now. She failed to stop thinking about him, but she had made cocoa so many times in her life, she could do what she needed to without much thought.

Finally she escaped to her room for a moment to catch her breath. As soon as she shut her door, she leaned against it. Remembering Josh's kiss, she closed her eyes. Why did she have this huge reaction to Josh, of all people, who would go out of her life as swiftly as he had come into it?

Three

Abby crossed the room to look into the mirror. She should look different, but she didn't. She felt different, as if Josh's kiss had somehow in some subtle manner changed her permanently.

She knew she had lived a sheltered, quiet life, but she had no idea a man's kiss could ignite a raging fire in her.

It was just as well he would soon leave. Occasionally men would stay at the inn who were charming and single. They would flirt and ask her out, and she had always turned them down. There had never been anybody she had particularly wanted to go out with, and she had never had a reason to cause any ripples in her relationship with Lamont. She had always felt secure, comfortable and reasonably happy with him, but was she cutting deep joy and fun out of her life? There were other nice guys in Beckett and areas close around. Answering Josh's questions about Lamont made her realize her romantic relationship with her old friend was almost nonexistent. Had she let the hurt caused by her father influence her too strongly? She went out with Lamont because it was convenient and easy.

Josh had not asked her out, and she didn't expect he would. Any day now he'd pack and go, and she would never see him again. How long would it take to forget his kiss?

Was that going to dim her relationship with Lamont, whose kisses were bland and far from exciting? Was she missing out on life, as Josh had accused her?

Was she settling for a dull, uneventful future with Lamont simply because it was safe and convenient? And was it even fair to Lamont?

Should she and Lamont date other people? If Josh asked her out, would she feel free to accept if she and Lamont didn't have an agreement to see others?

For the first time, she wanted out of the arrangement she had simply drifted into with Lamont. With uncustomary impulsiveness, she called him on his cell.

"Have you got a moment to talk, Lamont?"

"I need a short break, so yes, I'll take a minute. Why do taxes seem to have more rules each year?"

"I don't know much about that. Lamont, I've been thinking about us, that we should start going out with other people. We've sort of wandered into a relationship that I'm having some second thoughts about."

"Abby, we're just alike, so we're very compatible. And this is a terrible time for me to make major changes in my life. Maybe you should rethink this. I'm sorry if I've neglected you somewhat, but we don't usually go out during tax season, at least not in late March."

"I want to be free to date others, and I think it would do you good to do so, too. We may be in a rut." There was a long period of silence. She hated to upset him, but she still felt she should break it off with him, at least for a while.

"If that's what you want," he said. "Let's go to dinner and discuss it, but it will have to be in a few weeks."

"We can discuss it more when you're finished with taxes, but I want to agree to see others."

"Fine," he said and gave an audible sigh. "I better get back. We'll talk about this again."

"Sure, Lamont," she said, feeling better. She put away her phone, realizing she had just made what might be a life-changing decision. A decision based on a kiss from a man who was almost a stranger. Even so, she didn't regret it.

Taking a deep breath, she turned to go back and join the guests to see if anyone needed anything. Josh and Mr. Hickman had just finished their game as Abby joined them.

"We've each won a game now," Mr. Hickman said.

"Actually, you've won two and I've won one."

"We'll play again sometime, I hope." Mr. Hickman stood. "I think I should turn in. I'll see both of you at breakfast. I enjoyed the games, Josh. Thanks."

"You're welcome," Josh said. "I enjoyed them, too. We'll see you in the morning."

"Good night," Abby said. As soon as Mr. Hickman was gone, she turned to Josh. "There's hot cocoa and hot cider in the kitchen."

"At this point in my life, I'd like a cold beer."

"I think we can fill that order," she said as they walked to the kitchen. "Look in the fridge. If we're out, there's another fridge in the pantry."

"I'll find it." He got a beer, uncapped it and sipped, then set it on the counter. He picked up dishes people had left at the table, carrying them to the sink. "I'll check the dining room for dishes that need to be washed."

Five minutes later, dishwasher running, he pulled out a chair. "Sit here and we can talk where it's quiet. No cards, no piano, no movie."

She hesitated a moment. The more time she spent with him, the more she liked him. She should thank him and go because the man was a threat to her peaceful life, even though he didn't know it or intend to be. She stared at him as she debated with herself. Had Josh caused her to want to go out with others, to change her basic lifestyle? How much upheaval was he causing in her life?

"This isn't a monumental decision," he said, looking more intently at her. "Or is it? And if it's monumental—why? What are you concerned about?"

"Of course not," she said, her cheeks flushing. "I don't think anyone in there will miss me, so I'll stay. I'm ready for a little quiet." She sat quickly, sipping a cup of steaming cocoa, aware of his curious gaze on her.

"You've been good to play cards with Mr. Hickman," she said.

"He's a nice man. I haven't played cards since I was a little kid."

She smiled, relieved to be on an impersonal topic.

"By the way, Edwin asked me to come back and go fishing with him in about a week or later, depending on the weather. It's spring, and the weather should warm up. The snow will disappear soon."

"So, are you coming back?"

"Not to fish," he said. Even though she felt a twinge of disappointment over his answer, she was not surprised and knew it was for the best.

"Later this spring, I'll return to Beckett, but only to

pick up Edwin. I asked him to go fishing in Colorado for a weekend—we can stay in my cabin there. I'll fly us up. His health is good enough for him to go, isn't it?"

Startled that he would take Mr. Hickman to Colorado, she barely thought about her answer. "Yes, as far as I know. He seems fine, just elderly."

"He's enthused and sounds knowledgeable about fly-fishing, so we should have a good time. I'll ask him to check with his doc about the altitude change in case he needs to spend a night somewhere on the way."

"He goes to the doctor for regular checkups, so I'm pretty certain he wouldn't accept if he didn't think he was healthy enough to make the trip. He does like to fish. That's very nice of you," she said, staring at him. She would never have guessed that Josh would have asked Mr. Hickman to fly to Colorado to go fishing. "Frankly, I'm surprised. You don't seem the type to hang out with Mr. Hickman."

Josh smiled at her. "I'm a man of many facets—stick around and you'll see."

"I don't doubt you for a minute," she said. "Even so, that amazes me. I'm very impressed," she added, realizing Josh was not only appealing, helpful, fun, sexy—but also a very nice person. Once again, she thought that she should stop spending so much time with him because she could quickly and easily fall in love with him—a love that definitely would not be reciprocated.

"Well, now, that is satisfying. Interestingly, I've done some business with one of Edwin's sons in Dallas and see all three of his sons at parties. They have a successful business that Edwin started."

"I know he has five grandkids and he misses all of them."

"He likes it here because he has old friends here, but

he's beginning to think about moving to Dallas. To my way of thinking, he would be better off near his family, but that's Mr. Hickman's business. My folks are in California, so I'm in about the same situation, only younger. My parents are younger than Mr. Hickman, and they're very busy."

"He should have a wonderful time going fishing."

They sat in silence while Josh sipped his beer.

"Were your stories true tonight about the people you've known who have kissed in that shadow?"

"Yes, they were true," she said, surprised he would ask such a question. "Why would I make them up?"

"It's good for business. Sort of a special touch for this inn."

She laughed. "Goodness, no, I wouldn't make them up for business. I never know if that shadow will appear. We can go years when it doesn't. A lot of things have to be just right and shadows change as the earth turns, so it's very fleeting when it happens."

"Have people ever kissed in that shadow when they met each other barely twenty-four hours before?"

"No one whom I've known about."

"Has anyone you know about ever kissed in the shadow, married and then separated?"

"No. All of them stayed married, so see, you tempted fate. But take heart. We don't know each other, so I doubt if we would count. I expect our kiss to be meaningless."

"My kiss, meaningless—that's the first time I've been told that. I'm slipping. I used to get a better reaction," he said, his brown eyes twinkling. She had to fight the temptation to look at his mouth.

"You know you did get a better reaction," she flung

back at him, even though she had intended to stop flirting with him.

"Did I really now?" he asked.

"Don't act surprised," she said, then decided to change the subject to one that would keep her from kissing him again. "Tomorrow or the next day, the roads will be plowed and you can go on your way. And my brother and sister will be here to help."

There was a knock at the open door, and a guest stepped into the room. "I'm sorry to disturb you."

"We were just talking. Can I help you with something?" Abby asked.

"Do you have the old movie *The African Queen*?" the short blonde asked.

"Yes, we do. You can't find it?"

As she shook her head, Abby stood. "I'll come look. I'll be right back, Josh." She left the kitchen, leaving Josh sipping his beer, his eyes still twinkling.

Josh thought about their kiss. Her kiss had almost knocked him off his feet, and he hoped her reaction to him had been as intense. He'd thought she wasn't his type, but kissing her had changed his view of her. Her kisses melted him. There was no way he was flying out of Beckett without the certainty of coming back to be with her, to kiss her and to make love with her. As far as he was concerned, seduction was on his schedule.

He liked being with her. Maybe it was the laid-back atmosphere—no business, no calls, a different world for him—but he wanted to be with her. She had a big job running the inn and keeping people happy in this storm when they were stranded, and she did it with ease.

She returned to the kitchen, and he watched her ponytail swing as she walked across the room. She had a jaunty walk as if life were delightful and she intended to enjoy it. His gaze rested on her mouth while he thought about their kiss again.

"Did you find the movie?"

"Oh, yes. Someone had slipped it under the sofa." She smiled. "Pretty easy task."

"Do you ever take time off?" he asked, still studying her. What would she look like with her hair down and makeup on?

"I get someone in the family to cover for me if I need to take time off, but there are quiet days and times we only have two or three guests and some days when there are none, so it evens out. This is my life—always has been. I started helping my grandmother when I was about ten, maybe younger," she said.

"You don't ever want to go somewhere new? New York? Paris? London?" he asked, thinking there was nothing they had in common. "Is there something you'd like to do that you've never done?" He was certain he had never really known anyone with so few demands or wishes about life. He didn't date women who led the type of life Abby did. She was a homebody and shouldn't hold an instant's worth of attention from him, but all he had to do was think about kissing her and he got hot, shaken and lost in memories of their only kiss.

"I can't think of anything that I long to do."

He looked at her as if he had suddenly discovered someone from another world. "Surely there's something."

She smiled at him. "Sometimes I used to wonder what it would be like to go to Vienna to a castle or a palace. When I was little, I would imagine that I was in a palace at a ball. The music was always a waltz. I wore one of those beautiful dresses. I probably saw a movie with that scene, and I love music and particularly a waltz. Somehow at local dances, they never seem to play a waltz. Lots of two-steps, lots of square dances, no waltzes," she said, looking beyond him as if she had forgotten his presence.

He thought of the castles he had seen, the waltzes he had danced, thinking how waltzes were old-fashioned and not his favorite dance.

She smiled at him, focusing on him again. "No, I don't plan to go to foreign places. I see movies and it looks fun, but I don't really yearn to travel."

"You lead a simple life, and you're damn easy to please."

"Like I've said, my life is tied up in family and people here." She glanced around. "Want something to drink?"

"I still have my beer. What would you like?"

"One more cup of hot cocoa if I have any left. If not, just a glass of milk with a little honey in it."

"I can start another fire in my room—which is really your room," he said, wanting to be alone with her. "Why don't we sit there to talk? No one should need you the rest of this evening."

"Sure," she said as she poured her hot chocolate.

They finally settled on the floor in the living area of her suite with a blazing fire in the fireplace, cold beer, hot cocoa and a bowl of popcorn. Josh had pulled a coffee table near the hearth as a table for the drinks and popcorn.

They sat in silence a few moments. She watched the fire, her profile to him. His gaze traveled over her smooth skin, long, light-brown eyelashes, a straight nose and full, heart-shaped lips. He paused, looking at her lips while desire built and he fought an inner battle.

She wasn't his type of woman and he wasn't her type of man—in all ways except one. One that he couldn't resist as he thought about their kiss.

He could not stop wanting to kiss her again. Kiss her and more, so much more. She was sexy, responsive, plus a bundle of nice and capable traits. So many that she was beginning to seem like a very special woman with a lot more substance than some women he'd spent a great deal of time with.

"Tell me more about your family," she said, breaking into his thoughts. "Do they all live near you in Dallas? Do they work with you?"

"My brother Mike is a rancher. He just married a woman who is a neonatal nurse, although she's not working now. She's expecting, and Mike has a little boy, Scotty. Mike's first wife died of cancer."

"I'm so sorry to hear that. It's nice that he's remarried."

"He seems very happy, and so does Scotty. I think the marriage has been great for my brother and my nephew. It was good for Savannah, too, because she had a broken engagement and that ex-fiancé is the father of her child, although Mike will adopt the baby."

"That's a blessing for all concerned."

"My brother Jake is in the energy business and married to Madison Milan, an artist."

"I've met her. She stayed here once, and she's very nice. She wouldn't remember me."

"She is nice, and they're happy. It's a good marriage because for generations our two families have had a nasty feud, beginning with the cattlemen after the Civil War. The feud is fading, especially with Jake and Madison's marriage. And a distant relative of ours, Destiny, married a Milan—Wyatt Milan, the sheriff of Verity."

"Sounds as if the feud is over."

"Unfortunately, it's not. My sister, Lindsay, is neighbors with a Milan, and those two fight like two bears with one piece of meat. Since Wyatt became sheriff, he's been able to tone it down a little, but not much, so the old feud is alive and well."

"You have quite a history, and your Texas ancestors go back as far as ours do," she said, smiling at him. "Do you stay at your ranch often?"

"I don't. I'd like to, but I'm too busy. That's the life I really love, and I'll move to the ranch to live someday."

"The future has a way of becoming the past very quickly. Perhaps you should take more time for your ranch if you really like that life."

"Right now that day seems mighty far in the future."

"My family is close—as you can guess since Mom lives next door and my grandmother lives here at the inn, although she stays at Mom's house a lot of the time. That's where she has been a lot this winter, and right now she's gone to visit another relative."

"Is your mom okay in this storm? Does she need anything?"

"No. I checked, and she has groceries. Right now with everyone snowed in, she doesn't need the drive shoveled. I talk to her every day on the phone. This snow keeps her out of work, which is probably a much-needed rest for her. She has a hair salon and is usually busy."

"What about your siblings?"

"My brother and sister are both on spring break—and it's a good time to be gone. The snow is keeping them from getting back home."

Of all the women he had known, why was it a nurturer like Abby who set him on fire with her kisses?

The most unlikely female he had crossed paths with attracted him—and she must be attracted to some degree to him. He couldn't imagine why she would give him five seconds of attention, because she had already told him she avoided men who traveled or reminded her of the type of life her father had—but she *did* give him attention.

It was after one in the morning when she stood and picked up the tray of dishes. "It's late. I'll turn in now."

"I'll carry the tray," he said, taking it from her.

"I need to lock up and turn off lights. People leave them on." They walked down the hall to the kitchen.

"If the forecasts are correct," she said, "we should have better weather by Tuesday. Maybe they'll open the roads and you'll get to go home."

"Don't sound so hopeful," he said, teasing her, and she smiled at him.

"Believe me, I've always been aware that when the snow goes, you will, too. That's the way of all my guests, no matter how good a time they've had here."

"I'm guessing a lot of your guests have been here before or will come back again."

"You're right, fortunately. People like staying here. They do come back, and a lot of them keep in touch with us. We get Christmas cards from all over the United States, which makes me happy."

"I'll send you a card."

"By next Christmas, you may not remember me, much less remember to send a card," she said, sounding amused.

He turned to face her, blocking her way. "I'll remember you," he said in a husky voice, knowing that he would. He wondered how long it would take for him to forget her or if he ever really would, a thought that surprised him.

Her faint smile faded as her eyes widened. Heat streaked like lightning across his loins. He stood holding the tray of dishes with his hands full. He set the tray on the counter and turned to take her into his arms. "This is why I won't forget you for a long, long time," he said and kissed her, pulling her tightly against him as he leaned over her.

As before when he had kissed her, she held him just as tightly, pressing against him, kissing him in return, another hot kiss that blasted him with desire. He wanted her in his bed. Kisses to die for—the description flitted through his mind.

"Josh," she whispered, stepping out of his embrace. She was as breathless as he was, and her lips were red from his kiss. He wanted to wrap his arms around her again, but knew he shouldn't. She needed to lock up and turn off lights, and she would stick to that agenda. He placed the dishes in the dishwasher while she went to the sitting room to switch off lights. When she returned, she checked the back door.

"I think everything is off and locked, so with no more chores, let's go to bed," she said, switching off the kitchen light, leaving only the hall light.

"Oh, darlin', I am definitely ready," he drawled.

Glancing over her shoulder at him, she laughed. "Cool it—poor choice of words on my part. I'm going to bed—alone. You do as you please and cool your over-active—" she paused "—imagination."

He grinned as he strolled down the hall beside her. "You can't blame me. Hope springs eternal and all that."

"I might as well start planning tomorrow's activities, because I'm guessing it'll be a busy day."

"You're changing the subject."

"As fast as I can," she said as they walked into his room. She kept going to the adjoining door to the rest of her suite. She turned to face him. "It's been a fun and interesting day."

As he walked over to her, she opened the connecting door to her room. He caught her arm, turning her. "It's been an unforgettable day and night. We kissed in a shadow that is supposed to change our lives. Now we wait and see."

"It's a legend. That doesn't mean it comes true. I think it probably makes a difference if you're already in love when you kiss," she said. Her voice had softened and had a breathless quality now, a reaction to their conversation or to his touch or to his standing so close—he didn't know. All he knew was that she always had a response to him.

"We can't end this day without another kiss," he whispered. Before she could answer him or try to walk away, he placed his mouth on hers.

He stood kissing her until she finally moved out of his arms.

"I don't know why we have this effect on each other," she whispered.

"We do, and I find it fascinating and irresistible."

"Watch out. It may be as risky to your way of life as it is to mine. You tempted fate tonight, and you're still doing it."

"How am I still doing it when I'm just standing here?" he asked in a husky voice.

"Good night, Josh," she said a little more forcefully and stepped into her room, closing the door.

"Good night, Abby," he said, certain she stood close

enough on the other side of the door to hear him. "You didn't answer my question," he added.

He was hot, aroused, aching with desire. He wanted her, and he wanted to hold her and make love for hours. He did not want to tell her goodbye yet.

Later, as he lay on the sofa, he stared into the dark and tried to avoid thinking about her in bed only mere yards away with a door between them. In addition to the hot chemistry, she had jolted his busy lifestyle, moving him into a slower pace, making him think more about his life as a rancher. It had always seemed something in the far distant future when he was older, but was he missing out on life, as she had said? He definitely thought she was missing out on life in many ways, yet in others, she might have a happier lifestyle than he did. That thought shocked him.

He rose slightly to see if there was a light beneath her door. It was dark, so she was in bed. That thought was not conducive to his sleep.

What would happen if he knocked on the door? Some women would tell him to come in, but he was certain Abby would tell him to go away and she would see him in the morning.

He sat up and wondered if sleep would come. The firewood was ashes with a few glowing orange embers, and he watched them sparkle while he remembered holding her until he groaned and ran his hand through his hair. He looked at the door between them again. Was she on the other side sleeping peacefully without a thought about him?

As she pulled on flannel pajamas and then laid out her blue sweater, a fresh pair of jeans and thick knee socks with her suede boots for tomorrow, Abby could only think of Josh. She ached with wanting him. She wanted his arms around her, his kisses, his lovemaking. But that was hopeless and the way to big heartbreak.

She wanted to go on with her routine life when he left, as happy as she was before she met him. She had the feeling life as usual wasn't going to happen again. Josh had come into her world and changed everything.

She had known Lamont's kisses were not exciting, but she had thought perhaps no man's kisses would ever seem exciting to her. She enjoyed Lamont, but on a whole different level and to a lesser degree than she did Josh. Lamont had never sent her pulse galloping or kissed her until she shook with desire. She never sat talking and laughing for hours with Lamont. They were comfortable, but sometimes they sat together for an hour or more without saying ten words to each other.

She would never feel the same about any other man now that she had known Josh. His fiery kiss had changed her world, making her reconsider her relationship with Lamont. She was glad she had talked to Lamont. They could be cheating themselves by limiting themselves to such a dry, emotionally lacking relationship. After Josh's kiss, she didn't want to keep the status quo with Lamont.

She sighed as she contemplated how Josh had so swiftly changed her views of life. It was a good thing Josh would soon leave. Otherwise, she would fall in love—deeply in love—for the first time in her life. Josh was excitement, passion, dreams. How long would it take her to forget him?

Sunday morning Abby stirred to sunshine showing around the edges of the shutters that covered her windows. Stretching, she climbed out of bed to open the shutters and look out a partially frosted window at sparkling white snow. The sun was brilliant, dazzling on the glistening white. She smiled and hurried to shower and dress and start the day.

By the time she got to the kitchen, Josh already had the table set in the dining room, and he was outside, shoveling snow along the drive and walk. She stared at him a moment, shaking her head, thinking that Lamont would not be shoveling snow or setting a table. Her cell buzzed, and she saw it was Lamont, which surprised her. She read his text message and saw that he would come by to see Mr. Hickman tomorrow morning.

Soon enough, Mr. Hickman arrived, greeting Abby as he came through the buffet line in the kitchen.

"Good morning. It's a beautiful day even though everyone will still be snowed in."

"You're chipper this morning," she said, smiling at him.

"I'm thinking about the fishing trip Josh has promised. That's an exciting event in my life. I love to fish, and the thought of dropping a line in a Colorado stream—I can't tell you how marvelous that is. He's a remarkable young man to take me fishing. By the way, where is he this morning?"

"He's shoveling snow off the front drive. I'd tell him to stop since he's a guest, but he'll just go ahead, so I didn't even bother. If he'd waited, I could have called to get some boys to shovel it later."

"According to the news, everything in town is still closed, including the roads, so there's not a rush. The highway is shut down because of high drifts. It won't open until they can get it cleaned off."

"I suspect it's useless to tell Josh to stop."

"Ah, he's a good person. I would go help him, but I've reached a point in life where I can't."

"He wouldn't let you help. I wouldn't want you even to try, so don't think about it. He's doing what he wants to do, and neither you nor I can talk him out of it."

"I'm not about to talk him out of it. I just regret I can't join him."

"You're nice, too. Enjoy your breakfast. I'll bring coffee."

She was serving the coffee when she heard Josh come in the back door. Eagerness to see him made her smile. He had done one more thing to win her heart.

Four

"Thank you, but you shouldn't have cleared the drive. I could have found some kids to shovel it. Tomorrow Lamont is coming over if he can, but he would never think of shoveling the drive."

"He doesn't shovel for himself or his mother?" Josh asked as he pulled off snow-covered boots and removed his thick jacket. He had on his heavy knit brown sweater and jeans. Once again, he hadn't shaved, and it still took Abby's breath away to look at him.

"He pays a neighbor kid to shovel their walk and drive," she said. "Tommy is eleven years old and it takes him a while, but he gets it done and doesn't charge much."

"So Lamont is a tight accountant?" Josh asked.

"I guess you'd say so, yes. He's also Mr. Hickman's and my aunts' accountant, and that's why he's coming here."

Josh paused in hanging his gloves on a hat tree. "He's not coming to see you?"

"No," she answered, smiling. "We've grown up seeing each other. He's got some papers about taxes for Mr. Hickman. This is Lamont's busiest time of year." She headed toward the kitchen. "Come get breakfast. Everyone else has eaten or is finishing. You can sit in the kitchen with me if you want while I finish cleaning. Thanks again, Josh, for doing the drive. It's big, and that's a major job for anybody."

"I work out, and I don't mind. You'll need it clear tomorrow if people start leaving."

"You're right there," she said, walking into the kitchen with him. "Help yourself. I'll be back in a minute," she said as she went to the dining room. Everyone had finished eating, so she cleared the table and returned to the kitchen as Josh sat.

She rinsed dishes to place them in the dishwasher, washed and dried her hands and poured herself a cup of steaming coffee, which she carried to the table to sit across from Josh while he ate breakfast.

"Josh, Mr. Hickman is so happy about the fishing trip. He even sounds younger and peppier this morning."

"I'm glad. I'm looking forward to getting away for it myself."

"Oh, I meant to ask, did you buy the horse you came to Beckett to get?"

"Yes, I did, from Jim Lee Hearne."

"I know Jim. He recently married."

"Right. He and his wife are selling their horses and moving to California. He has one really promising cutting horse, and I bought it from him."

A woman appeared in the doorway. "Abby, I'm sorry

to interrupt you, but do you have a small bandage? Micah cut his finger on his broken toy."

"Sure," Abby replied, standing. "Excuse me, Josh," she said, leaving to help her guest.

When she returned, Josh had gone and had put her empty cup and saucer into the dishwasher. Of course, he had.

During the morning, Abby did chores, talked at length with her mother on the phone and then spent her time getting lunch ready. As soon as she started, Josh appeared. She was happy for his help and acutely aware of him.

In the afternoon, people played games while Josh helped her get dinner ready. He played checkers with Mr. Hickman and spent some time talking to various guests. She realized Josh had made a point to meet and talk to everyone staying at the inn, including the kids. One more facet so different from Lamont, who would have kept to himself.

Again, Abby was aware of him as he helped her with dinner. The more she knew him, the more the awareness grew, instead of diminishing as she kept expecting.

Finally, after all the chores were done, the food eaten and the kitchen cleaned, he turned to her. "Let's sit in your suite like we did last night. I've been with your guests and Edwin all day. I'm ready for some time with you where we're not working."

She smiled at him. "Sure. You've been great help."

"Let's go to your room and you can show me your appreciation," he said, leering at her in exaggeration and making her laugh.

"I'll give you a very nice pat on the back."

"A pat on the back isn't what I have in mind," he said,

getting a beer from the refrigerator. "We'll build a fire and have peace and quiet, just the two of us."

They sat talking in front of the fire with only one small lamp turned on. Josh was certain he would be able to leave tomorrow, and he kept thinking about telling her goodbye—something he didn't want to do.

Was his perspective warped because of his isolation, the storm, the full moon, the pressure he had been under for the past two weeks, the relaxation of being stranded in Beckett? Or was it her kisses that he couldn't stop thinking about?

His gaze ran over Abby, the blue sweater clinging to tempting curves, her low V-neck even more tempting. He'd like to take down her ponytail, but he didn't think she'd let him.

Goodbye seemed way too final.

"I hear the weather should clear tomorrow, so you may be able to go home."

"Now I have mixed feelings about that. This has been an unexpected holiday."

"Ah, that's good to hear. It's wonderful to sit back and enjoy life."

"I agree. It's also good to get out and really live," he said, touching her hand lightly with his fingers, even the slight contact electrifying.

When her lashes fluttered and her cheeks grew more pink, his pulse jumped a notch because of her instant response to his casual touch.

"Go to dinner with me Friday night," he said. The words were out as if the voice had come from somewhere besides himself, but once they were said, he wanted her to accept his invitation. He wanted her in his arms, and he wanted to kiss her again. He was traveling down a road he might regret, but he had no regrets about asking her out. She turned to stare at him with wide eyes and a slight frown. If he hadn't wanted her to accept so badly, he would have laughed over her expression—a disbelieving reaction he could not recall receiving in his adult life.

"You're coming back to Beckett?"

"Only to pick you up and take you someplace. You've worked hard these past days—why not enjoy a change? You get to relax for once."

"That's nice of you to ask. Where did you want to go?"

"You've rarely been out of Beckett," he said. "We can go to Dallas. We can go most anywhere you want to." They were silent a moment while he thought about where to take her that would be different for her.

"I have a new hotel opening this weekend in New York. I'll pick you up and we can fly to New York for the weekend. I can show you a tiny view of the city on Friday night, Saturday and early Sunday."

She laughed. "Me go to New York with you for the weekend? I think not, but thank you very much anyway."

"Wait a minute. Don't be so quick to say no," he said, deciding he had hit on something that would open up a whole new world for her. And give him a lot more time with her. "Think about it—I'll fly you to New York. I'm going anyway," he said. "You'll get to see things you've never seen before, and it'll be fun for both of us. No strings—just fun and getting to know each other better. You'll have your own suite, I promise. You'll be farther from me than you are tonight."

"Thank you, but I can't even imagine going off for the weekend with you or going to New York. You'll go home tomorrow and get back to your life, and you won't want to return to Beckett to take me to New York."

"Don't be so quick to turn me down," he said quietly, although a part of him thought she might be exactly right. "Get out and do something different for once and see if you like it. This might be the only time in your life you'll be in New York, the only time in your life you'll get out of your routine. I'll get you back home whenever you want. You can trust me."

She shook her head. "Our lives are too entirely different. I'm not the woman you want to take to New York for the weekend."

"You let me decide that one," he said. "The question is, do you want to go with me?"

The pink in her cheeks deepened, and he wondered if she blushed that easily all the time or if her blushes were only in reaction to him. "Give Lamont something to think about," Josh said, smiling at her. "C'mon, Abby, take a chance and live a little."

A faint smile flicked across her face. Impulsively, Josh reached over to take her cup of cocoa out of her hands. Her eyes widened as he set the cup on the table and turned back to pick her up and set her in his lap.

She opened her mouth, probably to protest. He kissed her before she could say anything. Wrapping his arms around her, he pulled her tightly against him. His heart pounded the minute his mouth covered hers. How could she turn him inside out like this? The question flitted through his thoughts and was gone. He wanted her. She responded instantly to him. She wound her arms around him and held him while she kissed him in return, a hot kiss that fanned the flames that had already been blazing.

As their kisses lengthened, desire thrummed, building to a heart-pounding need. He slid his hand beneath her thick sweater and up her smooth back, then around to her breast, caressing her so lightly through her bra. He cupped her full, warm breast, her softness making him hard. He was afraid to move too quickly because he didn't want her to stop him. He stroked her, shaking slightly with wanting her.

Her moan, her hip shifting against him, her softness and her wet, scalding kiss drove him to the edge. It took control to keep from peeling away her sweater or slipping his hand into her jeans—all moves that he suspected would end what she allowed right now.

Seduction, slow and sensual to build her need, was what he intended. As he kissed her he leaned away, slowly, caressing her with feathery strokes, her full breast a fiery temptation. She was warm, her skin smooth as velvet.

She tore her mouth from his. "Josh, you're going way too fast for me. I'm not ready for this. I can't—"

He raised his head to look at her. Her blue eyes were half-lidded, sultry, ready for sex. Again, she had a slight frown as if struggling with her own inner battle. He wanted to draw her back into his arms, hold her tightly and end her protests, which he suspected he might easily do.

He also wanted to please her, and he wanted her trust. He wanted her aching to make love as much as he did, so he sat quietly. He couldn't understand himself and his reaction to her. She shouldn't interest him in any way, for any reason. Her hair was in a perpetual ponytail and she wore no makeup. She had hardly been out of Beckett, never out of Texas. If she agreed to go to New York, she might not want more than a few kisses—hardly the sensual weekend he was hoping for.

He couldn't understand his own actions—something totally uncharacteristic for him. Why was he so attracted to her? Was it only the passionate kisses?

And yet he couldn't think of any other woman he had known whose kisses had had the effect on him that hers had. Plus, he liked to be with her.

She turned to face him. "My hot cocoa should be rather cold now, and your beer is probably warm. I'll go get some more."

He nodded and let her go, wanting to get some space between them, hoping to cool the strong urge to reach for her again.

He got up finally to go help her and met her as she was coming through the door. She carried a tray with cocoa, beer and popcorn and he took it from her, setting it on the coffee table and pulling it close as they sat on the floor in front of the fire again.

For a few minutes they made small talk. Then he lowered his beer. "You didn't give me an answer about the weekend. Go with me to New York." He leaned closer to her and caught her chin lightly in his hand. "Live a little, Abby. Life is a blast, so don't let it pass you by."

"Josh, it's crazy for me to think about going to New York with you."

"Why not with me? We have a good time together. It's just a weekend. No strings, Abby." He gazed into wide blue eyes filled with uncertainty.

"I promise you I will not sleep with you," she said in an earnest tone. "Knowing that, do you still want to take me to New York?"

He held back laughter that was as much at himself as her reaction. How did he get entangled with her? Worse, he was getting himself more involved by the minute. He had a chance right now to back off.

"I said no strings. We'll go and have fun."

She narrowed her eyes and leaned forward to stare intently at him. "Why do I suspect you of ulterior purposes?" she asked.

Amused, he leaned closer to her so their faces were only inches apart. "Because you like to kiss me, and you know I like to kiss you. I think you have to suspect yourself of ulterior purposes as well," he said softly, his gaze drifting down to her mouth.

"I guess I walked into that one," she said in a breathless voice. She sat back and gazed at him, looking as if she were thinking it over, so he remained quiet for a short time.

"Are you going with me?" he asked finally.

"Yes, I will," she said in a tone that sounded as if she had just agreed to rob a bank with him. "Friday night?"

"If you want to get in a little extra sightseeing, ask someone to cover for you and let's go Thursday. I'll bring you back when you want."

"Let's go Friday. That's long enough, and I can't believe I'm doing this."

He felt the same way, but he wouldn't tell her, ever. He smiled at her. "If you change your mind, that's fine, too. I'm adaptable." He sat back. "What would you like to eat on our first night there? Steak? Fish? Something foreign, exotic?"

She thought a moment. "Something French. French dishes always sound so delicious, and you know there's nowhere to eat any in Beckett. Cooking something from a recipe in a magazine doesn't always work out like I think it will. Something French would be fun, since you asked, but I can go anywhere you want."

"My house instead of New York?"

She laughed. "Now, that I hadn't thought about. I don't believe your house is on this trip's agenda. That one I'm not doing. It would be too intimate."

"I'm eating at your house this week."

"You and thirty-plus other people—that's a bit different. Only this weekend with you in New York. That's the same as if you'd told me you're taking me to the moon. It's just as unreal to me. I will be the talk of Beckett."

"They know you, and they know you'll still be you whether in New York or here."

"That's nice, Josh. I'm as dazzled as Edwin over the fishing trip. I'm going, but I can't believe it will happen."

He couldn't, either. "You've agreed. You've seen New York City in movies and on television—are there places you would particularly like to visit?"

"Maybe I should let you surprise me with your favorite places."

"I don't think so. I've been going since I was a little kid. You tell me what you want to see," he said, finding his thoughts drifting to where he could take her for dinner each night—someplace where they could dance. He was happy she said she would go. He would have her with him all weekend, and with her hot, sensual responses, he planned on seduction. By Saturday, she might even be eager.

It was two in the morning when Josh kissed her good-night and she went to her room. Finally she was alone and could think about the trip that she had accepted. As she changed into pajamas and took down her ponytail, she knew she couldn't cancel. She wanted to go. All too soon he would be out of her life forever, and she would be left with only memories of him and few of those. She intended to go to New York on Friday and have the time of her life, to store up memories for later.

She was too inexperienced to know much about men and love, but she suspected that she was already in love with Josh. When Josh kissed her beneath the rising moon, how could she resist him? And his appeal doubled when she found out he had asked Mr. Hickman to go fishing with him—something so many men Josh's age would never have taken time to do with someone elderly who was not a relative. All the help he had given her, the hours she had spent just sitting and talking to him—she liked him. He was handsome, sexy, exciting and a world of other good things. When he left, she would go back into the ordinary routine she had always had and would have for the rest of her life.

One weekend in New York—that was a thrill all by itself. One weekend in New York with Josh—that was beyond her wildest dreams. She thought of their kisses tonight and closed her eyes, tingling and wanting to be in his arms as she remembered his hand beneath her sweater, his caresses that she really hadn't wanted him to stop.

Even though she had broken off with Lamont, he was still in Beckett, still an old friend. Would this ruin a future relationship with Lamont? Did she really care if it would?

She would think about Lamont later. Right now the only man she wanted to think about was Josh.

Five

When she opened her eyes the next morning, she faced the realization that this was the day she would tell Josh goodbye—at least until Friday.

She went down early to get breakfast started, and Josh showed up looking like a rancher in his boots and jeans. A sizzling awareness of him gripped her. As usual, he began to help, working alongside her, as busy as she was until they finally sat to eat their own breakfast.

As they cleaned up the dining room and kitchen, the doorbell rang. "That's probably Lamont. I'll bring him in to meet you."

"This should be interesting," Josh stated.

When she opened the door, Lamont stepped inside, stamping his feet on the mat. He shrugged off his coat, removed his hat and gloves and crossed the hall to hang them on a coatrack that stood in the corner. He raked his fingers through his straight blond hair.

"The weather is better, but it's still cold and nasty out there. How are you doing?"

"Fine, considering we've been snowbound."

"It's slick out there, and we have deep drifts in spots. I have chains on my tires. I wanted to get here before other people get on the streets. Is Edwin around?"

"He's upstairs in his suite. But first, come meet one of the guests who's been very helpful since my brother and sister aren't here." She led him to the kitchen.

Josh put the lid on the coffeepot and turned when they entered, crossing the room to meet them.

"Josh, this is Lamont Nealey. Lamont, meet Josh Calhoun," she said, looking at the two together. Josh, with his brown hair, darker skin and dark eyes, looked more dynamic, but perhaps she thought that because she knew the personalities of both men. Lamont's paler skin was a reflection of his time spent indoors. He was seldom out, and as far as she knew, he did little physical exercise. He didn't convey the take-charge personality that Josh did, nor did he flirt. He was friendly, cooperative, intelligent and helpful about her bookkeeping, answering her questions when she had any. Lamont was absolutely reliable and he was hometown born and raised, just as she was. He was quiet, but she enjoyed the quiet, just as she had always enjoyed knowing Lamont.

"Can you sit and join us a minute?" Josh asked.

"I'd like to, but I better find Edwin. You're a little out of the way in Beckett, aren't you? I thought you lived in Dallas. I've seen your name in Texas magazines."

"I have a home in Dallas. I flew in here to see Jim Lee Hearne about buying a horse, and by the time we were through talking, it was all the cabbie could do to drive me back into town. The roads were closed and I had to stay in Beckett, which has proven to be nice."

"Good. Beckett is a very nice town." Lamont glanced at his watch.

"Well, it was nice to meet you, and I'm glad you found a place to stay. This has been a beast of a late snowstorm and I hope the last one for this year."

"It was nice to meet you, too, Lamont. I've heard a lot about you," Josh said as Lamont and Abby started toward the door.

"I hope it was all good," Lamont said, smiling and turning to look at Abby before he continued out of the room with her. She walked beside him up the stairs.

"I'm glad to see this weather clear," he said, "but it gave me a chance to get a lot of tax work done while people couldn't come to the office. It was a good time for uninterrupted work. You don't need to come up with me, Abby. Edwin is expecting me, and we'll be going over his taxes. I'll let you know when I'm leaving."

"Sure, Lamont," she said, pausing at the landing halfway up. She turned and walked back down to find Josh standing at the end of the hall, watching her.

A rising panic gripped her. Lamont had paled in so many ways next to Josh. Lamont was wrapped up in himself, his job, his own little world to an extent she had never noticed before. Perhaps it was just because it was tax season. This time of year, he always became tense, buried in work and preoccupied. He hadn't done the things Josh would have—asked if she needed help, inquired about when her brother and sister would return. Lamont was earnest, serious and reliable, and that had been enough to suit her until Josh crossed her path. How big a disaster was Josh turning out to be in her life? And was she contributing to it by agreeing to go to New York with him? Lamont would think she'd lost her wits or was sleeping with Josh, but she was glad she had suggested to Lamont they date other people.

Josh came forward with his phone in his hand. "The roads are being cleared, but Beckett isn't on a main highway, so it'll probably be tomorrow before I can get out of here."

She felt an emptiness over the thought of Josh leaving. He made his presence felt. She thought of her father and how charming he could be with the same type of personality, dynamic, charismatic, winning friends, yet so unreliable. He had broken her mother's heart, never being faithful, never able to stop charming everyone he came in contact with. She had always vowed she wanted the man in her life to be dependable, reliable, steady, scttled—like Lamont. Josh was a man like her father, and she was following in her mother's footsteps and should stop right now. Josh had helped her partly to be nice, but also to keep busy, and she was the only single woman around. He had turned on the charm and been helpful, but if she had shown up in his hometown, he would never have looked twice at her. She should back out of the New York trip, tell Josh goodbye and start trying to forget him. She suspected she wasn't going to forget him for a long time.

New York with Josh—letting him take her out and show her some of the things she had never dreamed of seeing in person—sounded so exciting. She sighed with indecision. She should back out, but she wanted to go. Josh would make sure she had a good time. And he was right—this would be a once-in-a-lifetime weekend.

"That's great," she said quietly. "I know you want to get home."

He pulled out his phone. "I need your cell number—tell me and I'll put it in my phone right now."

With a heavy heart, she watched him enter her number. Then she turned. "I better get back to the kitchen."

"I'll help you with the chores and we'll be through in no time."

"You're a guest, remember? You don't have to work constantly."

"Beats sitting still and doing nothing, and I've got my emails caught up and have taken care of all my business that I can from here. This weekend makes up for the past week," he said as they walked to the kitchen.

It was an hour later, as they had the table set for lunch, that Lamont appeared. "Am I interrupting?" he asked, frowning as he stared at Josh.

"No, not at all," Josh replied. He had been helping Abby put two trays of dessert into the refrigerator. He stepped away. "Did you finish with Mr. Hickman?" she asked while Lamont stood watching them.

"For now. He has some forms to fill out. I better get home and back to figuring taxes. This is my busiest time."

"I think right now it's Abby's busiest time," Josh remarked.

"Yes, I suppose. Good to have met you," Lamont said abruptly. As he walked out of the kitchen, Abby went with him to the front door.

"That Calhoun fellow is worth a billion," Lamont said while he shrugged into his coat. "I'd think he could have found somewhere else to stay. What in the world is he doing in Beckett? I know what he said, but why would he want a horse?"

"He's also a rancher."

Lamont glanced away. "Can you feed all the people you have here?"

"Yes. I couldn't if this storm lasted through today,

but someone can get me groceries today, or I can walk over there myself and carry some groceries back."

"Want me to send Tommy over? He cleared my driveway this morning. He could get your groceries."

"Thanks anyway. I'll get along, and I can probably get out tomorrow."

"If that Calhoun fellow is helping you out here, it's because he wants on your good side for some reason—to keep whatever room you have him in. He didn't become a billionaire by being nice. You should stay away from him."

"Being rich doesn't rule out being nice. He's been very helpful." She crossed her arms over her chest. "He asked me if you and I have ever talked about marriage."

"That's a personal question to ask you and none of his business," Lamont said, frowning even more. "Is he the reason for your call about wanting to go out with other people?"

"I just think maybe we'd both be better off if we see others at least a bit."

"We'll talk about it again after tax season," Lamont said. "Right now I've got all I can deal with."

"I know you do," she said, thinking how different Josh's remarks would be if she had a similar conversation with him. He would flirt, make light of the questions and ask more about her situation. She knew it wasn't fair to compare Lamont with Josh, but it was impossible to avoid noticing differences.

"Lamont, Josh has asked me to go to New York this weekend. He has a new hotel opening he wants to attend. It's just the weekend to see the sights, sort of a thank-you for taking him in out of the storm."

Lamont narrowed his eyes at her. "So that's why you called. You want to date Josh Calhoun."

"No. When I called, he hadn't asked me to go to New York. Being free to date others is something I've been thinking about and want to do. It may be better for both of us."

"It may be at that. I'm shocked if you're going out of town for a weekend with him, but that will make it clear to everyone in Beckett that we aren't exclusive."

The phone rang, and she pulled it from her pocket. "Excuse me, Lamont."

"You take your call. I've got to get back to work. I don't know when I'll see you again," he said and left.

She answered her phone and heard her brother's voice. While she talked and learned both her brother and sister might get home late that night, she stood by the window to watch Lamont get into his car and drive slowly away. She was certain he had already forgotten all about her and was thinking about taxes. How would Lamont react if she told him Josh had kissed her in the shadow of the trees under a full moon? Lamont didn't believe the old legend for one second. Twice he had been with her and others when the heart-shaped shadow had occurred, but he had merely shaken his head and said it was a silly story.

She finished the call with her brother and returned to the kitchen to find Josh making coffee.

"You're getting so you can do this all by yourself," she said, amused as she watched him.

"Has Lamont gone?"

"Yes. He's preoccupied when it's tax season."

"I've called Benny to come pick me up around three," Josh said, turning to her as soon as he finished with the coffee. "I've talked to my pilot. The weather is clear, so I can get home today."

"So you'll be gone today for sure."

"Yes, I will," he said, walking closer to her. "Miss me?"

"Of course, I'm going to miss you terribly—you're better help than my siblings." Her voice changed and became sultry as she ran her finger across his shoulder, feeling his soft brown sweater over hard muscles. "You're definitely better looking and more fun."

His dark eyes flickered. "Now I don't want to go," he said, sliding his arms around her.

Smiling, she pushed his arms away. "You bring that out in me. Maybe I've been cooped up too long."

"The weekend is coming, and it'll be fun. Abby, I don't know if you go out to eat much in Beckett—"

Smiling, she shook her head. "No, I don't. Sometimes the family drives to a chicken place along one of the county roads, and after church sometimes we'll eat at the hotel downtown, but not often. Actually, the food is better here or at Mom's."

"Do you and Lamont go out to dinner?"

"We rarely ever have. If we're going to something—a movie we want to see—we usually eat separately at home first and then go. It's easier."

"When you were in school, didn't boys besides Lamont ask you out?"

"Yes, but I really never had much fun with any of them, and we didn't like the same things. I don't know that I have so much fun with Lamont, but we do like the same things, so that works out. And Lamont doesn't make demands on me or my time."

"It surprises me that you didn't find anyone you had fun with," Josh said.

"Maybe a couple, but I'm wrapped up in my family, and I didn't go to college and have that chance to meet more people my age. Besides, in high school, I wasn't ready for sex with those guys, and I've been told more than once or twice that I'm very cold."

"That speaks volumes about them," Josh said.

She nodded. "And the few times I've gone out with someone besides Lamont, I think my family might have been a bit much for them. My relatives either live here or right next door. They're a huge part of my life."

"You said Lamont doesn't have a lot of family. He can deal with yours?"

"He just stays away. Like I said, we don't go out a lot."

"And you don't want to leave Beckett?"

"Oh, no. This is my home, my life, my livelihood. My family is here, which is the most important thing. Why would I want to leave Beckett?"

Josh smiled. "I can think of a few reasons why you might want to live elsewhere. Not getting snowbound, for one."

She could hear the laughter in his voice. "You don't understand because you're a cosmopolitan, sophisticated world traveler. You just can't imagine the satisfaction I find in my work and this town and the friends I have."

He seemed to take that in. "I'll bet I'm not the first single guy who has stayed here and wanted to take you out."

"You're just the first one I couldn't resist," she said as he started to put the dishes on a shelf. When he set them back on the counter and turned to look at her, she shrugged. "That's just a fact. Don't let it go to your head."

"It just went somewhere else," he said, crossing the room to her. "I find that a very candid, interesting statement." As he placed his hands on her waist, his gaze traveled over her features with curiosity in his dark eyes. "I can't wait for the weekend. I want to see if you can resist me then."

"This better be just a friendly, fun trip."

"I intend it to be," he said. "When I asked about eating out in Beckett, I had a purpose. In case you don't feel you have a dress for New York, when we arrive, I'll take you to a shop and you can get a dress to wear that night when we go out to dinner."

"You don't have to buy me a dress," she said, smiling at him.

"Of course I don't have to. I want to. You select it or I will, but you'll get a new dress, I promise you. Now I hear people coming."

"Probably looking for me," she said, turning to go into the hall, trying to even imagine herself in a fancy dress, let alone at a fancy New York City restaurant.

At two-thirty in the afternoon, Abby sat at the desk in her room. She heard the scrape of boot heels on the floor, and she glimpsed Josh enter and cross the room he had rented for his stay. He glanced through the open door and saw her. "Can I come in?"

"Sure. I'm working on records and very glad for an interruption."

"My plane is waiting. I'll check out and be on my way. Do you have enough help for dinner tonight?"

"Sure," she answered, wishing she didn't feel a loss, but certain she'd get over it soon. "Nearly everyone has checked out. One family will still be here tonight, plus Mr. Hickman."

"Good. You'll have a quiet night. I have to pack my things. I'll tell you when I'm ready to check out."

She nodded, feeling an emptiness and hating to see

him go. She couldn't recall feeling the same way about anyone who had ever stayed at the inn. Ideally by tomorrow she wouldn't feel this way. Josh hadn't been in her life long enough to make any giant difference. As quickly as the thought came, she considered the trip to New York. That trip might make a giant difference.

Once again, common sense said to back out of going with him. It wasn't like anything she had ever done in her life. She had to tell her family, and she suspected all of them would try to talk her out of going. As small a town as Beckett was, everyone knew what everyone else was doing most of the time. Particularly if someone left town. Her absence would be conspicuous because of where she had gone and whom she had gone with. She knew she'd better break the news to her mother and grandmother first.

Then again, would Josh really come back to get her on Friday and take her to New York?

For the first time, she realized that once he returned home to the world he was accustomed to, he might back out of the trip. With a sigh, she bent over the books open in front of her and tried to concentrate.

It was only a few minutes until he knocked again. "Hate to interrupt you, but I'm ready to check out."

Abby stood, a hollow feeling in her chest. "Since you worked constantly, I'm not charging you for your stay. You've earned it totally, and I really appreciate what you did."

He smiled and dropped the bag he carried, walking closer. "I didn't do that much, and I want to pay, so just give me the bill. C'mon, I insist."

"Josh, this is ridiculous when you worked the whole time."

"No, it's not. Now that's settled, there's something

else—I'll call you about when I'll be back Friday to get you. I'll bring you home Sunday—or Monday. I suspect you'll get to the city and decide you want to stay maybe one more night."

"I don't think so. I'm beginning to wonder about going, and I imagine you are, too. Here's your chance—I'll let you off the hook if you want. I will understand absolutely."

"No way. I'm looking forward to it and have already started making plans." He walked up to her and placed his hands on her waist. "I'm not backing out and I don't want you to, either. I'm going to do everything I can to see to it that you have a great time and don't regret going. Now, until Friday," he said and paused.

He slid an arm around her waist and drew her against him as he leaned close to kiss her. Without hesitation, she wrapped her arms around his waist and held him tightly, pressing against his solid length. She kissed him as if she would never see him again.

His arms tightened and he leaned over her, kissing her until all thought stopped. The only awareness she had was of Josh's kisses. Her heartbeat raced and desire enveloped her, making her tremble and want so much more with him. She wished she could keep him from going for just a while longer.

He raised his head slightly. "I won't ever forget this time here."

"Yes, you will, but that's nice to say," she whispered and stepped away from him.

"I'll call you about arrangements Friday."

She nodded. "Ready to go?"

"Sure," he said, his dark eyes intent on her. He walked with her to the front desk.

"I feel ridiculous charging you," she said.

"Go ahead. I meant it. Besides, I didn't really do that much or work that hard."

"We won't keep arguing that one," she said, typing in the figures, showing him the amount and printing out his bill after he had paid. "Here you are," she said. "Paid in full."

He smiled. "I'll call."

She walked around the counter to go with him to the door. The cab waited at the foot of the porch steps, and she waved at the driver. "Have a good flight, Josh."

"Bye, Abby," he said and hurried to climb into the cab. He waved again as they drove away. She had a sinking feeling that she had seen the last of him in spite of all his talk about going to New York. When she walked back inside, she met Mr. Hickman, who had just come from the dining room.

"Josh just left. He's invited me to go to New York with him this weekend for a new hotel opening he wants to attend."

"I hope you're going."

"I am, because it may be the only time I'll ever see New York."

"I hope you have a better reason than that. He's a special fellow, Abby."

"Yes, he is. I've told Lamont we ought to go out with other people for a while because we've never done that since high school."

"I think that's an excellent idea. Marriage for someone like you would be a lifetime bond. You should meet others now, while you're young. I'm glad Josh was snowbound here. Very glad, since I get a fishing trip out of his stay," he said, smiling. "You go to New York and have the time of your life."

"Mr. Hickman, I'm going to Mom's house. While

I'm gone, I'm closing the front desk. Will you be down-stairs?"

"Yes. I'll watch. If anyone comes in, I'll see what they want, and I can call you."

"I won't be gone long. Everyone has checked out except the Taylors, who aren't leaving until tomorrow, so it should be very quiet. Thanks for sitting here. I'll be home soon."

"Don't rush," Mr. Hickman said as she walked away to get her coat and gloves.

She needed to tell her mother about New York, even though she would believe it when it happened. She knew Josh would be back for Mr. Hickman's fishing trip, but would Josh really come back this Friday for her?

"Thanks for picking me up, Benny," Josh said as the cab pulled away from the curb, snow crunching beneath the tires.

"It's been a slow day. A lot of people are still not getting out because that snow is deep and the town's streets are covered and slick. How'd it go at the inn?"

"Great. Abby is nice, and it's been a good place to stay. The food is the best," he said, realizing it had been. "Abby is a good cook." He thought about her biscuits, which were the lightest he had ever eaten. Until Abby, he'd thought his cook and his mother made the best possible. Also, Abby's salmon cakes would be worth driving from Dallas back to Beckett.

"We have a town picnic in the summer. People come from all around, and whatever Abby cooks and brings is gone first," Benny said. "She's even better than her grandmother was when she ran the inn, and that's saying a lot."

Josh nodded. "Benny, have you ever thought of moving away from Beckett?"

"Move out of Beckett? Nah, I don't think so."

"Abby mentioned that you've worked in construction. I can get you on a construction crew. It would mean moving, though. Same thing with my brother, who has an energy business in Dallas. He might have a place for you in the oil field if you want to go talk to him."

"That's nice, thanks. I'll take his name. I've never even thought about moving away from here."

"It's still in Texas," Josh said, smiling as Benny glanced at him in the rearview mirror and gave him a thumbs-up.

"That's important. Doubt if my wife would leave Texas."

"When I get out, I'll give you my business card, and I'll put his name and number on it," he said, writing Jake's name on the back of a card.

"That's great. Thanks."

"Sure. You helped me." As they left the last houses in Beckett, Josh looked at the white world stretching all around him.

He listened to Benny talking, but his mind was on what he needed to do before the weekend trip to New York. He was amazed Abby had agreed to go with him, but glad. After meeting Lamont, he didn't think she would spend ten seconds worrying about Lamont's reaction to her going to New York with another man.

Sending a text to his secretary, Josh asked her to find the best possible French restaurant in New York and make reservations for two for Friday night. He called a private club he belonged to and made reservations for Saturday night.

He couldn't wait for Friday. He wanted Abby to have

the time of her life, and he wanted her in his arms, in his bed, to make love to her for hours. Was it possible for that to happen?

Next door, Abby found her mother in the kitchen putting a meat loaf in the oven.

"Can't I help with anything?" Abby asked, pouring herself a cup of coffee and sitting at the table.

"Just sit. I imagine you've been worked to pieces the past few days with the inn overflowing."

"I had a lot of help from one of the guests. I'll be glad to help you now."

"No, I'm almost ready for a break. I'll get some tea and sit with you. Grandma is napping, and if she doesn't get up in a little while, I'll wake her, because she'll want to see you while you're here. She said you might know who shoveled our drive and porch steps this morning."

Surprised, Abby looked out the window. "Mom, that was probably my guest. He was very helpful all the time he was here."

"That was really nice. Did he know I'm your mom?"

"Yes. And he probably knew you needed your drive cleared. You don't have any customers to get their hair or nails done today?"

"Heavens, no. Everyone canceled when snow began to fall a few days ago. I'm glad they did, because I've enjoyed the lull."

Having had a break, maybe her mother wouldn't mind covering for her at the inn while she was in New York. "Mom, can you cover for me this weekend? Justin and Arden said they can help if they get home by then."

"Sure, I'll cover. What's going on? Lamont is in tax season, so you're not doing anything with him."

"No, I'm not. Besides, I've talked to Lamont, and we're going to date other people for a while."

"That's a big change in your life," her mother said, her eyebrows arching in surprise. "What are you doing this weekend that I need to cover for you?"

"Josh Calhoun—he's the one who helped and shoveled the drives—has invited me to go out this weekend. Josh is from Dallas and Verity. He has his own hotel business with the headquarters in Dallas. Mom, he asked me to go with him to a new hotel he's opening this Friday in New York, and I said I would."

"New York City? My, oh, my," she said, her blue eyes widening. "Are you in love with him?"

"No, but I like being with him. I think part of it is, he feels sorry for me because I've never been out of Texas. And part of it is gratitude because I let him stay at the inn so he could get out of the blizzard."

"A trip to New York. That's a big deal. He must be important. I just don't want you hurt. He sounds a bit like your father, except wealthier."

Abby smiled. "I'll take care, but it's something I may never have a chance to do again. He's very nice. He's coming back in April or May and taking Edwin Hickman fishing in Colorado."

"I can't imagine. Have you checked on his background?"

"Yes, and Mr. Hickman has. He owns Calhoun Hotels and he's a rancher. He said I could call the sheriff of Verity, Texas, if I want a reference, because he's known him all his life."

Her mother gazed at her for a few moments and then nodded. "You're young, but a grown, intelligent woman, so go and have a wonderful time. Call me, will you?"

"I will. And I'll be careful. I'll tell Grandma about the trip."

"Let me tell her gently. I don't want her to have a heart attack."

"You're kidding me, aren't you? I hate to leave without saying hello to Grandma, but I'd better get back to the inn."

"I'm glad you came over and told me. My friend Marilee goes to Dallas a lot. Care if I ask her if she knows who Josh Calhoun is?"

"Of course not. Ask any of your friends or customers," she said, getting her coat and pulling it on again. "He's nice, Mom."

"Just don't fall in love with him. Men who have private planes and hotel chains do not fall in love with inn owners from places like Beckett, Texas. It would be heartbreak."

"I know. I'm going to see New York while I have a chance. At least as much as you can see in the blink of an eye. We'll just have a full day on Saturday. Fly in on Friday and out on Sunday."

"That's long enough to fall in love. You take care of yourself."

They hugged lightly, and Abby jammed her cap over her ponytail and left, calling over her shoulder, "Tell Grandma hi for me."

She walked through new snow back to the inn, thinking about what she would pack to wear for a weekend in New York City. Her wardrobe was simple.

By eight that evening, the only guests watched a movie and Mr. Hickman had disappeared upstairs, so she had the first chance to look at her clothes and lay things out to pack, aware that she might have to put them all back if Josh canceled.

Shortly after ten that night, Josh called, and they talked on the phone until past midnight. After the connection was broken, she stared at the phone, still wondering if she would regret going with him for the weekend, if her mother was right about it leading to heartbreak.

She couldn't back out. This trip to New York might be the one time in her life that she could step out and do something exciting, unforgettable, something she had never expected to do.

She was surprised that Josh had called and that they'd talked so long. Sure, they'd talked for hours at a time when he had been here, but he had been snow-bound. Now he was in Dallas, home where his friends lived, where he knew lots of people, so it surprised her that he called at all.

Would she come back from New York in love with him? He wasn't going to make any commitment—he had made that more than clear. And soon, he would want her in his bed, although she had told him plainly to not expect that.

What did he look forward to? Seduction? Maybe just a fun weekend together. She knew better than that, but she had warned him that was all she intended to do. Now she just had to resist him.

Six

At noon Wednesday when Josh walked into a restaurant for lunch, Lindsay and Jake were already waiting. He shook hands with Jake and hugged Lindsay. "Hey, this is good. Lindsay, you should come to Dallas more often."

"Heaven forbid," she said, smiling at him. "I come only when I absolutely have to." She turned to Jake. "You should have brought Madison."

"She had an appointment with a gallery in Fort Worth, and she's having lunch with the owner, so business first. Mike has an excuse for not making the Calhoun sibling lunch because of his honeymoon. Let's get our table."

After they were seated and had ordered, Jake turned to Josh. "You were snowbound for the weekend in some little town. I'll bet you went stir-crazy."

"Did you have trouble finding a place to stay?" Lindsay asked.

"Yes, I did. I was afraid I'd have to sleep in the park in Beckett. A very nice B and B owner let me have the front room of her personal suite—"

"Let me guess," Jake said. "She's single."

"As a matter of fact, she is. She had four others who were on the floor or sofas. That inn was packed. Be glad the storm veered north."

"We got a few flurries, some sleet and then rain," Lindsay said, "but nothing that would strand anyone, thank goodness. We've already had enough of that. I'm ready for spring."

"How're the horses?" Josh asked her.

"Beautiful. You'll have to see my new foal. He's perfect."

"Here comes the picture of her baby," Jake teased.

Lindsay stuck her tongue out at him as she pulled out her phone and handed it to Josh. "How's that? Isn't he adorable?"

"He is adorable," Josh agreed, smiling as he handed her phone back. The waiter came with their orders and placed burgers in front of Jake and Josh, while Lindsay had a tossed salad.

Jake sipped a tall glass of iced tea. "If Mike and Savannah get back this week, Madison and I'll have everybody for dinner Saturday night—how'll that work with both of you?"

"I'm out," Josh said instantly.

"I can't, either. I've already made arrangements to go to Austin to a horse sale this weekend," Lindsay said.

"And I'm going to a hotel opening in New York."

Jake turned to look at Josh. "You don't go to hotel openings. Not in a long, long time. In New York?"

"I'm going to this one," Josh said, looking at Jake's disbelieving brown eyes.

"So you're taking someone, is my guess. I'll bet it's someone who was staying at that B and B. Give you three days shut up somewhere if there is a single woman who is appealing, you'll have a date with her, although someone from Beckett, Texas, isn't your style."

"So it's one of the guests?" Lindsay asked, her blue eyes twinkling.

"You're so far off."

"I don't think I am. I'll buy lunch for us all if I'm wrong."

Josh grinned. "Okay. I'm taking the owner of the B and B."

"You wasted no time this past weekend," Jake said. "She's going with you to New York? I won't say what I'm thinking in front of Lindsay's delicate ears, but that's fast work."

Lindsay laughed with Josh. "Lindsay spends every day working alongside those cowboys at her ranch. There isn't anything Lindsay's delicate ears haven't heard," Josh said.

"You're right," Lindsay said, "but I don't have to listen to my brothers' raunchy remarks. So, Jake, can you have the dinner for Mike another time, please?"

"Sure. Mike and Savannah aren't due back from their honeymoon for a while anyway. Scotty is doing fine, though I'm sure he misses them. He's with his sitter, and Mom and Dad visited yesterday"

"Scotty is coming to my house soon to stay a week," Lindsay said. "We'll have a blast."

"Yes, you will. Scotty loves his aunt Lindsay. And vice versa. You're good with horses and little kids," Jake said.

"Thank you," she said, smiling at him.

Jake looked at Josh again. "So tell us about the latest

love in your life—she owns a bed-and-breakfast inn—what else? We never meet these women of yours, so I don't expect to meet this one."

"You'll probably never meet her," Josh said. "This is just a weekend trip. She's never been out of Texas so I'm taking her to New York."

Jake and Lindsay both laughed. "This doesn't sound like our cynical, worldly brother's type of lady," Jake observed. "Never flown and never out of Texas? What does she do in her spare moments?"

"I don't think she has many. Her life is tied up with her family—a sister, a brother, her mother, her two great-aunts, her grandmother—and running the inn."

"You met all these people at the B and B?" Lindsay asked.

"No, none of the above. All were snowed in or snowed out and couldn't get back home. The elderly aunts live in the B and B along with an elderly gentleman. You'll find out anyway, so I might as well tell you that I'm taking him fishing in a few weeks," Josh said.

Jake choked on his tea and set down his glass to stare at Josh. "I don't think I heard right."

"You heard right, and it's not that big a deal. You can come along if you want. I'm flying him to Colorado. He reminds me of Granddad."

"No kidding," Jake said, staring at Josh.

"Is the B and B owner going with you?" Lindsay asked, and both of them stared at Josh.

"No, she isn't," Josh said, smiling at them. "She's only going to New York this weekend. Lindsay, close your mouth. You're staring."

"No more than Jake is," she said, exchanging a glance with Jake.

"I'll be damned, you've fallen in love. I didn't think

that would happen for another ten years," Jake said while Lindsay continued to look wide-eyed at him.

"I have not fallen in love. Don't be ridiculous, either one of you. I just met her. She's nice and hasn't ever been anywhere, and elderly Edwin Hickman, who lives at the inn, loves fishing, so I asked him to go fishing. I don't know why I'm explaining this to the two of you. Suffice it to say, I'm being a nice guy."

"I'll be damned," Jake said again. "You're a nice guy, but in a different way. I can't recall you taking a senior fishing before. I can't believe it when I hear you say it."

"Don't sound like I'm an ogre. It just worked out that way. You plan your dinner after Mike gets back. No telling when that will be."

"I will, and I'll let you know."

"I think something happened to you out there in the snow in that blizzard," Lindsay said. "Josh, this is so totally unlike you that I'm like Jake—I can't believe what I hear you say. As much fun as all this is, I have to go because I have a dental appointment." She stood. "Josh, I've just seen a whole new side of you that I've never seen before. It's very nice of you to take the elderly man on a fishing trip and your lady friend who has never flown, never been out of Texas, to New York. Remind me to call you next time I need some help birthing a calf or some such."

"Forget it, Lindsay," Josh said. "You can do that blindfolded."

"Well, I'm impressed with my big brother and these charitable trips."

"He gets a pat on the back," Jake said.

"Enough of you two. I'll think twice before we have the next lunch."

"No, you won't," Lindsay said as her brothers stood.

She hugged them briefly. "See you both soon." She left, her blond hair swinging with each step as they sat again.

"We didn't hear about her latest fight with Tony Milan," Josh said.

"Maybe those two have let up a bit."

"Oh, yeah," Josh said, "and the sky is pink today. They keep the old Calhoun-Milan feud alive and well."

"Madison and I have done our part to end it," Jake said, glancing at his watch. "I've got to go, too. I'll get the check today."

"Thanks. Let me know about dinner."

"Sure. Have a great time in New York. She may be terrified of the big city."

"I don't think she'll be terrified, but she may not like it. It's a far cry from Beckett."

"I don't even know Beckett. It must be smaller than Verity," Jake said as they walked out of the restaurant.

"I'm sure it is. One small hotel and the bed-and-breakfast—that was it. No motels. It's not right on the highway, and my pilot and I were lucky they had a runway and a place to land—I'm guessing it's for the ranchers out in that area. Good to see you," he said, unlocking his car and climbing inside to drive to his office.

As he sat behind his desk, he shoved aside a stack of papers to read later. Restless, filled with an uncustomary lack of interest in business, he thought about the ranch and the possibilities of taking a couple of weeks off soon and staying there. He had great executives who could run the company, including an executive vice president who could take charge and wouldn't need his help or direction.

Was this corporate world really what he wanted to continue to do? Was he missing life as Abby had said? No one had ever told him that before, and he wouldn't have listened to most anyone else. In addition to the New York trip, he would like to take her to the ranch, because that was what he really considered his home.

The moment he thought of Abby with him at his ranch, he wanted to do that soon. Would she like the ranch? He turned to look out the window at other buildings in downtown Dallas, but he was seeing Abby. He wanted to be with her, and he wished the weekend would arrive. He turned back to his computer to look up a number and make a call to a dress shop in New York. After he hung up, he called Abby and talked for twenty minutes until she had a guest needing her attention and had to go.

She was his total opposite—small-town, wrapped up in her family and where she'd grown up, very simple tastes and wants, yet he couldn't get her out of his thoughts. Maybe after this weekend when he would see her in his world, he could. He thought about her in New York with her ponytail hairdo, her slacks and plain shirts buttoned to her chin—would she want him to take her home early?

He couldn't imagine that she would really interest him long. He wouldn't be surprised if she backed out of going before the weekend came.

Continuing to be surprised by the fact that he wanted to take Abby to New York, he had to admit his brother and sister were right—that was unlike him. At least in some ways. But when he thought about their kiss in the heart-shaped shadow in the snow, mere memories made him hot with desire. No woman's kisses had ever affected him the way Abby's had.

What had started as a fun, lighthearted, meaningless kiss had shaken him and changed his views of her forever. He couldn't imagine ever forgetting her. How long was that kiss going to be an influence in his life? Would he get her out of his system in New York? Just thinking about her made him want to talk to her and be with her. He picked up his phone to call her again, saw the stack of mail in front of him and resolved to wait until night to call her.

He pulled the stack in front of him to go through it, trying to get Abby out of his thoughts and get work done.

During their last phone call, they had agreed she would meet him Friday at Beckett's small airport that consisted only of a tiny office, one small hangar and runways that were too short for commercial jets. When she arrived and walked toward the office, Josh came out to meet her.

The minute she saw him, Abby's heart missed a beat. All her doubts about going with him fell away. She became slightly self-conscious as wind blew a few tendrils of her hair across her cheek.

For the flight to Dallas and then New York, she had dressed in navy slacks, a new pale-blue button-down long-sleeve shirt with a collar and a light jacket, and she had let down her hair. She was relieved to see Josh dressed as casually in chinos and a navy sweater and boots.

"Hi," he said. "I'm glad to see you."

"Hi, Josh. I'm still torn between wondering what I'm doing going to New York and anticipating seeing you and this trip. This is the most exciting thing in my life."

"More exciting than when we kissed in the heart-shaped shadow?" he asked, a slight smile lifting one corner of his mouth.

Startled, she blinked. "No, maybe not," she answered

truthfully. His smile vanished as his brown eyes darkened and his gaze lowered to her mouth.

"With an answer like that, what I'd like to do is take you home with me for the weekend," he said in a deeper voice.

She smiled again as she shook her head. "I don't believe so. That isn't what I agreed to do."

"New York it is. Let's board." As Josh took her arm, he smiled. "You look fantastic. I've never seen you with your hair down."

Keeping the thought to herself that he looked fantastic, too, she smiled. "Thank you. I'm glad you like it. It's naturally curly and a little difficult to manage."

"If you need to get it done in New York, I'll tell you where to go and you can use my credit card. It'll save you time for sightseeing and being with me."

She laughed. "I'll keep that in mind. I do my own hair except for haircuts. We have a shop in Beckett."

"You might like getting it done in New York. It'll be something else to tell your family you did."

As they boarded the plane, he motioned to her. "Sit by a window. You've never flown, and you'll like looking out. It's a sunny day between here and Dallas, so you'll have a view."

"I'm excited."

He smiled and took her hand. "I am, too, but not over the view of Texas. I'd rather you'd be excited for another reason, too. I've missed you, and I'm looking forward to this."

"Everything this weekend except you will be a first for me," she said, barely aware of what she told him, as her attention was on his hand holding hers. His hand was well-shaped, warm, callused in places, and though his touch was light, it sent a sizzling awareness of the physical contact.

"That's an interesting statement I've never heard from someone out with me before. So your family knows you're going with me?"

"Oh, yes. Even Grandma, who was reassured by Mr. Hickman that you're an okay guy and I'll be safe and have a good time. You better live up to all their descriptions and promises."

"Actually, I heard from Edwin. He called me. He didn't threaten me, but he clearly indicated he held me responsible for you. He told me that he was delighted I am taking you to New York and he knew you would have a wonderful, safe time."

"If that's what he said, then he certainly didn't threaten you, but I'm astounded he called you."

"It was a threat to see to it you have a good time and get home safely. A very subtle one, and I think you have a substitute grandfather."

They taxied to the end of the runway and in minutes were clear for takeoff. She turned to gaze out the window in fascination until Beckett was behind them.

"That was a thrill," she said.

He smiled. "I'm glad it's good weather and you can see for miles, even if all you're seeing now is mesquite, fields of grass or just bare ground and a rare stream."

"I can't believe this day is happening."

"It's happening, and I'm looking forward to going out tonight. This afternoon I'll have a limo that will take you to the dress shop. Get a dress for tonight and one for tomorrow night."

"Now it's two dresses you want to buy. That's a bit much."

"No, it's not. Stop worrying about something that I want to do. Tonight we'll go to a French restaurant."

"That sounds fabulous," she said.

"I think you look fabulous, and my after-dinner plans sound fabulous to me. A little dancing, a few kisses— you think I haven't been waiting for this weekend to come?"

"That's why I don't want you to buy dresses—I don't care to be obligated to you or anyone else except my family. Even my family, now that I'm an adult."

"You're free of any and all obligations," he said, his eyes twinkling. "I just hope you want a few kisses, too. That's the special part of the evening and has nothing to do with obligations and everything to do with desire."

"When you put it that way, it does sound like something to look forward to," she said in a sultry, breathless voice, flirting with him and enjoying herself. She never had this kind of fun with Lamont—or reactions out of him. The minute she spoke, Josh's amusement vanished, and he studied her intently while his chest expanded as he drew a deep breath.

"We have to stay buckled in right now, but what I'd like to do is pick you up and move you over here," he replied.

She tingled. "You wicked man," she teased, fanning herself with her hand. "Now I'm all hot and bothered, and you haven't even touched me." She laughed. "Stop flirting, Josh, before one of us does unbuckle and ends up somewhere we shouldn't."

His dark eyes were intent as he leaned forward, holding her chin with his hand. "There's no harm in flirting. It's fun and I know you think so, too, because you can't resist doing it."

She smiled. "You might be right. It does make the

time pass. Anticipation is exciting," she whispered, looking at his mouth.

His hand slipped behind her head, and he pulled her closer as his mouth covered hers. His kiss was deep, sending waves of heat, stirring desire until she finally leaned away to look at him again.

"Slow down—we have a weekend and we just got off the ground," she said. Her voice was weak and did not hold a shred of conviction to her own ears.

He sat back. "We're going to have a great weekend."

"Did you have trouble clearing your calendar to go?"

"Nope, because it's the weekend. Have you had many people check in since I left?"

"Not at all," she answered, telling him about the past few days, sitting back and enjoying the flight. It seemed short until they landed in Dallas and left the plane to board a larger one that was far more luxurious. While she was fascinated with the takeoff and the sensation of their speed and the lift of the plane, it all paled next to her awareness of Josh, which was sharp and constant.

Their topics of conversation had a wide range, and she learned more about his relatives and ancestors, as imbedded in Texas history as her own family.

He had a flight attendant serve soft drinks and sandwiches for lunch, and finally the pilot announced they were approaching New York. She was breathless over the view as they came in, flying over water, and suddenly they were on the ground and the flight was over.

Josh had a limo waiting. A uniformed driver stood and smiled when they walked up.

All the way to the hotel, she was mesmerized by the sights and sounds. "Josh, this is fantastic—all the noise and traffic and buildings. I've seen pictures, but it's different in real life." She turned to look at him. He sat smiling, watching her, his long legs stretched out, crossed at the ankles.

"You've seen it so much, it means nothing to you."

"I'm having more fun watching you, and I'm glad you like everything. It's a fabulous city."

"More than fabulous—absolutely awesome, as my sister would say. I'm going to be such a tourist and take a million pictures."

"I think I'll have to take a few pictures myself, but mine won't be of the city, except as a background for you."

"I might not want to go home."

He grinned. "Let me know and I'll see how long we can stay."

"You know I'm kidding. We go home Sunday," she said, turning back to look at everything, thankful she had accepted Josh's invitation. "I can't wait to get out there."

"I can't wait to get to the hotel room," he said in a husky voice that made her turn to look at him and forget the scenery.

"I won't ask why."

"You know exactly why, and I think you're a little eager yourself because your voice changes."

"I hoped you wouldn't notice, since I can't control that with you."

"I'm happier than ever you agreed to this weekend."

When the limo pulled to the front door of the hotel, she stepped out to walk into an elegant lobby with bouquets and sprays of flowers for the opening. People greeted Josh as he walked to the front desk.

On the top floor, they crossed a hall, and he unlocked a door. "This is your suite. Mine adjoins it, and the adjoining door locks on each side."

"Locked is fine." She smiled, looking at the beige and white decor. "This suite is beautiful, and so are the flowers," she said, glancing around a large living room. A bouquet of mixed fresh flowers and a clear-covered plate of cheeses, fruit and crackers were on a nearby table. There was a dining area and a spacious covered balcony with a high wall, potted plants and outdoor furniture. "Josh, this is breathtaking."

"Come see my suite. We'll have to go through the door from the hall."

She followed him down the short hall until he paused to unlock the door to his suite.

The living room was larger than hers, as was the dining area with luxurious furniture. He had a bigger balcony. Through an open door she saw a small kitchen, and she guessed a second open door led to a bedroom and bath. Another huge bouquet of mixed fresh flowers stood on the glass coffee table, and a covered spread of cheeses, fruit and crackers was on a table nearby. Champagne was on ice.

"This is beautiful, too," she said. He dropped his things and crossed the room to her to slip his arm around her waist.

"I've waited for this moment since I told you goodbye at the inn," he said, leaning down to kiss her. Both his arms banded her, holding her tightly pressed against him. His kiss spiraled to the center of her being, setting her ablaze as she slid her arms around his neck and clung tightly.

Was she speeding toward heartbreak, real heartbreak that might take a long time to get over and sour her relationship with dependable Lamont? The question was fleeting, dwindling to no importance because she wanted Josh's kisses. She wanted this exciting weekend that she otherwise might not ever have in her life. Just this once. Broken bones mended, so broken hearts must mend, too.

It could never be a relationship or much of anything except a few times out together, but she wanted what she could get. It might hurt later, but at least she wouldn't have giant regrets that she had let life pass her by.

Josh's kisses drove away all her inner worries and she yielded to him, returning his kiss as passionately as he kissed her. He was hard, strong, his lean body pressing against her.

He shifted, running his hand lightly along her throat, down over her breast, her waist and hip, lower along her thigh. He swung her up into his arms and carried her through the suite to place her on the bed.

He lowered himself, still holding his weight partially off her as he continued to kiss her until she pushed slightly and he raised his head.

She ran her finger along his clean-shaven jaw. "Watch out, Josh. The first thing you know, you're going to make that old Texas legend haunt you."

"At the moment, that doesn't sound like something to fear."

She smiled but changed the subject. "I think I have a dress appointment soon."

"You do, but I couldn't resist." He moved away and took her hand to help her up. "Want a moment to freshen up? We have about ten minutes before we have to leave."

"Yes, I do," she answered.

He nodded, falling into step beside her. "I'll come get you in ten minutes—how's that?" he said as he walked her back to her suite.

"See you then," she said, closing the door and turning to get ready for the afternoon, while her thoughts were on the evening with Josh. Anticipation built with every second—a dinner out in one of the most famous cities in the world—a dinner with Josh. And dancing with Josh, being in his arms. Her heart raced at the thought, and eagerness enveloped her. Tonight would be a night to remember forever.

Josh rode down in the elevator with her, taking her arm lightly to walk to the front door. "I'll be here at the hotel while you're gone. I have a couple of meetings. The limo is yours for the afternoon. Just head back to the hotel by five."

The driver, Reed, stood waiting, holding open the door of the limo. She told Josh goodbye, climbed in and glanced back to see Josh going in the front door of the hotel. Everything in New York reminded her of the differences in their lives. She still was astounded he had asked her up for the weekend. She couldn't imagine why he was drawn to her at all. The women he dated, she was certain, were sophisticated, like him, beautiful and accustomed to the same life as him. He was a man of mystery in a lot of ways. She was as surprised about his friendship with Mr. Hickman as she was by his interest in her.

The limo halted in front of a shop, and Reed came around to open the door for her.

"Thanks, Reed."

"Here's my number. Call me when you see you'll be done and I'll come get you."

"Thank you," she said, pocketing the number and turning to the boutique, feeling butterflies in her stomach. This was a far cry from Sandy Perkins's dress shop in Beckett.

The friendly woman named Hilda, who had been

expecting her, soon ended the butterflies she felt. Instead, she was dazzled by the array of dresses Hilda brought out to show her and the treatment that made her feel like royalty.

She finally selected two dresses, which seemed incredibly extravagant, but she suspected if she didn't, Josh would return to the store with her and see to it that she purchased the second dress.

At one point, Hilda stood looking at Abby in a maroon dress. "That is perfect on you. If you would like to get your hair done this afternoon, there's a salon that I might get you in. It's on the next block, so you could walk. They're good and very nice."

Abby laughed. "Josh told you to ask me, didn't he?"

"No, actually, he didn't. And your hair looks nice. I just thought with your new dresses, you might like your hair done."

Abby thought a moment and nodded. "If they can take me, I have time, and it might be fun."

Hilda left and in minutes was back. "You're in luck. I've written everything down for you, and she can take you in an hour."

"Thank you. I'll be glad I did, I'm sure."

Her purchases made, she was so curious about the city, she asked Hilda to hold her packages while she walked down the street.

Sunshine spilled over buildings, traffic and pedestrians. A man passed on a skateboard, weaving in and out of traffic. Horns honked, and she enjoyed strolling along the avenue to the end of the block immersed in all the traffic, people hurrying past her, the sounds and sights that were so different from her world. She crossed the street to stroll along the other side, finally returning, gathering her packages and thanking Hilda. She went to the hair salon and in another hour called Reed and said she was ready to be picked up.

Back at the hotel, her eagerness grew steadily until it was only a minute before time for Josh to appear at her door.

She made one more check of how she looked. She had taken several pictures of her reflection in a mirror to send home and had already heard back from her mother and sister, who had seen the pictures. Her hair, parted in the middle, fell freely on both sides of her face in loose spirals. She had selected a simple sleeveless black dress that ended just above her knees deceptively modest neckline in front, but her back was left bare. She wore high-heeled black sandals and silver bangle earrings.

She heard Josh's light knock and picked up her black envelope purse. When she opened the door, her breath caught at the sight of Josh in his charcoal suit, red tie and white dress shirt; she also noticed his eyes widen with a look of surprise. "Do you want to come in?

"You look stunning," he said in a husky voice that indicated the reaction he was having. "Yeah, I want to come in, but if I do, we'll never get to the restaurant."

"Then I'm coming out," she said, grabbing a lightweight black blazer from a nearby chair and closing the door behind her.

The corner of his mouth lifted in amusement. "You don't want me to come in?"

"Right now, I want the French dinner more than a kiss."

"It wouldn't be just a kiss," he said, stepping into the elevator with her. People got on at the next floor, and they rode quietly until they got out in the lobby.

Reed and the limo waited, and soon they were driving through New York traffic as the sun slid behind tall buildings.

"So you like the dress I selected today? And thank you very much. It was fun and exciting and they were all very nice to me, which makes me wonder about your life and how many women you've sent to that store to get dresses. But it's none of my business, so you don't have to tell me."

"Actually, you're the first, but my mother has shopped there, and on a rare occasions when my sister is in New York for a horse show, she goes there. Hilda always helps Mom and Lindsay. " He glanced at her black dress. "You look fantastic."

"Thank you," she replied. "You don't have hotel business tonight?"

"No, I took care of everything that needed my involvement for the opening of the hotel. I'm free for the rest of the weekend, which will be devoted to entertaining you."

"That's very nice, but it doesn't seem to me that you're really very involved," she said.

"I'm involved all I care to be. Don't be concerned."

"Fine. You know your business, and I don't."

The restaurant was on the top floor of a tall building, and the view was spectacular. They sat by floor-to-ceiling windows in a dimly lit dining area with black linen tablecloths, red roses, and candles in hurricane globes centered on the tables. A string quartet played, and there was a small dance floor, but no one dancing yet.

"This is lovely, Josh."

"Yes, it is," he said, studying her and indicating he meant her and not the view outside or the elegant restaurant.

A waiter came, and Josh ordered champagne. After they were alone, he turned to her. "We'll celebrate."

"What could we possibly be celebrating? That you're no longer snowbound in Beckett? That we made a safe flight to New York? That we're out in New York tonight? I can't guess."

The waiter returned to show Josh the selection. He uncorked it, went through all the traditional procedures and finally poured a glass for her and then one for Josh and set the remaining champagne in the bottle in the stand.

When they were alone, Josh raised his glass. "Here's to your first trip to New York. May you have many more. May it be a happy, unforgettable visit, in your memory for years to come, and may you begin to see how happy you've made me that you came to New York."

"That's a nice toast, but you can't be serious. You're not going to want to remember this night with me for years. Or care if I do."

"Oh, yes, I'll remember. You're unique in my life. I don't know anyone else like you. And I really do want you to have a fun trip. This is my gratitude for rescuing me from the blizzard."

"As helpful and resourceful as you are, you would have managed quite well." She touched his champagne flute lightly with hers and sipped the golden, bubbly liquid, looking into his brown eyes over the rim. She had a running current of excitement with him, but it was even stronger tonight. She expected to dance with him and to kiss him, and that kept excitement churning. On top of being in New York, she was completely dazzled. She raised her glass.

"May you have a great opening of your newest hotel and not get stranded in any more blizzards."

"Thank you." They touched glasses again and sipped. "Do you know when your inn first opened?" he asked as he set his flute on the table.

"Only the year—1887—a very long time ago."

They talked as tossed greens on crystal plates were served. When she finished her dinner of creamed lobster and grilled asparagus, she placed her fork across her plate.

"Are you ready to dance?" he asked.

"I'd love to," she said as he came around to hold her chair. On the dance floor, he turned to take her into his arms. Her heart thudded while she followed his lead, dancing with him to the string quartet playing an old ballad.

She was intensely aware of him pressed against her, holding her close as they moved together. His hand was on her bare back, sending tingles all through her. As they danced, his hand trailed down to her waist, slowly, a light caress. She couldn't get her breath and thought about kisses later.

They danced well together—that much even she could tell. The string quartet finally played a fast song. As she danced around him, watching his moves, she was certain he would want to make love this weekend, and she had to make a decision.

Until this week, she wouldn't have given ten seconds of thought to such a choice; she would not have been interested. Now she thought about her future with Lamont or another man from Beckett, a routine, quiet life with little change from the life she had always known and perhaps little attention from the man she might someday marry—never the excitement she had with Josh.

She watched Josh dance, his dark eyes steadily on her while every move he made was sexy. She stopped worrying about it—a decision to make another time, not yet—and gave herself to enjoying dancing with him. So far the weekend had been like a dream. She was going to go home in love with Josh even though she knew it would never be returned and wouldn't work out regardless.

Seven

At one in the morning, after a stroll around Times Square with a mob of people, they finally headed back to the hotel.

"Want a nightcap, Josh?" Abby asked as she placed her purse and her jacket on a chair in her room. Watching her, he shed his suit jacket and removed his tie, unbuttoning the top buttons of his shirt.

"Yes," he said as he dropped his tie on the chair. "There should be a cold beer in that fridge in your kitchen. If you don't find what you want, we can call room service."

They walked into the kitchen, and she opened the small refrigerator. "I see grape soda pop, which will be fine for me," she said, getting the soda and the beer.

"It's a nice night. Want to sit on the balcony?" he asked.

"I'd love to turn out the lights and sit on the balcony and look at the city, which is absolutely fascinating."

"I'm glad you like the city, and I'll have to admit that I'm surprised. I thought you wouldn't care for it very much. Sort of 'I want to see, and now I can go home.'"

"Oh, no. I think I could spend the year here and not see all I want to see. As it is, we have a day, so let's go sit, and you tell me what we're going to do tomorrow."

He switched off lights, leaving on one small light above the kitchen counter. They walked through the suite. In the living area, he set down their drinks to unlock and open the sliding glass door. A breeze swept in from the balcony.

"This is a beautiful hotel," she said.

He turned to slip his arm around her. "I've waited all week for this moment," he said in a husky voice. "I've dreamed of holding you and kissing you, and I don't want to wait another minute." He leaned closer to kiss her, and she wrapped her arms around him tightly to press against him.

He kissed her with such hunger and desperation that she trembled. His hand drifted lightly down her back until he found the zipper at the waist of her backless dress and unfastened it slowly. His hand slipped beneath her dress, down over her bottom.

The intimate caress made her moan as she unfastened the buttons on his shirt. She wanted to touch him as he touched her, to slide her hands over him and excite him as he did her.

He leaned forward to kiss her, his hands shifting beneath the top of her dress to push the material off her shoulders. When he moved away, her dress fell to her hips, and he stepped back to look at her. "You're beautiful," he said, tossing his shirt aside. He cupped her breasts and caressed her lightly with his thumbs. The sensations rocked her. Gasping, she closed her eyes and clung to him.

"Abby, I've dreamed of this moment," he whispered, straightening to frame her face with his hands. "I want you—you can't imagine how much," he said in a hoarse whisper.

Sliding her arms around his neck, she stood on tiptoe to kiss him. His arms banded her waist, crushing her to him as they kissed, hot passionate kisses that made her want to toss aside her caution. Kissing him was exciting beyond anything she had ever known or imagined.

She wanted him with her whole being while she felt it meant little to him, something casual that would not involve his heart. She didn't know whether she could deal with that.

She pulled away. "Josh, I didn't come to New York to sleep with you. It may happen, but I'm not ready at this point. I still feel we barely know each other. You said I had no obligations in accepting this trip."

"You don't," he said, caressing her throat, his breathing ragged as if he had run miles. "Absolutely not. I never want a woman in my arms out of a feeling of obligation." He pulled her dress back in place. "We'll slow down. We'll go sit on the balcony, sip our drinks and talk. How's that?" he asked. His voice was hoarse, and the hungry expression on his face made her want to step back into his embrace.

"For the moment, that may be a good idea," she replied in spite of what she felt.

He gazed at her a moment as if making a decision.

"Josh, this is amazing out here," she said. She stood at the rail of the balcony with her arms resting on it. Wind blew her long, wavy blond locks. Her back was bare, her legs shapely, and she looked beautiful. His mouth went dry. He had done what she wanted and what he should, but it had taken self-control. He wanted her in his arms and in his bed tonight, and he felt certain he could kiss away her objections, but he didn't want to go against her wishes.

"You don't have any vertigo, do you?" he asked.

"No, I love standing here and looking at the city, down below as well as far away. This is a fantastic view, and I'm enjoying it."

"I'm glad," he said, moving beside her and turning her to face him as he slipped an arm around her waist. "One kiss—just one, out here to remember this moment."

She didn't object, but stood looking at him with eyes open wide. He tightened his arm around her and leaned down to kiss her, opening her mouth with his, his tongue going over hers. She held him tightly, kissing him eagerly, making him almost regret his decision to limit himself to only one kiss.

He was aroused, wanting her, wishing he could unfasten her dress and toss it aside, take her to bed and make love to her.

Instead, at the first hint she was moving away, he released her. "Welcome to New York," he whispered.

"It's fabulous," she answered breathlessly.

"Want to sit?"

She moved to the chair by the table, and he sat beside her. "Josh, this hotel is so luxurious."

"I like it. This chain has done well, even though it's small next to two others I have. This is the deluxe line."

"This is like a dream."

"I'm glad. Part of this is a big thank you for taking me in out of that blizzard."

"It worked out, and you were so much help, I'm glad I did."

"Do you plan to always run the inn?"

"Probably so. Justin and Arden won't come back to run the place with me after they finish college, which is all right because I'm happy there. Justin is majoring in accounting and Arden is planning on law school. I expect them both to leave Beckett. They're on scholarships, and I help them with money from the inn, which is more profitable than Mom's hair shop."

"I think you told me that you didn't go to college."

"Right. I've always helped at the inn, and after high school I stepped in full-time, which I was happy to do. I've always planned to do that when I grew up. Pretty simple in your view, I'm sure. Your major was what?"

"Double major in accounting and agriculture. MBA in accounting. I played football and then pro ball until a shoulder injury sidelined me and I decided to move on. I invested my money in a small chain of hotels that I've been able to grow into a bigger chain, and I started the others. I've been fortunate to have inherited money, too."

"A very busy man."

"I've told you someday I'll be a rancher. I'd like you to see the ranch."

"I'd love that probably as much as this."

He smiled. "Right now, I thrive on business. I like my travels and making deals, the challenges and the satisfaction. But I do miss the ranch," he said with a wistful note in his voice.

"Josh, if you really love it, why are you staying in the business world when you can do what you really like best? I know you thrive in the corporate world, but you've said you love life on your ranch. You said I'm missing out on life. I still think you are, in a big way."

He ran his finger along her cheek. "You might be right," he said quietly. While they talked, he couldn't resist touching her. He held her hand, rubbing her knuckles lightly with his thumb. She had the softest skin, even though she worked with her hands constantly.

"Josh, the sun will come up in not too many hours. I should go to my suite."

"Sure," he said, draping his arm lightly across her shoulders. "I'll get the bottles—don't worry about them."

He walked her around to her door and waited while she unlocked it. He opened the door, held it for her and followed her inside, then caught her arm and turned her to face him. "I want a good-night kiss," he said, wanting even more to pick her up and carry her to bed. He wanted *her*. She was excited about their itinerary for tomorrow, but as far as he was concerned, they could chuck it and just make love all day.

Even more, he wanted her to be happy, so if it was seeing the sights that he had been to too many times to count since he was a kid, he would do that with her. She seemed dazzled by the city, while he was dazzled by her.

He poured his longing and passion into his kiss, which became kisses as he caressed her and ached to make love to her.

Finally she stopped him. "Josh, it really is late. You need to go."

He sighed. "Yeah, I know," he said in a gravelly voice. He ran his finger down her cheek. "Sometime I'm going to make love to you for hours," he whispered, determined that would happen before too long.

Wide-eyed and solemn, she gazed up at him. "It might happen, Josh. We both want that, even though that isn't the wisest course to follow. Once again, I had a wonderful time."

He barely heard her last words, because his heart pounded over her admission that she wanted the same lovemaking he did.

"I'm glad you had a good time. See you bright and early. We can do breakfast or bed," he said, teasing her.

She looked briefly startled and then laughed. "I believe I'll choose breakfast. You remember that."

"How could I forget?" He brushed her lips lightly with another kiss and left.

After saying good-night to Josh, Abby drifted through the suite and opened her balcony door to peep outside, seeing Josh wasn't out. She sat on the balcony, loving every minute of her stay at his hotel. He hadn't wanted to stop making love tonight and neither had she, but she didn't want to go home with big regrets. She wanted to be sure of what she did.

Finally, when she was about to fall asleep, she went inside, closing up and getting ready for bed. She left a wake-up call and fell asleep almost as soon as she stretched out in bed.

Josh had the entire day planned, and an early stop was the Empire State Building. She stood looking at the view. "It's a gorgeous morning, I'm at the Empire State Building and we have to take a selfie to send home."

"First let me take some pictures of you to send home. They'll want to see you," he said, snapping pictures with her phone. Impulsively, he pulled out his own phone and took her picture as she laughed.

She took a selfie of the two of them and looked at it. She had on black slacks and a black cotton shirt with a matching sweater on over it. Josh was dressed in his brown sweater, brown slacks and boots. Josh reached out to get her phone. "I'll take the next selfie of us," he said, wrapping his arms around her, snapping a picture while they kissed.

"I'm not sending that one home."

"You don't want to be seen kissing me?"

She smiled. "I'll answer that later today."

He grinned and took her arm. "On to the next tour stop."

They went to St. Patrick's Cathedral, saw Grand Central Terminal and walked up Fifth Avenue into Central Park. "Josh, this park is marvelous. I've seen it in movies, but real life is better."

As the day wore on, she took pictures of bridges she had also seen in movies while Josh patiently waited and then took her to the next thing to see.

It was late in the afternoon when they went to the Statue of Liberty. In the midst of the crowd, she took out her phone, wrapped her arm around his neck to kiss him and took a picture of them. The moment she kissed him, his arms circled her waist and he held her tightly, kissing her in return, making far more of the kiss than she had ever intended. When he released her, she had a moment when she was still lost in his kiss, forgetting everything around them.

"I told you I would give you an answer later. No, I don't mind being seen kissing you," she said, but he had turned the kiss into a fiery moment that ignited passion.

He smiled. "It's a good thing, because it'll probably happen again while we're out. Your enthusiasm and exuberance about everything makes you irresistible. Plus there are a few other reasons you're irresistible."

"No one has ever told me that before. We won't go into the other reasons. At least not out in public. You're a bit irresistible yourself. Maybe someday I'll tell you why."

"That's something I'd like to hear. C'mon, time to get the ferry back."

They returned to the hotel to change for dinner. She showered and dried her hair, trying to get her unruly curls under control, momentarily envious of Josh's short brown hair.

She slipped into the other dress she had bought. It was wine-colored with long sleeves, clinging, longer than the black dress, with a slit on one side of the skirt. The cowl neck was low-cut. She wore the black high-heeled sandals with it.

She pinned her hair back slightly on either side of her head, working to brush out the curls and leave it in soft waves falling freely a few inches over her shoulders as her stylist at the salon had done yesterday.

Picking up her phone, she looked at pictures from their day. She had had the most wonderful time possible with Josh, but that didn't change one bit of the huge differences in their lives, lifestyles, ambitions and future plans. He would never fall in love with her, and she had to keep that in mind, because she was already in love with him. She hated to view her feelings too closely this weekend when she was with him. She was having the time of her life, an unforgettable time, she was sure. Would heartbreak go with it?

She still hadn't made a decision whether they would make love or not. All her decisions about no sex before marriage had been made long ago without Josh in the equation, and she didn't want him to change them now.

She heard a knock and went to the door, opening it to face him. He made her heart thud. He was in a navy suit with a matching navy tie. Gold cuff links in his dress shirt French cuffs added a touch of elegance to his appearance.

"I have to say wow," he told her. "You look stunning."

"Thank you, thank you," she said, smiling at him. "And so do you."

"That's good to hear. Ready?"

"Oh, yes. You know I can't wait." She picked up her purse and jacket and closed her suite door.

He took her arm. "Tonight we're going to my favorite restaurant. American, steak and potatoes, but they have other choices. How's that?"

"As wonderful as French. I'll love it if you do."

"You're being happy and cooperative."

"Always," she said, laughing, and he smiled at her.

"We have this elevator all to ourselves," he said, holding her arm lightly and leaning close to kiss her.

Her heart missed a beat the minute his mouth touched hers. Even a light, quick elevator kiss set her pulse racing when it was Josh.

This restaurant, too, was high in a building with a spectacular view that she couldn't stop looking at as they walked through the carpeted, dimly lit dining room. A piano player provided soft music, and their table offered a view of the glittering city. A candle was on the white linen-covered table, and someone was there to wait on them almost instantly.

They both ordered steaks and Josh ordered wine. "I did see couples on the dance floor. Care to dance?"

"I'd love to," she said, taking his offered hand. She stepped into his arms, dancing with him, knowing she would remember this weekend the rest of her life.

They spent more time dancing than eating. Of all the men for her to enjoy being with, why was it a mogul whose life was so far removed from her own?

As she laughed at something he told her, she gazed into his dark eyes and knew she would never have more fun than she had had with him. She didn't think she could possibly ever have kisses as hot and passionate, either. And she didn't think she would ever go back to dating Lamont or ever marry him. After seeing New York, she realized there was way too much in life to go back to playing it safe and accepting the most convenient way of living. She had accused Josh of missing out on life, but she saw now that he wasn't the only one. She could get out and live a fuller life.

At midnight, as they finished a dance, Josh took her hand to walk back to their table. "Ready to go to the hotel? We'll talk, kiss and look at the view—or do you want to stay here longer?"

"Let's go back to the hotel."

"Good. That's what I'd hoped you would say."

At the hotel, when they walked toward the balcony with their drinks, he set their glasses on a table, her heart beating faster as she anticipated his kiss.

He drew her to him. "Before we go out on the balcony, which is relatively private, but not private enough, come here."

Her heart thudded as she walked into his embrace and raised her face for his kiss. Desire filled his dark eyes when he looked at her, and then his gaze shifted to her mouth. He leaned down to kiss her.

He held her tightly, bending over her so she had to

cling to him as she kissed him in return. She moaned softly with pleasure from his kisses that were endless, seemingly more passionate each time. She felt his fingers at her back and then felt the cool air as Josh drew the zipper of her dress slowly down her back, opening her dress to push it off. It fell with a soft whoosh around her ankles, and she stepped out of it and her high heels.

With trembling fingers, she unfastened his shirt and pushed it away, running her hands over his muscled chest while his kisses drove all thoughts from her mind. She just wanted to keep kissing him. She wanted the clothing barriers away. This whole weekend had been a once-in-a-lifetime experience, and she wasn't going to stop now. Josh would never fall in love with her. She would go home, get over this trip, settle back into her regular life and someday marry, living in Beckett for the rest of her life.

This one night was the exception to all of the life she had planned for so long. She wanted Josh's kisses, his loving, all of him. She didn't want to look back with regrets of what she'd missed or had denied herself. She unfastened his belt, then his trousers to push them off, and he stepped out of them. He was aroused, ready to love. She wanted his arms around her and his kisses. He peeled away her lace panties. Her bra was gone swiftly.

He cupped her breasts in his hands, caressing her as he ran his thumbs so lightly over her. "You're beautiful, every inch of you," he said in a voice hoarse with passion. As she touched him, his deep, sexy kisses made her tremble.

She ran her hands over his chest, up to touch his jaw, feeling slight stubble. Trailing her fingers over the angular planes of his face, she wanted to commit everything to memory that happened this night. His chest was hard with sculpted muscles, his biceps well-defined.

Could she let go of the restrictions she had always held to? This was the one chance in her life to make love wildly, passionately and in a manner she didn't expect to again.

He picked her up to carry her near the bed, switching on a small table lamp and yanking covers back before turning to look at her again. "Abby, you're gorgeous," he said in the same gruff voice.

Standing her on her feet, he embraced and kissed her. His erection pressed against her, hot, hard. She moved her hand down his smooth back over firm buttocks and down to muscled thighs.

He stepped back to look at her again, filling each hand with a breast and leaning down to kiss her, his tongue sending streaks of pleasure that made her gasp, close her eyes and cling to his shoulders. "Josh," she whispered, feeling on fire, wanting to spread her legs for him, wanting him to love her for hours.

He kissed first one breast and then the other, caressing her at the same time. She gasped as sensations rocked her. She wanted to press her hips against him, but he held her away as he fondled and kissed her breasts.

She was barely aware when Josh picked her up to place her on the bed. Kneeling beside her, he stroked her ankle, moving up her leg, his fingers stroking lightly, his tongue and lips following as he caressed behind her knee. He moved between her legs, his hands stroking her inner thighs, driving her wild with desire.

He leaned down to kiss her thighs, his tongue following where his hands had been.

"Josh," she gasped and sat up to hold him and kiss him, running her tongue over him. His rod was hot, thick and hard. As she stroked him, he wound his fingers in her hair. He groaned and kissed her passionately until they fell back on the bed, and he showered her with kisses while he caressed her.

"Wait," he said and stepped off the bed. He returned to move between her legs and put on a condom.

Breathlessly she gazed at him. He was handsome, thrilling, sexy. She wanted him, reaching out to rest her hands on his thighs, feeling the crisp short hairs beneath her palms.

He lowered himself, his dark eyes watching her as he kissed her. She closed her eyes, wrapping her arms around him.

He started to enter her, moving slowly, and then he stopped.

"Abby, are you sure you want this? You're a virgin," he said, frowning.

She locked her legs around him and held him more tightly to pull him to her. "Love me now. I know what I want." She ran her hands down his back and over his buttocks. "Josh, I want you."

He lowered himself again and thrust into her. She felt a sharp pain as he covered her mouth with his to kiss her, and then she moved with him. Pain and pleasure mixed and then urgency made her move wildly beneath him, rocking with him and finally having a burst of release with her climax while he shuddered with his at the same time.

They gradually slowed, and his breathing became normal when he turned to kiss her lightly.

"Abby, you're special," he whispered.

Wrapped in euphoria, she drew him to her to kiss him again. Holding her, he rolled on his side, keeping her close with him and their legs entwined.

She held him tightly, at the moment enveloped in bliss. Josh was hers right now, and tomorrow didn't exist. For tonight she would take the moments, cherish Josh, making love with him. This was perfection, what she had dreamed of, wanted, fantasized about, this never-to-be-forgotten night and weekend. She suspected no one would ever excite her as much as he did.

She was in love with him—or had she been in love with him before this weekend ever started? She didn't want him to know. When he walked away—and she was certain he would—she didn't want him to feel guilty. She wanted him to think her heart was no more involved than his was.

She stroked his back, feeling the solid muscles, his narrow waist. She was eager to hold and touch him the rest of the night.

"I'm glad you came to New York," he said in his husky voice. "A rare night, a unique woman in my arms." He kissed her lightly again.

"It's thrilling, and I'll always remember this weekend."

"Both of us will," he whispered.

He held her quietly for some time and finally shifted to look at her. "How about a hot tub?"

"I'm not sure I can move," she said.

"I'll carry you." Stepping out of bed, he picked her up. She wrapped her arms around his neck and kissed him as he walked toward the bathroom. Shortly they were in a tub of hot water. She sat back between his legs, leaning against him while they talked, going from topic to topic. She felt deeply relaxed, floating in euphoria, happy with him, with everything about the evening.

When they finally climbed out of the tub, they dried each other with slow, sensual strokes, Josh barely touching her with the towel as he drew it across her breasts while his dark gaze conveyed so much desire, she could barely get her breath.

Inhaling deeply, she reached for him. He stepped close to wrap his arms around her and kissed her passionately, a searing, possessive kiss as if she was the only woman ever to be in his life. How could he make her feel so special, so pretty in his eyes?

She responded to him, pouring her heart into her kisses, sliding her hands over him, caressing him, hoping to drive him to the trembling need she felt.

As he kissed her, his hands were all over her, touching her lightly, moving between her legs to touch and rub her intimately, building her need.

He carried her to bed to kiss and caress her, taking his time until she tugged at his shoulders. "Josh, I want you now," she whispered, looking up at him and then pulling him down to kiss him hungrily. He reached to the table by the bed to get protection.

Lowering himself, he entered her, moving slowly, letting desire and need build. She clung to him, aware only of Josh, his muscled body, his hands and mouth, his staff, thick, hot and hard, driving her to moving wildly beneath him until she reached a pounding climax.

She shook with release, sending Josh into his climax, as he held her tightly and they moved together. She heard his groan, felt his arms tighten around her. Her breathing was ragged, loud as she gasped for each breath and slowed, sinking into rapture that was even greater than the first time with him.

How could she not fall more deeply in love with him after this night? She wouldn't think about the answer. Instead, she kissed him and held him tightly. For tonight there were no problems, and that was enough for the moment.

* * *

When sunlight spilled through the windows in the morning, Josh held her close against him. He turned on his side to prop himself up to look at her. Short locks of brown hair fell over his forehead, and she combed them back gently with her fingers. Everything about him fascinated her, and she couldn't stop touching him. She ran her hand over his shoulder. "I can tell you work out."

"Yes. I'll return to ranch life someday, and I don't want to be too puny to do it."

She smiled. "I don't think you're in danger of being too puny. Definitely not too puny to make love."

He smiled. "We go home this afternoon. I thought I would take you out for breakfast, but would you like to have breakfast on our balcony? I'll call room service."

"I would love breakfast on our balcony if it isn't cold out there."

"If it is, we'll have breakfast in here. I'll get the menu, and you can tell me what you want."

He stepped out of bed and grabbed a towel he had dropped the night before to wrap around him, knotting it across his flat stomach.

She propped up pillows, sat up and pulled a sheet under her arms to cover her. He came back and handed her the menu as he slid beneath the covers and tossed away the towel.

"Now what do you see that you'd like?"

"What I see is a very handsome man, and I'd like him to kiss me," she said, studying him. His expression changed, and he turned to take her into his arms. He pulled her onto his lap as he wrapped his arms around her to kiss her.

Over an hour later, Josh asked her again what she'd like for breakfast. "That question worked out well last time, so I'll try it again," he said.

Smiling, she leaned over the edge of the bed to pull up the menu and look at it. "This time I'll order, because I'm definitely getting hungry."

In half an hour, they sat in plush bathrobes on the balcony while they ate.

"Josh, I love this view," she said, pulling her cell phone from her robe pocket. She turned to face him. "Can I take your picture?"

"In this robe?"

"Yes. Is that okay?"

"Sure, if this is what you want."

She took his picture, smiling at him. "Every minute has been special."

"I can say the same, Abby," he told her, suddenly looking at her with an earnest expression that faded into another smile as he reached for her. "Come home with me to the ranch. We can leave this afternoon and get in tonight. Stay a couple of nights, and then I'll take you home."

She stared at him while she debated what to do. He leaned close to caress her nape lightly. "Your family can work it out, and it's just this once. I want to show you my ranch."

She nodded. "If someone will cover for me, I will. I'll call now."

Taking her phone, she walked away from him to talk to her mother briefly about going with him to his ranch. She talked quietly, ending with thanks.

"Mom said the desk at the inn will be covered and to have a good time," she said, not mentioning that her mother had said, "Take real good care of yourself" before she ended the call. She was certain her mother worried about her having a broken heart over Josh. "I need to go home Tuesday," she said breathlessly, and his eyes narrowed slightly. "I've finished my breakfast."

He stood and came around to pick her up and carry her to the bedroom. Dropping the robe, she slid beneath the sheet with him and slipped her arm around his neck while her other hand moved beneath the sheet to fondle him. He was aroused, ready to love again. He lifted her over him, so she sat astride him.

She wrapped her arms around his neck and leaned in a few inches to look at him. "I can't get enough of you," she whispered.

"I hope you can't," he answered as he reached out to cup her breasts and shower kisses over first one and then the other. He moved her closer, entering her with urgency as if it were the first time they had loved.

Later they sat on the balcony again after ordering a light lunch. "Josh, this is wonderful," she said.

"You like the whole world. Have you ever been any-place you didn't like?" he asked, sounding amused, and she stopped viewing the skyline to turn to him.

"No, I suppose I haven't. I don't travel much, so when I do, I like the places I've gone. Some are more spectacular than others, and this is definitely the most spectacular of all and the best—as Arden would say, 'awesome.' It really is awesome. The description fits this city."

"I'll have to say, you've taken to it better than I thought you might. Maybe better than I ever have," he added, glancing out at the skyline. "When I think of New York City, I think of sirens through the night, crowds of people, trying to get a cab in a storm, al-though I usually have a limo now—"

"For a man who's so much fun to be with, that's a harsh outlook."

"I've been coming here off and on since I was about ten years old. My family came a lot when I was a kid and later, I have to come on business. Sometimes I get jaded about things and places that I've seen a lot."

"Well, keep your sunny side up while you're with me, please. I like that."

"If it pleases you, then I will do my best to do what you want."

She smiled at him. "Why do I have such fun with you? You're a charmer. I can answer my own question."

"And that's a negative in your view."

"It has a definite appeal. You know you make my heart go pitter-pat."

"I hope so, and in a minute we're going to forget about the food that's—" They heard knocking.

"There he is," Josh said, standing. "I'll take care of it." He left, and she turned back to look out over buildings. Some were taller than the hotel. She could see the rooftops of others, with penthouses, or gardens and trees growing in large planters, a life so different from her own that she still felt dazzled by the city. And dazzled by Josh, more in love with him each hour. She was certain his feelings for her were shallow and nothing like what she felt for him.

She hoped she could return to her plain way of life in Beckett easily and tuck this time with Josh away in her memories as once-in-a-lifetime fun, sexy and amazing. She knew her relationship with Lamont was over. She could never go back to that, and it wasn't fair for Lamont, either. They weren't in love or deeply attracted. It had just been convenient.

Her thoughts shifted to Josh. Even if he fell wildly

in love—which she was sensible enough to know he would not—she couldn't tie her life to a charmer, a worldly man who could sweet-talk her into doing what he wanted and then, like her father, just disappear out of her life someday. Or even if he didn't disappear, just want out of any relationship with her.

She expected them never to get to the relationship stage, though. She didn't want to risk that much. If she got into a relationship with Josh and then he ended it, she would be brokenhearted to the point that she could never get over it. She wasn't certain her mother had ever gotten over her father or stopped loving him.

Interrupting her thoughts, a waiter pushed a cart onto the balcony and began transferring covered dishes to the table in front of them, sandwiches, bowls of chips, various fruits and desserts.

As they ate, she was still lost in thought. Was this weekend something she would recall with joy, or would it always remind her of how plain her life was in Beckett? Was the handsome charmer sitting so close to her going to break her heart? Had she already set herself up for a lasting hurt?

Eight

They scrapped the sightseeing plans to start home to Josh's ranch at one that afternoon, arriving in Dallas and changing planes to fly to Verity, where Josh had a car waiting. Leaving Verity at dusk, he drove across mesquite-covered land much like land around Beckett.

When they left the county road to drive over the bumpy pipes of the cattle guard, they passed beneath a high black iron arch with a circle centered at the top. Inside the circle was JC Ranch in iron, showing clearly in the bright glow from a spotlight.

After he had driven ten minutes without a sign of life, she was surprised. "How far away is your house?"

"Pretty dang far," he answered. "I don't want to be living near the county road where I see traffic if I look out my windows or where people driving past can see my house and all the other structures. I want to be back where I see open land and country, not a highway."

"No danger of that," she replied, unable to imagine Josh living in isolation. Darkness enveloped them except for the sweep of his headlights until they topped a small hill. Far ahead she saw myriad lights.

In a short time, they began to pass lighted barns, corrals and outbuildings. Most of her attention went to a sprawling gray slate stacked stone ranch house with a wraparound porch, wood railings, two porch swings and old-fashioned rocking chairs. Lights illuminated massive live oaks that had to be older than Josh. In front of the house was a pond with lighted fountains.

"I don't know why you ever leave this." She viewed it as beautiful, peaceful and welcoming.

"I'm beginning to wonder myself," he said, sounding unusually solemn. "Have you ever ridden a horse?"

"Sure. You don't grow up in Beckett without knowing someone with horses."

"Want to ride early in the morning? I have a gentle horse for you."

"I'd like that," she said.

"Later we'll go out in the truck, and I'll show you more of the ranch. Tomorrow night, how about barbeque and a little dancing—two-stepping?"

"It all sounds fun," she answered. "Remember, I have to get home Tuesday. Mom has customers booked at her hair shop, and my sis and brother have school."

"I'll get you home early Tuesday, I promise."

Soon he drove on a circular drive to a back door and stepped out. A man got up from one of the rocking chairs and came toward them. "Howdy, Josh. Let me get your things."

"Told you that you didn't need to wait for us to come in," Josh said, taking her arm. "Abby, meet Hitch Watkinson, my foreman. Hitch, this is Abby Donovan from Beckett, Texas."

"Glad to meet you, Miss Donovan," Hitch said.

"I'm glad to meet you," she replied, smiling at the tall, black-haired man with a deeply tanned face and a black broad-brimmed hat on his head.

"Just set everything in the hall, Hitch. I'll take it from there."

"Sure. Glad to have you home."

Josh unlocked a door and opened it. "We'll have the house to ourselves until morning, and then my staff will appear."

Hitch brought their things inside, said goodbye and left.

She stood in a long hall with Western paintings on the walls, walnut furniture and potted plants. Various hallways branched off to different wings of the house. "I'll show you around."

"Did you leave all the lights on when you left?"

"No. Hitch has a key. He came in and turned lights on for us when I texted him that we were coming. There is also a very full fridge should we want anything to eat.

"This is a huge house," she said. "It seems far bigger than the inn. How many bedrooms?"

"Seven," he said. "Actually five suites plus two more bedrooms. Sometimes I have all the family here. I have company during hunting season. There are four guesthouses on the ranch. Some people who work here have homes on the property, too. Hitch for one. Let's take our things upstairs first, and then I'll give you a tour."

He shouldered bags, and she took one. They climbed a sweeping spiral staircase to the second floor and walked down another large hallway.

"Here's my bedroom," he said, leading her into a sitting room larger than the main living room at her inn. The furniture was Western with brown leather wing-back chairs and a long brown leather sofa that faced a massive stone fireplace. Bookshelves lined one wall while another wall was glass. In the light that spilled in from outside, she could see a broad covered balcony with black wrought iron furniture. He tossed bags onto a chair and closed the drapes before turning to walk back to her and take her bag to place it on another chair.

"Josh this is a beautiful home," she said, thinking about him sleeping on her short sofa for three nights.

She wondered again why Josh had asked her to go with him to New York. She couldn't imagine the man who lived in this palatial home wanting to spend a weekend with her. She suspected he'd dated models, maybe actresses, women who were breathtakingly beautiful and had lives far more interesting that running a bed-and-breakfast in a small west Texas town.

"I'm glad we didn't come here first. I think I would have backed out of the trip. I can't imagine why you would want to take someone like me to New York."

He slipped his arms around her waist and gazed into her eyes. "I asked you to go with me because I wanted to be with you more than anyone else. Anyone," he repeated with emphasis. "I've had a grand time, and I don't want the weekend to end. That's why I asked you here tonight. You're the first woman I've ever brought to stay in this house."

Startled, she stared at him while her heart pounded. If only he really cared. But she knew better, no matter what he said now. There was no way, and even if he did, he wasn't the man for her. He was the man she had vowed all her adult life that she would avoid falling in love with. She was already in love with him, but she didn't want to go any farther. This was not the man to settle and lead a quiet life with a woman like her. Not ever. She hadn't changed her feelings about men like her father.

"Josh, this has been a wonderful weekend. I don't expect any more than that, and you and I are definitely not right for each other."

He tightened his arms around her, his eyes darkening with passion. He leaned down to kiss her, his mouth covering hers. It was a demanding, possessive kiss that made her feel as if he was in love, as if she was the one woman he wanted, yet she still clung to the knowledge that she was fooling herself and he would never really feel that way.

And then she stopped thinking and tossed caution and wisdom aside, holding him and kissing him in return, spiraling into passion and forgetting the world and all problems.

She was barely aware when he picked her up to carry her to his big bed.

It was in the early hours of the morning when Josh stirred and shifted, looking at Abby in the crook of his arm, lying against him, warm and soft. He brushed a silky lock of her hair away from her face. He couldn't understand his own reactions to her. He couldn't get enough of her.

He thought this weekend would satisfy him and he would lose interest. He had lost interest fast in some women he had dated, but it hadn't worked that way with Abby. Why was she such a draw to him when she was so many things he didn't like? She had been a virgin, which had shocked him and still made him wonder how important their lovemaking was to her since he was the first and only man she had ever been intimate with.

Her reactions weren't what he would have guessed. When she let him seduce her, take her virginity, he thought she might expect a relationship with him. That hadn't happened. She still viewed him as an undesirable male for a long-term relationship. If he hadn't been so tied up in knots with wanting her, he would have laughed at himself and his ego for assuming she would be dazzled by the first man she had sex with. Along with being a caring person, she was a confident woman and knew what she wanted in life. He suspected she would stick to her principles and views of what she wanted and didn't want. Why was he so upset that he fell into the "didn't want" category? He shouldn't care and he should be relieved, but he did care and he wasn't relieved at all.

They shouldn't be compatible. Was it purely sex? Since there hadn't been any sex until Saturday night and he had spent time with her at the inn and Friday night in New York, he didn't see how it could be purely lust.

He hadn't thought beyond this weekend. His plan was a fun weekend in New York, then take her home and forget her. That was what she wanted him to do. She wasn't thrilled with him at all. He wasn't the type of man she wanted in her life. It was Lamont she wanted. How could he be so drawn to a woman who was drawn to a man like Lamont?

Josh looked at her smooth, flawless skin, her long lashes, her silky hair that fell in waves over her bare shoulders and the pillow. He shook his head. He couldn't figure out his own feelings. Right now he wanted to wake her and make love. It had to be pure lust because they had nothing else between them. But if there was nothing between them, why had he wanted to take her to his ranch?

He thought about making arrangements to see her again. Beckett, Texas, was not convenient for a relationship. He mulled over possibilities. He hadn't thought she would go to New York with him when he asked her, but she had. Perhaps she'd go on other adventures with him. He needed to get over wanting to be with her. She wasn't his type. He wasn't her type. Once he was back in his regular routine, he would forget her.

He lay on his back and stared into the room. A small lamp burned, and he reached over to switch it off. Darkness enveloped them, but he didn't think he would sleep much. He turned, taking her into his arms and holding her close.

She sighed, tightened her arms around him and held him. Her breathing was deep and even, so she still slept. He wanted to kiss her awake and make love, but he let her sleep while he tried to figure why he wanted so badly to be with her.

Monday morning had spun away into afternoon when they got out of bed for Josh to cook breakfast. She took over and he helped.

"Our horseback ride will have to be another day. Which means you'll have to come back again," he said, smiling at her with a flash of white teeth. He reached across the table to take her hand. "I'd like you to come back, Abby," he said.

"Thank you," she said, knowing she never would be back. She withdrew her hand to eat her breakfast. "When did you buy this ranch?"

"As soon as I could when I graduated from college," he said, telling her about the ranch as they ate toast and scrambled eggs. There were bowls of strawberries, blueberries and blackberries with slices of kiwi. China cups held steaming coffee, and tall glasses were chilled with orange juice.

"Maybe breakfast is lunch, too," she said. "It's late enough to be lunch."

"After we eat, we can drive around the ranch. Or we can just go back to my bedroom."

She paused and shook her head. "I'm going to opt to see the ranch because this will be my only chance."

"On this trip," he said.

It was an hour later when she met him in the hall, ready to see the property.

Looking very much the rancher, he wore a blue denim shirt and jeans, a broad-brimmed brown hat, a hand-tooled belt and his boots.

"You look great," he said, his gaze sweeping over her. She thought she didn't look any different in her pink sweater, jeans and suede boots from when he saw her at the inn except for her hair, which she still let fall freely.

It was a crisp spring afternoon with blue skies and a stiff breeze. As they headed out, Josh pulled on a denim jacket and gave her one of his to wear. In the truck, he talked about cattle and horses, and she could tell that he enjoyed the ranch and knew a lot about it for someone who was rarely there.

Josh pulled over to show her an ancient windmill that he had left standing because it was so old. They drove past a small sod house that was even older than the windmill and on the ranch when he bought it. Later he drove to a spot with three tall cottonwoods. They climbed out of the truck to walk to a creek that widened into a small pool before narrowing to a creek again. Jake sat on a boulder and helped her sit down beside him, keeping his arm around her.

"This is one of my favorite places. In the summer, it's cool here, shady and quiet except for the water spilling over those rocks and into the pool. Some former owner hauled these rocks in here to create this pool, and it's pleasant. Sometimes I come sit for a while, just sit and be quiet. It's a good place to think and just do nothing except enjoy the ranch."

"Maybe you're not missing out on life as much as I thought," she said, surprised he experienced such moments as he had just described.

"I have to admit, I haven't been in this spot for two or three years. Those times are coming more seldom now because I'm so damn busy."

"Maybe you should try to work the ranch into your schedule more often."

"I've been thinking about it more and more. Actually, you make me think about it more," he said.

"How so?" she asked.

"I guess all your talk about enjoying life. This is the life I really like."

"Yet you choose to live in the corporate world. I'm returning to my opinion that you're missing out on life."

He gave her a crooked smile. "After the way you've taken to New York and come here with me and a few other things, I have to take back my judgment that *you're* missing out on life. I suppose you're not so much because you wring the most satisfaction out of every minute. You're easy to please, which makes a difference."

As they lapsed into silence, she listened to water spilling out of the pool, meandering on downstream, and thought about Josh's life.

Finally he stood and offered his hand. "We'll head back and get ready for tonight." She couldn't help but notice that he seemed lost in thought.

It was almost eight that evening when they entered the noisy, crowded honky-tonk. Fiddlers and a guitar player with a keyboard accompaniment provided the music. As soon as they had ordered a beer and a lemonade, he took her hand to dance.

They scooted around the floor with other couples, Abby watching Josh and desire building. Tonight, with his white Stetson, a navy Western-style shirt, a wide hand-tooled belt, tight jeans and boots, he was the most handsome man in the place or whom she had ever known, for that matter, and he looked every inch the wealthy rancher.

He seemed to know more than half the people present, speaking briefly to folks when they'd walked in and all the way to their table, then, speaking to more as they'd walked to the dance floor.

She already anticipated leaving. This was their last night together, and she wanted his kisses more than ever, wanted to be in his arms and make love again. He had changed her life. Tomorrow held uncertainties and questions, yet she wouldn't go back and undo meeting Josh and all that had happened since for anything.

They danced three dances and the set ended. As they stood talking, waiting for the musicians to start again, a tall, brown-haired cowboy approached them.

"Howdy, Mr. Calhoun."

"Evening, Johnny Frank."

"Haven't seen you here in a long time."

"Nope. I haven't been home in a long time. This is Abby Donovan. Abby, meet Johnny Frank Smith."

"You're not from around here, are you?" Johnny Frank asked her.

"No, I'm from Beckett, Texas."

"Mr. Calhoun, would you mind if I dance with Miss Donovan?" Johnny Frank asked.

"That's up to her," Josh said.

Johnny Frank turned to smile at Abby, and she smiled in return. "Thank you. That's nice. Since I came with Josh, I better stay with Josh, but I do thank you for asking, and I'm glad to have met you."

"Sure, ma'am. Thanks. See you both," he said, grinning and walking away.

"Thank you for turning him down," Josh said. "I see other guys watching, and I think we may have an evening of invitations for you, although since you discouraged Johnny Frank, we might not. But I'm ready to toss in the towel and go back to the ranch, where I can have you all to myself. Would you mind?"

She laughed. "I don't mind. I'd prefer that, too."

"You don't have to tell me twice," he said, slipping his arm around her waist possessively and heading for the door.

Outside she laughed. "That was mighty short, but fun."

"Well, I think if we'd stayed, you could have been the belle of the ball. You watch. Johnny Frank will come to Beckett and look you up."

"I doubt that," she said.

His arm tightened around her waist as he halted and turned her to face him, wrapping both arms around her and leaning down to kiss her hard, possessively. Everything else ceased to exist except Josh as she clung to him and kissed him in return.

Finally, when he released her, both of them were

breathing hard. "Let's get home where we'll be alone," he said, holding her close as they hurried to his pickup.

As they sped back to the ranch along the dark county road, she watched him drive. Light from the dash reflected on his face, highlighting his prominent cheekbones, throwing his cheeks into shadow. He had not shaved and had a slight growth of dark stubble that fit with their entertainment for the evening and made him look more like one of the cowboys.

"You're very quiet," she said.

"Thanks again for turning Johnny Frank down. I wanted to punch him out."

"Good heavens. I'm glad you restrained yourself."

"I wouldn't have hit him. I've never done anything like that except to defend myself, but I still didn't want you to dance with him. You bring out reactions in me I've never had before, and I'm having experiences with you I've never had before."

"I can certainly say the same thing about you," she said, not about to tell him that he had changed her life. "The only new experiences I can think you've had are sleeping on my short sofa and maybe asking Mr. Hickman to go fishing. Perhaps washing dishes and shoveling my drive and all that work you did."

"Nope. I've done plenty of that kind of work as a kid. And I've slept in worse places. I was so thankful to have that short sofa—you'll never know how glad I was to find a place to stay."

She lapsed into quiet, gazing out the window at the dark landscape and a myriad of twinkling stars overhead while she thought about her weekend with him.

When they walked into his house, he turned to draw her close again. "I can't get enough of you," he whispered before his mouth covered hers and prevented an answer.

* * *

The next day, he took her to the plane that would fly her back to Beckett. He stood at the foot of the steps and faced her, unable to resist touching her. He rested his hands lightly on her slender shoulders. It surprised him how much he wanted her to stay longer. He touched a long lock of her silky hair and then pulled her woolen jacket closer under her chin, little touches he wasn't sure why he needed. All he knew was he didn't want to tell her goodbye. "The weekend was great and it was special," he said.

"It was for me, too, Josh. Thank you for everything."

"When you land in Beckett, Benny will meet you and take you to the inn." Josh pulled her to him to kiss her. When he released her, he gazed at her. "I don't want to let you go."

Her blue eyes darkened slightly. "I think you have to," she said.

"I really don't want to. Abby, travel with me. I can hire someone to run the inn for you," he said, his words spilling out fast. "Come travel with me and live with me. It'll be like the weekend only even better, and I can show you the world."

Her eyes widened until he felt as if he would be consumed by a look. "We would have a wonderful time together."

"Josh, I can't do that. I have family and responsibilities."

"I'd cover the responsibilities for you. You can see your family whenever you want. I can easily afford to hire people to run the bed-and-breakfast whenever you're not there."

"I can't live with you. I just can't. My answer is a definite no, and I don't even have to think about it."

"I want you to think about it."

She shook her head. "No, it would never work, and I wouldn't be happy. Don't make this weekend a mistake. It's been wonderful, like a dream. Let's keep it that way, but you and I don't have a future. I really don't have one that would include moving in and traveling with you," she said. The tone of her voice became frosty. "That's not my life and never will be."

Her words were firm, and he stepped back. "I'll be in touch. You take care," he said.

"Thank you." She turned to hurry up the steps into the plane and reappeared at a window. She waved and he returned the wave. He turned around to walk away because the plane would take off soon.

The invitation to move in with him and travel with him had been impulsive, not even like him, because he usually thought things through. But it hadn't mattered because she wouldn't accept his offer. Not only that, but he also had a feeling she was insulted that he would even ask. He hadn't meant to offend her—far from it. He wanted her with him and he wanted to see her again. He didn't want goodbye.

He took a deep breath. He needed to forget her and go on with his life because they had no future together. He suspected she would not go away for another weekend with him.

As he climbed into his vehicle the white Calhoun plane took off in the distance. He paused, certain she was flying out of his life.

In Beckett, Benny met her and took her things to place them in his cab. As they headed toward town and the inn, he glanced at her in the rearview mirror. "I heard you've been to New York. What was it like?"

She smiled, glancing at him in the mirror as he returned his attention to the road. "It's a wonderful city with so much to do. If I lived there, I don't think I could ever do all I want."

"So you had a good time. You were with Josh Calhoun. He's really a nice guy."

"Yes, he is, Benny. He helped me a lot at the inn while Justin and Arden were gone."

"That's him. He tipped me the biggest tip I've ever had or ever will have. I think that's mostly because I tried so hard to find him a place to stay."

"That was very nice of you, and he told me. He really appreciated your help."

"He made that obvious. What did you see in New York?"

While she told him, she thought about Josh and being with him for the weekend. It had been wonderful, a dream come true until time to board the plane, when he asked her to move in with him and travel with him. In that moment, he was clearly the man she had expected him to be all the time. The charmer who was not into lasting relationships. His invitation had been a big reminder that she needed to put some space between herself and Josh, which shouldn't be difficult to do because time and distance would separate them anyway. She tried to pay attention to Benny's questions about New York and knew she would have another barrage of questions at the inn.

To her relief, when she arrived, Justin was in charge. He would ask her fewer questions than her mom would have and go on with talking about his own life.

She went to her room to change and put away her things. When she entered her sitting room, she thought of Josh there, remembered kissing him in this room, memories now that hurt.

Her cell phone rang, and she saw it was call from him. She didn't feel like taking it, so she dropped the phone back into her pocket.

She changed, heard the phone again and saw it was Josh once more. She let it ring. She wasn't ready to talk yet. She felt on a rocky emotional edge. She would have to get Josh out of her life, and it was going to hurt to do so. It already hurt to have him ask her to travel with him and live with him, to have him ask her to toss her life and family aside for his pleasure. She was sure he would compensate her with dresses and other gifts that really weren't that important to her. At the moment, she didn't want either of the dresses he had bought for her. If only he had just ended their amazing weekend without asking her to travel with him. She was determined to get him out of her thoughts and out of her life. There was no way to ever get him out of her memories.

Carrying souvenirs for Justin and Arden, she left her suite. As she walked down the hall, the elevator doors opened and Lamont emerged with briefcase in hand.

"Lamont, hello," she said, smiling, feeling a sense of dread, which she hoped she hid.

He paused. "Abby. So you're back. How was New York?"

"I did a lot of tourist things and had fun. Are you here to see Mr. Hickman?"

"Yes. Edwin had to sign some papers, and it's quicker to just come by so I can answer questions. Abby, I think we should have dinner and talk and reconsider not seeing each other socially. I have some questions to ask you. Now isn't the time or place because we can be interrupted at any moment. Can you go to dinner tomorrow night?"

"I still feel we need time and space and to see other people, and for now I want to stick with that. We're not in love, and we never have been. Maybe we're cheating ourselves out of a very good future. Let's leave it as is for now."

"I think you've let this Calhoun fellow influence you. He won't marry you, Abby. You should rethink some of your decisions, because you may be making a big mistake."

"I don't plan to marry him or want to. Right now I stand by my decision about us, and anyway, you're really busy with work."

"That's the truth. We'll talk this spring, but if you change your mind and want to go out, call me."

"Thanks, Lamont. I will. I need to relieve Justin," she added, starting toward the front. Lamont walked beside her. He would look at the problem from all angles he could think of and then draw his conclusion and tell her.

He sighed and shifted. "Perhaps you're right and we should go out with others for a while."

"I think it's a good idea," she said.

"Beckett single men don't ask you out because they know we date. Once they see me out with someone else, they'll start asking you out. Also, most everyone in town knows you've been to New York with a man from Dallas."

She smiled at him. "I'm not eager to go out with other men in town."

"Maybe not," he replied, looking distracted. "Abby, don't forget that I'm around if you want to talk. We're friends, no matter what."

"Yes, we are," she said, hurting and trying to be

careful what she said. "That's nice, Lamont, and I value your friendship." Impulsively, she brushed a light kiss on his cheek. "Go back to your work and we'll talk again later."

He looked at her for a long moment. "I guess I should have done more, maybe taken you less for granted."

"Don't blame yourself. I think this will be better for you, too."

"Perhaps," he said cautiously. "Take care." Lamont left her in the lobby as he went out the front door. In that moment, she was more certain than ever that she would never marry Lamont. Had she fallen in love with Josh so much that she would never love any other man? Was this a love for a lifetime? She thought of the old legend of kissing in the heart-shaped shadow. She had never really believed in it and still didn't, but in her life, it might come true. It wouldn't be true for Josh.

When her phone buzzed, she saw Josh was calling again. She still didn't want to talk yet. She hurt and if she talked to him, she felt he would realize her unhappiness. She didn't want him to. In a couple of hours, she would get back into her routine and be better able to handle talking to him.

Maybe she would get over him much sooner than she thought because she had just told him goodbye today. By the time a week passed, she might feel better about everything and able to think about telling Josh goodbye without any sadness.

Right now that didn't seem possible. He wanted to talk to her, so he must feel something—lust came to mind. He didn't feel anything else or he would never have asked her to live with him and travel with him.

Josh put away his phone. He couldn't concentrate on catching up on emails and text messages because

Abby wouldn't pick up. He had talked to Benny and knew she was back at the inn. No matter how busy she was, she would normally answer her phone, so the only reason for no answer had to be that she didn't want to talk to him.

Surprising himself, he already missed her. He had had various women in his life, affairs, some lasting longer than others, but he couldn't recall ever missing any woman the way he missed Abby. Even though he couldn't get her out of his mind, he had to because there was no future for them. She had made that clear before she boarded the plane. He wondered if she wanted marriage—somehow he suspected he might have gotten the same flat refusal if he had proposed marriage. It wouldn't have been with anger, though. She had been annoyed by being asked to move in with him.

He didn't know why it surprised her or why it angered her. Even if she didn't want to move in, she should have understood why he asked her. She should have been pleased that he liked her enough to ask. He never had understood Abby, and he still didn't. As simple as her life was, she was in many ways a mystery to him.

He needed to get his mind back on his business and forget her. Impatiently he pulled a stack of papers in front of him, looked at his calendar and swore. He picked up the first paper to read, forgetting about Abby.

She was out of his thoughts about fifteen minutes, until he recalled making love with her.

"Dammit, Abby," he whispered. How could she permeate his thoughts and life to such an extent? He could not have fallen in love, and Abby was definitely not the woman for him. She would never reciprocate any love from him except on a physical level, and she had ended that as swiftly as it had begun. "Dammit," he repeated in the empty office. He suspected she would not go out with him again, which was unique in his experience with women. It annoyed him now because he wanted to see her.

He shook his head. "Get a grip, Calhoun," he told himself. He should forget her and go on with life. They'd had a weekend. A month from now, it would be nothing except a dim memory. He was not in love with her. It would not do him any good if he was. He ran through the reasons again. He bent over papers on his desk to focus on work. Thirty minutes later, he realized he was staring into space, wondering whether Abby could work without thinking about him.

Nine

Abby's mother wanted to see her pictures from New York, so Abby copied all her photos to her laptop and then deleted from her phone the ones with Josh, leaving only the most obvious tourist pictures.

She headed next door and found her mom in the kitchen peeling potatoes for dinner. "Have a seat. Grandma is at her friend Imogene's house. Imogene's son came by and picked up your grandmother since she hasn't been able to get out for so long. She will be back in a couple of days."

Abby gave her mother a light squeeze around the waist. "Let me help you. You sit and I'll peel."

"No, I'm through and ready for a break," she said, dumping a bowl of peeled potatoes into a slow cooker that had the delicious aroma of a cooking roast.

"That smells so good. It makes me want to go back and change my menu for tonight," she said, watching her mother put a lid on the cooker, then wash and dry her hands.

"Did you have a good time in New York and at the ranch?"

"I had a wonderful time. I saw so many sights. I brought you something," she said, handing her mother a package wrapped in white paper and tied in blue ribbon.

"How nice. Let's get a cup of tea and sit while I open this."

"When she gets back, I have something for Grandma, too," Abby said.

Her mother opened her present and raised the lid on a box to find a sterling necklace. "Abby, it's beautiful. I love it. Thank you." She smiled at her daughter. "Now I want to hear about the trip and see pictures."

"I had a wonderful time," she said again. "I had a suite in the new hotel. Look at my pictures and I'll show you where I went." She spent the next hour talking to her mother about her trip. Finally she put away her phone and stood. "I'd better get back."

"You don't think you'll see Josh again?" her mother asked.

Abby shook her head. "No, there wasn't anything between us. He just asked me because I'd never been anywhere and he was going anyway. Also, as I told you, he asked because he was grateful to me for letting him stay at the B and B the night of the blizzard. I think this whole trip was a thank you for that," she said, trying to make light of Josh's attention.

Her mother studied her as they walked to the back door and stepped outside. "You really don't think you'll see him again?"

"No, I won't. It was just a special trip, Mom—what I said before, there isn't anything between us."

"I'm glad you had a good time, and I'm glad you're not in love with him, honey. I think that's for the best."

"I agree. I'll see you tomorrow. Thanks again for covering for me while I was gone."

She hurried back to the inn to take over the front desk. Josh had stopped calling, and she wasn't surprised. She didn't expect to hear any more from him.

In the late afternoon the first Friday in April, Abby looked at her reflection in the mirror. She wore navy slacks and a matching navy blouse. Her hair was parted and fell around her face. Her mother had covered the front while she had bought groceries, and she went to the front desk to relieve her mother.

No one was in the lobby. She heard a television and someone on the piano in the living room. She went to her room and pulled out her phone to look at the old, unreturned calls from Josh. She deleted all of them and sat browsing through the New York pictures on her phone. Josh wasn't in them, but she could see him in every one of them.

She didn't know about her future. Right now she just wanted to forget Josh Calhoun and go on with her life.

She would rather stay in her room and not have to talk to everyone, but she should relieve her mom, so she placed her phone in a dresser drawer and went to find her mother.

She found her in the living room and walked with her to the lobby. As her mother slipped into her coat, she said, "Josh Calhoun called you. I can see why you enjoyed going to New York with him."

"He's nice."

"He was very friendly, and we talked awhile. He told me he was sorry he didn't get to meet me and Grandma, because he'd heard a lot about us. He said it had been a lifesaver for you to let him stay during the blizzard."

"Josh can be charming, Mom. I won't deny that."

"He asked me to tell you that he called."

"Thanks. It's not important."

Her mother let out a long sigh as she frowned. "Abby, maybe I was wrong in being worried. Not all charming men are like your father. Don't be too influenced by the past. Josh seems to want to talk to you very much."

"Maybe, Mom, but I don't want to move in with him."

Her mother's brows arched. "If that's what he wants, then I'm glad you're not talking to him. That you don't need. Call me when you want me to cover again. If I can't, I'll tell you."

"Thanks, Mom," she said, kissing her mother's cheek as she hugged her lightly.

She followed her mother out and watched until she went inside next door. Then Abby went to her room. Tonight the guests would just have to be on their own or come get her because she didn't want to talk to anyone.

The phone extension rang in her room, and she picked it up. She talked with Colleen Grimes, her best friend, for a long time. It was a relief to tell Colleen a bit about Josh as well as breaking it off with Lamont. She was closer in some ways to Colleen than anyone else. Her sister was young, so her views of some things were not the same as Abby's, but she and Colleen had grown up knowing each other and had been best friends since first grade. They talked for almost an hour until she finally told Colleen goodbye.

She could hear her cell phone ringing in the drawer. She had heard it once when she talked to Colleen. After it stopped, she crossed the room to turn it off.

Her mother would call on the inn's phone if she needed her. Otherwise, Abby couldn't think of any call she would want to take.

That night she didn't sleep much but lay in the dark, recalling being in Josh's arms, kissing him, making love. She couldn't forget the fun and laughter they had shared. She wouldn't even think about traveling with him and what that life would be like, because it would never happen.

It was almost dawn when she fell into a restless sleep that was filled with dreams of Josh.

When she stirred in the morning, she felt groggy. She thought of her night and of Josh, wondering when he would stop calling and start forgetting her.

She spent the next week trying to immerse herself in work. Signs of spring finally began to appear even though late this year. With spring, their business picked up with guests who traveled once the weather improved.

Josh had stopped calling, and she wondered if he had already started seeing someone else. She guessed that he usually had a woman in his life. Some probably longer and more important than others. No matter how much she hurt thinking about him, she couldn't stop remembering and wondering about him.

With the passing of another week, she didn't feel one degree less drawn to Josh. Actually, the hurt seemed to increase with each day instead of diminishing, but she still assumed that after a bit more time, it would fade until it was gone and he was an unimportant memory.

She hoped that's what would happen. Josh had stopped calling, so she assumed he was moving on with his life, and she felt certain he had stopped thinking about her or wanting to see her. She expected to get over Josh eventually and just have the wonderful memories of New York.

She busied herself baking a cake and a pie for tomorrow. When she went to her room, she sat at her computer. She went through and wiped out all the pictures with Josh, which were already gone from her phone. As she did, she was unable to keep from crying. Josh was out of her life. Even if he wanted to see her again, she wouldn't because it would just mean more hurt, but she knew he was gone for good when his calls stopped.

In spite of keeping busy, she still couldn't keep Josh out of her thoughts. Who was he taking out this weekend?

It was the last Friday in April, and Josh struggled to pay attention to what was happening around him. He was in the executive meeting room at his brother Jake's Dallas office for a board of directors meeting.

Hands went up and he had no idea what he was voting on, but fortunately, it looked as if it would be unanimous. Even though he tried to focus on what was being said, in minutes his thoughts drifted to Abby. He wanted to see her again, and he couldn't understand why she wouldn't at least talk to him on the phone. What harm could that be?

His own actions puzzled him. He had never pursued a woman who obviously didn't want him in her life. Never before Abby. He just couldn't forget her.

The meeting was adjourned, and he remained in his seat. He was going to lunch with Jake. He didn't know who else from the board would go with them to eat, and he hoped he could pay more attention through lunch and get Abby out of his thoughts.

One by one, the others left the meeting room until the sole person left was Jake, who looked at him.

"We're the only ones going to lunch?" Josh asked.

"Yes. Everyone else had something to do."

Josh stood. "Okay. I'm ready to go. What's the deal with Mike? I never heard another thing from you about seeing him and Savannah when they return from their honeymoon."

"They're taking longer on their honeymoon because Scotty is doing fine and very happy staying with Lindsay. He loves his aunt Lindsay and doesn't want to leave. Then we'll keep him for a couple of nights, so Mike and Savannah are getting an extended honeymoon. I'll have a family dinner when they come back. The minute I have a possible date for the dinner, I'll send a text to everyone and let all of you know."

"Very good."

They left Jake's office building and walked down the street to the restaurant where they usually ate. After they had ordered hamburgers, Jake studied Josh. "Are you having business problems?"

"No. What makes you ask that? Things couldn't be going better—well, I guess they could be better, but they're plenty okay right now. No complaints. Financially, if the way this year has started is any indication, this is going to be a very good year."

"That's good to hear."

"Why the question?"

"You didn't know what was going on in that meeting today."

"Now, how do you know that?"

Jake shook his head. "I'm your brother, remember? I've known you a long time. I know when your thoughts are somewhere else, and they were really somewhere else—not much like you in a business meeting."

"Guess I was just thinking about a small chain of boutique hotels that has been presented to me at work as a good buy. My staff thinks I need to make a decision soon if I really want this. We don't usually deal with boutique hotels—it's a new concept to me. I just want to know what I'm getting into."

"I'd think your staff could handle that."

"They can, but I've been thinking about it. You had a good meeting today."

"I hate to say I'm going to profit out of marrying Madison, but so far, all indications are that her land is going to be lucrative for drilling."

"You don't know yet, but I'm glad it's looking that way."

"You never count on anything until it's absolutely signed, sealed and delivered and completely done," Jake said with a smile.

"It's paid off to be cautious. As for Madison, she'll be as happy as you are if you're right about her land. She knows that isn't why you married her."

"That's right." They ate in silence for a few minutes until Jake set down his water glass. "How was your trip to New York? I know you didn't go for a hotel opening."

Josh smiled. "No, I didn't, and it was fun."

"Ah, so are you seeing the B and B owner regularly now?"

"No, I'm not. It was fun and it's over. She isn't exactly my type, but she was nice and she'd never been anywhere, so I took her to New York."

Jake shook his head. "I'm not going to ask any more. I'd better get back to the office. Are you ready?"

"Yeah, I am, and I'll get the check this time."

"Okay, thanks," Jake said.

They walked back to Jake's office, where Josh told him goodbye, got in his car and drove to his office. He was busy the rest of the afternoon and finally drove home after five. He worked out, swam and ate leftovers even though there were casseroles in the refrigerator for him. A lot of the time he thought about Abby until he grabbed his phone and called one of the women he considered a good friend. He asked her out for the following night. The minute he finished the call, he regretted it because he didn't really want to go out with any woman except Abby.

The next night, when he picked Emma up, he tried to focus on her, but all he could do was think about Abby. Making another effort, he gazed at Emma Picket, a statuesque blonde, striking, between husbands at the moment. She was fun to be with, and occasionally he took her out. He hoped tonight she would take his mind off Abby. He thought of the brief relationship he'd had so long ago with Emma. It finally ended in a mutual agreement because she wanted to get married, so she moved on, but they stayed friends through her two marriages and divorces.

As she climbed into his car, his gaze swept over her dark blue sleeveless dress with a low V-neck that revealed a lush figure. She had long, shapely legs and he wondered why she wasn't out with a prospect for husband number three. In spite of her stunning looks, his pulse didn't speed or his breath catch. No response occurred that Abby could stir with her ponytail and no makeup. What was the magic Abby held that attracted him?

He took Emma to dinner, and they ate outside because the evening was perfect. She smiled at him and reached across the table to take his hand. "Now whom are you trying to get out of your life, or what knotty business problem do you have?"

"What makes you think I have a problem?"

"You look totally preoccupied, and you call me when you do."

He laughed and rubbed her soft hand, lifting it to his lips to brush a kiss across her knuckles. "You know me too well, but I know you just as well. Why are you out with me? Trying to forget husband number two or trying to make prospective husband number three jealous?"

She laughed. "Touché. The latter, Josh. And you?"

"You were right the first time," he said. "Trying to get someone out of my life, sort of," he added. He was trying to get her out of his thoughts.

"Ah." Emma glanced around the restaurant's patio at other couples. "Is she supposed to be here tonight and see us together?"

"No, I just wanted you to take my mind off her. She—" he paused "—worries me a little."

"Worries you? You never worry about a woman. Is she stalking you?"

"Oh, no."

Emma smiled. "Whatever's going on, I'm delighted because I didn't want to stay home tonight, and the man I need to make jealous eats here often enough that he might even show up. I've already said hello to two of his friends as we came in. Word should get back to him that I was here with you. Just excellent, Josh."

He smiled. "You make me feel better. When the dancing starts, we'll dance and I'll give them reason to tell him we were here together."

She laughed with him and her eyes sparkled. "Wonderful, darling."

Their waiter came and they ordered. Josh felt better because he could help Emma with her problem, and maybe his would diminish slightly. As he talked with Emma and their dinner came and they ate, his expectations of getting Abby out of his thoughts faded. He missed her, and even a good friend who was a fun person could not take his mind off her. He had the best time with Abby, and no one was going to get her out of his thoughts.

"Josh?" He realized Emma had said his name and was staring intently at him.

"I'm sorry. I had a business deal today that is hanging fire," he said to cover whatever made her stare at him.

"You haven't heard me. This isn't like you," she said, cocking her head to one side while she looked intently at him.

"Don't make too much of it. I'm just preoccupied."

Her eyes narrowed. "What's her name?"

"Whose name?" he asked.

"Josh, your mind is far away. You asked me out to help you forget someone." Her eyes widened and her mouth dropped open. "It's finally happened. You're the one who got left behind, and she walked out."

"Don't make a big deal of it, because it isn't a big deal."

"When did you break up?"

"Never. There was nothing to break up," he said, aware from Emma's expression that she didn't believe him.

"You're in love," she said, sounding shocked.

"No, I'm not in love," he said. "I've never told her I love her. I haven't known her long enough or well enough to be in love."

She laughed. "I never thought I would see the day.

You're so in love and you don't even know it." She giggled.

He stood. "C'mon, let's dance," he said, taking her hand.

On the dance floor, he held her close. She was soft, voluptuous, her perfume enticing, and she simply made him miss Abby more than ever. What kind of spell had Abby woven? Maybe he had tempted fate when he kissed her in the shadow caused by the full moon. That was a better explanation than any other he could come up with.

He had wanted Emma to make him forget Abby, but that wasn't going to happen. But in spite of his dilemma, he could help Emma. "Are the friends still here?"

"Oh, yes. I just smiled at one of them."

Josh dipped low, and her hands tightened on his shoulders as she clung to him. He swung her up and kissed her, wanting her to kiss him and make him forget everything else, to put an end to this constant need to want to be with Abby.

Instead, he just wanted Abby in his arms. He wanted to kiss her. Emma's kiss was meaningless and did nothing to stir him. He released her to continue dancing, but he wanted the evening to end so he could take Emma home.

"I have a long day tomorrow," he said. "I'll take you home."

"That's fine, but you don't have to lie about the long day. You're trying to get over someone, and I didn't help." She patted his hand. "I have no doubt you'll get over her eventually, but Josh, this was bound to happen at some point in your charmed life. She must be quite a woman."

"Emma, don't—"

"Shh. Don't worry. I understand, and since you've never been through this, it has probably hit you like a meteorite zooming to your little patch of earth. You'll live, Josh. Maybe you'll even have to think about marriage. If you do," she said, laughter in her voice, "please be sure to send me an invitation to the wedding, because I want to meet her."

He took Emma home and for a moment they sat in his car. "You're just blowing this all out of proportion."

"I don't think so." She kissed his cheek. "I definitely think you're in love, and you never have been in your life, so you can't even recognize the signs. I had a good time, had a good dinner and accomplished my purpose tonight. I'm sorry I couldn't make you forget her, but if you're in love, no one and nothing short of a total disaster will make you forget her. Knowing you, you'll win over your fair maiden. She must really be something to tie you in knots."

"She is, Emma," he said, thinking he could see Emma as a beautiful woman, a friend, but nothing more. Abby dazzled him, took his breath, and he couldn't ever view her in an ordinary way.

Emma looked intently at him and patted him on the shoulder. "You're really in love. Don't forget to invite me to the wedding."

He got out of the car and opened her door for her. "Don't hold your breath. She won't even answer my phone calls. I'm not her type."

Emma looked as if she might be biting her lip as Josh walked her to her front door. She turned to face him and once again was composed as she smiled. "Thanks for tonight."

"You're a real friend, Emma. Good luck with your latest guy. I hope he's a good one. You deserve it."

"Thanks." She blew him a kiss as she stepped farther inside and closed her door.

He walked back to his car, already forgetting Emma and thinking about Abby. Was he in love and didn't even know it? He didn't think such a thing was possible. Should he look at engagement rings? The notion was so foreign to him, he shook his head. They didn't know each other well enough to get married. She would reject that as swiftly as she had his proposition.

If she wouldn't answer his calls, the only thing he could think to do was to go see her. He had to get her out of his system, but at the moment he wanted some more time with her. If an affair with her was impossible, he'd just take her out. He thought about getting her a gift and vetoed it. Abby had some very old-fashioned and strong ideas about what she thought appropriate and wanted and what she didn't. How in hell had he gotten attracted to her?

As swiftly as the question came, the answer came— he had the best time with her he had ever had with any woman. How could he have ruined that wonderful weekend so completely that she wouldn't even talk to him? He knew exactly how, and he wished he had given more thought to asking her to move in with him.

He focused on going to see her. He wished he had met her mother and made friends with her. Instead, he called Edwin Hickman. He needed to find out when he could catch Abby where she had to talk to him and wouldn't slam a door in his face.

His usual self-assurance with a woman was leaving him fast. He was lost with Abby, unable to figure her out and hoping he would do the right thing. If this failed, he didn't see any hope of another chance.

He thought about his situation all the way to his

house. Once inside, he sat in a darkened bedroom that had light only from the hall, staring into space, still lost in thought.

He thought about Emma laughing at him. Was he in love with Abby? Really in love? If he was, he sure as hell hadn't followed logic in falling in love. Abby didn't like his lifestyle—there were a million problems. He raked his fingers through his hair. Did he love her? Really love her in a lifetime-with-someone kind of way? And even if he did, how could he ever get her to accept a marriage proposal since she didn't like his lifestyle, didn't trust him to ever settle and didn't want a husband who traveled? He had to think this through before he botched it.

"Dammit to hell, Abby." That night of the blizzard he should have gone home with Benny and slept on the floor with the in-laws and the kids and the baby. He wasn't ready for marriage. He wasn't ready to lose Abby, either. And if he proposed marriage, she would turn him down. That thought tied him in knots.

For the first time in his life, he was in love, and she didn't love him back. And she had enough backbone, no matter how irresistible she found him physically, to resist him totally.

A lifetime with Abby—right now that looked like a really good future, but an impossible one. He couldn't even get her to talk to him. How would he get her to marry him?

He had to admit that he must be in love. He would have laughed at himself and the situation if he hadn't hurt so badly. His brothers and Lindsay would laugh at him and probably say he deserved this. Maybe Mike wouldn't, since he'd fallen in love recently, but Jake and Lindsay would.

He was in love with Abby, and he hadn't even known the extent of his feelings for her until everything blew up in his face. He wanted to get her an engagement ring, something old-fashioned and sentimental, if diamonds could ever be old-fashioned and sentimental.

He needed to start figuring out what he would have to do to convince her to marry him. She wasn't even talking to him. It seemed the most daunting task he had ever faced. He got up and went to his desk to switch on a light. He grabbed a sheet of paper and jotted down the arguments she would throw at him for reasons she could not marry him. He numbered them, writing carefully and then staring into space, thinking about all the things she had said to him.

The moment the decision was made, he started planning. He felt better except that for the first time in his life, he had a running current of worry that she wouldn't even talk to him in person and give him a chance to propose.

Ten

Abby had just checked in two guests, and Justin was helping so she didn't have to show the couple to their room. She left the desk. Glancing at the clock, she saw it was almost seven.

"Ah, Abby," Mr. Hickman said, coming into the lobby. "It is a lovely evening, and I hope I can interest you in sitting with me on the front porch."

She smiled and linked her arm with his. "Of course you can. I would love to sit in the swing and do nothing but talk to you and enjoy the evening. It's hard to believe that recently we had snow."

"That was a freak, late snowstorm, although they do happen. Mother Nature is trying to make up for it tonight."

Mr. Hickman sat in a rocker. Abby sat on the porch swing and began to swing slowly. "This is wonderful," she said. "There is something soothing about a porch swing."

"I hope you are feeling patient, my dear. Your friend called me and is coming to see you."

Startled, she turned to look at him. Just then a car entered the parking lot at the side of the front yard. She watched the black sports car whip into a space. When Josh stepped out, her heart thudded. He wore his white Stetson, a white dress shirt open at the throat, jeans and his boots, and he looked even more breathtaking to her than before. She curbed an impulse to run and throw herself into his arms. Instead, she sat very still, certain this visit would be a deeper hurt.

"Here he is, Mr. Hickman."

"Yes, indeed. You're so kind to me, Abby. Be kind to him tonight."

Not trusting herself to speak, she nodded. If she hadn't been hurting so badly, she would have laughed over Mr. Hickman's ridiculous request.

She wasn't even aware when Mr. Hickman left. Her heart pounded and a mixture of feelings tore at her, but excitement dominated. As Josh bounded to the porch, he looked filled with vitality.

She reminded herself that whatever he wanted to do, she had to say no. She couldn't go out with him again. She definitely would not take a trip again with him.

She clamped her mouth closed and clenched her fists, jamming them into her pockets to hide them. She wished she had changed. She had on the same pink knit shirt and jeans she had put on when she got up this morning. Her hair probably needed to be combed and her ponytail redone. She shouldn't even care, but she felt self-conscious in spite of knowing she should send him on his way.

When he walked up to her to stand close, her heart pounded.

"Hi. I saw Edwin when I turned into the lot, so he must have told you I called him."

"Yes. Until then I didn't know you were coming."

"You wouldn't answer your phone."

"No, we really don't have anything more to say to each other. I don't know why you came all the way to Beckett."

"I want to talk to you. Can we go to your suite?"

She started to say no, looked into his dark eyes and nodded in spite of wary feelings.

"Good. You won't be sorry," he said with his usual take-charge self-assurance.

Holding the door for her, he walked beside her. Intensely aware of him so close, she felt their shoulders lightly brush as they walked, and a tingle slithered down her arm from the faintest contact. In her suite, she closed the door behind her.

"Would you like to sit?" she asked.

"If you will," he said. She moved to a wingback chair so he couldn't sit beside her.

He pulled another chair close. "I've missed you, and I wanted to talk to you. Abby, I shouldn't have asked you to move in with me or travel with me."

"No, you shouldn't have. You know I'm old-fashioned, tied to the B and B, very close to my family. Under those circumstances, your invitation indicated to me that you really don't know me and you don't care a lot about me. I understand that part, Josh. I never expected you to fall in love. Frankly, I never expected to, either."

"I should have thought that one through, and I didn't. It was a spur-of-the-moment impulse because I didn't want to tell you goodbye or have you fly out of my life. I've thought things through this time, and I have definitely fallen in love with you."

His words stunned her, and her heart thudded.

Standing, he stepped in front of her, took her hand and knelt on one knee. "Abby, I love you."

With those four words, her heart began to pound as she stared at him in shock.

"Will you marry me?"

"Josh—" she whispered, even more stunned and barely able to get her breath or voice. He held up a hand as if motioning her to wait.

She wanted to stop him, yet she couldn't. She had never thought about the possibility of a marriage proposal. *I love you.* The words echoed in her mind. "You can't love me," she said, barely able to get out the words. "You don't know me that well."

"Yes, I do love you. We had that weekend. We've worked together, laughed together, danced, kissed, made love. I just know that I don't want to go through life without you," he said. "Please listen," he added quickly. "I've thought about this. You object to several things about my lifestyle, my traveling and my cosmopolitan life. I can change that. I can turn my business over to very competent people and retire now to the ranch. I have enough money that I don't need to step into my office ever again if I don't want to."

As he talked, her heart raced. She had turned to ice, but now she warmed. Feeling dazed, she listened to him while all she could think was that he loved her and he indicated he would change his life for her.

"Josh, I'm shocked. I can't believe you mean this or know what you're doing."

"I usually do know what I'm doing, and I'm sure I know this time. It's been hell without you in my life. Abby, marry me. I love you," he said.

Her heart pounded. "You would move to the ranch permanently?"

"Yes, whatever you want. You don't know how I love you. I'll be happy on the ranch. I was going to live there anyway. This way, I'm just moving there sooner, and I'd have you with me."

"Josh, you're not thinking. I have this bed-and-breakfast. I can't just walk out and leave the inn."

"No, you can't. I can buy it from you and run it just as it is. You can pay off your mother's house with the money and pay for your siblings to finish college. I have enough money that we can do whatever you want to do. If your family wants to be closer, I can move them to Verity. Abby, we can do whatever we want about your family." His dark eyes were intent on her, and his voice was filled with conviction. She felt stunned, amazed as she listened.

"I have enough money to take care of all of them, aunts included. We'll take care of Edwin, too. He won't be moved out. It's just no problem. If they want to stay here, I have family planes at my disposal, and you can fly back and forth. The problem is, I don't want to go through life without you."

She felt dizzy as she looked at him and tried to fathom what he was telling her.

"Josh, you've had a lot of women in your life. I can't see you settling down."

He stood and pulled her to her feet to wrap his arms around her. She placed her hands on his forearms.

"I love you with all my heart," he declared. "I want to live on the ranch with you or wherever you'd like to live. I want you with me, Abby. That's what's important. Will you marry me?"

"I just can't believe you really are in love and won't change your mind."

"I promise. I won't change my mind."

"I don't even know if you want children."

"Yes, I do," he said. "Abby, for heaven's sake, you're doing me in here—don't tell me you haven't missed me or thought about me."

Her heart pounded. Josh was in love with her. He wanted to marry her, and he would move to his ranch and take care of the inn. Lost in thought about all he had said, she stared at him another minute while all color drained from his face.

"Abby, I want to marry you," he repeated.

Hoping he meant every word, she threw her arms around his neck. "I guess you have to take chances in life. I love you, Josh." She stood on tiptoe to kiss him. It took one startled second before his arms tightened around her and he kissed her in return, a hard, possessive kiss that reaffirmed his declaration of love.

Suddenly she leaned back to look at him. "I haven't met your family. You don't know Mom or my grandmother."

"So we'll meet everybody. It'll work out."

"Suppose your family doesn't like me?"

"That's totally impossible," he said, kissing her again. He finally raised his head. "Abby, give me an answer—"

"Yes, I'll marry you. I love you with all my heart."

He kissed again, passionately, a long kiss that made her heart pound with joy and all doubts crumble and fade.

"We need to tell our families," Josh said when he released her. "Can I have a room for the night?"

She laughed. "Yes, you can stay in a room or on my

sofa. That's your choice. You don't get any other choice, because I don't have privacy here."

"I'll settle for whatever I can get. Oh, wait. I'm not doing this right," he said, reaching in his pocket to pull out a box. Another shock rocked her when she saw his hands shake. He fumbled trying to get the top off the box until she had to hold back a smile. He yanked off the top and tossed it to the floor, taking out a smaller black box, which he opened. "If this doesn't fit or you don't like it, we can change it," he said.

She stared at a huge, dazzling diamond. "Josh, that is so beautiful," she said.

He removed it from the box and dropped the box to take her hand and slip the ring on her finger.

"It's heart-shaped," she said.

"That's so you'll remember the night we kissed in the heart-shaped shadow," he said. "We'll work everything out, I promise."

She looked up, and his dark eyes were filled with love. "Josh," she whispered, throwing her arms around him tightly as she kissed him. "I love you."

He crushed her against him, kissing her possessively.

Finally he released her. "I can't ever express how much I've missed you. Let's go tell your relatives and then we'll call my family. We're planning a family dinner soon, so you can meet all of them."

She framed his face with her hands. "You're sure about giving up your business? That's an enormous life change. Maybe I can make some concessions."

"I'm sure. I love ranching, and I don't want to travel and be away from you. I'll see more of all my family, which is a plus. Think you can live in the boonies on a ranch?"

She laughed and waved her hand at her surroundings. "What do you think? Of course, I can. Look at the life I lead now."

"You always have people around you. You won't have a bunch at the ranch."

"Maybe we can work on that one," she said, smiling at him as she kissed him again.

After a few minutes, he raised his head. "We're engaged. You're sure I go on the sofa tonight?"

"On the sofa or in another room."

"Let's set this wedding date soon. The Colorado trip may have to be postponed slightly. I'll still go, just a little later."

"Mr. Hickman will understand."

She gazed into Josh's brown eyes, and her heart beat faster because love filled his expression. He had never looked at her the way he did now, with warmth and intense longing. He drew her close to kiss her once more, a long kiss that made her heart pound. When he raised his head to look at her, he touched her cheek, caressing her lightly with his fingertips. "I've been through hell without you."

"I've missed you, too," she whispered, certain she would remember this night for the rest of her life, even though at the moment it held a dreamlike quality.

He took her hand. "Who do we tell first?"

"If I get my choice, I'd say let's tell my mom right away. Let me call and see if she's home. She'll be happy, Josh." In minutes she put away her phone. "She said to come over."

"I want to get moving so we can start planning a wedding."

As they walked to her mother's house, Josh's cell phone rang and he answered. He took her wrist to stop her and put his phone on speaker. "This is my brother Jake. I'm going to tell him now."

She nodded and listened. "Jake, I have this on speaker. I'm with Abby Donovan."

"Hi, Abby Donovan," Jake said.

She smiled as Josh put his arm around her shoulders. "Jake, I was going to call you. You go first though."

"Mike and Savannah came home. We're having dinner a week from Friday night."

"I'll clear my calendar," Josh answered. "I'm bringing Abby." He looked at her.

"Abby, you're definitely invited," Jake said.

"Thank you. That date is fine with me," she said, looking at Josh.

"It'll be fun, and Abby can meet the family and vice versa."

"Look forward to it. Now what are you calling me about?"

"Jake, I've asked Abby to marry me, and she's accepted. We're engaged," Josh announced, smiling at Abby and kissing her briefly.

"Congratulations to you. Abby, we're delighted to have you in the family and look forward to meeting you. That's wonderful news."

"Thank you," she said, smiling. "I'm happy and I can't wait to meet Josh's family."

"I'll call the others tonight," Josh added. "You're the first person we've told."

"That's really good news, Josh. I'm glad."

"I'll talk to you later," Josh said. "We're on our way to tell Abby's mom and grandmom."

"Have fun. Talk to you, bro."

The call ended, and after giving Abby a hug, Josh dropped the phone into his pocket.

They reached her mother's house. Abby went ahead, calling to her mother, who appeared and ushered them into the kitchen.

"Mom, I want you to meet Josh Calhoun. Josh, this is my mother, Nell Donovan."

"I'm glad to meet you," Nell said. "Now I have a chance to thank you for clearing snow off my driveway."

"I was glad to do it, and I'm glad to meet you."

"Mom, Josh has asked me to marry him. We're engaged," she said, holding out her hand for her mother to see her ring.

"Oh, Abby, how marvelous," Nell said, hugging her daughter and turning to Josh. "Welcome to our family, Josh. Justin will be thrilled to have another male in the family." She looked at the ring. "What a gorgeous ring. That's breathtaking."

"Mrs. Donovan, I know it's old-fashioned, but since Abby's father is gone, maybe I should have asked your permission first."

"If you make Abby happy, you have my permission. I think this is wonderful. We need to tell Grandma. You know what she will worry about, but we'll work it out."

"Josh already has, Mom. Let's go tell Grandma and sit and let Josh tell you what he has offered." Abby smiled at him and linked her arm through his. "Come meet my grandmother. We both have a lot of relatives to meet."

"Arden is on her way here to pick up something. When you tell her, they'll probably hear her screaming with joy at the inn," her mother remarked. "She'll think this is very romantic."

"Mom's right. Hold your ears, Josh, when we tell her."

They all laughed as they went to the living room

to find her grandmother. Abby wanted to shout with joy herself, and she kept glancing at the ring that was merely a symbol of what she and Josh had found in each other.

Butterflies were in her stomach as she stood in the foyer with the wedding planner and Justin at her side. She couldn't believe the date had finally arrived—a Saturday morning, the fourth weekend in May. Arden was maid of honor, and her best friend, Colleen, and Josh's sister, Lindsay, were bridesmaids. They all wore ankle-length yellow silk crepe dresses with spaghetti straps and straight skirts.

Abby glanced briefly at the groomsmen: Josh's brother Jake was best man, and Mike and two of Josh's friends from college were groomsmen. When she looked at Josh, all her nervous jitters ceased. He was so handsome it took her breath away, and she still couldn't believe she was about to become his wife and move to his ranch. He had already bought the bed-and-breakfast, hired someone to run it and made arrangements to pay Arden's and Justin's college costs. He'd paid off her mother's house. He had flown all her family, including her aunts and Mr. Hickman, to Dallas, and they were staying at a large hotel owned by Josh.

Right now, all she wanted was to be with Josh and leave for their honeymoon.

Justin took her arm. "You look pretty, sis," he said quietly, and she smiled at him.

"Thank you. You look quite handsome yourself," she said, thinking he did look handsome in his black tux.

"I think all of Beckett has turned out for the wedding, including Lamont," he said. "I can't think of anyone we know who isn't here."

"I noticed, and I'm amazed they all came. Mom is friends with a lot of people."

"I believe you are, too," he said.

"It's time," the wedding planner stated. With a nod at Justin, they stepped off together to start down the aisle. Again, she could see only Josh.

She went through the ceremony in a daze, looking at the slim gold wedding band that held a row of diamonds.

Then they were introduced to the guests as Mr. and Mrs. Josh Calhoun. Josh kissed her briefly, smiling at her as he linked her arm in his to leave.

Later, at the reception at a Dallas club, Josh took her hand for the first dance. When the band began to play a Strauss waltz, she smiled at him. "You did this and didn't tell me."

"I did. I thought you'd want a waltz."

"I love it," she said. "And you waltz divinely."

"I don't know about that. No one's ever said that to me before, but great," he said, laughing. "Soon my dad will dance with you. My mom thinks you're wonderful and a very good influence on me."

Abby laughed. "I hope I'm a good influence and not a bad one."

"Never. My brothers will dance with you, too."

"Your sister has been so nice to me. They all are. You have a very nice family. There are also a lot of Milans here. I think that feud is dead."

"You're new to the family. It's not dead because Tony and Lindsay keep it going. If you'll notice, they stay on opposite sides of the room. He's a friend, so I put him on the wedding list, but he won't stay at this reception, and the sole reason he'll leave is Lindsay. The feud isn't over yet."

"Well, you still have a very nice family. All the Calhouns have been friendly and welcoming. They've been that way to my family, too."

"Thanks. They're glad to have you join the family. Everyone thinks you'll be good for me," he said, grinning.

"Maybe it's best I don't know a whole lot about your life."

"I'll tell you most anything you want to know."

"I'm quite happy with what I know now," she said. "Lamont will probably dance with me, and I'm sure you don't mind."

"Not at all."

"I hope Lamont finds someone who is really in love with him."

"He probably will now that you're out of the way. See the blonde standing at the edge of the dance floor and talking to three guys?"

"Yes. She came through the receiving line. Emma, I think."

He nodded. "She's an old, close friend. I took her out to try to get you out of my system when I came back from Beckett. She figured out before we got through dinner that I was in love with someone else and thought it very funny that I had finally fallen in love. She asked me to invite her to the wedding."

"She may be a close friend, but she's not old. She's stunning."

"Definitely not as stunning as my bride. When I was out with her, all I did was think about you and miss you. You're gorgeous, Abby, and you've made me the happiest man on earth today."

"I hope so. I love you, Josh. I love my beautiful heart ring. See, I told you that night you were tempting fate by following that old legend of kissing in the shadow. Once again it came true."

"I'm damn glad I did tempt fate," he said, smiling at her.

"We'll be leaving soon, and you said you would surprise me with the honeymoon you've planned. I think it's time to tell me."

"We fly to New York and then to Vienna, where you can waltz your way through this honeymoon."

"Josh, I'm thrilled. Thrilled with Vienna and the waltz prospects."

"We'll also go to Switzerland and Germany so you can see all the castles you want."

"I feel as if I'm dreaming."

"I do, too," he said, suddenly looking at her intently and losing his smile. "I love you more than I can show you, but I'm going to try every day of my life."

"Don't make promises you can't keep."

"I intend to keep that promise, Abby. I mean it. I need you more than you'll ever know."

"There are some things about you I'll never understand. You shouldn't have had a shred of interest in me."

"I told you to remember the old saying, 'opposites attract,' and believe me, you attracted me from the first moment I looked into your big, blue eyes."

She smiled. "I could say the same in reverse. I'll be glad when we can leave."

"Just let me know when. I was ready when we walked down the aisle."

It was eight that evening when he carried her into the penthouse at his New York hotel. He set her on her feet and looked at her a moment in a silent exchange, his dark eyes filled with love. Wrapping his arms around her, he kissed her. Abby clung to him, kissing him passionately, letting her love pour through. Happiness filled her. She was starting life with Josh, the only man she had ever really loved.

* * * * *

"If you're pregnant with my child, that changes things."

"What things, exactly?"

He hesitated. "I'm already engaged to be married."

Her jaw set. "If you got engaged so quickly, you must have known your fiancée."

Gabe parked in her driveway. "No. It was an arranged marriage."

Horror transfixed her. "So that's why you slept with me. It was a last fling."

"It wasn't like that."

"How was it, then?"

His gaze pinned hers for long seconds. "You know exactly how it was between us."

Sarah stared at him, needing to see the truth in his eyes, feeling crazily emotional and on the verge of tears. "So how was it, exactly, between us?"

"Like this." Gabe cupped her jaw and out of nowhere her heart began to pound and the humming, tingling attraction she'd fought to suppress shimmered through her.

He lowered his mouth, and foolishly she tossed away any thoughts of being sensible and controlled and let him kiss her.

THE SHEIKH'S PREGNANCY PROPOSAL

BY
FIONA BRAND

Published in Great Britain 2015
by Mills & Boon, an imprint of Harlequin (UK) Limited,
Eton House, 18-24 Paradise Road, Richmond, Surrey, TW9 1SR

© 2015 Fiona Gillibrand

ISBN: 978-0-263-25261-3

51-0515

Harlequin (UK) Limited's policy is to use papers that are natural, renewable and recyclable products and made from wood grown in sustainable forests. The logging and manufacturing processes conform to the legal environmental regulations of the country of origin.

Printed and bound in Spain
by CPI, Barcelona

Fiona Brand lives in the sunny Bay of Islands, New Zealand. Now that both her sons are grown, she continues to love writing books and gardening. After a life-changing time in which she met Christ, she has undertaken study for a bachelor of theology and has become a member of The Order of St. Luke, Christ's healing ministry.

To the Lord.

"Our Lord showed me an inward sight of His homely loving. I saw that He is everything that is good and comforting to us. He is our clothing. In His love He wraps us and holds us. He enfolds us in love and He will never let us go."
—*The Revelations of Divine Love*, Julian of Norwich

Heartfelt thanks to Stacy Boyd for inspirational suggestions, patience and grace in editing. It's always a joy to work with you.

One

Twenty-four hours away from the deadline to sign a marriage contract…

The stark thought shoved Sheikh Kadin Gabriel ben Kadir out of a restless sleep. Tossing crisp linen sheets aside, Gabe flowed to his feet and pulled on a pair of narrow dark jeans. The cool light of a New Zealand dawn flooded his suite, a floor above the Zahiri consulate in Wellington, as he broodingly considered the concept of once more entering into the intimacy of marriage.

Marrying a wealthy heiress would solve his country's financial problems. The problem was, after the disaster of his last marriage, he had no desire to ever immerse himself in that particular hell again.

The morning air cool against his torso, he padded barefoot to the French doors and dragged aside heavy linen curtains. Dark gaze somber, he surveyed the gray rain drenching his last day of bachelor freedom. At that moment, like a fiery omen, the sun pierced the thick veil of storm clouds that hung over Wellington Harbour, illuminating a large painting of his twelfth-century ancestors, which dominated one wall of his suite.

Gabe studied the painting of the original Sheikh Kadin on whose birthday he'd had the bad luck to be born. A battle-hardened Templar Knight, Kadin's main claim to fame was that he had taken someone else's bride along with her diamond-encrusted dowry. The captured bride, Camille de Vallois, a slim redhead with dark exotic eyes, had then proceeded to entrance his ancestor to the point of obsession. Gabe's stomach tightened at the remembrance of the obsession that had haunted his own youthful marriage, although in his case the possessive intensity hadn't emanated from him.

Once they were married, Jasmine, his childhood sweetheart, had become increasingly clingy and demanding, dissolving into tears or throwing tantrums when she didn't get her way. She had resented his busy work schedule, and had become convinced he was having affairs. When he had refused to start a family until their relationship was on a more even keel she had taken that as a sign that he regretted the marriage. The guilt she had inspired in him had taken on a haunting rawness when, after a tense exchange during a boat trip, Jasmine had stormed off in the yacht's tender, overturned on rocks and drowned.

The memory of the icy salt water dashing off rocks as he had attempted to save Jasmine started a dull ache in the scar that marred one cheekbone, a permanent reminder of that day.

Legend said Gabe's ancestor had a positive outcome

to his passionate involvement with the woman he had married. Gabe's experience had been such that he would not allow a woman to have that kind of power over him again. As far as he was concerned, passion had its place, but only in short, controllable liaisons. Love was another thing entirely; he would not be drawn into that maelstrom again.

A rap at the door of his suite was a welcome distraction. Shrugging into a T-shirt, he opened the door to his longtime friend and Zahir's chief of security.

Xavier, who had just flown in from Zahir, strolled into the spacious lounge that adjoined Gabe's bedroom and handed him an envelope. "Special delivery."

Slitting the envelope, Gabe extracted the marriage contract he had discussed with his lawyers before leaving Zahir.

Xavier stared at the contract as if it were a bomb about to explode. "I don't believe it. You're actually going to go through with it."

Gabe headed for the state-of-the-art kitchenette that opened off the lounge. "There aren't a whole lot of options."

With the cold winds of bankruptcy at their backs and the remains of Camille's extraordinary wealth lost during the confusion of the Second World War, it was up to Gabe to restore the country's fortunes with another arranged marriage to an extremely wealthy woman.

Xavier shook his head to the offer of a glass of orange juice. "I would have thought that after Jasmine—"

"That it was time I moved on?"

Xavier's expression became impatient. "When you married Jasmine you were both too young. It's time you had a *real* marriage."

"The marriage to Jasmine was real enough." Gabe drained his glass of juice and set the glass down on the counter with a sharp click. As far as he was concerned, their marriage had been all too real. He could still feel the familiar coldness in his gut, the tightness in his chest every time he thought about the past and how completely he had failed his wife when she had needed him most. "This marriage won't be." It was prescribed and controlled, preventing any possibility of destructive, manipulative emotion. "Remember, it's a business arrangement."

Xavier, who was happily married, didn't bother to hide his incredulity. "You can't seriously think you can keep it that way. What woman will ever allow that?"

Gabe lifted a brow as he flipped to the back pages of the contract. It contained a short list of candidates and photographs of the pretty young women from wealthy families who had expressed an interest in the prestige and business opportunities inherent in a marriage to the future Sheikh of Zahir.

Xavier frowned at the list. "I still think you're making a big mistake, but I guess it's your funeral."

Gabe saw the moment Xavier realized the import of his final comment about a funeral. He cut off Xavier's apology with a curt word. They had grown up together. Xavier had been his best man when he'd gotten married, and when Jasmine had died, he had kept the press and hordes of well-meaning friends and relatives at bay, gifting Gabe the privacy he had needed. Through it all, their friendship had endured. "I have to marry at some point. Don't forget, aside from the money, Zahir needs an heir."

After Xavier left, Gabe grabbed fresh clothing and headed for the shower. He considered Xavier's comment that he and Jasmine had been too young to marry. He had been twenty, Jasmine eighteen. The marriage had lasted two years.

Flicking on the shower, he waited until steam rose off the tiles before stripping and stepping beneath the water. Now he was thirty, and as his father's only son he needed to marry and continue the family line. The prospect of a second marriage made his jaw clench. He could think of other ways to raise the money Zahir needed, Westernized ways that weren't presently a part of Zahir's constitution. But with his father recovering from cancer and wary about new investments, Gabe had accepted his father's old-fashioned solution.

Minutes later, dressed in a white shirt, red tie and dark suit, he stood drinking the dark, aromatic coffee he preferred as he stared out at the heavy rain sweeping the harbor. As cold and alien as the view was, thousands of miles from sunny Zahir, it was nevertheless familiar. Not only had his mother been born in New Zealand, but Wellington had been a home away from home for him because he had gone to school here.

Checking his watch, he placed his empty mug on the coffee table next to the marriage contract. Right now he had a breakfast meeting with both the Zahiri and New Zealand ministers for tourism. That would be followed by a string of business meetings, then a cocktail party and presentation on Zahir's attractions as a tourist destination at the consulate tonight.

Despite Gabe's resolve, he could think of better ways to spend his last day of freedom.

One more day—and night—as a bachelor, before he committed to the marriage of convenience that was his destiny.

* * *

She was destined to be loved, truly loved...

The chime of her alarm almost pulled Sarah Duval out of her dream, but the irresistible passion that held her in its grip was too singular and addictive to relinquish just yet. Eyes firmly closed against the notion of another day of unvarying routine in her teaching job, she groped for the alarm and hit the sleep button. Dragging a fluffy feather pillow over her head, she sank back into the dream.

The directness of the warrior's gaze was laden with the focused intent she had waited years to experience, as if he thought she was beautiful, or more—as if he was actually fascinated by her.

Strong fingers cupped her chin. Sarah dragged her gaze from the fascinating scar that sliced a jagged line across one taut cheekbone and clamped down on the automatic caution that gripped her, the disbelief that after years of being let down by men an outrageously attractive man could truly want her. The searing heat blasting off his bronzed torso, the rapid thud of his heart beneath her palms, didn't feel like a lie.

In point of fact, the warrior wasn't saying a lot, but Sarah was okay with that. After years of carefully studying body language, because she had learned she could not always trust what was said, she had learned to place a measure of trust in the vocabulary of the senses.

Throwing her normal no-nonsense practicality to the winds she lifted up on her toes, buried her fingers in the thick night-dark silk of his hair, and pressed herself firmly against the muscular warmth of his body. His mouth closed over hers and emotion, almost painful in its intensity, shuddered through her.

Dimly, she acknowledged that this was it. The long years of waiting were over. She would find out what it felt like to be truly wanted, to finally make love—

The shrill of the alarm once more shoved Sarah out of the dream, although the warrior's voice seemed to hang in the air, as declarative as his dark gaze.

"You are mine to hold."

An electrifying quiver ran the length of her spine, lifting all the fine hairs at her nape as she silenced the alarm. Blinking at the grayness of the morning, she registered the comforting ticking of the oil heater she'd dragged beside the bed to keep out the winter chill. She sucked in a breath in an effort to release the tension that banded her chest and the sharp, hot ache at the back of her throat. As if she really had been the focus of a powerful male's desire...

A soft thud drew her gaze to the leather-bound cover of the family journal she had been reading before she'd gone to sleep. It had slipped off the edge of her bed and fallen to the floor. The journal, which had been partially transcribed from Old French by an erudite cousin, relegated the dream to its true context—fantasy.

None of it had been real. At least no more real to Sarah than the dramatic contents of the personal diary of Camille de Vallois. A spinster and academic who had lived more than eight hundred years ago, Camille had been sold into marriage by her family. However, when her ship had foundered on the rocks of Zahir, she had made herself over as an adventurous femme fatale and gone after the man she discovered she wanted, a sheikh who had also been a battle-hardened Templar Knight. Camille had risked all for love, admittedly with the help of an enormous dowry, and she had succeeded.

Frowning, Sarah reviewed the vivid dream and re-luctantly let the last remnants of the powerful emotions that had held her in thrall flicker and die. Camille's story had clearly formed the basis of the dream. Plus, the pre-vious day, caught up in the romance she'd been reading in the journal, she had called at the Zahiri consulate and picked up a pamphlet about a scheduled exhibition of Zahiri artifacts and a lecture on their history and cul-ture. While exiting the building in the middle of a rain shower, head down because she had forgotten her um-brella, she had run into a man so gorgeous that for long seconds her brain had refused to function.

By the time she had recovered the power of speech, he had picked up the pamphlets she'd dropped, handed them to her with a flashing grin and strode into the con-sulate. The hero of her dream, scar and all, had looked suspiciously like that man.

Her cheeks warmed at the memory of some of the graphic elements of the dream, the searing embrace and a toe-curling kiss that had practically melted her on the spot. It had definitely been the stuff of fantasies and noth-ing to do with her normal life as a staid history teacher.

In her ancestor's case, the dream had come true, but Sarah could never allow herself to forget that Camille's romance had been smoothed along by a great deal of cold hard cash. Love story or not, Sarah was willing to bet that Sheikh Kadin had known on which side his bread had been buttered.

Pushing upright in the cozy nest of her bed, she reached down and retrieved the journal, which included photocopied sheets of the original, written in Old French, plus the sections of the journal her cousin had so far transcribed.

A heavy gust hit the side of her cottage, rattling the windows and making the old kauri timbers groan. Pushing free of the heavy press of quilt and coverlet, Sarah inched her feet into fluffy slippers, belted a heavy robe around her waist and padded to the window to stare out at the stormy day.

The steep street she lived on was shrouded in gray. The sodium lamps still cast a murky glow on neatly trimmed hedges, white picket fences and the occasional wild tangle of an old rose. The houses, huddled together, cheek-by-jowl—some so close a person could barely walk between them—were neither graceful and old nor conveniently modern. Inhabited by solo homeowners like herself or young families, they were something much more useful: affordable.

Letting the drapes fall back into place, she walked to the kitchen to make herself a cup of tea before she showered and got ready for work. Her tiny kitchen, with its appliances fitted neatly to take up minimal space, was about as far away from the exotic isle of Zahir as she could get.

As she sipped hot tea, her reflection in the multipaned window over the counter bounced back at her and she found herself critically examining her appearance. With her hair bundled into a knot, her face bare of makeup, the thick robe making her look ten pounds heavier than she was, she looked washed-out, tired and...boring.

Frowning, chest tight at the thought that at twenty-eight she was no longer in the first flush of youth, she peered more closely at her reflection. Her eyes were blue; her skin was pale; her hair, when it was loose, was heavy, straight and dark. It was the faded robe that drained the color from her skin, and the tight way her hair was scraped back from her face that was so unflattering. She wasn't old.

Although she would be twenty-nine next month. In just over a year she would be thirty.

The pressurized feeling in her chest increased. She sucked in a breath, trying to ease the tension, but the thought of turning thirty made her heart hammer. She was abruptly aware of time passing, leaving her behind, of her failure to find someone special to love and who would love her back in return.

On the heels of those thoughts an old fear loomed out of the shadows. That her disastrous track record with men wasn't about bad luck or bad judgment, it was about *her*; she was the problem. Perhaps some aspect of her personality, maybe her academic bent and blunt manner, or more probably her old-fashioned insistence on being truly loved for herself before sex entered the equation, was the reason she would never be cherished by any man.

Grimly, she considered her two engagements, which had both fallen through. Her first fiancé, Roger, had gotten annoyed when she hadn't felt ready to sleep with him the week of their engagement, and so had called it off. Not a problem.

The second time she had chosen better, or so she had thought. Unfortunately, after months of dating a fellow teacher, Mark, who had seemed quite happy with her views on celibacy before marriage, she had discovered, on the morning of their wedding, that he had fallen in love with somebody else. A blonde and pretty somebody else with whom he had been sleeping for the past four months.

Normally, she didn't wallow in the painful details of those relationship mistakes. Burying her head in the sand and anaesthetizing herself with work had been a much more attractive option.

But reading the journal that had recently arrived from her cousin and dreaming that deeply sensual dream had changed her in some imperceptible way. Maybe what she was feeling was all tied up with the realization that her biological clock was ticking. Whatever the cause, she felt different this morning, tinglingly alive and acutely vulnerable, as if she were standing on the edge of a precipice.

And she knew what that precipice was: she was finally ready to try again. Her pulse sped up at the knowledge that after years of relationship limbo she wanted to love and be loved and this time, marriage or not, she wanted the passionate, heart-stopping sex. Adrenaline zinged through her veins at the thought of tossing her old relationship rulebook away. She was tired of waiting, of missing out. She wanted to take the risk, to find a man she could not just desire, but with whom she could fall recklessly, wildly in love.

A man like the dangerously handsome guy she had run into the day before.

Absently, she sipped her cooling tea. In the past, she had been black-and-white in her thinking. She had wanted all or nothing. She didn't understand how she had become that way. Maybe her deep need for emotional certainty had been fueled by the fact that her father had only ever been a sometime presence in her life. Or maybe it was because she was naturally passionate in her thinking. For most of her adult life "all or nothing" had been the catchphrase that had summed up her approach.

Whatever the cause, it had devastated her last two serious relationships and was already sounding the death knell for the lukewarm friendship she shared with an importer of antiquities and fellow history buff that was the closest thing to a romance on her dating horizon.

Her jaw firmed. If she was going to find someone to love, someone she could marry and have babies with, it was clear she would have to be more flexible than she had been in the past. She would have to change. She would have to bite the bullet and experiment with a casual affair.

And the clock was ticking.

Replacing the mug on the counter, she dragged her hair free of the elastic tie that held it in place. Feeling tense and a little shaky, she raked her fingers through the warm, heavy strands, trying to work some volume into her satin-smooth hair. With her hair tumbling loose to her waist, she looked younger and sexier. Relief made her feel ridiculously light-headed.

She dragged off the robe and let it drop to the floor. The nightie she was wearing didn't help matters. Made of cotton flannel in an unflattering shade of pale pink, it reminded her of the nightwear her grandmother used to wear. Great for cold nights, drinking hot chocolate and reading a book, but ultimately as sexy as a tent.

The only positive was that beneath the material she had a good figure. Her breasts were shapely, her waist narrow, her legs long and toned from all the walking she did.

Shivering at the chill, she dragged on the robe and returned to her bedroom. Flicking on a light, she flung her closet wide and began examining hangers of clothes she had bought for the honeymoon that hadn't happened.

Annoyed at how affected she still was by the canceled wedding and Mark's easy dismissal of her in favor of a woman who had been dishonest enough to sleep with an engaged man, she hauled out slinky clothes and dropped them on the bed. She needed to exorcise the past by either wearing the clothes as if they had not been bought for a special, life-changing occasion, or else give them away to a charity shop.

Sarah arrayed the collection of jewel-bright garments across her bed. With a start, she realized that almost four years had passed since Mark had jilted her.

Four years.

Jaw set at the time that had passed, she selected a red dress. The color was sensual and rich, the silk jersey warm to the touch. With three-quarter-length sleeves and a V-neck, the design was classic. Bought for the romantic honeymoon she had paid for in Paris then cancelled, it was also sexy and sophisticated.

Before she could change her mind, she stripped out of the robe and nightgown and pulled on the dress. The jersey settled against her skin, making her shiver. Strolling to her dressing table she examined the effect of the dress, which, worn without a bra and with her hair rumpled and loose, was startlingly sensual. The deep, rich color made her skin look creamy instead of pale, and turned her dark hair a rich shade of sable. She stared at the bold, definitely female image, feeling oddly electrified, like a sleeper waking up.

The woman in the mirror in no way looked boring or tired. She looked young and vibrant. *Available.*

Years had passed since Mark had ditched her practically at the altar. Years that she had wasted, and which had been her prime window in terms of finding a suitable mate. If she had been focused by now she would have met and married her Mr. Right, gotten pregnant and had at least one baby.

She had put her lack of success with relationships down to her heavy work schedule. According to her mother, Hannah, the real reason Sarah hadn't found a relationship was fear. Two engagements had fallen through and in her usual stubborn way Sarah had refused to go out on a limb a third time.

Hannah's solution had been to produce a constant supply of eligible men from among her interior-decorating business contacts, which was how Sarah had met Graham Southwell. Although, after several platonic dates, she had received the overwhelming impression that Graham was more interested in her connection to the missing de Vallois dowry than in an actual relationship.

As it happened she was meeting Graham that evening. After the revelation of the dream, she could not view tonight as just another dead-end date with a man who did not really see her. Tonight was an opportunity to effect the change that was already zinging through her.

She could not afford to wait any longer for her true love to find her; experience had taught her that might never happen. Like her ancestor Camille, she had to be bold. She had to formulate a plan.

By the time she was ready to leave for work she had settled on a strategy that was time-honored and uncannily close to Camille's plan to win her sheikh.

Sarah would dress to kill, and when she found the man of her dreams, she would seduce him.

Two

Sarah found a space in the parking lot next door to the historic old building that housed the Zahiri consulate. Situated just over the road from the waterfront, the entire block was dotted with grand Victorian and Edwardian buildings and a series of old warehouses that had been turned into bars and restaurants.

As she stepped out of the car, cold wind gusted in off the sea and spits of rain landed on her skin. Her hair, which she'd spent a good hour coaxing into trailing curls with a hot curling iron, swirled around her face. Turning up the collar of her coat and shivering a little, because the red silk jersey dress was not made for a cold Wellington night, she locked the car and started toward the consulate.

Feeling nervous and self-conscious about all the changes she'd made, especially her new makeup and a pair of black boots with heels a couple of inches higher than she normally wore, she hurried past a group of young men hanging around the covered area outside a bar.

The wind gusted again, making her coat flap open and lifting the flimsy skirt of her dress, revealing more leg than she was accustomed to showing. Her phone chimed as she clutched the lapels of her coat and dragged her hemline down. Ignoring a barrage of crude remarks and a piercing wolf whistle, she retrieved the phone and answered the call.

Graham had arrived early and was already inside on the off chance that he might actually get to meet the elusive Sheikh of Zahir, who was rumored to be in town. Since it was cold and on the verge of raining, he had decided not to hang around outside waiting for her as they had arranged.

Irritated but unsurprised by Graham's lack of consideration, Sarah walked up the steps to the consulate and strolled into the foyer, which was well lit and warm.

She was greeted by a burly man with a shaved head who was dressed in a beautifully cut suit. He checked her invitation and noted her name on a register. When he handed the invitation back, his gaze was piercing. In New Zealand it was unusual to be scrutinized so thoroughly. She was almost certain he wasn't just a consulate official. With the sheikh in residence it was more likely that the man was one of the sheikh's bodyguards. Though a Christian nation, Zahir, a Mediterranean island, was caught between the Middle East and Europe. The elderly sheikh had been kidnapped some years ago and so now was rumored to always travel with an armed escort.

She hung her coat on the rack provided. Ignoring an

attack of nerves caused by losing the cozy, protective outer layer that had mostly hidden the red dress, she walked through an elegant hallway and into a crowded reception room. It was a cocktail party and promotional evening aimed at selling Zahir, with its colorful history as a Templar outpost, as a tourist destination. Sarah had expected little black dresses and the rich exotic colors of the East to abound, but crisp business suits and black and gray dresses toned down by jackets created a subdued monochrome against which she stood out like an overbright bird of paradise.

Sarah's stomach sank. When she had read the pamphlet she hadn't seen the evening as focused on business, but if she didn't miss her guess, most of the guests were business types, probably tour operators and travel agents and no doubt a smattering of government officials.

Deciding to brazen it out, she moved to a display concerning the mysterious disappearance of the remains of Camille's dowry. Hidden by a member of the sheikh's family at the time of the evacuation during the Second World War, the location of the hiding place had been lost when the family member died in a bombing raid.

A short, balding man in a gray suit also stopped by the display, but seemed more mesmerized by the faint shadowy hollow of her cleavage. Annoyed by his rudeness, she sent him the kind of quelling glance that would have had her pupils scrambling to apply themselves to their study. As he scuttled away, she thought longingly about retrieving her coat and covering up the alluring brightness of the dress, but she refused to cut and run because she was attracting male attention. After all, that had been the whole point.

A waiter offered her a glass of wine. A little desperately, she took a glass and sipped slowly as she moved to a display of Templar weaponry. Instantly riveted by a history she found even more fascinating after immersing herself in Camille's journal, Sarah read the notes about the Templar band under the command of Sheikh Kadin. Setting her glass down on a nearby table, she stepped closer, irresistibly drawn to the largest weapon—a grim, pitted sword that had clearly seen hard use. A small label indicated the sword had belonged to the sheikh. In that moment she remembered a passage of the journal, which had outlined Camille's first meeting with Kadin.

"An overlarge warrior with a black, soaked mane, dark eyes narrowed against the wind, a workmanlike blade gripped in his battle-scarred hand."

The fascination that had gripped Sarah as she'd read Camille's account came back full force. A small sign warned against touching the displays, but the powerful compulsion to immerse herself in sensation, to touch the sword, far outweighed the officious red wording.

Breath held, her fingertips brushed the gleaming grip where the chasing etched into the bronze was worn smooth by use. The chill of the metal struck through her skin. A split second later, the bracket holding the sword came loose and the heavy weapon toppled, hitting the carpeted floor with a thud.

Mortified, Sarah reached for the sword, hoping to prop it against the display before anyone noticed. Before she could grab it, a large tanned hand closed around the bronze grip. With fluid grace, a tall, broad-shouldered man straightened, the blade in his hand, and her heart slammed once, hard, as her dream world and the present fused.

The warrior.

That seemed the only adequate description. The man was tall enough that her gaze was firmly centered on his jaw. Heart pounding, she tilted her head and stared directly into the amber gleam of eyes that, for a split second, she fully expected to be as passionately focused on her as those of the warrior who had haunted her dream.

Her breath caught in the back of her throat as she recognized the man she had run into the previous day. The curious tension that had invested the dream drew every muscle taut as she took in black hair cut crisp and short, the blade-straight nose and the intriguing scar on his cheekbone. The planes and angles of his face were mouthwateringly clean-cut, although any sense of perfection was lost in the grim line of his jaw and the lash of the scar.

His brows drew together as if he recognized her and was trying to remember from exactly where. A split second later his gaze shuttered and she had to wonder if she'd imagined that moment of intense interest.

Or, on a more practical note, if he was married. As a single woman with years of dating experience, it would not be the first time she had been checked out by a man who then suddenly recalled that he was committed elsewhere.

His gaze dropped to her hands. "Are you all right? For a moment, I thought you might have cut yourself."

The low, rough timbre of his voice, the cosmopolitan accent, was definitely European, but with a slow cadence that indicated he had spent time in the States. The accent, along with the short cut of his hair and the suit, added to the impression that had been forming, the only one that made sense—he was either an aide to the sheikh or a bodyguard. Given his muscular build, and the fact that he had arrived within seconds of her touching the sword, she would go with the security option.

She dredged up a smile and displayed her palms to show she wasn't injured. "I'm fine, just a little startled the sword wasn't secured. Especially since it belonged to Sheikh Kadin."

For another heart-pounding moment his gaze seemed riveted on her mouth. "You're right, the Wolf of Zahir would not have been so careless. I'll have a word with the staff who set up the display."

She dragged her gaze from the line of his jaw. "Oh no, really…it was completely my fault. I shouldn't have touched the sword." Shouldn't have allowed herself to be distracted by her ancestor's passionate love story when she needed to apply herself to establishing her own.

With an easy movement, he propped the weapon against the display board. As he did so an angled spotlight above gleamed over his damaged cheekbone, and cast a shadow over the inky curve of his lashes. Suddenly the dream warrior, as riveting as he had been, seemed too cosmetically perfect and lacking in personality. From memory, he had also been oddly compliant. In the way of dreams, he had done exactly what she had wanted, in contrast to this man who looked as seasoned and uncompromising as the Templar Knight who had originally wielded the sword.

To her surprise, instead of moving on, he held out his hand and introduced himself as Gabriel, Gabe for short.

Surprised at the informality and that he seemed to want to keep the conversation going, Sarah briefly gripped his hand as she supplied her name. Tingling warmth shot through her at the rough heat of his palm. "I'm a history teacher."

She caught the flash of surprise in his expression and her mood dropped like a stone. He was tall, gorgeous, *hot*—as different from Graham as a dark lion from a tabby cat. Incredibly, he also seemed to be interested in her, and she had just ruined the outward impression of sexy sophistication she'd spent hours creating. If she'd had her wits about her she would have relegated her teaching occupation to some dusty dark hole and claimed an interest in travelling to exotic places.

"I'm guessing since you're at the exhibition that it's Templar history?"

Her mood dropped even further when she realized she now had to tell him how boring and prosaic her subjects were. "I specialize in the industrial revolution and the First and Second World Wars." She let out a resigned breath, convinced they had nothing in common. "What about you?"

"Five years at Harvard. It was useful."

Hope flared anew. "Harvard. That sounds like law, or business."

"Business, I'm afraid."

He sounded almost as apologetic as she had been. Her heart beat faster. Not a bodyguard then, despite the muscle. Perhaps he was one of the sheikh's financial advisors. She was riveted by the thought that maybe all wasn't lost.

Just as she was searching for some small talk, two Arabic men in suits joined them. The taller one, carrying a screwdriver, immediately set about refixing the bracket that had held the sword. The other suit, a plump man with a tag that proclaimed he was Tarik ben Abdel, the consulate administration manager, sent her a disapproving glance. He then button-holed Gabe and launched into a tirade in a liquid tongue she recognized as Zahiri.

Gabe cut him off with a flat, soft phrase, although Sarah was distracted from the exchange. Graham had appeared just yards away, head swiveling as if he had finally remembered to search for her. His gaze passed over her then shot back to linger on the hint of cleavage at the V of her dress. When he fished in his pocket for his cell phone and turned away, an irritated look on his face, she realized that, aside from checking out her chest, he had failed to recognize her.

Tarik, with a last disapproving glance at her, marched away, the second suit trailing behind. She noticed that the sword was once again affixed to the display.

Sarah was suddenly blazingly aware that the tall dark man hadn't left as she had expected him to and that he was studying her with an enigmatic expression, as if he'd logged the exchange with Graham.

Still mortified at the fuss she'd created, she rushed to apologize. "I read the sign. I know I shouldn't have touched the sword, that artifacts can be vulnerable to skin oils and salts—"

"Tarik wasn't worried that the sword might be damaged. It survived the Third Crusade, so a fall onto soft carpet is hardly likely to cause harm. He was more concerned about the tradition that goes with the sword."

Understanding dawned. If there had been a pre-eminent symbol of manhood in the Middle Ages, it had been the sword, and this had been a Templar sword. "Of course, the Templar vow of chastity."

Amusement gleamed in his gaze. "And a superstition that a woman's touch would somehow disable a warrior's potency in battle."

A curious warmth hummed through her as she realized that, as nerve-racking as the exchange had started out, she was actually enjoying talking to the most dangerously attractive man she had ever met. "Sounds more like a convenient way of shifting blame for a lackluster performance on the battlefield."

"Possibly." Gabe's mouth kicked up at one corner, softening the line of his jaw and revealing the slightest hint of an indentation. "But, back then, on Zahir, if a woman handled a man's sword, it was also viewed as a declaration of intent."

Breath held, Sarah found herself waiting for the dimple to be more fully realized. "What if she was simply curious?"

His gaze locked with hers and a tension far more acute than any she had experienced in her dream flared to life. "Then the warrior might demand a forfeit. Although most of the Templars that landed on Zahir eventually gave up their vows."

"Including the sheikh, who married."

The cooling of his expression as she mentioned marriage was like a dash of cold water. For the second time she wondered if he was married. Disappointment cascaded through her at the thought. A glance at his left hand confirmed there was no ring, although that meant nothing. He could be married, with children, and never wear a ring.

A faint buzz emanated from his jacket pocket. With a frown that sent a dart of pleasure through her, because it conveyed that he didn't want to be interrupted, he excused himself and half turned away to take the call.

Unsettled and on edge because she was clearly developing an unhealthy fascination for a complete stranger,

Sarah remembered her glass of wine. As she took a steadying sip, her cell phone chimed. Setting the glass back down, she rummaged in her handbag and found the phone and another text from Graham. Although there was nothing romantic or even polite about the words. Where are you?

Annoyed at his blunt irritation, the cavalier way he hadn't bothered to meet her as they had arranged, Sarah punched the delete key. She might be a victim of the love game, but she would not be a doormat. Temper on a slow simmer, she shoved the phone back in her handbag.

Gabe terminated his call. "Are you with someone? I noticed you came in alone."

Suddenly the tension was thick enough to cut, although she couldn't invest the knowledge that he had noticed her entrance with too much importance. She was the only person dressed in red in a sea of black and gray; of course he had noticed her. "Uh, I was supposed to meet someone…"

"A man."

She crushed the urge to say she wasn't meeting another man; that would have been a lie. "Yes."

He nodded, his expression remote, but she was left with the unmistakable impression that if she had said she was alone the evening might have taken a more exciting turn than she could ever expect with Graham.

His expression suddenly neutral, Gabe checked his watch. "If you'll excuse me. I have a call to make."

Sarah squashed a plunging sense of disappointment. As he walked away, she forced herself to look around for Graham.

She spotted him across the room involved in an animated discussion with a man wearing a business suit and a kaffiyeh, the traditional Arabic headdress. She studied the Arab man, who she assumed must be the sheikh. She had read a lot about Zahir, but most of it had been history, since Zahir was a small, peaceful country that didn't normally make the news. She knew that the sheikh was on the elderly side, and that he had married a New Zealander, a woman who had originally come from Wellington, which explained Zahir's close ties with her country.

She strolled closer just as the man with the kaffiyeh moved away and finally managed to make eye contact with Graham.

The blankness of his expression changed to incredulity. *"You."*

Not for the first time Sarah looked at Graham and wondered how such a pleasantly handsome man could inspire little more in her than annoyance. "That's right, your date."

He shook his head as if he couldn't quite believe what he was seeing. "If you'd told me you were going to change your appearance—"

Her jaw locked at Graham's unflattering response, as if the act of putting on a dress, a little extra makeup and messing with her hair was some kind of disguise. "This *is* how I look."

He stared at her mouth, making her wonder if she'd been a little too heavy on the berry lip gloss. "Not usually. If you had, we might have hit it off a little better."

Sarah realized there was one very good reason she had never been able to really like Graham. Not only was he self-centered with a roving eye, he had a nasty streak. She had been looking for a prince and, as usual, had ended up dating a frog. "How about I make it easy for us both. From now on don't call and don't come around to my mother's house for dinner. A clean break would suit me."

His expression took on a shifty cast. "What about the journal? You said I could look at it."

"That was all you really wanted, wasn't it?"

"I wouldn't say that, exactly."

No, because what he really wanted was to find the lost dowry and cash in on it. Sarah drew a deep breath and let it out slowly. The first two men in her life had dumped her for other women; that she could accept. Graham preferring *a book* and the possibility of cold hard cash over her was the proverbial last straw. "Forget the journal. It's a private, family document. Hell would freeze solid before I'd give it to you."

Feeling angry and hurt, hating the fact that she had lost her temper but relieved she had finally finished with Graham, Sarah spun on her heel then froze as she spotted Gabe talking with an elderly lady. He was close enough that he had probably heard some of her conversation with Graham. His gaze locked with hers, sharp and uncomplicatedly male, and for a moment the room full of people ceased to exist. Then a waiter strolled past with a tray filled with glasses, breaking the spell.

Her stomach clenched on a sharp jab of feminine intuition, that despite knowing she had a date, after he had made his call, Gabe had come looking for her. When he'd seen her talking with Graham, he'd stopped far enough away to allow her privacy—*to allow her a choice*—but close enough to keep an eye on her.

Graham didn't find her attractive, but she was suddenly acutely aware that Gabe did. Talking to him at the sword display had been easy; there had been nothing at stake. Instinctively, she knew a second conversation meant a whole lot more. It meant she would have to make a decision. Suddenly the whole concept of abandoning her rule about no sex before commitment seemed full of holes when what she really wanted was love, not sex.

Feeling utterly out of her depth, her chest tight, she dragged her gaze away and made a beeline for the ladies' room and the chance to regroup.

Pushing the door open, she stepped into a pretty tiled bathroom. Her reflection bounced back at her, tousled hair and smoky eyes, sleek dress and black boots. Her cheeks flushed as she registered what Gabe was seeing. Graham was right. *She* barely recognized herself. The woman who stared back at her looked exotic and assured. Experienced.

She wondered if all Gabe saw was the outer package and the possibility of a night of no-strings passion. What if, like Graham, Gabe wouldn't be attracted to who she really was?

She found her lipstick and reapplied it, her fingers shaking very slightly. The knowledge that Gabe was attracted to her, that the improvement she had made to her appearance had worked, was unsettling. She hadn't expected such an instant response.

She should be buoyed by her success. Instead, she felt on edge and, for want of a better word, vulnerable. Maybe it was because in her mind Gabe had become linked with the dream that had been the catalyst for all of this change. She knew almost nothing about him, but in the moment he had picked up the sword, he had made an indelible impression; he had symbolized what she wanted.

She stopped dead as the final piece of the puzzle of

her dysfunction with men dropped neatly into place. She drew a deep breath. She felt like quietly banging her head against the nearest wall, but that would not be a good idea with all the security personnel roaming around. The reason she had not been intimate with anyone, even her fiancés, was because, hidden beneath the logic and practicality and years of academia, she was an idealist. Worse, she was a *romantic*.

Maybe all the years of burying her head in history books had changed her in some fundamental way because it was now blindingly clear why an ordinary, everyday kind of guy with a nine-to-five job had never been quite enough. Somehow, despite common sense, in her heart of hearts, she had wanted the kind of seasoned, bedrock strength and stirring romanticism that it was difficult to find in the twenty-first century.

She had wanted a knight.

When she stepped back into the reception room, despite giving herself a good talking-to about the dangers of projecting crazy romantic fantasies onto a man she barely knew, she found herself instantly looking for Gabe. When she couldn't find him, disappointment gripped her. In an adjacent room the lecture on Zahir was beginning. She strolled inside and saw him at the back, in conversation with a well-known government official.

The jolt in her stomach, the relief and the tingling heat that flooded her, should have been warning enough. In the space of an hour she had somehow fallen into a heady infatuation with a virtual stranger, but after years of emotional limbo the blood racing through her veins, the crazy cocktail of emotions, was addictive. Just as she debated what to do—brazenly approach Gabe or wimp out completely and ignore the intense emotions—an elegant young woman walked up to Gabe and flung her arms around him.

Numb with disappointment, Sarah turned on her heel, walked into the foyer and began searching for her coat. She was fiercely glad she hadn't approached Gabe, because he appeared to have a girlfriend, or, more probably, a wife.

Frowning, she flipped through the rack of coats again and pulled out a coat which looked like hers, but which wasn't. Someone had obviously left in a hurry and taken her coat by mistake. As much as she needed a coat, she drew the line at helping herself to one she knew wasn't hers. Besides, she still had her small telescopic umbrella, which fit in her handbag. In the wind, it probably wouldn't last long, but it was better than nothing.

Outside, lightning flickered and, in the distance, thunder crashed. As Murphy's Law would have it, the rain, which had been light earlier was now tropical.

Extracting the umbrella, Sarah paused by the antique double doors of the entrance, reluctant to step out into such a heavy downpour. A flicker of movement turned her head. She saw Gabe speaking to the tall, bald man who had checked her invitation.

Aware that in just a few seconds he could turn and see her standing in the foyer, watching him, she pushed open the doors and stepped outside.

As she descended the steps the wind, damp with rain and bitingly cold, sent a raw shiver through her. She came to a halt at the edge of the sheltered area. Flipping up her umbrella, she stepped into the wet and wild night.

The bottom half of her dress was almost instantly soaked. Water seeped into the soles of her boots as she threaded through cars that gleamed beneath streetlights.

The parking lot seemed farther away than when she had arrived. In the murky darkness, the garish lights from the nightclub were overbright, although the steady thud of music was now muted by the sound of the rain.

Dragging soaked hair from her eyes and glad she was wearing waterproof mascara, she fumbled in her bag, searching for keys. She depressed the key lock, suddenly wishing she hadn't parked quite so close to the nightclub. The lights of her car flashed and she headed for the welcome beacon of her small hatchback. As she opened the door, she became aware of a cluster of dark shadows congregated beneath the overhang of the warehouse-size building that housed the nightclub. Slamming the door closed, she immediately locked it, just in case the youths tried something silly.

She inserted her key into the ignition. The starter motor made its familiar high-pitched whine, but the motor itself refused to fire. Feeling a little desperate, she tried again, then a third time. When the starter took on a deeper, slower sound, as if the battery was becoming drained, she immediately stopped. She was no mechanic but, at a guess, the wind had driven rain under the hood and the electronics had gotten wet. The car wouldn't start until she managed to dry the motor. If she kept using the starter she would also end up with a flat battery.

She considered ringing her mother then immediately dismissed the thought. Hannah was overseas on a buying trip for her interior-decorating business. Graham was still inside. As much as she didn't want to ask him, he would have to help her. Groaning, she tried texting. When minutes passed with no reply, she bit the bullet and rang him. The call went through to voice mail.

Deciding that it would be a whole lot simpler to just walk back into the consulate to get help, Sarah grabbed her bag and stepped out into the rain, which had thankfully eased to a fine drizzle. A tap on her shoulder made her start.

"Having trouble, darlin'?"

She stiffened at the shock of being touched by a stranger and stepped away from the powerful whiff of alcohol fumes. "Nothing I can't handle, thanks."

He grinned hazily. "I'd sure like to help you."

There was a stifled laugh somewhere behind him. With a jolt Sarah realized they had been joined by two more men, both of them like the first, darkly dressed, wearing leather and decorated with tattoos and multiple piercings.

The taller of the two grinned. "Don't keep her to yourself, Ty. We'd *all* like to help the lady."

Jaw set, Sarah debated trying to get back into the car and locking the doors, but decided against that. If she did, they could prevent her from closing the door and before she knew where she was, they would be inside the car with her and she would be in a worse position.

Rape. The horrifying thought shuddered through her. She was a virgin. She had saved herself for love and marriage. The first time she was with a man could not be because she was being forced.

Footsteps sounded across the parking lot. They were no longer alone. Thinking quickly, Sarah's fingers tightened on her umbrella. It wasn't much of a weapon, but she would use it if she had to. "I don't need help. My boyfriend's here. He'll fix the car."

"What boyfriend?" The taller man grabbed her arm as she edged away.

Jaw gritted, Sara brought the umbrella's wooden handle crashing down on the man's fingers.

"This one," a dark voice murmured, as Gabe stepped around a chunky utility vehicle into the light.

Three

Rubbing bruised knuckles, the tall guy, who now didn't seem large at all compared to Gabe, stumbled backward. "Hey, sorry, man," he mumbled. "Didn't know she was taken."

Gabe glided closer. When he stretched out his hand, it seemed the most natural thing in the world to put her fingers in his. "Even if she wasn't 'taken' you shouldn't have gone near her. But, as you said, she is taken, so don't bother her again."

Tall Guy took another step backward. The other two had already climbed into a car decorated with dents. He held one hand up in a placating gesture as he fumbled open the rear passenger door. "Yeah, man. She's yours. Totally. We won't bother her again."

He clambered into the car, which jolted into motion with a squeal of tires.

Gabe released his grip on her hand. "Are you okay?"

Sarah replaced her car keys in her bag. She was cold and her fingers were shaking, but she barely noticed because she was so focused on the fact that Gabe had come after her. She didn't know how he had located her in the dark, or why he had walked out into the rain to find her, just that he had. "I am now, thank you."

"Problem with your car?"

She blinked at the shift of topic. His gaze was still fixed on the taillights of the retreating car. The steely remoteness of his expression sent a chill down her spine. He looked more than capable of backing his flatly delivered challenge with physical force.

A fierce, oddly primitive sense of satisfaction curled through her. Gabe had not only come to her aid, but he had been prepared to physically fight for her.

When he repeated the question about the car, she realized he was deliberately distracting her from the nastiness of the encounter. Suppressing a shiver, she replaced her umbrella in her bag. "I think the electronics got wet."

Gabe, who had walked around to the front of her car, took a sleek phone out of his pocket and stabbed a short dial. "Is there still a charge in the battery?"

"I stopped before it went flat."

"Good." Gabe spoke quietly into his phone in the same liquid Zahiri she had heard him use before then slipped the cell back in his jacket pocket. "Xavier will have a look at the car. He's not a mechanic, but he spends a lot of his spare time tinkering with cars."

She hooked the strap of her bag more securely over her shoulder. It was an odd moment to register that the wind had dropped, leaving an eerie calm after the storm. With mist rising off the wet concrete, wreathing the cars and forming a halo around the street lamps, the night now seemed peaceful.

With a reflexive shiver she rubbed at her chilled arms and tried not to let her teeth chatter. Now that she was no longer buzzing with adrenaline the cold seemed to be seeping into her bones. "I suppose Xavier is one of the sheikh's bodyguards." The remark was shamelessly probing but she didn't care. She suddenly needed to know more about Gabe, what he did for a living, how long he would be in Wellington, when or *if* he was coming back—

His gaze glittered over her, making her aware of the soaked red dress clinging to her skin, her hair trailing wetly around her cheeks. "Only when the sheikh leaves Zahir."

The answer was confusing, as if the sheikh was still in Zahir when Sarah knew him to be here, in Wellington. But with Gabe walking toward her, dark trousers clinging low on narrow hips, his jacket damply molded to broad shoulders, white shirt plastered to his chest so that the bronze of his skin glowed through, it was hard to concentrate on unraveling subtleties.

He frowned. "You're cold. Have you got a coat in the car?"

"No c-coat. Someone at the consulate took mine by mistake."

A moment later, his jacket dropped around her shoulders, swamping her with warmth and filling her nostrils with the scent of clean male and an enticing hint of sandalwood. An electrifying thrill shot through her, reminding her of the sharp, visceral jolt she had felt when Gabe had said she was his.

He was briefly close enough that she felt the heat radiating off his body, and she had to resist the urge to sway a few inches closer to that delicious warmth. Her fingers closed on the fine weave of the jacket lapels, hugging the fabric closer. Despite everything, all of the warnings she was giving herself, she couldn't help loving that she was wearing his jacket, which was so large the sleeves dropped almost to her knees. After the nasty scenes with Graham and the leather-clad thugs, Gabe's chivalry—his consideration, as if she truly mattered to him—was a soothing balm.

Gabe checked his watch. "Xavier's on his way. If you'll give me your car keys, he'll take a look. In the meantime I suggest you come with me back to the consulate. There's a guest suite there, so you can dry off while you wait."

A vivid flash of the young woman flinging her arms around him made Sarah stiffen. "Won't your…girlfriend mind?'

His expression registered his surprise at the question. "I don't have a girlfriend. If you're referring to the young woman who came into the lecture, she was a cousin I haven't seen in years. She dropped in because she knew I was leaving in the morning."

The relief that the pretty girl wasn't a love interest was almost instantly replaced by the depressing confirmation that Gabe was leaving in a matter of hours.

His hand briefly cupped her elbow as he helped her step up onto the higher level of the consulate parking lot. "Is she the reason you left the lecture?"

Her mouth went dry at the bluntness of the question but after everything that had happened, somehow it didn't seem as intrusive as it should have been. It would have been easy to say she'd had a fight with Graham and was upset, but the truth was, whatever she had felt for Graham had been utterly overshadowed by her response to Gabe.

He was leaving in just a few hours.

Lifting her chin, she met his gaze. There was no point trying to hide what was already clear to him. She had been hurt and disappointed when she had thought he was committed to another woman. "Yes."

There was a moment of vibrating silence, filled by the muted sound of their footfalls on wet pavement, the distant wash of the sea and the slow drip of water splashing off a gutter. Sarah's stomach tightened as Gabe directed her to a door at the side of the consulate building and held it for her. Somehow, in the space of a little over an hour they had achieved a level of intimacy that made her stomach tighten and her pulse pound. But her time alone with him was almost up. Soon they would be joined by other people and a conversation that had become unexpectedly important would be over.

As if to underscore her thoughts, the plump administrative official, Tarik, strode down the corridor toward them, disapproval pulling his brows into a dark line. She drew a breath, but it was already too late to ask Gabe the question that was burning inside her.

He knew she was strongly attracted to him and that was why she had left the consulate so quickly. But was attraction the reason he had come looking for her?

Gabe left Sarah freshening up in the guest room that opened onto his study and strode along the hall to his suite. The moment he had seen the thug lay hands on her replayed through his mind, making him tense. When he had registered the danger, the half-formed desires and intentions that had driven him out into the stormy night had coalesced into one burning reality.

He wanted Sarah Duval.

He hadn't liked the fact that she'd had a date. He had liked it even less that the drunk thought he could simply reach out and touch her. Crazily, because Gabe barely knew her and had no interest in emotional attachments, his attraction to Sarah had coalesced into the kind of knee-jerk possessiveness he could not afford on the eve of his engagement. But, as hard as he tried to shake it, he couldn't—for one simple reason. In his mind he had already claimed her.

As he unlocked the door, Xavier stepped out of the elevator and followed Gabe into the suite. Gabe grabbed a towel from the bathroom and began blotting his hair and face. "What's the verdict on the car?"

Xavier shrugged. "We could have it going in half an hour if we put it in the consulate garage, but to get it there we'll need to tow it and none of the hire vehicles have tow bars. The best-case scenario is that I call her a taxi."

"No." Gabe unknotted his tie and peeled out of his wet shirt and tossed both in the laundry basket.

The sensible thing was to do what Xavier suggested. The last thing he needed was a complication that would make the commitment he had to make in the morning even more difficult. But ever since Sarah had walked into the reception room, glowing like a fiery beacon in red, her dark hair a sexy tousled mass, the obligation and duty of his impending marriage had seemed secondary. When she had disobeyed all instructions and laid her hand on his ancestor's sword, he had been entranced.

Somehow, the fact that she had knocked the sword,

which was practically a sacred object on Zahir, off its bracket had only made her more interesting.

She was a *history* teacher. Against all odds, he found himself grinning.

Like no history teacher he'd ever seen.

Gabe strolled into his bedroom to find a clean shirt. In the past hour something curious had happened. He felt lighter and more carefree, as if a weight had lifted off him.

Because for the first time in years when he had looked at another woman, he hadn't been haunted by thoughts of Jasmine.

He guessed the fact that Sarah was literally Jasmine's polar opposite—tall and curvy with a steady, resolute gaze and hints of a fiery temper, instead of tiny and fragile and sweetly feminine—had helped. When Sarah had toppled Kadin's sword, in some odd way the separation from his past had seemed complete. Jasmine had hated all of the old Templar relics and the violent history that went with them. Sarah had seemed fascinated. From the way she had wielded her umbrella in the parking lot, he was willing to bet she would not be averse to holding a sword.

He stared at his crisply starched shirts in the closet, looking for something that didn't belong in a boardroom. Clothing that might indicate that he had a life. "I'm taking her home."

Xavier muttered something soft and short. "I don't think that's a good idea. Neither will your father."

Gabe shrugged into a dark shirt and buttoned it. The searing attraction that had sent him walking out into the night to find Sarah settled into grim determination. Xavier's unease mirrored his own because it was a fact that Gabe didn't want to just spend time with Sarah—he wanted her. Period. But just hours out from signing his life away, he was in no mood to deny a response he thought he would never feel again. "Right now a whole lot of things are happening that are not exactly good ideas."

An outmoded financial system that did not allow for the foreign investment Gabe had been advocating for years, and the marriage that *was* Zahir's financial rescue plan.

"The marriage is just an arrangement, you could have an—"

"No." Zahir was Western, but it was also extremely conservative. And Gabe was clear on one fact: once he was married he would not dishonor his vows or his family's integrity.

Xavier looked uncomfortable. "Sometimes I forget the pressure you're under. But what do you know about this woman? She could be some hard-nosed journalist angling for a story."

"Sarah's not a journalist." Gabe shrugged into a soft black leather jacket. "And she won't go to the press."

"You can't know that. You've only just met her. You have no idea what she'll do."

Gabe went still inside as a memory flickered. Cold rain scything, a dark-haired woman, head down against the weather, stepping around a corner. As his hands had shot out to stop her caroming into him he had noticed that her hair had been scraped back and her face had been almost bare of makeup. *She* had looked like a history teacher. But it had been Sarah, her eyes that deep, pure blue, the faintly imperious nose and exquisite cheekbones, the soft, generous mouth.

Instead of tempering his attraction, the recollection had the disconcerting effect of deepening it. In that moment, Gabe recognized the quality that drew him to Sarah most of all—the fact that in the midst of all the superficiality of the social world he usually moved in she was exactly what she seemed, a refreshingly direct woman unafraid to reach out and take what she wanted. "I met her yesterday."

Xavier's brows jerked together. "That makes it even worse."

Everything Xavier was saying was true. Normally he didn't pursue women he had only just met. Because of his position, he accepted that security checks on the women he dated were a fact of life. But ever since he had woken up that morning he had been restless and in no mood to be controlled. "Relax. She doesn't know who I am."

"How is that possible?"

"I think she expected my father to be here." Gabe walked through to the sitting room and pointedly held the door for Xavier. "I don't need an escort. As of now you're off duty. Take the rest of the night off."

Gabe waited until Xavier disappeared into the elevator before walking down the corridor to check on Sarah's progress in the guest suite. He could hear the sound of the hair dryer in the bathroom, so he returned to his suite to check his laptop. There was a message from his father and one from their lawyer, Hadad. Both messages, naturally, were centered on the contract Xavier had delivered.

He replied briefly to both then, jaw set, sat down to examine the list of marriage candidates that was clipped to the back of the contract. The candidate his parents preferred was at the top of the list.

He studied the color photo of Nadia Fortier. She was

slim and beautifully dressed, with long dark hair. She had to be all of eighteen.

He checked the basic information that had been provided. He saw he had been wrong about Nadia's age; she was twenty, a whole two years older than he had thought. And a good ten years his junior.

He flipped through the rest of the candidates. There were four in all. Extremely wealthy and young, all from good families, most of them with either noble or royal connections. Girls straight from exclusive finishing schools, groomed to make very good marriages as their designated career paths.

His gaze snagged on another notation: "guaranteed pure."

His jaw tensed. He realized that the situation was probably even more stressful for the girls, but he was beginning to feel like a prize stallion being led to stud. Broodingly, he wondered what kind of description of him they had received.

Tossing the document down on the coffee table, he strolled to one of the tall sash windows that looked out over the city streets. On a personal level he would not have dated any one of those candidates purely on the grounds that they were too young. He doubted they had any interests in common on which to build a marriage. The notation about purity explained the emphasis on youth, but as perfect and beautiful as each one was, none of them inspired even the remotest flicker of desire.

Unlike Sarah.

In that moment, the urge to do the unthinkable, to bail out of the arranged marriage and immerse himself in a tangled, messy, flamboyant affair with the very interesting Ms. Duval was irresistibly, powerfully appealing.

Massaging the taut muscles at his nape, he strode into his bedroom and found the keys to the Jeep that had been rented for him while he was in New Zealand. As he did so, his gaze snagged on the portrait of Kadin and Camille. Camille was dressed in flamboyant red, her dark gaze composed and direct, and for a split second he had an inkling of the fascination that had dominated his ancestor's life. The thought was like a dash of cold water. It was an obsession Gabe was determined would not dominate him.

He had already had a taste of the manipulation that went hand in hand with emotional excess. As tempting as it would be to toss tradition and his country's need and do exactly what he wanted, he could not walk away from his responsibilities.

Exiting the suite, he walked back to the guest room, his mood once again remote. He could understand Xavier's anxiety, because Gabe's behavior was distinctly out of character. Normally he took responsibility and did the right thing, and tomorrow he would choose which candidate he would marry. He had given his word.

But right now, tonight, he didn't want to think about the future. He was determined to accept the invitation he had seen in Sarah's eyes.

He was going to spend his last few hours of freedom with his quirky, fascinating lady in red.

Sarah finished blow-drying her hair and stared at the result in the gilt-framed mirror that dominated the ivory marble bathroom. With its gold taps and step-down bath, the room was utterly decadent. Her makeup was gone, washed off in the rain, and her hair had lost all of its curl. It fell in a shiny but depressingly straight waterfall to her waist. Her dress was still damp and clinging to her skin, but thankfully the silk seemed to be drying fast.

With all the glamor and magic of the makeover gone, there was no getting past the fact that, like Cinderella at the stroke of midnight, she was once again plain-Jane Sarah Duval. Although, she no longer felt like a plain-Jane. Her cheeks were softly flushed, and her eyes had a depth and sparkle she had never noticed.

Maybe that was because, just when she had thought there was no chance with Gabe, he had walked out of the night and rescued her. Now, she had been admitted to the hushed elegance of one of the sheikh's private apartments and suddenly the scenario she had planned seemed terrifyingly possible.

Placing the fluffy oversize towel she'd used in a laundry hamper, she checked that she hadn't left anything behind, hooked the strap of her bag over her shoulder and walked out into the luxuriously furnished bedroom, which opened onto a study.

Her heart slammed hard in her chest when she spotted Gabe standing at one of the tall sash windows in the study, watching the rain, which was once again pounding down. As he turned, she caught the flare of appreciation in his gaze and at the same time noticed that he had changed into dry clothes. If he'd looked formidable and just a little remote in a suit, the dark, soft shirt and black leather jacket, narrow trousers and black boots achieved the exact opposite, making him look younger and infinitely more approachable.

He indicated the rain streaming down the window. "With this weather, there's nothing we can do about the car tonight. If you want a lift home I can drop you. Or if you'd prefer I'll call a taxi."

Her heart sped up at the offer. The sensible thing, of course, would be to call a taxi but the instant she considered that option, she knew she wasn't going to take it. "If you could drop me, I'd appreciate it."

"No problem." Gabe picked up a set of keys he must have placed on a side table.

As he opened the door, she noticed an oil painting of a man dressed in robes on the wall. "Is that the sheikh?"

He glanced at the painting, but didn't seem inclined to linger. "Yes."

The painting had obviously been done when the sheikh was a lot younger, but even so, with his clipped beard and wearing traditional robes, it was difficult to see exactly what he looked like. He didn't look a lot like the man Graham had been talking to at the reception, but with the facial hair it was hard to tell. "Are there any paintings of Sheikh Kadin?"

Gabe went very still as he held the door for her. "The first Sheikh Kadin?"

She stepped out into the corridor, distracted by the sudden curtness of his tone. "I didn't realize there was more than one."

Gabe pressed a button on a sleek, private elevator and gestured that she precede him. "The name reoccurs practically every second generation in the sheikh's family." He pressed the button for the ground floor. "The name is also popular on Zahir, mostly because it's linked with prosperity."

She frowned at the flatness of his tone. "You don't sound overly impressed by the first sheikh."

"It's ancient history."

"And an ancient love story."

The doors slid open. Gabe waited for her to exit first. "According to tradition."

Her head came up at the implication. "You don't think love was involved?"

Gabe indicated a gleaming Jeep Cherokee situated at the far end of the cavernous garage, next to the doors. "Kadin was broke, Camille was wealthy. What are the odds?"

Even though she had entertained similar thoughts about Kadin's motives, she frowned as they strolled through the dim shadows. After reading Camille's very personal revelations about how strongly she had been attracted to Kadin, she couldn't help taking his comments personally. "So I suppose you think that just because Kadin was a knight and good-looking, Camille was lucky to get him? That the money somehow made up for her defects?"

He came to a halt beside the Jeep, his expression enigmatic. "Let's just say that if Camille hadn't been traveling with approximately a metric ton of gold and jewels that history would probably have taken a different turn."

He opened the door for her, his consideration taking the sting out of his words and dampening down the knee-jerk urge to spring to her ancestor's defense. His hand cupping her elbow as she climbed into the passenger seat further distracted her. After Graham's dismissive treatment, Gabe's manners and the feeling that while she was with him she was the absolute focus of his attention were a much-needed balm.

Feeling breathless, she fastened her seat belt. As Gabe swung into the driver's seat, the cab of the Jeep seemed to shrink, suddenly claustrophobically small and disturbingly intimate.

Sarah attempted to relax as Gabe accelerated out of the garage into the murky night, but the easy camaraderie of earlier in the evening had evaporated. Bludgeoned out of existence by her usual bluntness, she thought grimly.

Minutes later, when he pulled into a parking space on the road above her rain-drenched cottage, her stomach tightened at the knowledge that whatever she and Gabe had shared would be over in a matter of seconds. "Thank you for the lift."

She fumbled at the door handle, but before she could push it wide, Gabe swung out of the cab and walked around to hold the door. Rain swirled down, shimmering in the pooling light of street lamps as she retrieved her bag.

Once she was out, Gabe closed the door with a discreet *thunk*. "I'll see you to your door." A beep and flash of lights indicated that he had locked the vehicle.

Feeling breathless and chilled after the warmth of the cab, Sarah led the way to her porch with its single glowing light. She paused in the shelter of the wide, old-fashioned porch and extracted her house key from her bag. A moment later, she pushed the door wide. The house was softly lit and comforting, with lamps burning in the sitting room. Warm air flowed out, making the night seem even colder and damper.

She glanced at Gabe, suddenly awkward. A restless part of her wished for the boldness that had arisen out of nowhere earlier in the evening. She longed to have the confidence to do what she had planned and fling herself into a wild, passionate affair, to curl her fingers into the soft lapels of his jacket, go up on her toes and kiss him. But as nice as Gabe had been in looking out for her and giving her a lift home, she was determined not to make a fool of herself by misreading the situation. "Thank you for everything. I'll collect my car in the morning."

"No problem." He produced a card from his pocket and scribbled a name and number on the back of it. "Xavier will be gone, but a receptionist will be there. She'll have your keys."

She took the card, careful not to touch his fingers, and tucked it in her bag. "You're leaving first thing?"

"I have business to attend to on Zahir."

A little desperate that he was about to leave, she searched for a reason to detain him, if only for a few seconds. The question that had consumed her earlier, resurfaced. Heart beating a rapid tattoo, she lifted her chin. "Why did you follow me when I left the lecture?"

Something flared in his gaze, the electrifying intensity she had been aware of at the reception, as if he were searching for something intangible but utterly necessary to him. As if he had found that necessary quality in *her*.

His gaze connected with hers. "I couldn't let you go."

The words sent a bolt of pure sensation through her. In that moment her mind cleared on the whole issue of risk. She had gone out tonight specifically looking for a wild fling to break herself out of the emotional rut she'd fallen into. Her mother would count it a victory if Sarah married Graham. In Sarah's mind that would be the ultimate relationship train wreck because Graham would never give her the one thing she craved: true love.

But with Gabe, on some instinctive level, she knew the opposite to be true. The connection sizzled between them. She could see it in his eyes, *feel* it with every cell of her body. There was no logic or sense to it. They barely knew each other, and yet she knew in her heart that something deep and essential was right between them.

He was edgy and utterly male, and he'd been ready to go to war for her. At times he had been grim and re- mote, but there had been a softness and humor she had loved. She didn't know him, and yet every instinct she possessed informed her that he was everything and more she wanted in a man.

He was perfect, and in a few minutes she was going to lose him.

She drew a swift breath. "Don't go. Not yet."

Four

Gabe said something low and soft then his mouth was on hers.

Heat and sensation seared through her, time seemed to slow and stop as she lifted up on her toes, wound her arms around his neck and fitted herself more fully against him. She logged the solid wall of muscle that was his chest, the warmth of his arms as he pulled her in close, the firm swell of his arousal.

The kiss was soft and lingering and the intimacy of it rocked her. She had been kissed before, more times than she could count, but in other kisses she had been aware of an element of recoil in the process. Either she didn't like the way her date touched her, his taste or smell, or she didn't like her date, period.

There had been times when she had wondered if she was the tiniest bit frigid, but with Gabe the details that registered were all on the plus side. He smelled clean and male and delicious and his touch and taste shivered through her senses, making her feel boneless and weak. While every other kiss she'd ever experienced had been wrong in some way, this kiss was somehow right, filling her with an absorbing, dissolving heat so that she wanted to press herself even more firmly against him.

His mouth lifted then sank again, taking her under. Dimly she was aware of the strap of her handbag slipping off one shoulder. Misty rain swirled around the enclosure of the porch, triggering disorienting flashes of the sensual dream she had experienced just that morning.

Gabe lifted his head. His gaze locked with hers. "If you want me to leave, you should say so now."

The cool separation when only moments before she had been held against the muscled heat of his body was faintly shocking. He wanted her. That thought alone was enough to anchor her, when for years she had felt rejected as a woman and intrinsically undesirable.

Now she knew that none of those past relationships had been right because she had been waiting for the deep connection she needed. It had never happened with anyone else, but through some strange alchemy it had happened with Gabe.

The knowledge filled her with dizzying relief. She had begun to think she was odd, different, that she would never marry, never have the warm family chaos, the husband and babies that were at the center of most of her friends' lives. She had begun to believe that she would never be truly loved.

It was a huge leap to go from one kiss to thinking that Gabe could be hers. Making love with him would be a risk, but *not* making love would be an even bigger risk.

She might miss her only chance to feel this way—loved and desired by the man of her choice.

Sarah touched Gabe's jaw, loving the rough feel of his five-o'clock shadow. Drawn by an impulse that had its roots in the dream, she allowed her fingers to drift over the smooth, ridged scar that marred his cheekbone.

Something flared in his eyes, gone almost as swiftly as it had appeared, then his mouth was on hers. A split second later, the world went sideways as Sarah found herself swung into his arms.

One step and they were inside her house. She heard the door slam shut then they were moving.

Gabe lifted his head. "Which way is the bedroom?"

She indicated a left turn. Moments later he carried her into the dim shadows of her room lit only by the lamp-light washing down the hall and the glow of a street-light flowing through her window. Setting her down, he shrugged out of his jacket, letting it drop to the floor. He kissed her again, drawing her against him as he slowly drew the zipper that fastened her dress down the sensitive curve of her spine. Cool air circulated against her skin as she stepped out of the dress and set to work on the buttons of Gabe's shirt, although that work was momentarily halted as Gabe dispensed with her bra and cupped her breasts.

Long dizzying seconds passed as he bent and took first one breast, then the other into his mouth, the sensation pulling every muscle tight and starting a heavy ache low in her belly. Despite the coolness of the air against her skin and the chilly sound of the rain on the windows, heat flushed her skin making her feel restless and hot.

Lifting his mouth, Gabe dispensed with the remaining buttons of his shirt and shrugged out of it, before pulling her close. Drawing in a breath at the seductive heat of skin on skin, Sarah coiled her arms around his neck and pulled his mouth to hers, the kiss deepening as he walked her backward to the bed. She felt the soft give of the mattress at the back of her knees then she sank back onto the down-filled white quilt, Gabe sprawled beside her.

He moved over her, his weight pressing her down. Little more than fifteen minutes ago she had been on the verge of saying good-night out on the porch, now they were on the verge of making love. Disorientation hit her at how fast things had moved, but the night had an odd dreamlike quality and the dizzying intensity of emotion that burst through her with every touch of his hands, his mouth, was too addictive to relinquish.

She felt his fingers tugging at her panties and shifted restlessly, helping him strip them down her legs. The faintly rough weave of his pants brushed against her sensitive skin.

Frustrated that while she was naked Gabe was still half dressed, she reached down and tugged at the fastening of his pants. She dragged the zipper down and felt the blunt, silky shape of him in her hands. He muttered something taut beneath his breath as he moved between her legs. A split second later she felt him lodged against her. Hot, irresistible sensation burst through her as she instinctively pressed against him, inviting him deeper.

He tensed and attempted to withdraw but, utterly mesmerized by a burning maelstrom of sensation, Sarah's arms coiled tighter as she pressed closer still. An agonizing second later he shoved deep and the irresistible, coiling heat shimmered and dissolved along with the night.

* * *

Long minutes later, Gabe propped himself on one elbow, his gaze in the darkened room brooding and reflective. He stroked one fingertip over her tender bottom lip in a lingering caress that sent a shiver through her. "How likely is it that you'll get pregnant?"

The question was shocking. Although it was a possibility Sarah had been turning over while she'd attempted to adjust to the intimacy of what they'd just done and the shameless way she had pressed herself against him before he'd had a chance to use a condom.

The possibility of an unplanned pregnancy. It was not a problem she had ever thought she would face. Along with the thought of a pregnancy and all that entailed, Gabe's practicality in asking the question brought her back to earth with a thump. For long minutes she had been caught up in her own very private fantasy, but with every second that passed it was becoming increasingly obvious that Gabe did not share her longings.

She swallowed against the sudden ache at the back of her throat and made an effort to dismiss the hurt. She needed to be as practical as Gabe. She had wanted to make love and they had. It had been a huge risk and, whatever the outcome, she refused to regret what had happened.

A baby. The thought that in the past few minutes they could have made a tiny human life together was stunning.

Gabe might have no interest in anything more than an interlude, *a one-night stand*, but if there was a baby, Sarah would want it. She loved kids and adored babies. She had always wanted at least one of her own, and the way things had been going she had begun to think she would never be a mother.

She drew a deep breath. Gabe's silence spoke louder than words, there was no way he wanted the complication of a baby. Since he was leaving in the morning, and he hadn't indicated that he was coming back to New Zealand, she had to assume that it was entirely possible that they would never see each other again. "Don't worry about a baby. It won't be a problem."

If she was pregnant, it was too late now; it was done. And if Gabe did not want an actual relationship with her then so be it. She would take sole responsibility for the child.

Gabe cupped her jaw, his gaze intent. What he saw in her eyes must have satisfied him. "I've never done that before, so you don't have to worry about STDs."

She suppressed the sharp hurt that Gabe was clearly used to making love with women, and the jab of guilt that he obviously thought she had taken care of contraception. "Ditto."

Something like relief flickered in his gaze. "Good."

As Gabe climbed from the bed and drew the curtains against the rain still spattering the windows, it registered that he hadn't noticed she was a virgin. That small point shouldn't have mattered, but somehow it did. Although, with the swiftness with which they'd come together, Gabe probably hadn't had time to process anything beyond the fact that they'd had unprotected sex.

As he peeled out of his boots and pants, items she hadn't given him time to fully dispense with, Sarah surreptitiously pulled back the quilt and shimmied beneath it.

Gabe, who was in the process of tearing open a foil

packet, prevented her cover up by the simple expedient of stripping back the quilt. "Don't," he said softly. "I want to remember you like this."

The finality of the words—as if they'd already said goodbye—struck her forcibly.

Despite her innate caution, while they'd been kissing, undressing, hope had formed. She and Gabe would swap numbers. He would call her from Zahir and somehow they would form a relationship. And maybe, just maybe, sometime in the misty future there would be the possibility of something real and enduring.

Tension gripped her as she watched Gabe sheath himself in the dim light. With his biceps bronzed and gleaming, chest and abs tautly muscled, he was beautiful in a fierce, completely male way and she wanted him.

But he wasn't hers. The truth was there in the faint remoteness of his gaze, a subtle distance she could feel even in the midst of passion.

As he joined her on the bed, she propped herself on one elbow and looked directly into his eyes. "Are you married?"

"No."

Relief filled her. "Good." She suspected that Gabe wasn't as free as he seemed but she didn't want to know that there was a girlfriend or significant other back on Zahir. If there was, what was between them obviously wasn't strong enough to hold Gabe. To her mind that meant it wasn't love.

Love. The concept burned through her, initiating a new tension. Everything she had felt for Gabe had been new, intense and passionate. She drew a swift breath as the reality hit home of how affected she had been by him. She didn't see how anyone could fall in love in the space of a few hours, but she had.

Her chest squeezed tight. Swallowing the impending hurt, the silly desire to cry, she leaned down and kissed Gabe, her hair sliding like a curtain around them.

The thought that she could be pregnant already made her feel even more unsettled. As his hands moved to her waist, drawing her down to him, she forced herself to forget about the possibility of a pregnancy, forget about the fact that Gabe was leaving.

If they only had one night, she was determined that it would be a night to remember.

Sarah woke to sun streaming through a gap in the curtains. Yawning, she turned over, reaching for Gabe only to find cool rumpled sheets and a pillow with an indentation. She glanced around the room. The certainty that he had gone was there in the absence of any of his clothing.

A knock at the front door had her jackknifing out of bed. Shrugging into her robe, she tightened the belt around her waist and dragged fingers through her tangled hair. Her first thought was that Gabe must have gone out for a walk, or maybe to buy some breakfast.

When she opened the door, a uniformed courier was standing on her porch with a huge bunch of dark red, perfectly formed roses.

Her mood plunging, Sarah took the flowers and set them on a side table just inside the hall while she signed an electronic pad to confirm she had received them. Closing the door, she leaned against it and stared at the beautiful, expensive bouquet. A quick check revealed there was no card.

Stomach tightening, she picked up the heavy bunch

and carried them to her small kitchen. She had received roses only twice before in her life. Roger had given her a modest bunch on her birthday, once, but they had been pink and wrapped in yellow paper with the unmistakable tag of a local supermarket. Mark had sent her one lone rose on a Valentine's Day. Neither man had thought to send her two-dozen roses that hinted at the passionate, sensual bond she now knew could exist between a man and a woman.

But then, she hadn't slept with either of them.

She found a vase large enough to hold the flowers, although a part of her didn't want to either keep them or display them just in case they did represent "goodbye."

It occurred to her then that she didn't know Gabe's full name, and she had somehow forgotten to give him her phone number. Although he knew her name and address, so it should be easy enough for him to find her.

She bent forward and inhaled the fragrance. She would stay positive, hang on to hope. All of her instincts told her that Gabe was special, that despite that touch of remoteness—a caution she well knew—he had valued their passionate hours together as much as she.

He would call; it was just a matter of time.

Gabe could not afford to contact Sarah, ever.

The thought made his mood even grimmer as he boarded his chartered flight, late.

Xavier, who had been waiting in the departure lounge, strode alongside him, his expression taut. "I thought I was going to have to come and get you."

Gabe took his seat in the small jet's luxury cabin, resignation settling in at his friend's implication. "Don't tell me, there was a GPS tracker on the Jeep."

Xavier dropped into the seat beside him. "There's always a GPS. You're the son of the sheikh, thc heir apparent. If I hired vehicles that didn't have that facility, I'd be fired."

Gabe fastened his seat belt for take-off and concentrated on resisting the insane urge to disembark and drive back to the small seaside suburb where Sarah lived.

"Please tell me you won't be seeing her again."

Gabe didn't bother answering. Xavier was justifiably upset because he had been tasked with Gabe's security. He had slipped the leash and given Xavier a difficult night. But the whole point had been that Gabe had one last night to himself.

Only it had been a little more complicated than that.

He had hoped that when hc made love with Sarah the attraction would lose its potency. He had been wrong. Despite the short length of time they had spent together, he still felt the force of their connection, the emotional pull, which was even more reason to leave.

As the jet leveled out, a pretty Zahiri air hostess dressed in an elegant blue uniform, her hair caught up in a glossy knot, served coffee.

Gabe set his briefcase down on the fold-down tray, flipped it open and extracted the marriage contract. Xavier pretended to be immersed in a newspaper while Gabe once again read through the list of marriage candidates. His jaw tightened as he came back to the young woman his parents had rated number one.

Dispassionately, he studied her face, which was beautiful but, to Gabe, lacking in personality. There was no hint of stormy emotions or engaging boldness. There was absolutely no evidence of the sharp, take-no-prisoners intellect that would make life interesting. It was a face he would be seeing on a daily basis once they were married.

Xavier put down his paper. "If you really are going ahead with a marriage of convenience you shouldn't have had a one-night stand with a twenty-eight year old history teacher."

"Twenty-eight?"

"Almost twenty-nine."

Controlling his irritation that Xavier had referred to the hours Gabe had spent with Sarah as a one-night stand, Gabe flipped to the legalese of the agreement. "I suppose you had to do the security check."

"I was worried. You don't normally go off the grid like that."

"Normally I'm too busy." Trying to finesse the traditional approach to finances his father clung to into a system that would bring his country out of its financial nosedive. Now their lack of solvency had reached a critical state, stopping a resort development vital for Zahir's continued prosperity in its tracks.

And yet, despite his country's problems, his mind returned to Sarah. She was almost twenty-nine. The small snippet of information was intriguing, and made sense. She had been far too interesting to be younger and yet, with her moonlight-pale skin and silky hair, her passionate intensity when they had made love, she had seemed much younger. No wonder they had clicked so instantly. Besides the college education, the fact that they were close in age was one more thing they had in common.

As the jet gathered speed, Gabe closed out an image of Sarah lying in a tumble of sheets, her hair spread out over the pillow and applied himself to reading through the fine print. He hit the clause that stipulated his bride had to be pure, which was why each of the candidates was so young. With every year that passed, logic dictated that it was more difficult to find a suitable candidate for marriage who was still a virgin. A twenty-eight-year-old virgin was an impossibility.

Or, maybe not.

Gabe's heart slammed once, hard, against the wall of his chest as the engines reached a crescendo and the jet leaped into the air. Pressed back into his seat for the ascent, he felt electrified, every nerve ending in his body on fire as the missing piece of the puzzle that was Sarah fell into place.

She had been a virgin.

Nothing else explained her unusual behavior. She had been at once bold and shy, and she hadn't employed any exotic techniques. She had simply made love to him. In all the years he had been involved in relationships, no woman he had ever been with had ever made love to him like they meant it, including his wife.

He could kick himself. He had felt the initial constriction, noted the moment of discomfort on her face but, stunned by the knowledge that he had been so caught up in her passionate response that he had failed to protect them both, the significance of those sensations had bypassed him. Given that the first time had been over almost before it had begun, maybe he could be forgiven for the oversight.

"What's wrong?" Xavier must have picked up something in his expression. "Please tell me you protected yourself."

Eventually. Although he hadn't wanted to, and that had been a first. But from the moment he had seen Sarah at the reception he had been thrown off balance. Grimly he noted that if the jet wasn't in the air, he would have done something precipitate and obsessive, like walk off the flight and refuse a marriage arrangement that, long-term, would provide the stability and the heir both his family and Zahir needed. He would have behaved emotionally—in a way that he knew from bitter experience destroyed happiness and lives.

Letting out a breath, he forced himself to once more study Nadia's profile. He knew her family, of course. Her father was a French billionaire who had made his money in shipping. No doubt those two details had appealed to Gabe's father who, with the onset of his illness, had become a little obsessed with the legend of Sheikh Kadin. No doubt he thought there was a satisfying symmetry to the idea of Gabe marrying a shipping magnate's daughter. After all, that was how Zahir had made its money in the first place.

Gabe replied to the email, accepting the preferred candidate, Nadia Fortier.

His father had decreed a short engagement to give them time to get to know one another. A few months' grace in which to get to know and accept the woman he would marry.

And to forget Sarah Duval.

Five

Four months later Sarah double-checked the results her doctor handed her.

"You're absolutely sure I'm pregnant?"

Evelyn lifted a brow. "You're not just pregnant, you're very pregnant and I think you knew that. You should have come to see me sooner."

Caught between resignation, dismay and the dizzying sense of wonder that had gripped her over the past few weeks as she'd logged the undeniable symptoms of a pregnancy, Sarah tucked the sheet of paper in her handbag.

Of course she had noticed that she had missed her first period. But, caught stubbornly in denial, she had waited another month. When her cycle missed for the second time and she had begun to feel faintly nauseous, she had begun to accept that what she had thought would never happen had happened.

She sent Evelyn an apologetic look. "Sorry. I needed some adjustment time."

To her credit, Evelyn, who was an old friend, didn't comment on the fact that Sarah was pregnant and didn't have a husband or even a boyfriend. "I presume you want to keep the baby?"

The words were discreetly put while Evelyn pretended to be busy shuffling papers and checking something on her computer screen.

"Yes." The answer was unequivocal.

"Can you supply me with any history of the father?"

Despite bracing herself for this question, Sarah's cheeks warmed. This was the part she'd been dreading. She had done some research on the whole business of having a baby and knew that sometimes details about the father, such as blood type and genetic conditions, were important. "No."

There was a small, vibrating silence. Evelyn ducked her head, her own cheeks flushed, but not before Sarah caught the flash of compassion in her friend's eyes. Evelyn knew Sarah's past, vividly. Evelyn was supposed to be Sarah's bridesmaid at the first wedding, her maid of honor at the second. Instead, Sarah had cried on Evelyn's shoulder over men, twice.

She wouldn't be crying on Evelyn's shoulder a third time because this mistake was in a whole new league.

Sarah hadn't been sedately courted by a man she and her family and friends knew well. She'd had a wildly romantic night of passion with an exotic stranger, a one-night stand, and then he had disappeared, leaving her flat.

She had committed every mistake in the book within the space of a few hours, literally picking up a guy, having unprotected sex with him and getting pregnant, and she didn't even know Gabe's full name. All she knew was that he lived thousands of miles away on an island in the Mediterranean and that he worked for the Sheikh of Zahir. Since Gabe had been careful not to supply her with any contact details, or even his full name, it was clear that he did not want further interaction with her.

Her behavior had not just been uncharacteristic, it had been dumb, and all because she'd been seduced by a romantic dream and frightened by the thought that she would end up thirty and alone.

She should have been a lot smarter than she had turned out to be. Becoming a mother was going to have a huge effect on her life. For a start, she would have to quit her full-time teaching job, because she wanted to stay home with her child. That meant she would have to find alternative employment, something she could do from home. Although she had already come up with an idea which was, crazily enough, based on Camille's journal.

Sarah forced herself to relax. There was no need to panic. She would work it all out one step at a time. "Okay, what do I do now?"

Evelyn scribbled her signature on a form and handed it to Sarah. "You'll need to have a blood test and make an appointment to come and see me in a week's time, but you've always been in great health so I don't anticipate any problems."

She opened a drawer and took out a bunch of pamphlets, selected several and slipped them across the surface of her desk. "Do some reading, don't drink alcohol and don't take any medication unless you run it by me, not even a painkiller. If you've been feeling sick, that's normal, but if it gets too bad come and see me right away."

Evelyn pulled up a file on her laptop and tapped briskly before hitting the print button. When the copy printed out, she handed it to Sarah. "It's an application for a scan. Since it looks like you're at least four months pregnant, you should have one of those. The clinic will contact you with a date and time."

Sarah took the form. A tentative, dawning delight began to spread through her. If anything could make the baby real, this was it. "Thanks."

Slipping the paperwork inside her handbag, she pushed to her feet.

Evelyn walked Sarah to the door. "If you need to stay longer and talk, I can stall the next appointment for a few minutes. And if you just want to talk, call me at home. Anytime."

Sarah pinned a smile on her face. She had been coming to Evelyn for years. Aside from the friendship that had developed between them at university, they had the perfect doctor/patient relationship. But if Sarah had to admit to Evelyn how naive she'd been, the relationship would be permanently dented. "I'll be fine, thanks. Don't forget I have a mother."

"Of course."

The relief on Evelyn's face confirmed Sarah's thoughts. Evelyn was smart, successful and married to another doctor. They had three children, a nanny and what looked like a perfectly organized life. As compassionate as Evelyn would try to be, there was no way she could understand why Sarah had slept with Gabe.

As Sarah walked out of the medical center into the warmth of a summer's day, she felt a tiny flutter, like butterfly wings, in her stomach. She froze, her hand going to her abdomen. The flutter came again and a sense of wonder spread through her. In just a few months she would be a mother.

Joy, heady and a little incredulous, hit her. For long moments she simply stood on the sidewalk, foot traffic flowing around her. She didn't have everything she wanted out of life. She didn't have a husband to love and who would love her, but she was going to have a baby, something she'd thought she would miss out on altogether.

Feeling disoriented and shaky, she took dark glasses from her bag, slid them onto the bridge of her nose and strolled to where she'd parked the car. She unlocked the driver's-side door, opened it and waited a few seconds for the heat that had built up inside to dissipate before climbing in. Instead of driving home, she drove by the Zahiri consulate.

On impulse, she pulled into the parking lot and found a space just outside the main entrance. Heart pounding at the idea that had blossomed, that she should at least think about contacting Gabe, she checked her appearance in the rearview mirror before exiting the car. Her hair was coiled in the messy knot she had perfected and her skin was positively glowing. Rummaging in her bag, she found her makeup kit, retouched around her eyes and applied fresh gloss to her mouth.

Stepping out of the car, she smoothed the loose white shirt she had teamed with a pair of camel pants, both items classic and stylish, but loose enough to fit comfortably, given that her waist had started to thicken.

A dark-haired receptionist, different from the one she had collected her car keys from the morning after she had slept with Gabe, listened to her enquiry. "We don't have anyone named Gabe working here. Do you have a surname?"

Sarah explained that Gabe had only been in the country for a short time, with the sheikh's entourage.

The woman's gaze grew oddly evasive. Sarah was almost certain she knew exactly to whom Sarah was referring.

She pushed to her feet. "Just one moment."

Frowning, Sarah watched her disappear into a side office. Moments later she reappeared with a small, plump man—Tarik. Sarah's stomach dropped.

After an unsatisfactory interview in which Tarik had first pretended not to recognize Sarah, and had then feigned confusion over which Gabe she was referring to, Sarah lost her temper. "The Gabe who picked up the sword after I dropped it at the reception. The man you appeared to know very well."

There was a small silence. "Do you have a photograph of him?"

Sarah's brows jerked together at the odd question. "No."

Tarik seemed to relax at that point, his voice turning as smooth as butter. "He doesn't work for the sheikh. He was just on…assignment."

Her fingers tightened on the strap of her bag. "What does that mean?"

Tarik fixed her with a bland stare. "It means he is not in the sheikh's employ."

"So you won't help me contact him?"

"No."

Annoyed at being treated like some kind of groupie, or worse, a stalker, Sarah turned on her heel and left the consulate, aware of two sets of eyes boring into her back. She was convinced they knew exactly who Gabe was, and where he was, and that for some unfathomable reason they were protecting him.

Grimly she decided that reason was probably that Gabe was married, even though he'd said he wasn't. Maybe her judgment in sleeping with him had been more skewed than she'd thought.

Her temper, held on a tight leash for most of the interview, boiled over again as she unlocked her car door. Lately, with the pregnancy, she had noticed a tendency toward mood swings. It no doubt had something to do with the hormones rioting through her body. Whatever the cause, her personality had definitely found another gear.

Fuming, she drove home and walked into her front room. Her plan was to find the first Zahiri ornament that came to hand and smash it in the hopes that small satisfying act of destruction would make her feel better. Instead she found Graham in her house.

Graham's head jerked up guiltily. He had a sheaf of papers in his hand. "I thought you'd be at work."

Sarah dropped her bag on a side table. "Normally I would be, and—" she checked her wristwatch "—that would have given you another good two hours to steal whatever it was you came to steal."

Graham tried for a smile. "You're looking good, Sarah, positively blooming. We should go out sometime."

She couldn't believe his nerve. She noticed Camille de Vallois's journal on a coffee table, the spine broken. "You've copied the journal." And by the looks of things, he'd been cheeky enough to use her paper and copier.

"I didn't think you'd mind—"

"You mean you hoped I'd never find out."

His cheeks reddened. He glanced at his watch as if he was suddenly in a hurry. "Uh—I need to go. I'm flying out to Zahir in a few hours, so I need to pack."

Sarah pointedly held the front door open. "Good luck finding the missing dowry. And if I ever find you in my house again, I'll call the police."

Graham's expression turned decidedly unpleasant. "I won't be back. Why would I when I've got what I wanted?"

Sarah slammed the door as Graham scuttled up the drive. She hooked the chain for good measure then walked back into her tiny sitting room, picked up the journal and sat down. She took a calming breath, then another, as she heard the whine of Graham's sports car, which must have been sneakily parked outside someone else's house, accelerate away.

The interview with Tarik, followed by the altercation with Graham, had worn her out.

She strolled through to her bedroom to put away the journal, but on the way down the hallway, something went curiously wrong with her balance. Head spinning, skin flushing with perspiration, she clung to the wall for long seconds before making a dash for the bathroom.

Minutes later, she rinsed out her mouth and staggered the rest of the way to the bedroom. Up until a few minutes ago she had felt healthy and alert and even more energetic than she normally did. But now that she had finally acknowledged the pregnancy, it seemed her body had decided to catch up on a few symptoms.

Opening her closet door, she put the journal on a shelf. As she did so, she glimpsed a flash of red on the floor of the closet. The dress she had worn the night she had made love with Gabe.

Jaw clenched against another wave of nausea, she retrieved the crumpled dress and sat on the edge of the bed as she waited for her stomach to settle. She should get rid of the dress, get rid of every last association with Gabe, but a part of her couldn't. In her heart of hearts she had been sure that there was a genuine connection between them. What she'd felt and experienced had been too real to be fake.

Annoyed with herself for mooning over the past, Sarah bundled up the red dress, strode to the kitchen and jammed it into the trash.

Another wave of dizziness hit her. She gripped the kitchen counter. She felt so washed out. Would she really be able to do this alone?

Yes. She was determined to be positive. She loved kids and she adored babies. This baby was hers and she would love it within an inch of its life. And concentrating on being a mother rather than a wife or lover suited her perfectly, because she was definitely off men!

Three days later, Sarah went for her ultrasound and stared, hypnotized, at the tiny life growing inside her.

The nurse, a cheerful middle-aged woman, peered at the screen. "Do you want to know the sex of the baby?"

Mesmerized by the clearly discernible arms and legs, the delicate, sleepy face, Sarah instantly said, "Yes."

"You're having a girl."

Sarah's throat tightened and her chest swelled. She was no longer just having a baby; she was having a daughter. She wasn't a crier. She hated crying, but these days tears seemed to well at the drop of a hat.

Smiling, the nurse handed her a wad of tissues. "I'll bet your husband will be pleased. Or did he want a boy?"

Sarah mopped her eyes and blew her nose and tried not to imagine what Gabe might want. "I don't have a husband."

She had developed a new and far more satisfying focus in life than searching for her own personal knight in shining armor. She was determined to learn all she could about childbirth and parenting, to enjoy the changes to her body, the weird cravings and the myriad discomforts. Once the baby was born, she would then put theory into practice and do her very best as a mother.

As she stepped out of the clinic into the glaring heat, the copy of the scan tucked into her bag, a tall lean guy in a suit strolled by, caught her eye and smiled. Automatically, Sarah smiled back, although she didn't know him at all. When she turned her head, he was still watching her, his expression appreciative. With a jolt, she realized he was flirting with her.

Feeling dazed, she unlocked her car. As she slid into the driver's seat she stared at her reflection in the rearview mirror. Her hair, piled as it was into a loose knot, looked tousled and sexy. Her eyes were a deep, pure blue and her skin had a definite glow, as if she was illuminated from within.

With a start she realized that despite the bouts of tiredness and sickness she had never looked better. She wasn't just attractive; she was beautiful. An odd sense of lightness assailed her. For the first time in years, her failed engagements didn't seem important. Gabe's defection was too recent to discount, but that disappointment was, also, no longer crushing.

She felt stronger, more confident. Maybe someday she

would meet a man she could fall for and who would actually fall for her in return, but if that didn't happen, she wasn't going to fret about it. The moment was freeing.

Fastening her seat belt, she started the car and pulled out into traffic. All that was left to resolve was the mystery that surrounded Gabe. She needed to decide whether or not she should allow him to be a part of her baby's life.

And find out what kind of man she had slept with.

Six

Gabe boarded his chartered flight out of Dubai, following his meeting with the construction CEO who had agreed to build the stalled resort complex on Zahir. With Gabe's engagement now formalized, a partial financial settlement had been made into Zahir's accounts and he had been able to transfer the funds, enabling the contractor to resume work.

Xavier was waiting for him in the small jet's luxury cabin. "I've been trying to call you."

Gabe frowned at Xavier's presence as he dropped into a seat beside him. "Cell phone coverage is sketchy in Buraimi, but then you knew that." His gaze sharpened. "What's wrong? Is my father okay?"

"He's fine. Your mother oversees every medical detail. He wouldn't dare not recover."

Gabe found himself grinning. "It's hard to say no to

Mom." The eldest of a family of eight and with a law degree, she had the kind of immovable, steely calm that was hard to mess with.

Xavier was silent for a moment. "Have you been in contact with the Duval woman?"

Gabe froze as he fastened his seat belt for takeoff. *The Duval woman.* As if Sarah was hardened and manipulative, when Gabe knew the opposite to be true.

A picture of the way Sarah had looked, asleep, as he'd quietly dressed and left her cottage in the early morning hours shimmered in his mind. Dark silky hair sliding over one flushed cheek, the outline of her body graceful beneath tangled bedclothes. Every muscle in his body tightened at the vivid memory of what it had felt like to make love with her, a memory he had worked hard to obliterate. "You know I haven't. What's wrong? Is she all right?"

"Uh—nothing's wrong. She's fine." There was a vibrating pause. "Tarik thinks she might be pregnant."

Gabe's heart slammed against the wall of his chest. "I thought we were past the point where there was a possibility of a pregnancy."

It was a thought that had consumed him for some weeks after they had made love. Despite the major complication a pregnancy would have been, a part of him had been crazily, irresistibly attracted to the idea that Sarah could be pregnant with his child. His fingers tightened on the arms of his seat. It had been another indication that, despite his efforts to distance himself from that night with Sarah, he had become entangled in the kind of obsessive emotion he had vowed to avoid.

Xavier shrugged. "I talked to Tarik a couple of hours ago. He practically had a heart attack over the phone."

Gabe dragged at his tie, loosening the knot. "What makes him think she could be pregnant now? It's been over four months."

"A few days ago she walked into the consulate looking for you. Why would she wait so long to do that?"

Gabe's pulse rate lifted a notch at the visual of Sarah confronting Tarik and trying to prise Gabe's contact details out of the man. Gabe would have liked to have seen that battle of wills. Out of nowhere a lightness he hadn't felt for a very long time—*four months and eleven days to be exact*—flooded him, dissolving the tension that had gripped him since spending a large chunk of the marriage settlement funds. Spending the money had sealed him even more completely into the agreement. Worse, it had made *him* feel bought and paid for. "Maybe she just wanted to contact me."

Xavier looked frustrated. "This is why you need a bodyguard. Sometimes, I think you and I live in different universes. The consulate receptionist agreed with Tarik. She thought Sarah *looked* pregnant. Something about a loose blouse and a glow."

"A glow isn't exactly evidence." Although he found himself suddenly ensnared by the idea of Sarah glowing.

"Tarik uncovered something else interesting. Sarah is a descendent of Camille de Vallois's family."

Gabe frowned. "There have got to be thousands of descendants of the de Vallois family. As I recall they were wealthy and prolific."

"Granted, but you don't normally sleep with one of them."

On edge and unsettled, Gabe glanced out of the jet's window as the glittering city and blue-green sea of Dubai receded. He knew what Xavier was getting at.

Maybe Sarah was somehow fascinated by the old legend. Maybe that had been her motivation for sleeping with him. The only difficulty with that scenario was that four months ago Sarah hadn't known he was a sheikh. She had thought he was an employee.

Added to that, she had made no attempt to contact him—until she had walked into the consulate and spoken to Tarik. For long moments, Gabe became lost in the riveting concept of Sarah, *pregnant with his child* and searching for him.

When the jet leveled out, he released his safety belt and retrieved his laptop. He opened the surveillance report that he had commissioned precisely so that Xavier would have no excuse to do so. Although he already knew Sarah's daily routine by heart, including the fact that she had recently joined a gym, changed her hairdresser and added a weekly visit to a beauty therapist. Although, the factual report, fascinating as it was, didn't interest him. It was the photographs attached that he wanted to examine. Snapshots of Sarah going about her normal life, which he had perused more times than he cared to count.

He studied Sarah wearing a sleek red suit and a pair of black-rimmed glasses that made her look corporate and outrageously sexy. Sarah in jeans and a tight sweater going shopping. Another shot where she was wearing a pink dress with a slit on one side that showed off long, tanned legs. He frowned at how increasingly alluring and feminine she looked as the months had gone by. Another more disturbing word popped into his mind—*available*.

He stared at an image of Sara sunbathing on the beach below her cottage, wearing an ultra-skimpy floral bikini. Annoyance gripped him that the PI who took the photo had spied on her when she was practically naked, even though Gabe had ordered it.

He sat back in his seat, jaw tight, annoyed at the whole concept of Sarah being available. Not for the first time it occurred to him that now that Sarah was sexually awakened she would feel free to sleep with other men.

Over his dead body.

Not that he had any rights over Sarah. But if she was pregnant with his child, that would change.

The primitive surge of possessiveness took him by surprise and formed a decision that settled smoothly into place. If Sarah was pregnant, they would work something out. She wouldn't be happy with him. He had left her, and the reason he'd had to do so was still in place. Even so, if there was a child involved, *his child*, he wasn't prepared to walk away.

The ramifications of becoming a father made his heart pound. "I'm going to New Zealand."

Xavier's head jerked up. "You can't. Your wedding date is set and besides, your father will have a stroke if he finds out you had a one-night stand with a twenty-eight-year-old history teacher."

"Twenty-nine," Gabe muttered absently, as he wrote a brief email to his personal assistant to arrange the flight. "She had a birthday a few weeks ago."

"You remembered her birthday?" There was another tense silence. "I knew it. You're falling for her."

Gabe's stomach tightened at the idea of falling in love again. "Love doesn't come into the equation. Sarah's birthday was on the security report."

"You're supposed to be trying to form a relationship with your fiancée. Nadia's smart, beautiful—most men would kill to spend just one night with her."

Gabe pressed the send button.

When the jet landed, Gabe gave in to an uncharacteristic surge of impatience and rang Sarah's number which had been conveniently supplied in the report. With the time and date difference, he didn't know if she would be at home or at work. Long seconds passed. Convinced that she wasn't home, he was about to terminate the call when she picked up, her voice husky and soft as if he'd woken her from sleep.

Gabe's stomach tightened at the thought of Sarah lying in bed. For a moment he felt tongue-tied and almost entirely bereft of English. "Sarah, it's Gabe."

There was an echoing moment of silence. "Gabe who?"

The phone slammed down, the noise loud enough to make him jerk his cell from his ear.

Xavier shot him a horrified look. "You just called her. You should let me deal with this. If she really is pregnant—"

"No. Go near Sarah Duval and you're fired."

"You can't afford a scandal."

Neither could he afford to lose a child.

Gabe called Sarah again. This time the line was engaged, which meant she had left the phone off the hook.

As he stepped outside into the hot Zahiri sun he replayed the all-too-brief conversation, the small silence then the husky curtness of Sarah's voice, as if she was hurt. Even though the evidence was sketchy, he was abruptly certain that Sarah was pregnant.

When he reached the palace, he confirmed his flight and travel arrangements and cleared his schedule for the next four days, including canceling a formal dinner with his fiancée and her parents. Feeling restless and on edge, he stepped onto the balcony of his private suite and paced.

Gripping the still sun-warmed balustrade, he stared at the smooth sweep of sea glimmering beneath the rising moon, buttery gold and huge on the horizon.

Sarah trying to contact him and hitting a wall would explain why she might not feel like talking to him now. In her mind, he had abandoned her. Worse, he had made sure she couldn't find him.

Once Sarah knew his situation, she would understand the need for discretion. She would understand why he'd had to leave her.

She was a mature, educated woman. He was certain they could work it out.

Sarah stared at the shadowy shape of the phone in the dark, shock and a sharp jolt of anger running through her. Dragging tumbled hair from her face, she flicked the switch on her bedside lamp and sat up in bed. Her digital clock said it was close to midnight. She had been asleep for two hours, more or less.

She should feel exhausted, but within the space of a couple of seconds any hint of exhaustion and nausea had been vaporized. She felt alert, her mind crystal clear, the heady charge of adrenaline still zinging through her veins.

On impulse, she took the phone off the hook in case Gabe tried to call again. Maybe that didn't make sense when just days ago she had tried to contact him. But lately she had been on a roller-coaster ride of emotions. One minute she wanted Gabe in her life, the next she recoiled from that particular weakness and didn't want to know. When she had slammed the phone down, it had been a knee-jerk reaction. Now that she'd hung up, she was beginning to wonder what, exactly, Gabe had wanted.

Could he possibly want *her*?

Her heart thumped hard in her chest. Somewhere deep in her abdomen the baby kicked. It was still the merest flutter, but it served to remind her that she had turned a corner with her thinking. She was no longer hurt and vulnerable, and she was over Gabe. There was a whole lot more at stake now than romance and passion.

Tossing the bedclothes aside, she headed for the kitchen. Now that the adrenaline was wearing off, her stomach was starting to turn somersaults again. Her mother had told her to munch on a supply of salty crackers. Since they went perfectly with the other things Sarah craved—pickles and cheese—she had complied.

After piling a plate and making herself a cup of weak tea, because now anything with milk made her stomach queasy, she strolled back to bed. While she worked her way through the crackers and tea she picked up the book of baby names she'd been reading before she'd fallen asleep. So far she had isolated fifty or so names and noted them on a pad on her bedside table.

Yawning, she picked up the pad and grimly ignored the way her mind kept constantly replaying Gabe's few words, the curtness of his voice, which had sent an automatic thrill through her. She began reading through the names she'd so far chosen, mentally linking each of the names with Duval because without a husband that would be her baby's surname.

Hours later, the doorbell chimed, pulling Sarah out of a restless sleep. Belting on her robe, she dragged fingers through her hair and hurried to the door. Her heart sped up at the breathless thought that it could be Gabe, that the reason he had rung was that he was back in New Zealand and wanted to see her again.

Flinging open the door she was met by an enormous basket of fragrant red roses that matched the other bunches filling her porch. A short, bald deliveryman stared at her with undisguised curiosity as he requested her signature for the flowers.

Feeling dazed, confused and angry—because the dark red, deeply fragrant tea roses sent from the same expensive florist that had delivered the last lot, had to be from Gabe—Sarah scribbled her name. When the deliveryman had driven away, she lugged the flowers inside. After a brief search, she found a note attached to the enormous basket filled with roses and boxes of expensive chocolates. When she opened the note she stared blankly at Gabe's full name, which was unexpectedly long, and a number.

A red mist obscured her vision for long seconds. She was finally over him and *now* he decided to provide his phone number? When the mist cleared she found herself out on her deck, the myriad shreds of paper that had once been the note whipping away in the wind.

Legs suddenly weak, she walked back inside and sat down. Her skin kept going hot then cold. Her heart was beating way too fast. Rage, she decided, was definitely not good for the baby. Taking a deep breath, Sarah stared at the small fortune in roses and chocolates. She felt stunned that after all this time Gabe had decided not only to contact her, but apparently, to woo her.

Squashing the weak, wimpy kernel of hope that was unfurling irresistibly inside her, she decided that if Gabe had wanted to send her roses, he was too late.

Just like he was way late sending his contact details.

If he had genuinely cared for her and valued her, he would have given her his number months ago, or showed up at her door. Neither of those things had happened. He hadn't even bothered to check to see if she had gotten pregnant.

She went still inside. Or maybe he finally had.

That would explain the flowers and the sudden desire to be in contact, which, now that she was thinking straight, smacked of damage control.

Mood plummeting, she unconsciously cradled her abdomen, protecting the small life inside. She frowned at the thought that Tarik had seen through her visit to the consulate, that he had been suspicious enough to contact Gabe. The scenario seemed a likely explanation for both the call and the roses, given Gabe's unreliable behavior in disappearing so completely after their one night together.

Pushing to her feet, she decided that under those circumstances she didn't want the roses Gabe had deliberately chosen to remind her of the night they had spent together.

She began ferrying the roses back out onto the porch. She would give them to the pretty little church down the road, and the chocolates could go to the rest home near her school. If Gabe thought he could charm her and buy her off so she wouldn't make trouble, he could think again.

The following morning, just as she'd finished dressing for work, a knock at the door made Sarah tense. Assailed by a curious sense of déjà vu, as if she would find the same deliveryman with a new consignment of flowers, she opened the door. When she saw Gabe, she froze, too shocked to speak.

Before she could slam the door, he jammed his foot in place and planted one large palm flat on the door, holding it open. "I just need a few minutes of your time."

Chest tight, heart pounding, she did her best not to be mesmerized by his amber gaze or his fascinating scar. She was fiercely glad she had made an effort with her hair, which was wound up in a sexy knot that showed off the new caramel streaks her hairdresser had insisted she try. She was also wearing a high-waisted pale turquoise dress that was not only short enough to show off her legs, but also cleverly disguised the thickening at her waist. "You sound like a salesman."

"Technically, I'm an accountant, not a salesman."

The freely given fact about his life startled her enough that she almost weakened and let him in before she remembered that was one of the ways he had gotten her before. He had told her he had gone to Harvard to study business and she had been silly enough to think that with the prosaic nature of both of their occupations they had something in common. Determined to ignore the fascination of a man who looked like a battle-hardened warrior but had an affinity for figures—*and who had been a breathtaking lover*—she kept a firm grip on the door. "Why are you here?"

His gaze locked with hers for a burning moment that transported her back to a pitch-black night, rain pounding on her window, a breathless tangle of sheets and the heat of his skin against hers...

"I had to see you."

For a split second she was startled enough by the flat, declarative timbre of his voice that she almost weakened.

It almost seemed as if he had missed her and really had desperately needed to see her.

He frowned at her stubborn lack of response. "Did you get my roses?"

"I did."

"Let me guess, you gave them away."

"They were not exactly a happy reminder, since you left without saying goodbye and haven't bothered to keep in touch."

"But you knew I had to leave."

And she'd known that there were no promises made, on either side. Avoiding his gaze and concentrating instead on a point somewhere to the right of one mouth-watering cheekbone, she tried to nurture the fiery anger that flared whenever she considered just how much time had passed. But it was a fact that the night had been what it was: two people recognizing a mutual attraction and agreeing to sleep together. The only problem was she had been emotionally involved from the beginning.

"Thanks for reminding me." She glanced at her watch, which had a pretty turquoise band to match her dress. She tried to look as if she really was in a hurry even though the school term had ended days ago, and all she needed to do for the day was prep work for next term. "Now if that's all you have to say, I think you should go. I need to leave for work in just a few minutes." Besides that, she was beginning to feel nauseous and dizzy all over again.

Gabe's gaze seemed to pierce her, pinning her in place. "You're still working?"

His voice sounded oddly muffled, as if it were coming from a distance, although the thing that concerned her most was that something weird was happening to her vision. Vaguely, she realized she had lost her grip on the door and that Gabe had taken advantage of that fact by swinging it wide-open. Stumbling slightly, she reached for the solidity of the wall. "Why wouldn't I be?"

"I checked with your school. The receptionist said the school holidays had started."

Outrage that he had been sneaking around, poking into her life was tempered by a scary delight that he had wanted to do so. Suddenly, Gabe was close enough that she could feel the warmth of his body. It seemed the most natural thing in the world to clutch at one shoulder in a bid to stay upright. "This doesn't mean I've forgiven you." She tried to be crisp and stern, but the words sounded muffled.

His arm came around her waist. Just as everything faded to black she heard him mutter, "Damn, you are pregnant with my child."

When she came around she was lying on her couch in the sitting room and Gabe was in her house.

Tense and on edge that he had slipped past all of her defenses she cautiously levered into a sitting position. Apparently the sluggish maneuver had been way too fast, because her head started to spin again.

Gabe handed her a glass of water, which she would have refused on principle if she wasn't so thirsty all the time, and right now her mouth was as dry as a desert. Draining the glass, she set it down on the coffee table and glared at him. She was suddenly glad she had gotten rid of the roses, and hadn't allowed herself to weaken and keep any. "I don't remember inviting you into my house."

"That would be because you were too busy fainting." He loomed over her, the dark jeans and loose shirt he wore making him look lean and muscular and vital, while she felt limp and rung out. "I found your doctor's number by the phone and made an appointment." He consulted his watch. "If we leave now we might just make it."

"I don't need a doctor, there's nothing wrong with me—"

"You're pregnant."

She crossed her arms over her chest, which successfully minimized her tiny bump. "What makes you think I'm pregnant?"

Gabe dragged distracted fingers through his hair, making him look disheveled, younger and infinitely cuter. "Tarik."

Sarah's jaw tightened. That little man. It was a further confirmation she should never have gone near the consulate.

Gabe's gaze flashed broodingly over her. "Are you pregnant?"

Heat filled her cheeks. She couldn't lie. No matter how much she wanted to conceal the truth and keep the baby her secret. "Yes."

Seven

Forty minutes later Sarah was sitting in Evelyn's office while Gabe stood at a window, staring out at a slice of suburban Kilbirnie.

Evelyn strolled back into the room, throwing Gabe a glance filled with thinly veiled curiosity. Despite the fact that Sarah was still unhappy with Gabe and the way he had bulldozed her into seeing Evelyn, she couldn't help but feel a tiny glow of satisfaction that he was with her. If nothing else, it proved to Evelyn that while Sarah might have had bad luck with men in the past, at least this time she had chosen one who was certifiably gorgeous.

Evelyn handed Sarah a slip of paper with the results of her urine test. "It's not the best news. Your blood sugar is high, which makes you pre-diabetic. That accounts for the dizzy spells. It happens to some women in pregnancy."

Sarah stared at the test result. "That would also explain the thirst."

Evelyn gave Sarah a sharp look. "From now on you need to call me about anything unusual that happens. You'll need to manage your diet and I want you to have regular blood tests." Rummaging in her desk she found a diet sheet, which Gabe commandeered.

Gabe sent her a narrow-eyed glance then began asking Evelyn rapid-fire questions that indicated he had studied up on pregnancy. Evelyn crossed one elegant leg over the other and sat back in her chair, visibly preening as she smoothly answered his every question. Beginning to feel sidelined, even though she was the patient, Sarah pointedly got to her feet.

Evelyn stopped midsentence and blushed. Gabe instantly rose and cupped Sarah's elbow, in case she needed steadying. She didn't, she felt fine now, but it wasn't such a bad thing for Evelyn to understand that Gabe was here for her. Although the fact that Sarah should want to make any kind of statement at all was ridiculous because it smacked of jealousy.

When they reached Gabe's Jeep, he helped her up into the passenger seat. "You don't need to be jealous."

Sarah busied herself fastening her seat belt to disguise the fact that she was blushing furiously. "Why on earth would I be jealous?"

There was an odd, tense silence then Gabe closed her door with a soft *thunk*, walked around the bonnet and slid behind the wheel.

Enclosed in the intimacy of the Jeep the one burning question she hadn't had time to ask pushed to the fore. Jaw taut, she stared at Gabe's faintly hawkish profile as he turned into traffic. "Why are you here?"

He had already said he'd suspected she was pregnant, but she would have thought that news would make him run, not come back to her.

"If you're pregnant with my child that changes things."

"What things, exactly?"

He braked for a set of traffic lights. "I'm engaged to be married."

Fury channeled through her. If she could have found something to break in that moment, she would have broken it. Her reaction upset her. This unstable, passionate creature she seemed to be turning into wasn't her. She was normally calm and collected; she thought things through. She did not fly into rages. "I knew it. Although my guess was that you were married."

His brows jerked together. "I do not have affairs."

"But you cheated on your fiancée."

"I wasn't engaged at the time."

Her heart pounded even harder. What Gabe had said should have made the situation better, so why did it feel worse? "Let me get this right. You had sex with me then you went back to Zahir and got engaged. At least that explains why you never bothered to call."

He'd had more exciting options than a twenty-eight-year-old history teacher.

Her jaw set. "If you got engaged so quickly, you must have known your fiancée already."

Gabe pulled into her driveway. "No. It was an arranged marriage."

Horror transfixed her. "So that's why you slept with me. It was a last fling." She dragged at her seat belt, trying to unfasten it, but the mechanism wouldn't cooperate.

Gabe half turned in his seat, frowning, which only made him look more gorgeous. "It wasn't like that."

She fought against the lure of his fierce, warrior's gaze. "How was it then?"

There was a vibrating silence. "You know exactly how it was between us."

He tried to help her with the seat belt. Incensed, she pushed his hands away. "I can do this. I'm used to doing things on my own."

"You're not on your own any longer."

Even though she didn't want to feel anything at all for Gabe, his flat statement sent a dangerous hope spiraling through her. He had used the word *was* with his marriage, as if it was in the past tense. Added to that fact, he *could* have stayed on Zahir and simply ignored her. Instead he was here, *because* she was pregnant, taking charge, getting involved.

She stared at him, feeling crazily emotional, still angry but also on the verge of tears. "So how was it, exactly, between us?"

"Like this." Gabe cupped her jaw and out of nowhere the humming, tingling attraction she'd fought to suppress burst into fiery life.

He lowered his mouth, and foolishly she tossed away any thoughts of being sensible and controlled and let him kiss her.

Gabe closed Sarah's front door behind him and followed her into her sitting room. The heat that had surged through him at the kiss was still pulling every muscle in his body taut. But, aware of how badly he had mishandled things so far, he grimly controlled the need that had hit him.

As she opened French doors to let a cooling breeze in, he noticed a pad on the coffee table. Picking it up, he examined a list of names. "Tiffany, Tanesha, Tempeste…" He glanced at Sarah as she strolled out of the kitchen with two glasses of water in her hands. "Are these names for the baby?"

Setting the water down, she snatched the pad from his fingers. "They're just ideas."

"Any favorites so far?"

She snapped the pad closed. "It's just at the formulation stage. Names are important. You can't just choose any old thing."

While Sarah jammed the pad into the drawer of an antique sideboard, Gabe strolled to the French doors that opened onto a tiny deck and stared at the view over Wellington's harbor and hills. The fact that he was going to be a father hit him again, even more strongly than when Sarah had fainted. The situation was unbelievably complicated because it involved his commitment to Nadia and his country. But Sarah carrying his child changed everything.

He desperately needed to order his thoughts, to think like a Sheikh of Zahir and control the dangerous, possessive emotions that surged through him.

He needed to provide for Sarah and the baby, therefore the only possible solution was marriage. In order to marry Sarah, he would have to end his current engagement and solve Zahir's financial problems another way.

Given that his father would finally be a grandfather, and with the possibility of a future male heir to the sheikhdom in the pipeline, Gabe did not foresee that his father would hold to his stance against foreign investment.

His mind made up, Gabe turned from the view. Sarah was busy plumping cushions and tidying magazines. As she straightened, sexy tendrils of dark hair clung to her flushed cheeks, making her look both gorgeous and vulnerable. The light fabric of her dress swung against her abdomen, giving him his first real glimpse of the gentle swell of her belly. Another surge of fierce possessiveness hit him, and he frowned. Zahir's financial situation, tricky as it was, would not be a problem, but if he wasn't vigilant, what he was feeling could be. Marriage was a solution, but it could not be an unstable, emotionally based, marriage. Like the arrangement with Nadia Fortier, this too would be a marriage of convenience.

"So," he said carefully, "you're having a girl."

Sarah took a deep breath, repressing an uncharacteristic flash of temper that Gabe was extracting information from her about the baby before she was quite ready to tell him. "That's what showed up on the scan."

A curious emotion darkened his expression. Was it disappointment? Instantly she was up in arms on behalf of her child, a female baby who no doubt, in his country, was not as celebrated as a male child.

"Evelyn said you have a copy of the ultrasound. I'd like to see it."

He watched the video file through without a word then almost immediately replayed it again.

He closed her laptop. "The baby changes things. We need to make arrangements."

Her heart pounded out of control at his words, because in that moment she realized he was going to suggest the one thing she had wanted from him over four months ago: a relationship.

Although she wasn't sure how she felt about any of that now. Half of her was melting inside, teetering on the brink of hope, the other half still blazing mad that he had left her alone for so long. "What did you have in mind?"

He extracted a platinum card from his pocket.

The temper she had been trying to keep a lid on spilled out. "If you think you're going to start paying my bills, you can think again."

Before he could stop her, she grabbed the card, marched out on the deck and threw it over the side, down onto the lawn below. "I don't want your money, so you can forget it. Forget me—"

"I can't." With a swift movement, he pulled her toward him so that she found herself plastered against his chest.

His mouth came down on hers. She could have ducked her head or pulled away, but her precarious mood had taken another swing, from fury straight to desire. She didn't like what was happening. She didn't want his money. But after the sweet, tender moments in his Jeep, which had spun back the clock, with every cell in her body she wanted him to kiss her again.

Long, dizzying minutes later, she pulled free. Her mouth tingled; her body was on fire. She loved that he still wanted her, but they had been in this place once before. That time she had gotten pregnant. Before anything else life-changing happened, she had to be clear about whether or not they had a chance at the one thing that was important to her in a relationship: love. "Where, exactly, are you in this scenario?"

She finally identified the glimpse of emotion in his eyes that had baffled her from the moment she'd first seen him at her door—not quite cool detachment, but wariness. "I'm proposing marriage."

Her legs went weak at his blunt statement. "What about your fiancée?"

"First I'll need to go back to Zahir and terminate the agreement with Nadia."

The word *terminate* sent a chill through her. Had he not felt anything for his fiancée? At the name Nadia, alarm bells rang. Sarah walked back inside and sat down, her legs feeling wobbly. She had read something about an engagement in Zahir online. Suddenly the way Tarik and the consulate receptionist had behaved in protecting Gabe began to make perfect sense.

Gabe had said he was an accountant. It was possible he simply worked for the sheikh as part of his business team, but she was beginning to think Gabe was something more than that.

She remembered the piece of paper with Gabe's full name on it, which she had ripped up and tossed away before she'd read it properly. She thought she might have glimpsed the name Kadin somewhere. Her stomach plunged as a wild notion occurred to her, a notion that made sense of all the cloak-and-dagger behavior surrounding Gabe's identity and whereabouts. "Who are you, exactly?"

"My full name is Sheikh Kadin Gabriel ben Kadir. I'm not the ruling sheikh. That's my father, but I will rule one day."

Eight

Gabe, *Sheikh Kadin Gabriel ben Kadir*, insisted he take her to lunch while they talked over the situation. Too shocked by his announcement to refuse, Sarah found herself courteously helped into a gleaming Jeep. As Gabe pulled away from the curb, she took better note of the vehicle, which was brand-new and luxurious. Now, too late, all the subtle clues about him registered, like the way he had spoken to Tarik—not as a subordinate, but as someone in command. The fact that he'd had accommodations at the consulate, and that he'd gone to Harvard. Of course he was a member of Zahir's ruling family.

His gaze touched on hers. "How do you feel?"

"I'll feel fine when you explain why you didn't let me know who you are."

She noticed they were heading away from the city into the wilder hill country.

Gabe stopped for an intersection. "The same way you didn't let me know you're an ancestor of Camille's?"

She flushed at the quiet statement, although it wasn't as if she had concealed *her* identity. "How did you find that out? No, wait, let me take a wild guess. The son of a sheikh, with bodyguards and an impenetrable security force field around you? I'm betting you had me investigated."

"We had unprotected sex—"

"So you had to find out exactly who you had gotten entangled with." A horrified thought occurred to her. "I suppose you thought I was some kind of adventurer, maybe even a journalist."

He turned into a very beautiful, secluded drive that, from the signage, led to an exclusive private resort. "I didn't tell you I was a sheikh because I thought all we would share was the one night. And I knew you were exactly what you said, a history teacher, but the investigative process went ahead because security protocols still needed to be satisfied."

"And you were worried about a pregnancy." Her fingers tightened on the strap of her handbag as he parked beneath a shaded portico and a uniformed valet opened her door. "If you had left me your contact details, you could have saved yourself the trouble. I would have told you."

There was an uncomfortable silence as she climbed out of the Jeep. Gabe handed the keys to the valet. They were shown to a restaurant with a fabulous cliff-top view of the ocean. As he took a seat opposite her, she glanced around at the other diners. They were without exception beautiful, very well-groomed people with perfect tans. Most of them, even the men, were dressed in shades of white and cool pastels. Dressed as she was in vibrant turquoise, with her hair wisping damply around her face, all of the elegant restraint made her feel overly bright. It shouldn't have mattered, but the restaurant suddenly made her see the gulf in lifestyles that existed between her and Gabe.

"What's wrong?"

She frowned, hating that she was actually allowing herself to be stressed-out by surroundings that were formal and just a little pretentious. "I can't relax in this place. What if I need to be sick?" Just the thought made her feel queasy.

His gaze sharpened. "Do you feel unwell?"

"A little. It comes on suddenly."

The waiter who was delivering beautiful leather-bound, gold-embossed menus, blanched. Within minutes Gabe had canceled their reservation and the valet had delivered the Jeep to the portico. Gabe opened the passenger-side door, but instead of simply helping her up, he clasped her waist and boosted her into her seat.

Breathlessly, she released her hold on his shoulders. "I could have gotten in by myself."

"Since we're engaged, I thought we should start getting used to the idea of being a couple."

She blinked at the subtle way he was trying to bulldoze her into agreeing to marry him. "I haven't said yes yet."

He released her, but there was a curious relief in his gaze as if he liked that she wasn't jumping at his proposal. Although, she wasn't so sure *she* liked the idea that if they were to marry he would be happy with a certain distance in their relationship.

When Gabe slid behind the wheel, she directed him to

a small beachside café in Lyall Bay that was casual and cheerful, with enough background noise that they could have a conversation without being overheard.

Gabe shrugged out of his jacket and dragged off his tie. With the sea breeze ruffling his hair, he looked breathtakingly handsome. While they ate he asked questions about her family and supplied details about his. It shouldn't have surprised her that he knew her cousin, Laine—who had sent Sarah the journal—and who was married to the Sheikh of Jahir, a distant relative of Gabe's. But the fact that he was close to that branch of her family was reassuring. As big a leap as it was, it somehow made it easier to imagine being married to the next Sheikh of Zahir.

Marriage to Gabe. For a split second, her heart pounded out of control. Her last two attempts at getting married had both ended in disaster and she couldn't quite believe that this one would work out.

When they'd finished, Gabe suggested they take a walk on the beach. When he clasped her hand in a loose hold, a dangerous thrill went through her because even if Gabe didn't feel the romance of what they were doing, she did, and she was afraid of being too happy. Her experience of happiness was that once you thought you had it in your grasp, it was snatched away. "Are you certain you want marriage?" Taking a breath, she offered him an alternative that would dispense with the need for a relationship altogether. "Sharing custody is an option."

Gabe stopped and pulled her into a loose hold, his gaze oddly fierce. He hooked a loose strand of hair behind one ear, the small possessive gesture sending another sharp little thrill through her. "We're both mature, educated people. There's no reason we can't have a... successful marriage."

Sarah frowned at the way Gabe framed marriage, as if it was something one had to be qualified for, even while his measured response reassured. After all, with a baby on the way, if she was going to marry, she needed her husband to be responsible and trustworthy.

When Gabe dipped his head, she allowed the kiss and tried not to love it too much. Reluctantly, she planted her palms on his chest and kept her gaze fixed on the pulse jumping along the side of his jaw, because if she looked at his mouth or into his eyes, she would kiss him again. "We can't make love until...things are settled."

"Until you've agreed to marry me."

Her chin came up and this time she met his gaze. "Yes."

It was a fact that they couldn't get engaged until Gabe had ended his current arrangement. And Sarah knew better than anyone, a lot could go wrong between an engagement and the altar.

Two weeks later, Sarah, finding her state of relationship limbo a little too lonely after Gabe had gone back to Zahir went online to indulge her new favorite hobby, searching out news about Zahir and the ruling family.

During the two days they had spent together, they had eaten out and gone for walks. Gabe had sketched in brief details of his life, including the startling fact that he was a widower. When he'd flown out they'd agreed to stay in contact by phone. However, he hadn't called for a whole week now, and the silence after the long, cozy calls had her worried even though he had mentioned the possibility of sketchy cell phone coverage. With time passing she was beginning to have flashbacks to the silent, empty months that had followed the one night they had spent together.

Worse, she was beginning to think she had been foolishly optimistic in trusting that Gabe would choose her over Nadia Fortier. She needed to know more about his engagement, even if it was just internet gossip. And she needed to know more about the wife he had lost.

Her mother, who made a habit of dropping in unexpectedly, walked through the door, just as Sarah found a reference site. Hannah, who was naturally suspicious of Gabe, paused beside the screen, which was currently displaying a dated story about Gabe's engagement. "If you were having a boy, he would have put a ring on your finger immediately."

Sarah blinked at the flamboyant outfit her mother was wearing. A saffron-yellow dress over blue leggings. Cobalt-blue earrings made her short, spiked blond hair look even more startling. "What makes you say that?"

Hannah fished in her bag and placed cold cups of fresh fruit smoothies on the table. "Stands to reason. The sheikhdom is patriarchal, so only male children can rule, specifically the first male child. If the baby was a boy, he would be the next sheikh."

Sarah picked up her smoothie, took a sip and decided she would have to tell her mother the truth. "Gabe proposed. I'm the one who hasn't agreed, yet."

Hannah stared at her as if she'd just landed from Mars. "I thought you wanted to marry him?"

"I do." But only if Gabe truly valued her and their baby girl. Only if there was the possibility of love.

Hannah dug two salad rolls out from the depths of her bag and plunked them down on the table. "You've wanted to get married for years. Now you're dangling one of the most eligible, *hot* men on the planet?" she sat down and peeled plastic wrap off a roll. "Sometimes I don't know you."

With difficulty Sarah refrained from pointing out that her mother had just expressed two conflicting views about Gabriel. "Is it such a bad thing to not want to make another mistake?"

Too irritable to eat, she searched a site she normally never bothered with, because it was full of the kind of magazine articles and sensationalized gossip that normally didn't interest her. Moments later she found a short article posted just two days ago. She stared at a photo of Nadia Fortier in a skimpy bikini lying on a dazzling beach, a glass of champagne in one hand.

Nadia was accompanied by a broad-shouldered, dark-haired man who had his back to the camera. Sarah's heart stuttered to a halt in her chest. It looked like Gabe, and the text confirmed it. Apparently, Gabe and Nadia were spending some quality alone-time at a secret hideaway in Tuscany before the wedding.

Sarah pushed to her feet so fast the chair went flying. So much for angsting about Gabe's dead wife, when it was the gorgeous young fiancée she should have been worrying about.

At the periphery of her vision she was aware of her mother, staring at her with a frown. Sarah righted the chair, too focused on Gabe's blatant betrayal to try to appear normal or calm.

She had begun to trust him again. She had liked his phone calls, especially when he'd called late at night and she'd been snuggled up in bed.

His behavior during their two days together had made

her think he would be a wonderful father. She had seen it in his absorption with all the aspects of her pregnancy. She had loved it when he had fussed over her when she'd felt tired and ordered takeout. The next day he had insisted on stocking her pantry with healthy low-fat food.

But it had all been a smokescreen. He had lied. He hadn't gone back to Zahir to make any kind of arrangement that would benefit her and the baby. He was spending his time wining and dining his beautiful, slim fiancée at some swanky Italian *castello*.

And in that moment Sarah knew why she had been both ecstatic and miserable for the past two weeks. It wasn't just that her hormones had been running riot. She had been busy falling head over heels in love with Gabe all over again—the father of her child and a man who would be marrying someone else in three months' time.

Her mind was spinning. She could scarcely believe how completely Gabe had deceived her. Although this kind of betrayal had happened to her before.

Sarah glared at the grainy, blurred photo, which had obviously been taken with a telephoto lens, and clicked on the mouse to close the site. Caught between fierce anger and utter misery, she walked out onto her small deck, barely registering the humid grayness of the day, which was a whole lot different from the arching blue sky and blistering heat of Tuscany. A brisk wind laced with spits of rain flattened her dress against her body and sent her hair flying. So much for her improbable daydreams of moving to Zahir, of Gabe really and truly falling for her once they had time to spend together.

Trying to stay calm, she walked back into her sitting room, which was cluttered with baby paraphernalia: a pretty white bassinet and piles of bright fluffy toys. She picked up a pink bear Gabe had sent, and which was so ridiculously large it occupied its own chair. Fury boiling over, she marched the bear through to the spare room and jammed it in the closet, out of sight.

Slamming the door, she leaned against it, breathing hard.

Hannah, who had been making tea in the kitchen poked her head around the corner, looking concerned. "Are you all right?"

"Yes." No. "Eat your lunch, I'll be out soon. Promise."

Maybe the photo and the article hadn't portrayed the absolute truth. She had to stop reacting emotionally and start operating on the facts. The only way she could reliably gather facts was to go to Zahir.

Returning to the computer, she found a travel site and searched for fares. Once she had made bookings, she felt shaky but glad she had acted. She had lost two potential husbands because she had not cared enough to actively claim her man. But this time was different. Her heart and her baby's future happiness were both at stake.

She was over sitting quietly at home. Whether Gabe liked it or not, she was joining him on Zahir.

In just two days' time she would no longer be Sheik Kadin Gabriel ben Kadir's guilty secret.

Nine

Gabe walked into Gerald Fortier's office in Paris flanked by Xavier and Hasim, Gabe's personal assistant, just ten minutes short of midnight. They were all wearing the formal business attire of Zahir: well-cut suits, white shirts with ties and white kaffiyeh headdresses fastened with black rope *agals*. Kadin's *agal* was differentiated by the badge of his family, a lion rampant.

This was a meeting he had demanded ten days ago, after he'd received information that Nadia was not staying with an aunt in the South of France as her family had claimed but instead was shacked up with an Italian count in Tuscany. Fortier, clearly aware that Gabe could declare the marriage contract null and void on the basis of it, had ducked the meeting until now.

Gabe presented his ID to a doorman who seemed mesmerized by his scar, the headdress and the entourage.

Seconds later, they stepped into the elevator to the penthouse suite. When they emerged, Fortier was standing at a large plate-glass window, staring out at the spectacular view of Paris at night and the glittering landmark of the Eiffel Tower.

Fortier turned to face Gabe. As always the older man's expression was smooth and urbane, although when he noted the kaffiyehs, something usually reserved for formal or ceremonial occasions, his dark gaze became wary. He consulted his wristwatch, as if he were in a hurry to leave despite the late hour. "You're lucky you caught me, I have a plane to catch."

"To Tuscany?"

Fortier's expression paled as he indicated they should sit down on the comfortable black leather chairs grouped around a coffee table.

Gabe ignored the offer of a seat. He produced a photocopy of a snippet from a French newspaper where Fortier had stated Gabe was holidaying in Tuscany with his daughter. "You know very well I've been in New York and the United Arab Emirates for the past few days."

Fortier placed the page on the coffee table. "It was a solution. Damage control."

"Only if I still wished to marry your daughter."

Fortier stiffened. "There's no reason our agreement can't stand, especially since a substantial partial payment has been made. The agreement is sealed."

"Not any longer."

Fortier plowed on as if Gabe hadn't spoken. "Of course I can compensate you for a certain…breach of the conditions."

The breach being that Nadia was no longer a virgin and, according to the report Gabe had received, hadn't been for quite some time. Gabe also happened to know that Gerald Fortier had been well aware of that fact when he'd signed the marriage agreement.

Until Gabe had spent that one night with Sarah he hadn't realized just how much integrity in his relationships mattered. "I'm afraid," he said softly, "that part of the agreement is nonnegotiable."

There was a small, tense silence. Fortier's gaze flickered over Xavier and Hasim, who were flanking Gabe in an unmistakably military fashion. Fortier jerked at his tie. "In that case I will require immediate and full repayment of the funds you've received."

Gabe kept his expression neutral. With the small constitutional change Gabe's father had made, repaying Fortier would not be a problem. "You'll have the money as soon as the finance I've arranged with a New York bank is approved. In return I'll make certain that the information that Nadia is having an affair is not leaked to the press."

Fortier's face went dead white then flushed bright red. "Thank you."

The man's momentary loss of control informed Gabe that, for all his faults, Fortier cared about his daughter's reputation.

Turning on his heel, Gabe led the way to the elevator. Within an hour he was back on the small jet he had chartered. The engagement was now null and void, although he couldn't allow himself to celebrate just yet.

His mother was quietly over the moon that Gabe wanted to marry a New Zealand girl and that there was a grandchild already on the way. Breaking the news to the general populace of Zahir, however, would be a more delicate issue.

Preparations for the wedding were almost complete. Invitations had been sent and hotels had been booked out. The cancellation was a matter that would have to be handled by the public relations experts. Although Gabe was certain that once the tourism minister got hold of the fact that Sarah was a descendent of Camille de Vallois, he would leverage the information into a wave of public approval that would smooth over the fact that he was changing brides.

Grinning at the thought that finally there was a practical application for the romantic story of Kadin and Camille, he dropped into a leather seat. Taking out his cell he logged the string of missed calls from Sarah and tried to call her before the jet taxied onto the runway. It was something he hadn't been able to do while in the remote hill country of Buraimi.

When the call went to voice mail and Sarah didn't respond on her cell, he checked his messages. There were two from Sarah. He listened to the cool, low register of her voice as she requested that he contact her. The last message had been left four days ago.

Grimly, he tried calling Sarah again. When there was no reply, he turned his cell off. If there was an issue with the pregnancy, Sarah would have said so in one of the two messages she'd left, and which he hadn't been able to pick up because there was no cell phone service in Buraimi.

Xavier, who had been talking to the pilot, dropped into the seat beside him. "A problem?"

"Nothing I can't handle."

He'd been away from Sarah for two weeks. Two weeks too long. He had missed her.

His jaw tightened at just how much, because a part

of him didn't want to be subject to the whims of desire and the havoc it could wreak.

While the other part of him couldn't wait to have her back in his arms.

Zahir glittered beneath the scorching noonday sun as Sarah paid the bellhop who had delivered her bags then strolled through the cool, spacious hotel suite she had reserved for the next ten days.

After changing into a white cotton dress, she collected her camera and a notebook and took the elevator to the ground floor. Evelyn had reluctantly given her the all-clear to travel after her blood test had been much improved. Now that Sarah had moderated her diet the dizzy spells had abated and she was feeling much more energetic.

She strolled out onto one of Zahir's narrow, quirky streets, loving the heat and the quaint lime-washed buildings clinging to the hills and cliffs that rimmed most of the bay. Zahir was also home to a cluster of beautiful resorts, all owned by the sheikh. The resorts had all been built to blend with the historic old city and looked more like ancient villas and palaces than actual hotels.

Lifting her camera, she took several shots to catch the panoramic view then started down the steep hill to the main street, which ran along the shoreline and was famous for its cafes and souks. As she strolled, she frowned at the sight of a sign in Zahiri and English congratulating Sheikh Kadin on his upcoming marriage. Festive ribbons and lights strung across the streets and huge planters spilled richly scented flowers in celebration. Her mood dropping, she lifted her camera and snapped a photo. If she had wanted confirmation that the wedding had not been called off, this was it.

The zeal she'd had to gather information then fling it at Gabe when next he contacted her abruptly flatlined. It was all very well playing detective, but it didn't feel so good when the results seemed to confirm her worst fears. Feeling deflated, she stopped to buy a cold drink at a small bustling café.

The pretty English waitress who served her was breezy and chatty and happy enough to answer the few halting questions Sarah asked.

She set a cool drink in front of Sarah. "Almost no one's actually seen Nadia. I think her family are keeping her under wraps until the day, you know? Although, if you go online you'll find a few photos. She's young and drop-dead gorgeous. Apparently she used to be on social media until the engagement was set in concrete, then—" she made a slicing gesture across her throat "—nothing."

Sarah took a desultory sip of her drink, which was a delicious sweet-sour concoction of plum and lemon, laden with ice. "I guess Gabe—the sheikh, can be controlling."

The waitress gave her a disbelieving look. "I was talking about Nadia's father. Kadin is a whole different kettle of fish, a total babe. A lot of women have tried to entice him into marriage, but since he lost his wife, he hasn't been interested." She shrugged, her gaze turning soft and a little dreamy. "I guess he must have really loved her. Rumor is that's why he agreed to an arranged marriage this time around. He can't have Jasmine, but he needs an heir. Oh, and of course, the Fortiers are rich. I'm guessing that helps."

Sarah set her glass down, suddenly losing any desire

for the drink or the conversation that had gone with it.
The pipe dream that she could have a marriage, maybe
even true and lasting love, with Gabe was receding fast.
She had thought Nadia Fortier was the only problem but,
according to the waitress, Nadia came in a bad second
because he was still in love with a first wife that he'd
almost never mentioned!

Tired and on edge after the night flight from Paris,
Gabe negotiated Zahir's main street traffic, his temper
on a tight rein as he noted the displays of ribbons and
strings of colored lights, and the congratulatory messages that were appearing despite the wedding date being
weeks away. His phone vibrated. He took the call while
he waited at a traffic light.

Xavier, who had been met by his wife when they'd
landed, sounded weary. "An Italian tabloid has gotten
hold of the story that you're supposed to be holed up in
a *castello* in Tuscany with Nadia. What do you want
me to do?"

"What we always do, nothing." With any luck the fact
that he had openly spent two days in New York and the
past week in Dubai would discredit the gossip. "Any luck
getting hold of Sarah?"

"Same luck you had. She's not answering her phone.
Tarik went around. She wasn't home."

The sense of unease that had gripped him when he
hadn't been able to get hold of Sarah before the flight
from Paris returned full force. He tensed at the thought
that she might have had another fainting episode. Maybe
the diabetes had worsened and she'd been admitted to
the hospital. He had thought she was okay now that her

diet was under control. But it was always possible she had suffered some other complication.

Suddenly the distance between them, a distance he had thought he needed in order to control his own emotions—was a barrier he was no longer prepared to tolerate. As soon as he could locate Sarah, he would make arrangements to have her fly out to Zahir. Jaw taut, he instructed Xavier to keep trying to locate Sarah, including checking the hospitals.

A thought occurred. Sarah had told him the man she'd dated the night she and Gabe met at the consulate, Southwell, had once broken into her house. It was possible he'd come back to harass her again. "And check on Southwell."

Even though Sarah had finished with him, Gabe couldn't rule out the fact that Southwell might try to make another move on Sarah. "One more thing, ask Tarik to check the airport manifests just in case Sarah has left the country."

Gabe hung up as the light changed. He inched forward in the heavy traffic. He was probably overreacting. It was possible Sarah had gone away for a few days, although that didn't explain why she hadn't called or answered her phone. Wherever she was, she would still have a cell phone, which meant she was choosing to be out of contact with him.

He frowned at that thought. Usually, Sarah was more than happy to talk for as long as he wanted to stay on the phone. For her to close off all communication meant something had happened. His fingers tightened on the wheel. At a guess, she had picked up on the scandal brewing around Nadia.

The fact that Sarah had reacted by closing him out,

the kind of manipulative tactic Jasmine had often used, should have had him backing off from the relationship. Instead, he thought grimly, it was having the opposite effect and for good reason. Even though he was certain Sarah was emotionally involved with him, she had also made it crystal clear that vulnerability was optional: she could get along without him.

Gabe braked as a truck pulled out from the curb and brooded on the prospect that Sarah might have made the kind of bold, declarative decision she seemed prone to make and ditched him. Caught in traffic, surrounded by the hubbub of a hot Zahiri day, Gerald Fortier's manipulation still leaving a bad taste, it was an odd moment for Gabe to reach a point of absolute clarity about the future.

He had made a mistake in leaving Sarah alone for so long. It was a mistake he would not make again. Now that he had terminated the agreement with Fortier, he was going to insist he and Sarah get engaged immediately.

Gabe had almost reached the palace when Xavier rang with the news that Sarah had left New Zealand and landed in Zahir that morning.

Fierce satisfaction curled through Gabe. Sarah hadn't run from him, she was here, on his island. And there could be only one reason: she had come after him.

She loved him, he was suddenly certain of it. Nothing else explained why she had let him make love to her in the first place and then been willing to take him back, even after he had left her flat.

The thought that Sarah was committed enough to come to Zahir in search of him should have sounded alarm bells, but the relief that she had done so somehow canceled out any recoil he should feel. He had dreaded Jasmine's brand of intense, cloying love, but he found he did not feel the same way about Sarah. If Sarah was in love with him then, as far as he was concerned, that provided a counterbalance to her strong will and a measure of certainty he needed. The desire to consolidate their relationship with marriage settled even more firmly into place. He registered that Xavier was still talking.

"Uh—as it happens Southwell is also on Zahir, but they're not staying at the same hotel and they didn't travel together."

Frowning at the irritating specter of Southwell, Gabe did a U-turn and headed for the hotel. He braked for a stream of pedestrians crossing to a waterfront souk. A woman dressed in white with dark, caramel-streaked hair arranged in a sexy knot caught his eye. He couldn't see her face, but something about the confident feminine stride spun him back to a stormy night in Wellington.

Traffic moved at a snail's pace as the woman in white paused at the entrance to the souk. Hitching the strap of her handbag a little higher on her shoulder, she checked her watch. Gabe's heart slammed against the wall of his chest. He would recognize the elegant shape of her cheekbones, the smoky slant of her eyes and that delicate, faintly imperious nose anywhere. It was Sarah.

There was no place to park on the congested street, so he backed up a few feet, waited on traffic then turned down a narrow lane that ran down one side of the souk. There was no official parking, just dedicated loading bays for the stallholders. He found a space at the back of a diamond merchant's shop and parked.

As he locked the car, the security guard for the merchant, a tall heavyset man dressed in a suit, stepped into the loading bay. His grim expression changed when he noted Gabe's signature kaffiyeh and *agal*. Moments later, the security guard was joined by the owner, who assured Gabe he could leave his car for as long as he wanted. The effusive offer was followed by a sales pitch on a line of diamond earrings that would make Gabe's future bride melt with desire.

Gabe assured the owner of the souk that if he required diamonds, he would be sure to consider him. It was a fact that now that the way was clear to marry Sarah, he would need a ring. It would seal the engagement and be a tangible sign that Sarah was his.

He found himself wondering what kind of diamond Sarah would like. It was not the kind of question that had ever consumed him before. Jasmine had insisted on choosing her own ring, and he had never known what Nadia liked; the ring she had received had been chosen by Hasim. But Gabe had an intimate knowledge of Sarah's tastes: fresh flowers and spicy food; old-fashioned, mismatched dinner plates; colorful, funky kids' clothes. *His* kid's clothes.

Stepping out into the main thoroughfare, Gabe skimmed the press of shoppers that flowed like colorful flotsam through the streets. Most were Western tourists, drawn here by a media campaign that had been formulated by Zahir's young and aggressive minister of tourism. A Harvard graduate Gabe had met while he was studying, Faruq Malik was intent on selling Zahir as an island of romance, history and mysticism.

Faruq had left no stone unturned in his attempt to resurrect the mystery of Camille's lost bridal dowry and the first Sheikh Kadin's ancient romance. He had even invented new aspects to the story, claiming that the moon had been full the night of the wedding and that the vows had been exchanged at midnight.

Gabe glimpsed a cool flash of white in a sea of vibrant reds, blues, oranges and glaring pinks. He made his way through eager streams of shoppers, all avid for gold and silks, jewel-bright rugs and exotic spices, until he reached the silk merchant's shop that Sarah had entered.

A group of Japanese tourists were clustered around the counter. Sarah half turned as he entered the shop, a sumptuous drift of berry-red silk held draped against her body. For a split second, Gabe was riveted. The sensual richness of the cloth seemed to make her skin glow and her eyes seem even darker and more exotic.

Red. It was her color.

Sarah's gaze passed blithely over him then zapped back. *"You."*

The fiery glare spun him back to the conversation in his Jeep when Sarah had discovered he had gotten engaged straight after they had made love. She had been angry and then she had kissed him.

A purely masculine satisfaction filled him. If Sarah had been disconnected and indifferent, he would be worried, but she wasn't. She was mad, her glare pointed and highly personal as if everything that was wrong was his fault. Which, if she had read the gutter-press story claiming that he was holed up with Nadia in Italy, was understandable.

In the heat of that glare, he found himself feeling oddly at home, as if they had just picked up on a half-finished conversation. In that moment he realized how much he'd missed the long phone calls and the electrical connection that seemed to hum between them. Crazily, putting distance between them had done nothing to lessen what he felt for her.

"Sarah. What a surprise to find you on Zahir."

Ten

Unwillingly arrested by the traditional kaffiyeh and *agal*, which had distracted her from recognizing that it was Gabe filling the shop doorway, Sarah dumped the red cloth back in a bin filled with colored silks. The low timbre of his voice shivered through her, but she refused to be seduced by it. Been there, done that, she thought grimly. Didn't want the T-shirt.

She dredged up a cool smile. "I'd hate to miss your wedding."

In the dim interior of the shop, dressed in a dark suit with the kaffiyeh, his jaw stubbled as if he hadn't had time to shave, his amber eyes gleaming in the shadows, he looked exotic and even larger and edgier than she remembered.

Her anger and hurt that he had not canceled his wedding and had spent the past couple of weeks at some

Italian *castello* with Nadia dropped to a slow simmer as Sarah registered how utterly out of place Gabe was in a silk merchant's shop. That could only mean that he had seen her and followed her into the shop. The thought instigated a flicker of pleasure that she could not allow to make headway, given that Gabe had betrayed both her and their baby and from all accounts had enjoyed every moment of it.

Her anger bolstered by that thought, she lifted her chin another notch and decided she had nothing to lose by the direct approach. "Where's Nadia?"

A deathly silence descended on the shop.

Gabe glanced at the number of women filling the shop. "We need to talk…elsewhere."

Dimly, Sarah realized there seemed to be a lot of women holding cell phones. Cell phones equaled photographs, social media, maybe even a video of the conversation. She imagined it was the kind of situation that had happened to him in Tuscany.

When she didn't immediately follow his order, Gabe gave her the kind of irritated look that made her feel like *she* had betrayed *him*. A split second later she found herself hustled out into blazing sunlight.

Gabe gave her a searing glance as he threaded his way through a stream of shoppers and into a shaded alleyway between merchants' shops. "I haven't been with Nadia. I've been in the Emirates negotiating with a building contractor for most of the past week. Finding cell phone coverage is difficult. Does that answer your question?"

She dug in her heels, halting them both and tried not to notice that with the snowy-white kaffiyeh framing the masculine planes of his face, Gabe looked almost fiercely beautiful and completely at home in the sun-drenched souk. "So that wasn't you at the *castello* in Tuscany?"

He said something curt beneath his breath. She was fairly certain it was one of his swear words. "Since I've never been to Tuscany, no, it wasn't."

He hadn't been with Nadia. Relief surged through Sarah, making her feel faintly dizzy. Silly, emotional tears pricked at the backs of her eyes.

Blinking furiously, she searched in her bag and found a tissue. "Who was it, then?"

"Raoul Fabrizio. Some Italian count." Gabe ducked down and peered into her eyes. "Damn, you're crying."

As she dabbed her eyes and blew her nose, she found herself eased into a loose embrace. The deep rumble of his voice and the steady thud of his heart were oddly soothing. She drew a shallow breath, and the clean scent of his skin laced with the irresistible whiff of sandalwood that she had worked so hard to forget made her tense. After days of stress and fury it was hard to adjust to the fact that he wasn't the villain she'd been building up in her mind.

Sniffing, she blew her nose again. "I never cry. It must be the pregnancy."

When she searched for a second tissue, he handed her a beautifully folded handkerchief. "How have you been? Have you put on weight?"

She stared at the monogramed handkerchief, which was too beautiful to use, and tried not to be seduced by the deep, velvety timbre of his voice. She glared at him. "Do you really care?"

A couple of tourists strolling in the direction of the beach, towels slung over their shoulders, glanced at them curiously.

Gabe frowned. "We can't talk here. If you'll come with me now, I know a place where we can be private."

Sarah checked her wristwatch and tried to look like she was on a schedule and wasn't quite sure if she could fit Gabe in. "Will it take long?"

"You've got other appointments?"

A fresh wave of hurt and anger fountained up at the note of incredulity in Gabe's voice, as if pregnant, abandoned history teachers did not have appointments. "I'm not on Zahir for a holiday. Now that I've got a child to support, I'm starting a new career as a travel writer."

His brows jerked together. "You don't need a job. I'll support you and the baby."

She pulled free of his hold, fire shooting from her eyes. "I will not be dependent on you."

"I didn't ask you to be."

The calm timbre of his voice somehow defused the anger that kept trying to erupt, conversely leaving her feeling vulnerable and unsure. Sarah decided she preferred the anger.

Gabe indicated they should follow the couple with the towels. Aware of him close behind her, a few steps later Sarah found herself in a service lane lined with vans and small trucks.

The sidelights of a sleek black sedan with darkly tinted windows flashed as Gabe unlocked the vehicle. Sarah stopped in her tracks. "You said we would talk somewhere in private, not that you wanted to put me in a car and drive me somewhere."

He looked momentarily arrested as he held the passenger-side door. "It's not that sinister. All I want to do is find somewhere private to talk where we won't be overheard. I've got a beach house five minutes away. If you don't want to go there, we could go to your hotel."

Her eyes widened. "You know where I'm staying?"

Frustration burned in his gaze. "Zahir's not exactly a big country—"

"So you sicced some kind of Zahiri secret service on me."

"It wasn't that high-tech. Xavier called the airport."

Sarah climbed into the luxurious Audi and tried not to like the chill of air-conditioned air and the smell of new leather. "Your henchman. I should have known."

Gabe closed the door then walked around and slid behind the wheel. "Xavier's not a henchman. We decided not to have those a few years back. He's head of palace security. Mostly he checks locks and alarm systems. Occasionally he checks out people who are close to the family."

She fastened her seat belt and tried not to love the sexy quirk to Gabe's mouth as he took off the *kaffiyeh* and *agal* and tossed them on the backseat. Instead she needed to remember how easy he found it to forget about her.

His comment about people close to the family got her attention. "But your family doesn't actually know about me."

His gaze dropped to her mouth, making her heart pound. "Of course they know about you and the baby."

Feeling mollified and altogether calmer now that she knew he had actually told his parents about her, she relaxed back into the cloud-like seat. Deliciously cool air washed over her as Gabe accelerated into traffic. He stopped for a stream of pedestrians heading for the souks and Sarah stiffened as her cell phone chimed. Aware of

Gabe's proximity and that he would hear every word she spoke, she picked up the call from her mother.

The conversation was brief. Hannah wanted to know how Sarah was and if she'd checked into her hotel. She also wanted to let her know that she had heard from a mutual acquaintance that Graham was on Zahir.

Sarah frowned at the mention of Graham, who must still be on his wild-goose hunt for the missing dowry. After their last meeting when he had broken into her home, she had no interest in seeing him ever again. Luckily, with all the holidaymakers on Zahir, the chances that she and Graham would actually cross paths were slim.

Gabe turned down a narrow driveway that flowed beneath a shady grove of ancient olives. He brought the car to a halt outside a villa built on a small rise overlooking a tiny, jewel-like bay. "Was that Southwell?"

Sarah grasped the door handle. It would be a simple matter to say it was her mother, but after the past week of turmoil and uncertainty, she still felt ruffled and hurt. "I don't think that's any of your business."

Leaning across, he pulled the door shut, trapping her in place. "I don't want you seeing Southwell."

For a moment she was close enough that she could see the faint shadows under his eyes, as if he hadn't gotten a lot of sleep, and the intriguing roughness of his five-o'clock shadow. "I wouldn't see Graham Southwell if he was the last man on earth."

He let go of his hold on the door. "Who were you talking to, then?"

She wanted to stick to her resolve to leave Gabe in the dark about her personal life, and let him experience a little uncertainty. But with Gabe close enough that she could feel the heat blasting off his body and breathe in his clean masculine scent it was difficult to think straight. Unfortunately, she was also seduced by the dizzying notion that Gabe was jealous. If he was jealous, that meant he did care for her. "It was my mother."

His gaze dropped to her mouth, sending a sharp tingle of heat through her. "My apologies," he said curtly. "But I was worried about you. Southwell is on Zahir, too."

She tried not to stare into his irises, which really were a mesmerizing hue of amber, striped with chocolate brown. "Graham comes here a lot. Besides being an importer, he's obsessed with finding Camille's dowry."

He *was* jealous. A dizzying surge of pleasure flowed through her, warming her from the inside out so that she was practically purring. "Did Xavier make a call to find out where Graham is?"

Gabe's gaze narrowed, signaling that she was playing with fire, but she didn't care. As wary as she was about what he might feel for her, she loved him. He was the father of her child and he'd been gone for over two weeks, and in that time she had *missed* him. Added to that, she had thought she was on the brink of losing him to a woman she was certain he did not love. As far as she was concerned she had a right to the truth.

"To be strictly accurate, Xavier asked an investigative firm to confirm Southwell's movements."

But Gabe had paid for the report. She had to suppress the sappy desire to grin. "Isn't that a bit paranoid?"

"Not from where I'm standing. I needed to know that he wouldn't come near you."

He *was* jealous.

Feeling suddenly giddy that not only had Gabe not slept with Nadia, but that in the time he'd been absent, he had actually worried about her, she pushed the door wide and stepped out onto a pristine white shell drive.

Gabe gestured at a path that led to a shady patio overlooking the sea. He unlocked and opened a set of French doors. She stepped into a sitting room shaded by shutters. Tiled floors were strewn with bright Zahiri rugs and low, comfortable couches were strategically placed to make the most of the stunning view.

Gabe walked through to a sleek kitchen that opened off the sitting room. "Would you like a drink?"

The polite request distracted her from checking out the beautiful house that was obviously not Gabe's primary residence since it had been shut up for some time. "Water will be fine."

She heard the opening of the refrigerator, the chink of ice. Gabe indicated she should take a seat. When she did so, she found herself staring at a vivid oil painting of a woman seated in an enclosed garden, wearing a vivid flame red dress.

"Camille." Gabe handed Sarah a frosted glass then strolled to the open doors to stare out at the view.

Gaze drawn to the broad width of his shoulders emphasized by the snug fit of his suit jacket, Sarah sipped a mouthful of water. Unable to bear the silence, she asked, "What did you want to talk about?"

He turned, his expression oddly neutral. "Us. As of last night I'm no longer obligated to marry Nadia. I'm proposing that we should get married next month."

Eleven

For long moments, Sarah thought she had heard wrong. She set her glass down on the beautiful ebony table, careful not to spill any water on what looked like a precious antique. "You really mean it, you want to marry me?"

Gabe's expression was still curiously neutral. She realized the descriptive she should be using was "guarded."

Given his worry over Graham, she knew Gabe had feelings for her. But she was also aware that his approach to marriage was just a little too businesslike. He hadn't said he loved her, and he very probably didn't at this stage. Her stomach dipped when she realized he almost never mentioned his first wife.

The reality was that for now the pregnancy was dictating what happened next, but Sarah had hoped for something more, a glimpse of the warmth and love they could share once they were living together.

Despite her efforts to stay just as guarded as he, her heart swelled with emotion. The problem was, she thought a little desperately, that she loved him and she wanted to marry him—even if he didn't feel the same right now. "Next month?"

He mentioned a date and her stomach plunged. She knew that date. It was engraved in fiery letters on her heart. Despite her effort to stay calm, she found herself on her feet, too upset to sit. "I presume you mean the same date you were going to marry Nadia?"

"Yes."

The cautious joy that he did still want to marry her was swamped by annoyance. "Let me guess, the wedding venue is booked, the guests are invited and there's no wedding without a bride?" She knew how that went, since she'd had to cancel wedding plans, twice.

"I know it's not ideal, but it's a fact that we need to get married soon, and the wedding, which is important for Zahir, has been arranged."

"I understand the practicalities." But it was hard to feel cherished and special when the proposal sounded as forced as Gabe's last engagement, and when she was being offered a second-hand wedding.

Still caught in the curious ambivalence of receiving the proposal she wanted from Gabe but in a way that sounded more like a transaction than a relationship, Sarah paced to the portrait of Camille.

A small heated tingle shot down her spine as she registered Gabe close behind her. Determined to control her response to him, she concentrated on the painting. "She had style."

"She was a woman who knew what she wanted."

Sarah couldn't help wondering if that was how Gabe

viewed her. "Is there anything wrong with knowing what you want?"

"Not as long as it means you'll say yes and marry me."

She swung around, his words sending a bittersweet pang through her. She had thought he hadn't noticed that she hadn't actually agreed to marry him yet. They had made plans back in New Zealand, but all of that had been tentative, knowing he had to end things with Nadia first.

Sarah wanted marriage, but only because she truly believed he might fall for her over time. She guessed she had hoped he might view their relationship as more than just a solution. "Do you want to marry me?"

His expression closed up and she wondered if she'd said something wrong, then his hands curved around her upper arms, seductively warm against her skin.

"We're good together. We like one another. We're going to have a child."

And the lovemaking had been off the register. Two weeks ago it had seemed almost enough. "What about the money?"

"Money is no longer an issue for Zahir." Gabe's fingers meshed with her's, pulling her close. "I want you, Sarah, and I think you know that. I have spent weeks making and breaking deals to have you. Will you marry me?"

Time seemed to slow, stop. She had wanted to change her life, to take risks, and she had. Now there was no way she could go back to the flat and endless routine of her old life. This version of life might be hurtful, but at least she knew she was alive.

Above all, she had to think about the baby. If there was a chance for them to be a real family, she had to take it. "Yes."

Relief flared in his gaze. He bent and touched his mouth to hers.

The slow, lingering kiss sent a hot pang all the way to her toes. Before she could stop herself, she clutched his shoulders, lifted up and deepened the kiss. This was what she had wanted, what she had longed for even when trying to be cautious.

Gabe's arms closed around her, fitting her even more closely against him. Relief flooded her as she felt the firm shape of his arousal pressing against her hip. His blunt, masculine response was a reassurance that, in the wake of the article claiming that he was with Nadia, she badly needed.

When he lifted his head, she boldly wound her arms around his neck and instigated another lingering kiss. When Gabe dragged pins from her hair so that it cascaded around her shoulders then lifted her against him so that her feet left the ground, the eroticism of it sent a flush of heat through her.

When he lowered her to the floor, she felt the cool leather of a couch at the backs of her knees. With a tingle of excitement, she realized he had carried her there while they'd kissed.

He tangled his fingers in her hair, his gaze burned into hers. "Are you well enough to make love?"

Heat burned through her at the question. "I'm fine, never better."

He kissed her again. They were going to make love. The reality of it, when an hour ago she was in the depths of despair, was faintly shocking.

With fingers that fumbled slightly, she unknotted his silk tie then started on the buttons of his shirt. Irresistible flashes of the last time they'd made love kept mak-

ing her heart pound out of control. There were a lot of
things about their relationship that needed working on,
but she couldn't help thinking that this part was absolutely perfect.

Minutes later, with her dress lying puddled on the
floor, Gabe lowered her to the leather couch. He had already dispensed with his jacket and shirt, and now eased
out of his pants. As he tossed stretchy gray boxers on the
floor, she drank in the sight of him, naked. In her bedroom, at night, he had been beautiful. In full daylight,
the hot Zahiri sunlight making him look bronzed and
sleek and muscular, he was breathtaking.

He joined her on the couch, his weight pressing her
down. Automatically, she moved to accommodate him.
His gaze locked with hers and a faint tension assailed
her as she felt him lodged against her. Now that marriage
and a baby were part of their equation, she was worried
that she might disappoint him in some way. After all,
she was not a glamorous jet-setter like Nadia, or a fragile beauty like his first wife.

A split second later the worry ceased to be important
as she held her breath against the exquisite moment of
their joining. He kissed her then pulled her closer still,
holding her tight against him as if he needed her, as if
she truly mattered to him, as they moved together and
the afternoon dissolved in a blinding shimmer of heat.

Much later, after they'd both showered and dressed,
Gabe found his cell and pressed a speed dial. "Hasim will
take care of the change to the invitations. Meantime, I'll
need you to stay on in your hotel and keep our engagement under wraps until the palace issues a press release."

Still caught in the rosy aftermath of lovemaking, the

sudden switch to the "business" of the wedding was a little jarring. Sarah picked up her handbag and adjusted the strap over one shoulder. "Stay in the hotel, as in lay low?"

Gabe's gaze settled on her mouth and lingered. Not quite all business, then, she thought with relief.

"It would be expedient. Once the press get hold of this they'll go crazy—"

Whoever Gabe was calling picked up. He half turned away while he spoke in rapid Zahiri. A few minutes later, he hung up and slipped the phone back in his shirt pocket. "That was Faruq, the minister of tourism. He'll take care of the press release. Once the announcement is made, we can move you into the palace."

Gabe drove Sarah back to her hotel, taking the time to question her about her and the baby's health, wanting verbatim accounts of exactly what Evelyn had said. Sarah couldn't help basking in his concern. To her mind, like the beautiful, off-the-register lovemaking, it was a sign that he was falling for her.

Feeling bemused and a little dreamy after the hours they'd spent making love, Sarah strolled into the deep shade of the hotel's portico. Graham's sudden appearance as he popped up from a café table caught her completely off guard.

His gaze swept her with that hint of disbelief she still found irritating. As if updating her look had somehow changed her beyond all recognition. Still intensely annoyed with Graham for breaking into her house and copying the journal, she fixed him with a flat glare. "What do you want?"

"Do I have to want something?"

When he opened his arms as if they were actually going to hug, Sarah stepped back, neatly avoiding the fake intimacy. "In my experience, yes. Although I thought you'd already gotten what you wanted."

Unfazed, Graham fell into step beside her as she strolled into the gorgeous mosaic tile lobby.

"Mostly. I think I'm finally onto something, I just need you to decipher the piece of the journal that's still written in Old French—"

"No." Sarah stepped into an elevator. As the doors slid closed, Graham's expression was red-faced and belligerent, but she didn't care. She was too absorbed with Gabe to pay attention to Graham.

The elevator doors opened on her floor and she found herself staring blankly at a pair of probable honeymooners, their eyes starry, skin tanned, bright new wedding rings gleaming on their fingers.

As she strolled to her suite, she checked her watch, dazed at how little time had passed. Just over three hours since she had left. And yet in that time Gabe had found her, proved their attraction was still fiery and tingling with life. They had made love and the engagement had been confirmed.

Pulse speeding up at the memory of their lovemaking, she stepped into her suite and caught a glimpse of her reflection in the mirror by the door. She touched a red mark on the side of her neck. She remembered Gabe's jaw scraping her tender skin, the ripple of sensation that had gone through her at the utterly sensual caress, as if he couldn't get enough of her.

She drew a deep breath as it sank in just how much she had changed.

She was no longer the dry, low-key history teacher who had stayed in Friday, Saturday…let's face it, *every night.* She was the kind of risk-taking woman who attracted a sheikh and who, after one wildly passionate night, was carrying his child.

Gabe had made love to her as if she was desirable, as if he couldn't resist her. As if she belonged to him.

Just as she knew that Gabe was hers.

A little startled by the clear, bold thought, she set her bag down and strolled to the refrigerator to get herself a cold drink. Carrying the ice water back to the sitting room, she sat down on the sofa and booted up her tablet. After the conversation with the waitress in the café, she was even more curious about Gabe's first marriage. Maybe she should have asked him about it, but she hadn't quite been able to broach the subject because she had wanted him to confide in her.

Minutes later, she had turned up an old tabloid report that seemed to confirm everything she'd heard. Gabe and Jasmine had been childhood sweethearts and married young. She had died tragically in a boating accident.

Another search turned up a series of photographs of Jasmine, fragile and breathtakingly pretty, an enormous diamond solitaire sparkled on her finger.

A ring. It was a small detail and something Sarah and Gabe hadn't spoken about, something they hadn't had time for, yet.

The phone rang. When Graham's voice registered, she slammed the receiver down then took the phone off the hook. For good measure she also turned her cell off then went back to her tablet.

A couple of hours later, a rap on the door woke her from a nap. She checked the peephole in case it was Graham. It was Gabe.

Still feeling on edge about Gabe's almost complete

silence about his first wife, she opened the door. Gabe was obviously freshly showered and looked utterly gorgeous in dark pants and a light, gauzy shirt. "I didn't expect to see you so soon."

His gaze narrowed as he picked up on the coolness in her voice. "I tried to ring but your cell seems to be turned off, and the hotel phone is off the hook. There's been a change of plan. I've arranged a house for you to move into. It was originally a fortress, so it's more secure than the hotel. If you can collect your things I'll take you out now, then I thought we might go out for dinner."

She stiffened at the calm way he was making arrangements, as if he'd smoothly moved past the minor glitch of almost losing her. Before she could stop herself, the question she'd promised herself she would not ask burst out of her. "Why don't you ever talk about your first wife?"

His expression turned bleak. "The marriage ended years ago."

Her fingers tightened on the doorknob. "But you haven't forgotten her."

"My wife died, that's not something I'm likely to forget."

Instantly, she felt guilty and contrite that she'd stirred up painful memories. Although that didn't stop her wondering if the reason Gabe wasn't falling for her was because he was still in love with his dead wife.

A group of cleaners, one pushing a trolley filled with cleaning products, strolled past, their expressions openly curious.

Gabe kept his gaze firmly fixed on her. "Why did you turn your phones off?"

Her brows jerked together at the probing question. She had only had her phones off for a couple of hours, while Gabe had been incommunicado for a whole week. "I bumped into Graham in the foyer. He tried to follow me to my room, then he started calling."

"Southwell." Gabe straightened, a grim fire burning in his gaze. "That's why I've arranged the shift to the old fortress."

He glanced at the cleaners who had stopped a short distance away and who seemed fascinated by their conversation. "We can't discuss this in the corridor. Are you going to let me in?"

A little thrill shooting down her spine, she stepped back as Gabe stalked into her suite.

Closing the door, he crossed his arms over his chest. "What did Southwell want?"

"He wanted me to translate some Old French from the journal."

Gabe looked briefly arrested. "You know Old French?"

"I did a couple of papers in historical linguistics." She shrugged. "I'm not as good as Laine."

He shook his head, the grimness morphing into an expression that made her heart race, as if he liked her quirky, oddball education, more, as if he liked *her*.

He shook his head slightly. "Damn," he muttered. "Back to Southwell. If he ever comes near you again, call me immediately. And if you're thinking of arguing about the move out to the house, you can forget it. I need you safe."

Another small thrill shot down her spine at the flat series of commands, most especially the last statement, that Gabe needed her safe, as if her safety was personally important to him. And in that moment she knew that Gabe's feelings toward her were neither neutral nor businesslike.

She had a sudden flashback to the night of the cocktail party at the Zahiri consulate, the moment when Gabe had walked out of the stormy night to rescue her.

The gloom that had enshrouded her when she had been focused on Gabe's wife, Jasmine, dissipated. She had been concentrating on the past, but what was happening right now was significant. Gabe had gone out on a limb for her. He had changed his country's constitution, brokered deals and canceled his marriage contract. He wanted her—enough that he'd made her pregnant. Now he wanted to put her in a fortress to keep her safe.

They were not the actions of a businessman wanting a marriage of convenience; they were the actions of a warrior with a passionate heart. A heart that had *not* been buried with his wife.

Twelve

The drive out to the house, which was situated on a cliff above Salamander Bay, took fifteen minutes along a narrow, winding road. The house itself stole Sarah's breath, because although it had been extensively remodeled it was clear that the original structure had once been a cliff-top fortress.

Gabe introduced her to the resident housekeeper and gardener, Marie and Carlos.

She chose a room that had white walls and dark floorboards strewn with jewel-bright rugs, and which contained a huge four-poster bed draped with a filmy mosquito net. Light and airy French doors opened onto a stone balcony, and like many of the rooms she'd glimpsed, there was a spectacular view of the sea.

Sarah quickly unpacked then dressed for dinner in a softly draped red chiffon dress that floated off her shoulders and clung in all the right places. When she walked downstairs, Gabe strolled in from the terrace, which opened off a large sitting room that seemed filled with antique furniture and artwork.

Her interest piqued, she examined the carving on a chest that inhabited one corner of the room. "This must be a twelfth-century piece if it's a day. Looks like it came off a ship."

"It came off Camille's ship, the *Salamander*. It's one of the few objects that survived the wreck." He nodded in the direction of the terrace. "If you want to see the remains of the *Salamander*, the outline of the hull, which is mostly buried, is still visible."

Sarah followed Gabe out onto the windswept terrace.

Gabe leaned on the parapet, as he pointed out the shadowy outline of her ancestor's ship, still visible where it had foundered in the rocky shallows of Salamander Bay.

Once she had seen the wreck, he hurried her back inside. "We need to discuss meeting my parents and we need to do it fast, because they're on their way here."

The sharp chiming of the doorbell sounded in the distance.

Gabe's expression turned rueful. "Too late. They've already arrived."

Moments later Sarah heard the click of high heels on ancient flagstones as Maria showed the Sheikh of Zahir and Gabe's mother into the great room.

The sheikh was tall and lean with a dark, penetrating gaze. Forty years on, Gabe would look exactly like him. Gabe's mother was slim and medium height. Despite being in her fifties, with her dark blond hair smoothed into a stylish short cut, she looked a good ten years younger than her husband.

The instant Hilary Kadir saw Sarah her face softened, and Sarah knew it was going to be all right.

Hilary gave Sarah a hug. "Your name's Sarah?" Sarah barely had time to nod before Hilary continued. "Are you all right? Is he treating you okay?" She shot Gabe a faintly accusing look then smiled apologetically before introducing herself and her husband.

The sheikh was kind, but formal. From the paleness of his skin, Sarah guessed he was still unwell, so she hurried to offer him a seat then blushed because she'd been here less than an hour, and the house belonged to the Kadir family.

Hilary smiled. "We're sorry for the ambush, but when I heard you were pregnant I couldn't stay away. Since Jasmine—"

"Mom."

Hilary frowned at Gabe and sent Sarah an apologetic look. "If we'd known there was a baby, we would have been in contact a whole lot sooner."

Marie arrived with a tea tray.

Broodingly, Gabe watched as Sarah fielded his mother's questions. Until that moment he hadn't realized how on edge he had been about this particular meeting.

The turnaround in his thinking was immense and complete. He had gone from an organized, convenient marriage to marrying a woman he wanted. It was the exact opposite of the situation he had planned.

Gabe's father was understandably cautious about the relationship, even with a baby on the way. Gabe knew that the biggest obstacle for his father right now was accepting the money situation, but he had finally handed the financial reins over to Gabe with his blessing.

His gaze rested on Sarah as she talked with his mother, who was a talented linguist. Whimsically, he wondered what his mother would think when she found out that, like her, Sarah could read Old French. Sarah reached up and adjusted a pin in her hair, and the memory of what it had felt like to have those strands cascade over his hands in a silky mass made him tense.

Dispassionately, he examined why he was so attracted to Sarah. Possibly it was because, with her double degree and forthright manner, she was as unlike Jasmine as it was possible to be. Although that wasn't the whole of it, and the way he reacted to Southwell was a case in point.

Gabe considered the thought that he was jealous and dismissed it. Sarah was pregnant with his child, she was going to be his wife and Southwell was an unsavory character. There would be something wrong with him if he didn't react possessively.

Hilary smiled at Sarah, her gaze narrowed shrewdly as she and her husband got ready to leave. "You love him, don't you? I can tell."

Sarah felt heat rise up in her cheeks. "Yes."

She let out a breath, gripped by the thought that it was really that simple. She loved Gabe and she had from the first. A lot of things had happened that should have killed that love, but through all the reversals and the stinging betrayal of finding out he was engaged to Nadia, she hadn't let go. Somehow her emotions were stubbornly anchored. She couldn't imagine losing interest in Gabe; everything about him fascinated and drew her. She even loved his occasional bad temper because when it came down to it she would rather fight with Gabe than spend time with anyone else.

Although she had to be careful not to let him know that.

"He likes you," Hilary said quietly. "And I think he's over the moon that you're pregnant. A lot of marriages have started with less."

Gabe took Sarah to a small restaurant down on the waterfront, which had a private room. Seated on a balcony right over the water, the setting couldn't have been more romantic. Although the dinner had a practical aspect. While they ate, Gabe filled her in on more family information, including the names of about twenty cousins, most of them female, and a raft of children.

"After meeting my mother you'll understand why you need to know this stuff. She's big on family."

"I like your mother." They'd chatted for ages, and Sarah had hemorrhaged most of her life story, including the two failed engagements. As appalled as she'd been over spilling those kinds of details, in the end she hadn't minded because there had been a genuinely compassionate streak to Hilary Kadir.

After dinner, Gabe took her for a walk along the waterfront. The romanticism of the moonlit walk was somewhat marred by the fact that a very large bodyguard trailed them all the way.

She glanced at the guard, who was trying to look inconspicuous, but at six feet eight inches, with huge shoulders, that was difficult. "Do you always have a bodyguard?" Offhand she couldn't remember seeing one in New Zealand.

Gabe looped his arm around her shoulders, drawing her close. "It depends. Sometimes I slip the leash."

Half an hour later, Gabe dropped her off at the fortress house. He hadn't suggested they sleep together, which had been obsessing her through the evening, because after what had happened at the beach house that afternoon she had assumed they would continue to sleep together. When his fingers tangled with hers when she opened the door, relief made her feel a little shaky and she found herself inviting him in.

The house was dark except for a couple of lamps left burning in the sitting room. Sarah automatically gravitated to the balcony, with its view. Gabe's arms came around her and it seemed the most natural thing in the world to turn and kiss him. Long minutes later, he pulled her inside with him.

The perfumed warmth of the night air flowed around them as they undressed in her room. Somehow the more leisurely pace, so different from the fierce interlude in the beach house that afternoon, seemed even more intimate. Breathlessly she realized that this time they had all night.

With easy strength, Gabe swung her into his arms, lowered her to the bed and came down beside her. He cupped the small mound of her stomach then one rounded breast and she logged his curiosity.

"These are different."

"They changed almost immediately."

He bent his head and kissed each breast. The sensations low in her stomach coiled, tightened.

He lifted his head. "Do you want me to use a condom?"

The roughness of his voice and the jolting practicality of his question registered, but somehow couldn't mar the magic of the night. He hadn't asked the question when they'd made love earlier. She ran her hand down his chest, loving the heated feel of his skin. "Why use one when we don't need it?"

He went very still. "Are you sure?"

Her breath suddenly locked in her throat. "Unless there's a reason that you should use one."

"There isn't. I haven't been with anyone since you."

Out of nowhere joy hit her. His words weren't a declaration of love, but they were significant. She touched the scar on his cheekbone, running the tips of her fingers gently across the smooth tissue. He captured her hand, deliberately possessive as he bent and kissed her again. She clutched at Gabe's shoulders, drawing him close, lifting against him. This time their lovemaking was quieter, deeper, and as the night slowly unraveled around them she felt that something precious and right had flared to life between them.

She woke to gray morning light and the sound of Gabe in her shower. He dressed in the clothing he'd worn the previous night and dropped a kiss on her cheek. Since he didn't have any clothes at the house he had to return to his apartment at the palace to change. Feeling sleepy and bemused, Sarah agreed to meet him for lunch.

Gabe made a quick call to the guard who had looked after them last night, arranging for him to pick her up around eleven.

After Gabe had gone, Sarah had a leisurely breakfast out on the terrace then checked the palace's events online, noting that there was an open day today. It was part of the tourism promotion around the wedding, so the palace was bound to be crowded. Some spin doctor called Faruq seemed to be running everything.

Since it was now supposed to be her wedding, she decided to take a risk and join a tour, despite Gabe's warning to stay out of sight for now. A tour of the palace as an anonymous tourist would fill in time before lunch, and provide more background information about Gabe's family before she became an official part of it.

After changing into an ice-blue dress that looked fabulous with her new tan and a pair of sexy heels that were comfortable for walking she strolled downstairs, talked to Maria about the car in the garage and managed to get the keys.

The sun burned down on the acres of perfectly manicured grounds and the elaborate wings and towers of the palace. The building itself was impossibly beautiful and romantic. To imagine that she would live there one day soon seemed a dream.

Humming beneath her breath, Sarah took the tour, journal in hand. Despite seeing photos, the palace took her breath away with its vaulted ceilings, marble columns and mosaic floors. Most of the tour seemed concentrated in the reception rooms that would be used for the wedding, and those rooms were filled with a buzz of activity as exquisite furniture was polished, fresh paint applied to paneling and the gilding on the high, ornately plastered ceilings was retouched.

As she lingered in a hallway that resembled an art gallery, a slender young woman, accompanied by two large men in suits with the unmistakable look of bodyguards, strolled by.

Shock reverberated through Sarah as she recognized

Nadia. With her hair trailing in loose, sexy tendrils, a gold-and-diamond pendant hanging suspended in the faint shadow of her cleavage, her wrists coiled with elegant bracelets, she looked more like a fashion model than the young heiress portrayed in her engagement photo.

Sarah's stomach lurched. There could only be one reason for her to be here; Nadia was trying to get Gabe back.

After all Sarah and Gabe had shared yesterday and last night, she shouldn't worry about Nadia's machinations. Yet she couldn't help but wonder—was this why Gabe hadn't wanted Sarah to come to the palace?

Thirteen

Frowning, Sarah watched where Nadia went as the tour trailed into a formal library that was in use by the family. Sarah glanced into a room that opened off the library and caught a glimpse of a familiar set of broad shoulders.

A small shock went through her. She hadn't expected to see Gabe. He had told her he would be in meetings all morning. Although of course, he hadn't said with *whom* he was meeting. Adrenaline zinged through her as Nadia strolled into view and it became obvious that Gabe was meeting with his ex-fiancée. In that moment the door to what must be Gabe's office closed, blocking Sarah's view.

Feeling ruffled and upset, because she had thought Nadia was out of the picture completely, she found herself marching toward the closed door. Popping it open, she breezed inside as if she was expected.

Gabe, who was leaning against a gleaming mahogany desk, turned his head, his gaze clashing with hers. Nadia stared at Sarah, clearly annoyed at the interruption.

Sarah plastered a steely smile on her face and kept her gaze on Gabe. "Darling, I hope I'm not interrupting anything important. I just wanted to check what time we were going to buy the engagement ring, before lunch or after?"

Marching up to Gabe, who looked taut and sleekly urban in a dark suit and pristine white shirt, a royal-blue tie at his throat, she went up on her toes. Curling her fingers into the lapels of his jacket, she kissed him on the mouth, noting the glint of amusement in his gaze.

His arm curled around her waist, holding her close. "How about before lunch?"

"Good, I'll just go and finish the…research I was doing next door." Kissing him one more time for good measure, Sarah made a beeline for the door.

Gabe's voice stopped her in her tracks. "How long will the research take?"

"I'll be researching until you're finished in here."

"That's what I thought."

Nadia started speaking in low, rapid French. Sarah, who spoke French fluently, understood fighting words when she heard them, then the door swung closed behind her, cutting off Gabe's reply.

Adrenaline pumping, Sarah walked straight into the tour group again, but she was no longer interested in the architectural and interior wonders of the palace. Peeling off, she practically jogged through the large library toward a set of French doors that opened onto a courtyard. Since the library was next to Gabe's office, if she walked outside, she should be able to hear what was going on between him and Nadia.

Tiptoeing over the paved courtyard outside, she sidled through a thick tropical shrub and peered into Gabe's office. Frustrated when she couldn't see anything, and wondering if somehow she had gotten the wrong office, she circumnavigated a tub of flowers and a trellis festooned with a dark, glossy creeper, to peer into the window.

"See anything interesting?"

The rough timbre of Gabe's voice spun Sarah around. When the heel of one shoe caught in the gap between pavers, she grabbed at a bunch of foliage to keep herself upright. "Not yet."

Gabe pulled her out of the shrubbery and picked a leaf out of her hair. "I thought we agreed you wouldn't come to the palace—"

"Because I'd find out you're meeting with your fiancée?"

"Ex-fiancée."

Sarah extracted herself from his hold. "It didn't look that way a few minutes ago."

"What you just saw was Gerald Fortier sending his daughter in to apply pressure. Apparently, he thought if I received a little 'encouragement' and an extra financial carrot, I'd go ahead with the marriage."

She stared at Gabe's stubbled jaw and an intriguing mark on the side of his neck. She could feel herself blushing at the memory of just how he had gotten that mark. "And were you encouraged?"

He cupped her nape, drawing her close. Dipping his head, he touched his mouth to hers, the kiss tingling all the way to her toes. He lifted his head. "If I was 'encouraged' do you think I'd be out here with you?"

She clutched at the lapels of his jacket again, using them as a convenient anchor. "I'm not going to apologize for making a scene." She had lost her last fiancée to another woman; she would not risk losing Gabe.

"Nadia Fortier's gone. Xavier's taken her back to her hotel. He's putting her on a chartered flight back to Paris this afternoon."

Gabe ushered her back through the library and into his office. "Now that you're here, I have something for you. I was going to give it to you at lunch, but with the damage Fortier's caused with leaked photos and documents, it needs to happen now. Faruq has set up a press conference straight after lunch, and I'd like you to attend it with me."

"You're going to officially announce our engagement?"

Gabe opened a wall safe and extracted a set of keys. In succinct tones he outlined the information that would be given to the media. In light of the fact that both he and Nadia had discovered they were not as compatible as they had first thought, they had ended their engagement. But, after the deepening of a relationship with a previous flame, a descendent of the de Vallois family, the wedding would proceed, just with a different bride. "We won't announce the pregnancy straight off. We can do that a few days before the wedding."

Sarah stiffened at the sanitized version of how the whole tangled situation had unfolded. There was nothing untruthful in the statement, but it was definitely constructed to distract attention away from the more scandalous aspects of the story.

Indicating that she should precede him, Sarah stepped out into the beautiful, echoing hall. Closing the door behind him, Gabe's hand dropped to the small of her back. A small tingle of pleasure went through her at his casual possessiveness as they strolled past tourists and palace staff who now stared at her with open curiosity.

A man in a suit acknowledged Gabe with a lift of his hand and fell into step behind them and the reality of her situation struck home. As Gabe's wife she would have to get used to security.

Gabe opened a heavy wooden slab of a door and they descended an ancient stone stairwell, leaving the brightness of day for the hard glow of artificial lighting. The dry coolness grew, enough to raise gooseflesh on her arms.

Gabe glanced at her, shrugged out of his jacket and dropped it around her shoulders. "I forget how cold it gets down here."

The jacket instantly swamped her with heat, sending a reflexive shiver through her. They stopped at another door, this one smaller in size and alarmed.

When Gabe had disarmed the door, she followed him into a room that had probably once been a cellar. He halted at a steel door that was utterly twenty-first century high-tech, unmistakably a vault, and tapped in a code. Depressing the handle, he pushed open the thick door.

The small room was lit with halogen bulbs and lined with metal shelves containing glass-fronted cabinets filled with ancient books, scrolls and archives that instantly piqued Sarah's interest. As an historian she loved examining original documents, although she seldom got the chance since most ancient texts were too fragile to be handled. There was also a series of locked steel cabinets and boxes. "Is this where the dowry used to be kept?"

Gabe checked through the ring of keys and found the one he wanted. "It was kept here, but in those days the security was primitive, just two locked doors and old-fashioned iron keys, which was why the dowry needed moving when the island was evacuated."

Gabe chose a cabinet, unlocked it then withdrew two midnight blue velvet cases. Setting them down on a sleek metal table that occupied the center of the vault, he opened the smallest. Already prepared for the fact that he was probably going to give her a ring because they were in the palace vault and she would be presented as Gabe's fiancée that afternoon, Sarah was still stunned.

The ring wasn't the old family jewel she had expected, borrowed for convenience. Made by a staggeringly exclusive jeweler, the oval-shaped sapphire rimmed with diamonds was modern and breathtakingly gorgeous.

Extracting the ring, Gabe picked up her left hand. "May I?"

Sarah blinked back ridiculously sentimental tears as he slipped the ring onto her third finger. It was a moment she had experienced twice before but which had never been more important or filled with emotion. "It's beautiful." And it fitted perfectly.

He opened the other flat velvet box, which contained equally gorgeous drop earrings and a pendant. "You'll need these, as well. After lunch, Faruq's arranged for one of the designer boutiques to outfit you for the press conference."

Still feeling a little misty, the businesslike necessity of the press conference grounded her. Sarah tucked the velvet boxes in her bag and minutes later they walked out of the dim lower rooms and back into the airy lightness and clamor of the palace.

In the end, lunch with Gabe was canceled because Faruq, a small quick man who looked more like an accountant than a marketing genius, insisted Sarah not only needed an outfit, but that she must have her hair, nails and makeup done. Hilary Kadir, who had joined them, agreed to take Sarah to her stylist. Surrounded by palace staff, suddenly the responsibility Gabe carried hit home. It explained his calm, measured manner, the lack of outward emotion that sometimes felt like coldness. She knew for a fact that he was neither cold nor emotionless, but with cameras constantly pointed at him and literally thousands of people dependent on him, he would have learned early on to maintain that steely self-control.

Two hours of relentless pampering later, wearing a slim-fitting royal blue jacket and skirt that deepened the color of her eyes, her hair smoothed into a glossy, thick swathe and tucked behind her ears to show off the earrings, Sarah walked into the press conference with Gabe. Already warned about the hot lights and the camera flashes, and prepped on what she should and should not say, she did her best to keep her expression serene.

The questions came thick and fast, although Gabe blocked most of them with a flat "No comment."

Thanks to the genius of Faruq, who had also briefed the press beforehand and had plied them with champagne and canapés, the sticky territory of their fling before Gabe had gotten engaged to Nadia was barely touched upon. Apparently, Nadia was now old news. The story everyone wanted was the love affair between the sheikh and the schoolteacher, a mismatch that carried echoes of Zahir's romantic past.

Annoyed by the idea that they were a mismatch, but bolstered by the positive atmosphere, Sarah allowed the beautiful ring to be photographed. When one of the journalists asked Gabe if he had finally gotten over Jasmine, and wanted to know what it felt like to be getting married again, Gabe pushed to his feet, pulling her with him. Thanking the press, his expression cold, he propelled her from the room.

A security guard fell into step behind them. When they reached Gabe's study, he took a call. His already grim expression turned icy. He glanced at Sarah, but seemed to barely see her. Curtly, he informed her that something urgent had come up then instructed the guard to see Sarah back to the cliff-top house.

As Sarah followed the guard out of the palace, the fact that Gabe had some emergency to cope with took second place to the question that was burned into her mind. The one that had abruptly ended the press conference and which she had hoped she had put behind her.

Was Gabe over Jasmine?

Fourteen

Sarah glanced in the rearview mirror as a sleek black sedan nosed out of the parking lot behind her. Feeling more and more upset as the minutes ticked by, Sarah pulled into the parking lot of the cliff house. She needed some air, without her guard, the six foot eight, Yusuf.

Changing into light jeans and a cotton camisole with a tight white cardigan buttoned over top, she checked to see where Yusuf had gone. When she heard his voice in the kitchen, she picked up her camera and bag and sneaked out a side door. When she reached the car, still in the clear, she turned the key in the ignition and pointed it down the drive. In her rearview mirror, she saw Yusuf race out onto the drive.

Adrenaline pumping, she turned onto the coast road. Her phone rang, but she didn't answer. Once she got to the bottom of the cliff, she would text the number he had given her before she had left the palace and let him know she would be an hour at most. A second turn and she was winding down the hill to the parking lot at the beach.

She drew a swift breath as Salamander Bay came into view, wild and beautiful and still almost devoid of habitation. As she brought the car to a halt in a parking lot occupied by half a dozen vehicles, she climbed from the car, feeling miserable, but consoled by the wildness of the spectacularly beautiful white sand beach with its high rock promontory that ran like a dark finger out to sea.

After texting Yusuf, she took a photo of the beach, which was occupied by sporadic bathers and the occasional bright umbrella. Turning, she took a shot of the rock promontory, which was brooding and spectacular, then she walked down onto the sand. She took a couple of snaps of the dark, brooding cliff face crowned by the fortress, which occupied the highest point in the bay, a square set against the onslaught of the wind with a sole crenellated tower.

Still feeling terminally unsettled because she was worried that Gabe was still in love with Jasmine, and that he wasn't willing to trust Sarah with that truth, she walked out along the rock promontory. The extra height gave her a better view of the beach and the place that was the wreck site of the *Salamander*. Sunlight glittering off polished metal caught her attention. A black sedan had just pulled into the parking lot.

She couldn't believe it when Graham emerged from the car and had the nerve to wave at her. She pretended not to see him and continued taking photos.

Irritated beyond belief that he seemed to find ways to insert himself into her life, she walked a little farther along the rocks. A wave, larger than any she'd yet seen, almost completely submerged the rocks ahead. Spray exploded, close enough to wet her. Suddenly aware of the danger and kicking herself for not being more careful, she tucked the camera in its the bag and started for shore.

Her stomach tightened as a flash of movement alerted her to the fact that someone was walking toward her. A curious sense of inevitability gripped her as she turned to see Gabe, still dressed in his formal suit. "Let me guess. Yusuf called you."

"You weren't supposed to leave the house without him." His gaze was trained steadily seaward. "Didn't you read the sign?"

"What sign?"

The sound of another large wave hitting rock spun her around, cold spray drenched her.

Gabe's arm snaked around her waist, steadying her. "The sign that said don't go out on the rocks." There was small, bleak silence. "This is where Jasmine died when her boat overturned."

The shock of his statement—of his finally mentioning Jasmine—was canceled out as the next wave flowed toward them, this one even larger. Fingers laced with hers, he pulled her onto a higher shelf of rock and back toward shore.

Breathless, Sarah worked to keep up with Gabe's smooth, gliding stride, glad that she was wearing sneakers and that she had kept up her walking during the pregnancy and was still reasonably fit. "I suppose people get swept off."

The wave broke sending more spray flying. The distraction took her attention from the uneven rock surface for a split second, making her wobble.

Gabe said something hard and sharp beneath his

breath as he reeled her in close again then swung her into his arms. "Not today."

Coiling her arms around his neck, she held on tight, worried that she had provided another painful reminder of Jasmine, but loving that Gabe had come to her rescue. Water dripped from his hair and clung to his lashes. His gaze rested on hers for a moment, the glint of masculine satisfaction sending a warm surge through her. She was soaked, they both were, but suddenly she didn't care. For a few moments they were alone, and like the hours they'd spent together last night, he was *hers*. "I'm sorry. I should have kept a better watch out. Graham arrived at the beach and I got a bit creeped out. I thought he would try and follow me."

Gabe's expression turned grim. "Don't worry about Southwell. Xavier has him under surveillance."

Resting her head in the curve of his neck and shoulder, she breathed in his warm scent. "I suppose that's how you found me? I ran into your secret service?"

She felt his smile rather than saw it. "What did you expect when you gave Yusuf the slip? Tell me, *kalila*, are you always this difficult?"

She was startled by his rueful expression, the softness of his gaze, as if he liked it that she was giving him such a hard time. "Only when I get engaged."

"And when you're pulling swords off displays, assaulting thugs with your umbrella and giving Tarik a hard time."

She blinked at the picture of herself. "Maybe I am difficult."

A curious expression crossed his face. "Don't change, I like it." Bending, he kissed her.

Her heart thumped at the kiss and the tone of his voice. "What does *kalila* mean?"

Stopping at the edge of the rock promontory where it flowed into the smooth, broad curve of the beach, he set her on her feet. "It's an endearment. On Zahir we use it much as you would honey or darling."

Feeling suddenly self-conscious, she smoothed wet straggling hair back from her cheeks. When his gaze flickered to her chest she glanced down and realized that her thin white cardigan and camisole were wet. Luckily, she had a bikini top beneath, so she could afford to ignore the wet T-shirt effect.

Gabe glanced along the cliff face. Graham was still there somewhere because his car was in the parking lot, although he was nowhere to be seen. At a guess he had disappeared into the warren of caves that riddled the rock.

When Gabe spoke his voice was terse. "I'm moving you into the palace tonight."

Gabe arranged for all of their belongings to be transferred to the palace.

Night was falling with a pretty sickle moon, the sky studded with brilliant stars as he drove into a cavernous garage beneath the palace.

He gave her a quick tour of the residential area, which used to be the old harem quarters and which had been remodeled into a series of family apartments. He pointed out where his parents stayed and two other empty apartments. "There are also a whole bunch of single and double rooms, but those are mostly empty unless family or guests come to stay."

He opened the door to their apartment and a warm

glow suffused her as she walked into the main sitting room, which was filled with comfortable leather couches and low coffee tables. A dining table was positioned in an alcove next to a gleaming kitchen. The dining table was set, candles lit, giving the room a welcoming elegance while the warm aromas of the meal that had been kept hot in silver chafing dishes drifted on the air.

Gabe gave her a quick tour. The next room, which Gabe indicated as they walked past, looked like a beautifully appointed guest room. That was followed by a large bathroom tiled in cream marble with a tub big enough to swim in.

She examined the large walk-in shower and the supply of fluffy white towels. "We'll have to block off the bathroom once the baby starts walking."

"Good point." He stared at the marble bath, which had steps that would be slippery when wet. "Even better, we'll get a house. This place is a death trap for kids."

The casual comment about getting a house made her heart glow with happiness. More and more they were starting to feel like a regular couple. She stepped inside what looked like the master bedroom, since it had its own bathroom and dressing room opening off it. This was confirmed by the masculine bedspread, the faint scent of Gabe's cologne and one of his shirts slung over the back of a chair.

Sarah checked out the dressing room, a faint tension she hadn't realized was there dissipating when she saw her suitcase. "I take it I'm staying in this room."

Gabe was leaning against the doorjamb watching her. "That's right, with me. Although, you can have the guest room if you want."

She strolled toward him and when he didn't move

aside she took another half step, which brought her up against him. She wound her fingers in the smooth silk of his tie. "I choose this room."

"I was hoping you were going to say that."

His phone hummed. Looking frustrated, he took the phone from his pocket, checked the screen and frowned. "I need to take this."

"No problem." While Gabe sat at a desk in a small study that opened off the lounge and took a series of calls, Sarah unpacked then had a quick shower to remove the salty residue from that afternoon. Toweling herself dry, she put on fresh underwear. Instead of dressing in the cotton shift she'd chosen, she decided to wear an exquisite rose-pink silk kaftan she had bought in the souk the morning Gabe had found her. The kaftan was gossamer fine and flowing but when belted with a silk sash became a gorgeous Eastern dress.

She combed out her hair and used the blow-dryer. When her hair was mostly dry and trailing down her back, she quickly applied a little eye makeup. Now that she finally knew how the makeup should look and what products to buy, she was determined not to go back to dashing on a bit of dark brown eyeliner and rose-pink lip gloss, both of which usually faded into invisibility within an hour.

Rummaging through her suitcase she found the pashmina that went with the outfit, an exquisitely fine woven cashmere stole in rich hues of purple and pink with splashes of deep red that added a sensual grace to the pretty kaftan. She examined the effect in the bathroom mirror. The outfit was more modest than the red dress she'd worn the night she'd met Gabe, there was only the barest hint of shadowy cleavage, yet somehow it was in-finitely more feminine and mysterious.

With her hair dropping around her shoulders in a dark curtain, her eyes taking on a smoky, exotic slant cour-tesy of the eye shadow and mascara, she didn't look re-motely like a sensible history teacher, neither did she feel like one anymore. The clothing seemed to underline the inner change that had taken place, almost without her being aware of it.

When she walked out into the lounge, Gabe was dish-ing up food. He must have had a shower in the other bathroom because his hair was damp and he'd changed into a pair of dark pants and a polo shirt. His gaze met hers as he set the plate he'd just filled on the table. Her pulse sped up at the intensity of his gaze as he took in the softly sensual outfit. "Are you hungry?"

"Starved."

They ate, although as delicious as the food was, Sarah could barely concentrate because she was so aware of Gabe.

When she was finished, he took her plate and set it in the sink in the kitchen, his expression taut. "Would you like dessert?"

She followed him and placed an empty salad bowl on the counter. "Not really."

"Me neither." With a grin, he picked her up and car-ried her through to the bedroom. "When you walked out of the bedroom like that, I didn't think I'd make it through dinner."

He set her on her feet. The Pashmina slid to the floor as she reached up to kiss him. One kiss followed another. She felt the silk sash loosen then slip off her shoulders and puddle at her feet. Two steps back and they were on the bed and somehow, this time, she was on top, her hair sliding silkily around them. Long drugging minutes later she was naked and so was Gabe.

Tension gripped her as she studied Gabe in the wash of light from the hall. For the first time, she was actually beginning to believe that he could be hers.

Cupping his face, she looked directly into his eyes. "I love you." The words were bald and declarative, leaving her nowhere to hide.

Instead of the words she wanted in return, she felt his instant tension and knew she shouldn't have made the declaration, shouldn't have pushed him. Even if he had mentioned Jasmine today, it was still too soon. A split second later, he kissed her and, determined not to fret, she relaxed into the kiss and let the warmth and heat of lovemaking encompass them both.

A phone call in the early hours brought Sarah out of a deep, dreamless sleep. Rolling over in bed, she slipped an arm around Gabe's taut waist as he lay, propped on one elbow, speaking in rapid Zahiri. When he hung up, the gray light of dawn illuminated the grim expression on his face. "That was Xavier. They've been keeping Southwell under surveillance. Apparently, he's found the lost dowry, which was sealed in a side cave in Salamander Bay. That's what he was doing there today, repacking the caskets and getting ready to transport them to the loading docks at the port where he has an export container waiting." Expression taut, Gabe set the phone down. "Damn Southwell and the dowry. Why did he have to find it *now*?"

Climbing out of bed, Gabe dressed and was gone within minutes.

Unable to go back to sleep, Sarah belted on the beautiful silk kaftan, freshened up in the bathroom then walked through to the sitting room. Gabe's words kept echoing through her mind.

Damn Southwell and the dowry. Why did he have to find it now?

As if Gabe had wished the dowry had been found some other time. Probably months ago, a year ago, so he would never have given way to the pressure of an arranged marriage in the first place. Because if that hadn't happened, he would never have spent a dangerous night of passion with her that had resulted in a pregnancy, and what could only be termed a marriage of convenience.

Dragging fingers through her tangled hair, she paced through the huge apartment, strolling through moonlit rooms only to find herself in Gabe's study, the one room she hadn't seen on their tour. Curious, she flicked on a light and strolled to tall French doors and looked out onto a beautiful patio. When she turned, she noted a rich leather photograph album on top of a polished mahogany desk.

Knowing that she shouldn't, she flipped the album open. The first section had Gabe and Jasmine's engagement photos. Lavish wedding shots followed and the final section was filled with romantic honeymoon photos. Feeling a little sick, because Jasmine looked glowingly happy in every photo, her arms either draped around Gabe's neck or his waist, as if she couldn't bear not to touch him.

She closed the album with a snap. As she did so, she noticed a folder beside it, carrying her name.

Feeling like an automaton, she picked up the file and opened it. Fifteen minutes later, feeling sick, she set the file back in its place. She had known that Gabe had had her investigated, but this file was a detailed *surveillance* record that Gabe had ordered after their first night together. He had expressly stated that he wanted her watched in case she was pregnant.

Seeing the truth about how Gabe had viewed her, in stark contrast to his romantic, loving relationship with Jasmine, was hard to take. It *hurt*.

She guessed that, given he was a sheikh's son and the future ruler of Zahir, she could understand his approach. But that didn't change the fact that she had given up everything for Gabe, including her heart, and he had given up very little for her. He still hadn't shared even the bare facts about his marriage.

Feeling numb, she replaced the file. As understanding as she had tried to be, she wasn't stupid, she had limits, and her limits had just been breached.

She had taken a risk in loving Gabe, moving in with him and agreeing to marriage. She knew he'd been hurt in the past, but even so she had believed there was a possibility that he would come to love her someday.

But she couldn't stomach marriage on such compromised terms, with someone who had seen her as predatory. It underlined the fact that if she hadn't gotten pregnant and forced his hand, she would never have seen Gabe again.

Face burning at the humiliation of seeing the basis of their relationship laid bare, of having her life sifted through, *by the man she loved*, she left the study and found her way back to the bedroom. Their bedroom, but not any longer.

Lamplight pooled like liquid gold, casting a soft glow on the beautiful plastered walls and delicate frescoes.

Chest tight, she opened a set of doors and stepped onto the balcony, staring out over the moonlit city to the sea. It was all unspeakably beautiful and she loved it, but she was going to have to leave.

She finally understood why Gabe had agreed to a marriage of convenience to Nadia and why he'd never confided in her about his past with Jasmine. It was because he didn't want the one thing she craved: intimacy.

The moment was defining. She had said she would marry Gabe, but how could she when his heart wasn't in it? When his heart might *never* be in it?

She knew what it felt like to be second best, to be passed over. It hadn't been a good feeling, but she had gotten over it. She didn't think she could get over Gabe, but neither would she be second best for him.

She had always thought she was lacking in passion, but when Gabe had entered her life she had discovered that she was passionate and volatile. She wanted a real love with Gabe with a fierceness that shimmered and burned and made her want to cry.

Knowing now that she would never have his love, she had to act. When she had the baby Gabe would love their daughter and want to be a father to her, but that was a scenario with a modern solution. He might not like the idea, but the only sensible thing to do was to share custody.

Working quickly, she retrieved her bags from the closet. She didn't know how much time she had before Gabe returned, so she simply stuffed clothing into them. She found her engagement ring, which she'd left on the bedside table, and replaced it in its velvet case. She put the case along with the second case containing the pendant and earrings on the dressing table. On impulse, she walked through to Gabe's study, found the photo album and the surveillance report and placed them beside the jewelry boxes.

She checked her watch. An hour had flown by. She needed to leave before she weakened and changed her mind.

Gabe would hate it that she'd walked out on him. He was an alpha male. But the very strengths that made him such a good leader were the qualities that would push them apart in the end. He would continue to sacrifice his free choice, and perhaps his happiness, and she couldn't bear that.

Walking through to the bathroom, she splashed cold water on her face. Feeling chilled despite the balmy warmth, she used her cell to call a local taxi firm and arranged to meet the cab in the residential street that backed onto the palace grounds.

Fumbling slightly in her haste, she changed into cotton jeans and a sweater and pulled on sneakers. She found a scarf and on impulse used it to cover her hair, tying it under her chin. After all the media coverage she was now recognizable on Zahir. It wasn't much of a disguise, but it would have to do.

She carried the luggage downstairs and outside to the street, leaving it in the shadow of a huge flowering rhododendron. Walking back to the apartment, she did a last check of the rooms, picked up her handbag, hooked the strap over her shoulder and walked out onto the landing. Headlights beamed up the driveway. Heart in her mouth, feeling sick to her stomach at what she was doing, Sarah walked quickly down the stairs.

Fifteen

Gabe locked the car and headed for the stairs. Now that the situation with Southwell and the dowry was resolved, with Southwell in custody and the dowry in safekeeping, all Gabe wanted was to go back to bed with Sarah and preserve what time they had before the major news companies picked up on the story and all hell broke loose.

Faruq was coordinating the press releases. With any luck, he would finesse the timing of the discovery of the ancient treasure as a "sign" that the marriage to Sarah was propitious for Zahir. The romantic tale of his ancestor's love affair with Camille de Vallois would do the rest.

As Gabe stepped inside the apartment, the curious quality of the silence made him frown. Somewhere outside he heard a car door close, the sound of an engine. On edge he walked into the bedroom. Moonlight slanted over the rumpled bed, which was empty. Stomach tight, he checked the bathroom, which was also empty.

Out of the corner of his eye he saw the two velvet cases on the dresser and the photograph album and surveillance report he had left on his desk with the intention of destroying them that morning.

He went cold inside. For the album and the file to be where they were, Sarah had clearly found and perused them. A quick glance in the spare room confirmed that Sarah hadn't just moved out of his bedroom. She had left him.

For long moments he couldn't think. Then he remembered the slamming of the car door out in the street. Sarah must have called a taxi.

Heart slamming against the wall of his chest, he picked up the phone, called Xavier and arranged to detain her at the airport.

With distaste, he forced himself to look at one of Jasmine's last gifts to him, an album filled with photos that portrayed a love story that had grown to be cloying and unhealthy.

Jaw taut, he opened the surveillance file and skimmed the damning evidence of his letter requesting a watch on Sarah in case she was pregnant. The report included an extensive back history on Sarah's life because for some reason Tarik had gotten a little overzealous and had requested the private investigator dig back several years.

Reading through the bare facts, Sarah had looked like a woman who had amassed a certain experience with men, but Gabe knew the truth. The reason none of the relationships had stuck was because she had refused to sleep with them. But she had slept with him, after little more than a few hours.

Because she had fallen in love with him.

Grimly, he remembered her saying the words to him tonight, his complete lack of response because, even then, in a sheer knee-jerk reaction he had automatically closed himself off.

She loved him.

He felt like he'd been kicked in the chest. Sarah wasn't like Jasmine, wavering with every breeze, clinging and resenting at the same time and wanting to be spoiled and cosseted. She was independent and fierce. Used to making her own way through life, for years she had refused to give in to relationship pressure and have sex. She had waited and chosen, and she had chosen him.

Once she had found she was pregnant, she hadn't panicked. She had gone in search of him, not to coerce him into a relationship, but to ascertain whether she should include him in her life. Those were the actions of a rational, independent woman who had fallen in love.

Tossing the report down on the desk, he found his keys and headed for his car. He felt electrified, every nerve ending in his body on fire. Sarah had told him, but now he knew in his gut—and his heart—exactly why she had agreed to marry him, and why she had left. She loved him but she had given up on the hope that he could love her back.

And suddenly he realized what he had done to himself, and to Sarah. After Jasmine had died he had spent years consumed by guilt, not because he had failed to save her life, but because he had never been able to *love her*.

He and Jasmine had been wrong together and that tension had reverberated through their marriage, ending in a tragedy that he had allowed to color the rest of his life.

Panic gripped him. He felt as if the scales had just been ripped from his eyes. Too late, he now realized that he did love Sarah. And now he had lost her.

He was partway to the airport when he knew it was the wrong destination. Sarah was smart. She would have known how easy it would be for him to stop her flying.

Turning the car around, he headed for the ferry terminal, the only other way off Zahir other than chartering a yacht or boarding a cruise ship. There were no cruise ships leaving today, and chartering a yacht was a lengthy process because it involved customs declarations. Boarding a ferry to the neighboring island of Al Jahir was a much simpler option.

His stomach churned at the thought that she had chosen the sea as a way to escape him. *Jasmine's choice.*

As he drove he went through every nuance of their last conversation, which had been about the dowry. He knew that, like him, Sarah placed no stock in money or possessions. Southwell had chased the treasure for its own sake, but Sarah, who should have been more interested in it than most with her family background, had barely shown a flicker of interest.

From memory the only thing about the past that had interested her had been whether or not his ancestor had loved hers.

His fingers tightened on the wheel as he turned down the street that led to the docks. Jaw tight, he found a space and slammed out of the car. Sarah was simple and declarative. She had told him she loved him, but he had failed to reciprocate. He had taken the easy way out, *the cowardly way out*, because then he didn't have to expose his own emotions. He didn't have to take any risks.

That would have to change; he couldn't lose her.

Gabe faced the raw depth of emotions that in the past had caused him more pain than happiness.

He wouldn't let Sarah go without a fight.

Sarah boarded the early-morning ferry to Al Jahir.

Stepping inside the lower deck cabin, which was already half-filled with passengers drinking coffee and watching TV, Sarah made a beeline for a seat near a window. She stopped when she noticed a large TV was on and that the coverage riveting most of the passengers was a news story on the crates of gold and jewels that Graham had tried to steal.

In no mood to listen to the story she was on the point of walking out onto the ferry deck when Gabe's deep voice kept her riveted to the screen. She recognized footage of an earlier interview that had been linked with the segment about the dowry, but even so, when Gabe was asked about his impending marriage his curt "no comment" stung.

The reporter smoothed over the awkwardness of the moment by stating that in Zahir any marriage by the ruling family was necessarily an affair of state.

Shivering slightly and hugging her cotton jersey closer against her skin, she walked to the upper deck and ducked inside out of the brisk wind. She stared through one of the large windows at the palace, which gleamed in the first golden touches of morning light, and the terraced jumble of streets and villas that gave Zahir such charm. Feeling miserable, she forced herself to look in the direction of Al Jahir, a misty lump on the horizon. She had made the right decision, even if it made her feel ill.

She was tired, so she bought a cup of tea from the

small cafeteria. She guessed she should eat something, but her stomach was still churning and unsettled, and the faint wallow of the sea swell wasn't helping.

She chose a seat that overlooked the docks, just in case Gabe arrived before the ferry left. She hoped he wouldn't come after her because if he did she didn't know if she'd have the strength to resist him.

Gabe walked inside the ferry building. He had missed the sailing by about twenty minutes. He could still see the ferry in the distance. He asked to see the manifest. His jaw tightened when he spotted Sarah's name.

Thanking the clerk, he left the building and made a call. Al Jahir was ruled by his cousin several times removed, Kalil. The relationship was distant, but that didn't matter. They were family. A second call and he had arranged a helicopter.

Half an hour later he landed on the docks of Al Jahir. When the ferry anchored just offshore, embargoed from landing until he had retrieved Sarah, Gabe took the launch Kalil had provided and climbed on board.

When Sarah saw him, her stricken expression gave him a small measure of hope. Although, he had mishandled their relationship so badly he had to wonder if he had finally destroyed her love.

Ignoring the disgruntled crowd of ferry passengers, he concentrated on Sarah. "Will you come with me?"

She shot to her feet, clutching her handbag. "Why?"

"Because you belong on Zahir, with me."

The sleepy-eyed tourist next to her muttered, "Last I heard slavery went out of fashion a few years back."

Someone else grunted agreement and added, "*And* piracy. Honey, if you need backup just say the word."

Jaw locked, Gabe kept his focus on Sarah. "You're free to leave anytime. But I need you to hear me out, in private."

Minutes later, caught halfway between misery and delight that Gabe had come after her, Sarah allowed Gabe to hand her down into the launch.

A short helicopter ride and they landed on the roof of the palace, which had a helipad.

As Sarah walked back into the familiarity of Gabe's apartment, her stomach tightened. "I left because I didn't want you to feel you had to marry me just to have access to the baby." She lifted her chin. "You're her father, so it's only right that you should have a part in her upbringing. We just need to reach agreement on how that will work."

Gabe shrugged out of his jacket and tossed it over the back of a chair. He ran lean fingers through his hair, looking suddenly unutterably weary. "Zahir is an old-fashioned country. The only agreement that will work here is marriage, and that's what I want."

She blinked at the intensity of his gaze. "I found the surveillance report."

His expression turned raw. "It was something I had to do, because I knew I couldn't afford to contact you again unless there was a child. If I hadn't instigated the report, Xavier would have. At least that way I could make sure the information came only to me and ensure your privacy."

The tension when she had discovered the report relaxed a little. She still hated that she'd been spied upon, but viewed that way, Gabe's actions had a protective element. "I thought you hated it that you were being forced to marry at all. If the dowry had been found months ago—"

"I would never have gotten engaged to Nadia. And since I was always going to New Zealand for the promotional tour our relationship would probably have followed a more normal path."

She stared at a pulse jumping along the side of his jaw. "But, when Graham found the dowry—"

"I was annoyed because I'd finally gotten you to myself, and then Southwell put himself in the frame again." He grimaced. "In case you hadn't noticed the dowry is a media circus. I knew I'd be out for hours."

Sarah took a deep breath. She was starting to feel happy, but she couldn't allow herself to relax just yet. "What about Jasmine?"

"I married Jasmine because I thought I loved her, but that was years ago."

The words *thought I loved her* seemed to reverberate. Her throat closed up so that when she spoke the words came out in a husky croak. "Do you still love her?"

Something cleared in his expression. "She was a childhood sweetheart. The media blew it up into a big love affair, but the marriage was a mistake. Jasmine was stuck on Zahir while I traveled. She hated it."

In terse, halting words he supplied a brief outline of the day Jasmine had drowned. He'd been spending more and more time away on business, tired of the fights and Jasmine's unhappiness. When Jasmine had insisted on accompanying him on a diving trip he had let her and when another fiery argument had ensued, he had suggested they end the marriage. Jasmine had lost her temper and in desperation had clung to him. Tired of her manipulative tactics and the clinging, he had gone below to study the navigation maps. When he had come back on deck, Jasmine, who had never handled a boat in her life, had taken the small dinghy, determined to row to shore. The dinghy had been swept onto a rock shelf and the boat had capsized on top of her. Gabe had dove down to search for her.

Sarah touched his cheek. "And that's how you got this."

His hand covered hers, holding it against the scar. "I had to get her off the rocks."

And the scar had become a permanent reminder that he hadn't been able to save his wife—more, that he had no longer loved her. It was no wonder he hadn't wanted anything to do with love again. "You can't believe it was your fault."

"I shouldn't have argued with her on the boat."

"And she shouldn't have taken the dinghy." Sarah unlocked her jaw. "I'm sorry she died, but it's a fact that she endangered your life as well as her own."

By the startled acknowledgment in his eyes she knew he hadn't considered that angle, preferring to take all the blame on his own shoulders. The only problem was that the guilt had morphed into an aversion toward emotional commitment that had almost destroyed their chance at love.

He threaded his fingers through hers, pulling her closer. "When it came to you, I knew I was in trouble, but I tried to channel the emotion into a purely sexual connection. It didn't work."

"Then I got pregnant." And he had attempted to transfer the "safe" relationship model he had settled on to her, and that hadn't worked either.

She cupped his jaw, suddenly seeing him, his tenderness and depth. "Even though I was a lot of trouble, you didn't let me go." She tried to breathe deeply, but her chest felt banded and tight. "Why?"

His hands closed around her arms, his palms warm through the cotton pullover. "That would be because I'm in love with you."

Happiness flared deep inside. Not just love, but *in love*. "Since when?"

"Since the moment I saw you completely ignore the don't-touch sign and knock my ancestor's sword to the floor." He pulled her snug against him. "I suppose you think because I'm a guy I'm incapable of that kind of depth."

She spread her palms over the warm solidity of his chest, loving the steady beat of his heart, the heat and strength of him. "It was a fact that I was a last fling before you got engaged." Flickers of the old hurt came back to haunt her at the words.

"I was on the point of getting engaged. It was an arrangement that had taken months to negotiate then I blew it by sleeping with you. That should tell you something."

She went still inside. Somewhere in all of this she realized she had lost the ability to stand back and look at the big picture, or to read between the lines. The one thing she had learned about Gabe was that for most of his adult life he had put Zahir ahead of his own wants and desires. The only times he had departed from that pattern were when he had married Jasmine, then again when he had slept with Sarah.

She stared at the clean, strong planes and angles of his face, the steadiness of his gaze. "You really did fall for me."

He cupped her face, his thumbs drifting over her

cheekbones, giving her goose bumps. "Like a ton of bricks."

"The way I fell for you."

His gaze connected with hers in a poignant moment of recognition.

She coiled her arms around his neck, holding him tight, loving the rock-solid quality that had frustrated her so often but which carried its own assurance. She knew without doubt that she and their daughter could trust Gabe with their hearts.

They had finally come home.

Sixteen

They didn't delay the wedding, even though Gabe was happy to do so. Sarah, now secure in his love, decided she had to do her bit for Zahir, and upsetting the travel plans of hundreds of people wasn't a good way to start.

The next day Gabe ushered Sarah into his study, where Faruq was impatiently waiting to find out just how the new wedding would affect his promotional efforts.

He was visibly relieved when Sarah informed him she was prepared to accept the current wedding date. She fixed him with the calm, level look she used in the classroom. "But I'm not getting married in the dead of night, like it's some kind of secret—"

"It's hardly a secret with four hundred guests."

Sarah frowned at the interruption. "—since it's my wedding." She softened the statement with a blinding smile that, to Gabe's mind, seemed to light up the room.

"Also," she continued, "I want my cousin Laine's son to be a page and her three daughters to be flower girls. Since they're family, and on the next island, that should happen."

Sarah kept her attention on Faruq as he took notes. "I'm thinking one o'clock is a good time for the ceremony. Midnight might have suited Nadia, but it doesn't suit me or my nephew or nieces. Laine's youngest has only just started to sleep through the night. You can't expect us to upset that pattern when it's taken so long to put in place."

Faruq looked suitably chastened. "Uh—of course not—"

"Good." She sent him an affirming smile. "It's also crucially important that people should understand that Gabe is not being *forced* to marry me."

Gabe hid a grin.

"Um—I don't think Sheikh Kadin was being forced as such, it was more of a service to the country."

"With a financial benefit." Sarah favored Faruq with another brilliant smile. "My point exactly. Gabe is not marrying me for money. He's marrying me because—"

"You're irresistible to him." Gabe thought he would just toss that one in.

Sarah's gaze locked with his. "Irresistible?"

Gabe pulled her into his arms. "Absolutely."

When she went up on her toes and rewarded him with a kiss, he heard the door close softly as Faruq let himself out. The meeting had ended a little precipitately, but it didn't matter. Faruq was a creative genius and he was already excited about the promotional potential in Gabe's marriage to a descendant of Camille, especially when combined with the recovery of the ancient dowry.

According to Faruq those two aspects could only enhance Zahir's new image as a destination for romantic getaways, and would make it relatively easy to gloss over the small detail that Gabe and Sarah had already made a start on a family. For Zahir the formula was win-win, but for Gabe those two elements held little importance to him when he finally had what he wanted—the gorgeous, fascinating love of his life and their first child together.

The day of the wedding dawned fine and clear. The ceremony was held in the ancient stone church next door to the palace. Golden sunlight poured through the rose window at the western end. Jewel-bright colors illuminated thick flagstones and the gleam of dark oak pews. The church overflowed with guests, so seats had been placed outside along with two very modern screens with speakers.

A restive murmur ran through the guests as Gabe's parents arrived and took their places. His father looked tanned and relaxed after a recent holiday and was no longer walking with the aid of a cane. His mother looked elegant and happier than he had seen her for years. She sent Gabe a beaming smile and a small thumbs-up.

Although Gabe couldn't quite relax until Sarah arrived. It was an insecurity that shouldn't have existed after the days and nights they'd spent together, but he couldn't quite forget the stark moment when he'd found out she'd left him just weeks ago.

Xavier checked his watch and frowned. "She's late."

"Tradition." Gabe's gaze was drawn to the priest, robed in white, as he also checked his watch. "Probably caught up in traffic."

The noise level outside increased. An usher at the front doors gave Gabe a nod. He let out a breath and relaxed. She was here.

Sarah stepped into the church, a little frazzled after the frustration of sitting in the back of a limousine that seemed to spend large amounts of time stuck in heavy traffic or at a standstill because of the crush of pedestrians. All wanting to get to *her* wedding.

A liltingly beautiful wedding march started, and the hum of conversation died. Gabe turned, looking tall and handsome in a gray morning suit and wearing the traditional *kaffiyeh* and *agal*. His gaze connected with hers through the drift of her veil. The quiet joy that he was hers seemed to swell inside her, forming an ache at the back of her throat.

Gripping the elegant bouquet that matched the simple lines of her designer gown, she began the slow, measured walk toward her husband-to-be.

With every step memories flickered. Gabe straightening with the sword in his hand at the reception in Wellington, the rescue in the parking lot, their first kiss, the first night they had spent together.

Blinking back tears, she halted at the ancient altar, which had seen the flow of centuries, bowed her head, made the sign of the cross and turned to her husband-to-be.

Sheikh Kadin Gabriel ben Kadir, heir to the Sheikhdom of Zahir.

For a moment, her composure wobbled, but when he lifted the veil from her face and took her hands in his, the warmth of his gaze held her steady.

The hush of the church, the beauty of the words of the

ceremony, filled her with an emotion that was piercing. When Gabe slipped the simple gold band on her finger, tears finally spilled.

His mouth brushed hers; his hands at her waist burned through the silk of her gown. Beeswax candles guttered in the faint breeze that blew through windows and suddenly the air was filled with the wild sweet scents of honey and thyme.

Sarah's head spun dizzily as she went up on her toes to kiss him back.

She finally had it all, more than she had ever dreamed—the father of her child and the love she had waited for, the husband of her heart.

* * * * *

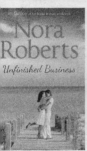
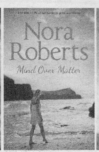
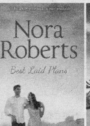
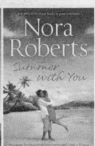
115_ST_11

MILLS & BOON®

The Thirty List

* cover in development

At thirty, Rachel has slid down every ladder she has
ever climbed. Jobless, broke and ditched by her
husband, she has to move in with grumpy
Patrick and his four-year-old son.

Patrick is also getting divorced, so to cheer them
selves up the two decide to draw up buck[et]
Soon they are learning to tango, abseili[ng]
stand-up com[edy] and more. But, a[s]
closer to P[atrick]
relations[hip]

www.mil[ls]

MILLS & BOON®

PASSIONATE AND DRAMATIC LOVE STORIES

A sneak peek at next month's titles…

In stores from 15th May 2015:

- **Carrying A King's Child** – Katherine Garbera
  and **What the Prince Wants** – Jules Bennett

- **Pursued by the Rich Rancher** – Catherine Mann
  and **The Sheikh's Secret Heir** – Kristi Gold

- **The Wife He Couldn't Forget** – Yvonne Lindsay
  and **Seduced by the CEO** – Pamela Yaye